T5-AQR-041

"This is historical fiction at its best, imaginatively filling the gaps and bringing us intimately into a portrait of marriage."

—Times Literary Supplement

"*Beautiful Fools* is the work of a genuine literary talent . . . Spargo's characters transcend reality and become rich and fictional, and the novel, in the form's paradoxical brilliance (at its best, as often here) speaks truth through invention." *—Spectator*

"*Beautiful Fools* is F. Scott's story as well as Zelda's, and a Fitzgeraldian wistfulness prevails. This approach to the Fitzgeralds' story is the most successful . . . With its contained arc and energetic plotting, *Beautiful Fools* takes the focus off more familiar episodes in the couple's history." *—The New Yorker*

"Spargo's voice is entirely his own and is capable of articulating certain ranges of experience only rarely now available to us. His work seems to me marked for permanence." *—Harold Bloom*

"Spargo's novel certainly succeeds in providing a timely reminder that the love between Scott and Zelda Fitzgerald, even in destructive decline, was a force to be reckoned with beyond the experience of many—maybe most—human beings." *—Wall Street Journal*

"In Spargo's hands, the Fitzgeralds emerge as fully human as they trade back and forth a valueless currency of hopes, promises and vows of loyalty. It's the one version of the story that resists the temptation to glamorize Scott and Zelda out of their humanity." *—The Washington Post*

"*Beautiful Fools* skillfully evokes Cuba at the end of the 1930s, redolent of the music and scents and tastes of the tropics. Beyond the customary tourist haunts, adventure and danger seem to lurk in every bar and cafe, along every road and deserted beachfront." *—Boston Globe*

"Spargo's book is richly imagined, and paints a delightfully detailed portrait of Cuba of 1939. It's a positively delicious travelogue." *—Chicago Tribune*

"It takes a brave novelist to tackle Scott and Zelda, those mythic ghosts of the Jazz Age. Luckily, Spargo is more than just brave—*Beautiful Fools* is a vivid and revealing look at two charismatic, self-destructive people, and the love that sustained and ruined them. It's a real feat of historical imagination and novelistic empathy." —Tom Perrotta, author of *Election* and *Little Children*

"While reading both Spargo's novel and Hemingway's [*Garden of Eden*], I felt (guiltily) privy to the private conversations and consternations of a couple inside their locked hotel room. Spargo's portrayal of a couple in crisis . . . offers two people not so much against each other as against the world." —*Bookslut*

"If you're looking for a *Great Gatsby* retelling with more substance than Baz Luhrmann's latest, *Beautiful Fools* is it." —*Miami New Times*

"Here is a writer possessing the greatest talent: that of fully inhabiting the lives of others. Spargo conjures up these two as no one has done before. Scott and Zelda, surrounded by the poignancy of last words, last things, become, in Spargo's remarkable novel, not people of history but of literature, and reminders of what we fight for, what we fail to win, and the beauty that abides between. A marvel of a book." —Andrew Sean Greer, author of *The Story of a Marriage*

"In a voice both intimate and expansive, tender and shrewd, R. Clifton Spargo manages to do the near impossible: craft a story worthy of his iconic subjects." —Holly Goddard Jones, author of *The Next Time You See Me*

"Spargo writes with animation and fervor, a style conducive to the heat generated by his subjects." —*Kirkus Reviews*

"Meticulously researched, *Beautiful Fools* is a wonderful exploration of a great American writer and his marriage: both what it was and what it could have been." —*Cedar Rapids Gazette*

For BRYU —
WITH ADMIRATION
FOR YOUR
KIND AND
COURAGEOUS
PERSON AND
VOICE.

BEAUTIFUL FOOLS

The **LAST AFFAIR** of
ZELDA and **SCOTT FITZGERALD**

a novel

R. CLIFTON SPARGO

OVERLOOK DUCKWORTH
NEW YORK · LONDON

This edition first published in paperback in the United States and the
United Kingdom in 2014 by Overlook Duckworth, Peter Mayer Publishers, Inc.

NEW YORK
141 Wooster Street
New York, NY 10012
www.overlookpress.com
For bulk and special sales, please contact sales@overlookny.com,
or write us at the above address.

LONDON
30 Calvin Street
London E1 6NW
info@duckworth-publishers.co.uk
www.ducknet.co.uk
For bulk and special sales, please contact sales@duckworth-publishers.co.uk,
or write us at the above address.

Copyright © 2013 by R. Clifton Spargo

All rights reserved. No part of this publication may be reproduced
or transmitted in any form or by any means, electronic or mechanical,
including photocopy, recording, or any information storage and
retrieval system now known or to be invented, without permission
in writing from the publisher, except by a reviewer who wishes
to quote brief passages in connection with a review written
for inclusion in a magazine, newspaper, or broadcast.

Cataloging-in-Publication Data is available from the Library of Congress

Book design and type formatting by Bernard Schleifer
Manufactured in the United States of America
ISBN US: 978-1-4683-0880-8
ISBN UK: 978-0-7156-4746-2

For Anne

BEAUTIFUL FOOLS

FEBRUARY 12, 1932

SOME MEN, NO MATTER HOW MUCH TIME AND ENERGY THEY EXPEND on other men, no matter how deeply they invest themselves in rivalries with peers, can only discover their true selves in the company of women. Scott Fitzgerald was such a man, and for that reason he spent an inordinate amount of time listening to women, even those he didn't know, believing that in their conversations he would learn something about himself. Just now, seated across the aisle from two working-class Irish women, the older of whom kept using the younger one's name at the beginning or end of every few sentences, he jotted down fragments of an argument. Mother and daughter, most likely—they debated a topic of mutual concern, except the daughter never once returned the personal address. On first glance the mother might have been fifty-nine or sixty, but, no, she was working-class and not all that well kept, so subtract a few years. One minute she was peremptory, haughty, conducting herself as someone used to getting her way; the next she was docile and supplicating, aware that her wishes could not prevail.

"What are you writing, Scott?" From the seat nearer the window Zelda raised herself, eyelids heavy, having nodded off for a few minutes but now pulling upright to grab at the corner of the Moleskine notebook he tucked inside his jacket. "Is it about me?" In her voice the old touch of paranoia, the worry she could not master. Asleep for only a short while, she did not trust the world to have remained the same. For all she knew he'd reached his limit while she napped, vowing once and for all to be rid of her.

"I wish you wouldn't," she said, and the remark startled him. "Wouldn't what?"

"I'm not sure what I meant." She mulled it over for several seconds. "Give up on me, I suppose. I wish you wouldn't."

"Zelda, no one's giving up on you."

They had come to the decision to check her into the hospital together, cabling Dr. Forel, who thought she might do best back in Switzerland, but when Scott saw the panic enter his wife's eyes at the prospect of a return to Les Rives de Prangins clinic, he promised Forel she hadn't backslid quite so far. No, all she required was a restful month, maybe two, in which to regain her equilibrium. So Forel recommended the Phipps Clinic in Baltimore, familiar territory, a city they already knew, where Scott might establish residence without much trouble.

"I want you to understand I'm only doing this so you'll stop worrying about me," she started to say, her words swallowed by the squeal of metal on metal, the shrieking release of air announcing yet another station. It bothered him, this habit she had of seizing the most inopportune moments for intimate conversation, as if there were no difference between things you could say in a railway passenger car and things that ought to be whispered, if ever, in a church confessional.

But is it really so odd she should choose this moment to speak of such matters? Only consider the situation from her perspective. Over the past few weeks she has been convinced for hours, sometimes days on end, that this time round the voices won't be silenced, this time they won't cease until they've wrung from her every last ounce of soulfulness, rendered her incapable of retrieving the self she has twice salvaged these past two years. There were stretches of clarity during which she couldn't remember the hallucinations, or her own desperate words, or why she allowed Scott to label her "sick" and submit her to evaluation by so-called experts altogether hostile to the premises by which she wished to conduct her life. But what galled her most, what stayed with her, were the broken promises. Almost two years ago she'd entered Prangins voluntarily, expecting to be released within weeks, only to be kept there against her will for sixteen long months, not knowing if she would ever be allowed to leave. A year and a half of her life stolen from her. She vowed during the fourth month of imprisonment never again to surrender her freedom without a fight. Here she is today, seated beside a husband mired in an alcoholic tailspin altogether as self-destructive as her own slow unraveling, and yet no one arrives to propose stowing him in an asylum. No one so much as notices that as he sits there primly, playing the role of jailor and deliverer, there is alcohol on his breath. Every time he turns his head she can smell it on him, the sweet, pungent stench of his own ruin.

What happened to her wasn't so unusual. With Scott two thousand miles away, gone for weeks on end, working on that movie in Hollywood that was never going to get made, Zelda remained in Alabama with her family, her mother and sister watching her every move, her father dying under the mask of his terrible dignity, leaving her with graveside thoughts of how she was like him and also (she hoped) not like him. "Please tell me what normal looks like under those circumstances," she pled on her own behalf. "Please tell me how you're supposed to grieve without knowing how far inside the pain you can venture before everybody starts barking, fussing, trying to determine whether or not you've lost your mind."

"It's always so exhausting," she remarked, as he shifted in his seat, "for you too, I suppose, when I start to go crazy."

"Zelda, don't be so dramatic, please. You'll be fine."

"Oh, I can stop if I concentrate. It's only your constant worrying that wears me out."

"Would you like it better if I didn't care?"

"Honestly?" she asked, catching herself, making sure she didn't say anything that might prove irrevocable. They have uttered such words before, each of them many times. Even now she could trace the damage, if she cared to.

The train came to a halt, the departing passengers lining up at the front of the car. Still others stood before their berths, shuffling and twisting to face one another, yawning, stretching indolent limbs as newcomers filed down the aisle in search of empty seats.

Zelda clutched at his sleeve, asking him how long she would have to stay at Phipps and if afterward they could travel to Europe as a family. The three of them—Scott, Zelda, and their daughter Scottie—could have dinners in Montparnasse and make a study of how Paris was changed since the mid-1920s when they'd known it so well. Except this time, unlike the miserable return three years ago, they wouldn't mind the changes so much, since they were older, wiser, sobered by life. In the final years of the twenties they had indeed gone back to find their once-cosmopolitan city a travesty of its former grandeur, the cafés reeking of decades of spilled alcohol, the salons populated by hackneyed hangers-on, everything they stumbled on seeming gaudy, motley, or crass. So Zelda had dedicated herself to the regimen of ballet, one last chance to become more than an amateur, all hopes distilled into a passionate crush on her mentor, Madame Egorova, and, oh, if after that she couldn't remember details, maybe she just didn't wish to remember. Suffice it to say she pushed herself to the dire end while foreseeing it clearly, knowing full well how much it was going to cost her, this love of dance.

"If the novel earns what it should," he said, "I don't see why we couldn't visit Paris."

"We'll have room to move about," she mused without glancing his way, as if talking to herself, "and do the things we were going to do. We could purchase the home I've bought for us a thousand times in my head, which I've decorated and redecorated as many times, the one secure place I always wanted and we're probably never going to have. I could take up ballet again—"

Scott twisted in his seat, studying her, warning her without words that she was straying beyond permissible bounds.

"Yes, Scott, I was only speaking hypothetically," she said in a spirit of concession, and then, taking a deep dancer's breath and heaving cheerfulness into her voice, added, "I've decided to concentrate my energies on becoming a writer such as yourself and Ernest. Someone who spends his time observing life pass him by and puts poignant remarks on the page about the many activities, such as fighting in wars or killing bulls, he himself cannot do."

"True enough," Scott said, "writers are like parasites."

"Please don't become melancholic on my account." She waited on a reply and when it wasn't forthcoming resumed. "About Paris, then, where will we live this time? Maybe, if I were well enough, you could cut down on the drinking."

Here was the reliable reprimand, the fight for not only power but first principles. Hadn't his drinking and antics provoked her mad search for a vocation of her own because what they'd built wasn't sound enough? And if she pushed too fast, too hard, pressed her body to do things it had never done, stretched her mind to the breaking point, wasn't he in the end the cause of it all?

The train was in motion again, passing under a viaduct, the percussive roll of its wheels amplified and played back against the funnel-like walls. When they emerged from beneath the overpass, the voice of the older woman across the aisle could be heard distinctly. "Listen to me, he was always so fond of you, but you could never believe him after that one night, not that I entirely blame you. Don't you see, Clara, you'll put me in a bad sit—"

"You imagine I care," the younger woman cried, facing forward. Several passengers in the berths near the front of the car jerked their heads, fixing rubbernecking stares on the two women.

"You know what," the older woman said, her voice heavy with exasperation. "You're sick; your memories and thoughts are so twisted, it's shocking."

A nearby passenger rose from her seat, seeking out the conductor in order to direct his attention to the ruckus. The conductor looked over the woman's shoulder as he listened, eyeing the two women, and a minute later he made his way toward them.

"Isn't it dramatic?" Zelda whispered. "What's your theory as to the cause of the row? I'll tell you my surmise. The older one is a stepmother, and the younger a victim of incest by the hands of the father. Though the stepmother tried her best to protect the girl from violence, she nevertheless failed to do what a guardian ought to have done."

"Zelda, you shouldn't speculate so wildly."

"Oh," she said, a mischievous smile lighting her face, "now I recognize the girl; she is to be my roommate for the next several weeks at the Phipps Clinic at Johns Hopkins. She and I and perhaps several other crazy people on this train are on a journey to be cured of our neuroses and dementia praecox and assorted afflictions of the soul. We're all of us on a pilgrimage."

He could tell from the tone of her voice that there was nothing truly precipitous in these speculations. She was playing with her own story, imagining it as dispersed among the masses and somehow less terrifying for its typicality. Today was one of her good days, and there hadn't been many of those since the middle of December. No telling how long the clarity would last, of course. The break had been building since the onset of the holidays and when it caught up to her these past few weeks it overwhelmed her with predictable brutality. Scott had observed the irregularity in her behavior on his return from the West Coast. She would start down wild trails of thought, obsessing over the smallest details, unable to relinquish arbitrary desires, no matter how contrary to common sense they were. As a Christmas gift for Scottie she re-created the world of their travels on the scale of model trains—a tour of the globe from Rome to Paris to New York, wooden and papier-mâché constructions of St. Peter's Cathedral, the Eiffel Tower, the Empire State Building, all positioned along the Lionel train tracks encircling the Christmas tree. Weeks and weeks of desperate craftsmanship went into the gift, as she distracted herself from her father's final absence from the world by attending to the minutiae of the models. Though she was far inside the disease by the time he returned from California, their reunion brought about a détente. For a while she was happy and spoke magnificently in the collective—*We will do this, we will do that*—but at the end of a trip to Florida in early January they quarreled and the next day she was kneading the tender skin above her eyes in an effort to roll back the spikes of pain that nibbled at tranquillity, her vision newly troubled by halos, also a sudden tightness in her lungs that manifested in wheezing breaths; and there appeared on her lovely cream skin a patch of eczema, starting at the neck, spreading like poison ivy down over her shoulder, across her breasts, upward to the shadow line of her round, China-doll jaw.

On the return trip she admitted defeat, but only to him. "Oh, Scott, I'm broken again." When they arrived in Montgomery she pretended he'd invented it all, claimed never to have said any such thing, wishing to expose him to her family as her cruel jailor. It might have worked, except the eczema was by then climbing her cheek, contradicting her declarations of health and autonomy. For an entire Sunday afternoon she waded imaginatively through the bare grass of a field that ran behind her parents' estate and accused Scott of being brutal for not letting her fulfill her wishes, as though it never occurred to her that it was the dead of winter. In her mind's eye she saw her dancer's callused feet and strong naked calves sporting in the grass and it was always summer. She spent whole days languishing in nostalgia, settled on the porch, remembering the soldiers stationed in Montgomery who'd once come to her door attired in military costume, also the dozens of local boys who'd religiously courted her. She was susceptible to visions—of Judas Iscariot, Napoléon, Jeanne d'Arc, and the Spanish artist El Greco, whom Scott loved so much and she thought merely another Mediterranean mystic. Her visitors told her secrets: Judas was Christ's favorite for several hours after the betrayal; Jeanne had always suspected the voices she heard were from the devil.

Since leaving her mother's house in Montgomery, Zelda had been positively exuberant, not in itself cause for concern, but Scott had to watch her all the same. She wished to gossip about the two women across the aisle, but he interrupted to report that he was headed to the dining car for some coffee, would she like anything, and she reminded him that she rarely drank coffee.

He reclaimed the seat next to his wife. Across the aisle the berth was empty, the two Irishwomen nowhere in sight. For several minutes Zelda remained silent, eyes clamped shut in fake sleep, until she leaned forward, yawning, extending her arms in exaggerated languor into a fully stretched Y, turning to him with mouth half open, a shy smile on her lips. Expressing no curiosity as to the whereabouts of the two women, she instead commented on his shoes. "I've been meaning to tell you how much I like your new shoes." She knew how to play to his vanity. "You strike such a fine figure in the world, Scott.

"Sometimes I see you from afar as if I didn't know you and my heart runs fast like a young girl's as I entertain a perfectly meretricious thought. 'Oh, how handsome he is,' I say to myself, 'a stranger come to seduce me.' Then I take a second peek, embarrassed not to have recognized you, 'Oh, but it is only my husband,' reprimanding myself for the intent to cheat on the good solid you who stood by me when I was cracked and doubted I could ever again fake wholeness. Poor you, I think, to be married to a sexually tawdry wife who is ready to run off with the first man she sees, regardless of his station in life, owing only to his handsome face. He could be a waiter for all I care."

"Which should I find more flattering," he asked, "your dutiful loyalty to a tired old partner or the flash of excitement I now and then inspire from afar?"

"You needn't be so analytical, I only meant to compliment your shoes."

"Which you, of course, helped pick out."

They had discovered the shoes, independently, months ago, in an advertisement in *Esquire,* Scott lifting the magazine after Zelda laid it down, then asking minutes later what she thought of the two-toned leather brogue shoes the man in the photograph was wearing. She uttered a small cry of joy, delighted by their like-mindedness, having instructed herself that if he commented on the pair of Florsheim shoes, she would have to buy them for him at Christmas.

"Still, you're the one who wears them well," Zelda observed, "and now I'll be able to imagine what you are like in the wide world while I am tucked away in the insane asylum."

There was such excitement in a pair of new shoes. You looked down at your feet and detected the shine on them, unblemished, undiminished, and it was the beginning of experience all over again, the promise of falling in love, the thrill of imagining what he would be like under his clothes. After that came the worry. How long could the newness last? So you kept track, wondering at what point the shoes would no longer be mistaken as freshly purchased, at what point they would require polish to restore their luster so that you might venture onto the streets with a pair of shoes that looked as good as new—except you would know better.

"You make me want to take them off." Scott smiled and she put her hand in his lap.

He was still so charming, she told herself. All he had to do was let the affect back into his voice and he was again irresistible.

Look at her in that pose, the hand in his lap asking to be taken up, this small ritual by which they unburden themselves of history all at once. There is style in her gesture, one might almost call it a moral style. It is their style as a couple, and it has seen them through so much adversity, this penchant for reconciliation in the midst of ongoing conflict. The charm and lightness with which she faces down illness; his stubborn habit of perceiving her latest breakdown as merely one more setback in a string of soul-wearying events. Neither of them, Zelda no more than Scott, ready to admit defeat, their optimism unflagging despite all that has proven contrary to it. They have always been this way, he might tell himself, and their life not always so tragic. Never mind what people saw from the outside: everything could be forgiven, the past converted, all might be made new. If only, she reasoned, improvising a test, if only he will pick up my hand. He has done it so many times before, intertwined his fingers in mine, turned his wrist and mine inward, together.

"So," Zelda said after a long silence, withdrawing her hand from where it lay unembraced, "I suppose you're wondering what became of the lousy old Irishwoman and her daughter."

He wouldn't listen to her anymore if she insisted on using that word.

"Please, Scott. Lousy, lousy, lousy, you're so damned fastidi-ous." But when she looked up and saw that he wasn't going to be teased out of his mood, she gave in. "Oh, all right, *haggard,* that haggard Irishwoman, is that better? I thought they were both perfectly dreadful, making a spectacle of themselves in front of the entire train."

"They weren't so bad. I felt rather sorry for them, especially the mother."

"When it was she who wronged her own ward," Zelda exclaimed. "Oh, let's not talk about it." Here for the first time all afternoon he recognized the illness in her voice, otherworldly in its intensity, capable of expanding in several directions at once and leading almost anywhere except toward that which could be reasonably deduced. "While I'm stuck in bedlam you'll befriend such women, and their unseemly daughters will attempt to steal your heart."

"Zelda, control yourself. You don't believe a word you're saying."

"It was probably the new shoes," she conceded, adopting a philosophical tone. "People buy new shoes and suits and dresses when they're ready to fall in love with somebody else. I know you still love me, but you must often be overcome with buyer's remorse. Excuse me, but I didn't notice the cracks in her porcelain skin or that her mind was so fitful, some might say fundamentally impaired—do you suppose I might trade her in? Oh, wait, maybe I better not."

"Zelda, I'm not listening to any more of this."

"In the end you always decide to stick by me because you're loyal and you would rather that I get well than have to start over with some new woman and train her to put up with the insanity of living with a writer and his neuroses."

The conductor came down the aisle, calling, "Next stop Baltimore, folks," his voice trailing off as he passed to the rear of the car.

"I don't believe this emptiness is all I am," she said, snaring Scott's arm, digging into his biceps with her fingernails even as she pressed against him.

"Of course not." He ran his fingers along her forehead close to the hairline. "You're a mother, a writer, an artist—mostly, you are my own girl whom I always love."

"And you'll come visit and remind me of who I was and who I'm going to be again afterward, won't you?"

Scott watched the terror sweep across her face and take refuge in the corners of her eyes.

"Do you suppose," she asked, making an effort, toying with abstraction, as though observing herself from the outside, "Trouble has followed us all the way from Montgomery?"

"What will he do if he catches up to the train?"

"Well, he spends most of his time chasing us. It's a game to him, the pleasure in pursuit."

Here she lifted her face to Scott so he could study the line of her chin in profile, the soft skin marred by the eczema only partly masked by face powder. He put his hand on her shoulder, but she pushed it away, so he asked, "Where is Trouble now? What is he doing?"

"Oh, probably running alongside the train, panting heavily. It has been a long chase and he will be there, I imagine, waiting for me at the Phipps Clinic."

"Trouble is always waiting for you, isn't he?"

"Yes, he likes me better than you. But you also deserve your share of Trouble."

"You always were generous about sharing your Trouble with me."

A white-haired woman in the seat ahead cast a reproachful glance. Zelda, with her round Indian face and slightly slanted eyes, returned the woman's scrutiny with such dread intensity that she turned forward again without uttering a word.

They had invented the game on that trip to Florida before everything went bad. Only this past fall they had purchased a bloodhound to whom they gave the name Trouble ("Like a character from Hawthorne," Zelda declared in a burst of inspiration). Late one night in Florida Zelda was feeling blue and began to pine for her dog, recalling Trouble's droopy face and fond way of following at her heels, and she said aloud, with childish simplicity, "Oh, I wish Trouble were here with us." Without missing a beat Scott answered, "Haven't we had trouble enough the past few years?" and Zelda thrilled at his off-the-cuff double entendre. Within minutes they had concocted her new favorite pastime, which involved using their dog's name in a string of sentences that might as readily refer to a blood-hound's behavior as the rough lot in life of a black blues singer.

"Maybe that nosy woman is angling to take ownership of our Trouble," Zelda said in a voice loud enough that the eavesdropping woman ahead of them might hear.

"Oh, he'd be too much for her," Scott said.

Soon the train was braking and everywhere at once air seeped upward through the floorboards, like the last exhalations of a military truck on which the tires have been shot out. But when Scott declared his intent to see the conductor about the luggage, Zelda lurched for his elbow, saying, "Don't leave me," her antics at once staged and altogether sincere.

"Oh, all right, we'll both go."

Along the train passengers disembarked, throngs of working-class people from the cars farther down, the blacks in even greater numbers at the rear. On the platform white men in suits stood erectly, waiting for the next departure.

"Zelda, do you need anything? Otherwise we should find a taxi and start for Phipps."

"Yes, whatever you think best," she said, trying to sound cooperative even though her stomach was tumbling in on itself. Humming a song, slowly recovering its words—*Oh, I got that trouble in mind, it's true*—she trailed Scott through the turnstiles into the main concourse of Baltimore's Penn Station, scouting for exits as they crossed its cold, marbled, cavernous center and now headed through one of the high arched doorways that led to Charles Street.

I'm gonna lay my head on some lonesome railroad line
And let that midnight train satisfy my mind—

"Stop that, Zelda," Scott insisted. "Do you hear what you're singing?"

A taxi pulled forward and the driver took the bags from Scott.

"I was playing the game without you," she explained once they were in the cab. "What else shall we talk about? Let's pretend we're a young couple starting out, the two of us newly on our own, heading to the theater and dinner because you've sold your first book."

"I would rather that we concentrate on the near future. Let's at least agree on what we should say about what happened and how you slipped back."

"Get our stories straight, you mean."

"Not that we have anything to hide, but if we point the doctors in the right direction, maybe the cure will be easier on you this time."

"They're very strong-minded."

"Zelda, they're doctors, people of reason. Of course they'll want to know everything that can be of help."

"They have a strange way of showing their love."

"What do you mean?"

"Morphine, numbing doses of chloral hydrate, solitary confinement, restraints—"

"Stop it, Zelda. It's not love they're supposed to show—"

"No, that's your job."

"They're supposed to make you stronger, better able to cope with—"

"With you," she interrupted him. "Yes, I know all of that. What I should have said is that *you* have a strange way of showing your love."

She looked at him then, holding his granite jaw away from her. *Why do you hate me?* she wanted to cry. *How did I become your opponent?* For hate was radiating from his body, the desperate sense of lost destiny, which was and always would be her fault. Fierce and uncompromising, he wanted back the dream of uninterrupted existence, the writerly life to which she was the obstacle. If he were a harder man, such as Ernest, he would have abandoned her years ago and maybe it would have been better for everyone all around.

"I don't want to be their child again, Scott," Zelda said softly, but his heart was hardened against her. So she reached two fingers to his chest, stroking his shirt beneath the tie. He resented her when she was strong and defiant and troublesome, but could never resist her when she was falling apart. He could not stand to watch her suffer at the hands of anyone but himself.

"It's only a short time, Zelda dear," he said, his voice an arch-angel of mercy, come to her rescue—true, first he must hand her over to the enemy, but in time he will return to deliver her and she must remember to be grateful for what he will one day do for her.

"Just 'til you're well," he added.

"How will they know?" she asked after riding several minutes in silence, as though sound belonged only to the world beyond their windows, the metal shrieks of electric streetcars and the constant banter of car horns. "The doctors begin from a presumption of guilt, not innocence."

The patient must prove herself, show perfect docility, sometimes by performing the impossible, like witches with limbs tied together who must make their bodies sink even at the risk of drowning, who if they continued merely as they were, floating on the surface of the ordinary world, were still wrong. Only when she agreed to play the part expected of her—of wife, of mother, of artist in moderation—only then could they begin to talk of her release.

"It's not like that at all." He was tempted to believe her, but what good would that do? "It's also up to you to determine when you're well."

"If that's the case, if it's up to me to say when," she said, reasoning like a character out of Plato's dialogues, perhaps one of the sophists, "then I'm well right now."

"I know, Zelda, but you must maintain it," he said. He ran back over the day, able to recall only a single instance in which she had caused him to lose his patience. "You weren't at all well two days ago."

"But you see for yourself I am now," she said, maybe for the first time believing she might convince him to turn the taxi around and drive to a hotel for several days of necessary respite, away from her family. "Scott, what's it for? Am I going to the asylum to expiate my sins?"

"Is that your opinion of me?" he asked sharply. "I suppose that's why I work round the clock writing stories, so many of which I hate, just to be able to pay your medical bills."

"I only meant that the doctors see it that way, Scott."

But he could remember all those letters from Prangins, accusing him of being in league with the doctors and serving as her private inquisitor, plotting the barbaric things they would do to make her a true believer—though of what he'd like to know, since, he assured her, he had no doctrine anymore. Nothing in which he still believed.

"Please don't say that," she pleaded. "You scare me when you speak like that."

"I'm through with consolations, Zelda."

"Please, Scott, you must be consoled."

"For what?"

"For my sake. Please, I'll make myself better and I'll let the doctors believe they did it and then I will come and I will be your consolation."

Zelda tilted forward to ask the taxi driver, an Italian man with a heavy mustache and olive-dark skin smelling of soil, sun, and garlic, how far to the clinic.

"Three to five minutes, *signora*," the cabbie said, rolling his vowels in that wonderful Italianate manner, his words far more elegant than he himself could ever be.

So she slackened in her seat, thinking of how long she would have to wait for deliverance. Scott looked at her and he was kind again.

Studying her face, patient and gentle, youthful today as when he first met her, he could remember the possibilities he'd written for them. Last year at Prangins, with Zelda getting worse by the minute, Scott banned from seeing her, Dr. Forel had taken him aside and said, "I have read your stories. You are like the sculptor Pygmalion in the ancient myth, creating your wife and yourself in the image of what you might be, believing in youth as a promise. To be young is to be invulnerable. And neither of you—she more desperately than you, perhaps—can let go of what you were promised. Imagine, a grown woman taking up ballet, eight to ten hours a day, in her late twenties. Only a woman who doesn't believe in the mortal body, who believes in fables of youthful lore told by her husband, could do such a thing." It had made Scott angry for weeks afterward just to think of Forel's harangue.

To hell with them, the psychoanalysts were the booboosie, Zelda was right.

Why not order the driver to turn the car around and drive them to Lexington Market to pick up wine, cheese, and fruit? He formed the proposal in his head. *Zelda, if you'll only discipline yourself, we can skip the doctors.* He would take her on a picnic. She would be grateful and all his again, concentrating on his every word, able like any normal person to anticipate what should come next, assembling words and actions and their consequences into a story of self that held together. It might go on for days, weeks. He could remember seasons of terrific performance, the way she attended to him as ardent wife, doted on Scottie, kept things in balance, not indulging the wild habits of thought, the incessant dancing. Always, though, it unraveled, slowly at first, maybe in the wake of a critical remark he made after a glass of wine at the end of a long day of writing. "Zelda, why does it have be so hard?" he would ask, and it was as though a member of the audience had hurled an insult at her, drawing her out of character. In the face of criticism she was awful—breezy, lax in her duties, asking why it was that everyone had to slip through the house quiet as church mice until three in the afternoon each day, and when he said, "You know the answer to that," she'd say, "Oh, yes, because you're the great writer."

Then it would be over. She would prod and prod until she got him to admit his egomaniacal ambition, wresting from him a confession that he was in competition with the immortals, all of whom were, in her view, merely self-adoring seekers of fame. One stray remark and she was ruinous to herself and those nearest her, everything crashing down in its usual manner, as though she relished nothing more than her ability to make him stop writing. "I won't be responsible for your failure," she would scream. "I won't let you use me as an excuse."

"Scott, listen," Zelda said, tugging at the sleeve of his jacket, nudging him into the present, her lips pressed against his jaw in a seductive, husky whisper, "we could still escape."

Again she asked the taxi driver how much farther.

"At the end of this street, ma'am."

"Scott?"

"What, Zelda?"

She stared into his eyes but could discern only judgment there.

"You're not better than me."

He didn't say a word.

"Only please don't say the bad things," she begged. "Those are just between us."

"Zelda, we have to be honest."

"I'll tell them everything, on my terms, in my way. It's so much worse coming from you. Please, Scott, promise you'll let me say the bad things, let me tell them what it's like when I suddenly realize I'm not there anymore, that this woman who kisses her writer-husband and tells him she adores him or reads a book to her daughter is like a made-up character—I can pretend to be her for a while, but it's just pretend."

"As long as you say all that."

"I will," she said, "and more."

And maybe he hears the threat in this last remark, remembering the words she's already said and those she might yet say about him, everything on record in some psychoanalyst's office for people to read years later when he is dead.

"But I don't have to say any of it," she now whispers, as the driver curbs the taxi before the austere five-storied red brick building and its tight, enclosed arcade with heavy roman arches. The driver removes their bags from the trunk to set them inside the front door of the clinic. "There's still time," she says. "Let's make our escape." But Scott has already paid the taxi driver and made arrangements to be picked up in two hours and driven to the Belvedere Hotel. And now her husband turns and cradles her arm, her knees folding in dread as they climb the wide, shallow stairs like worshippers at the altar of some unforgiving god.

"I will be sad," she says as he holds the door for her and she listens for their heels clicking on the mosaic tiles, "watching you walk away in your new shoes."

I

April 1939

MORNINGS WERE A SUMMONS, THE URGENCY OF GUILT AND INDI-
gestion as he lay in bed not nearly as rested as he ought
to be, the precarious act of swinging his feet to the
ground, raising his head slowly so as to fend off the vertigo. His
routine was monkish. A good morning included the absence of
other people, casual neglect of the body's needs, the ability (never
to be taken for granted) to string together enough sentences that
he might deem himself worthy of companionship. He started each
day on the sentences he had been mulling over in his sleep, those
unbidden gifts of the unconscious. The longer he remained at his
desk, the longer he was able to suspend his visceral disgust in the
presence of food, activity, optimism, any of which in even mod-
erate doses might provoke a fit of vomiting. No matter what he
did the nausea stayed with him, constant for months now, relenting in brief stretches, mostly while he was eating sweet foods
or drinking hard liquor. In the kitchen he would bring himself to
life on Benzedrine, on cups of coffee laced with cocoa and sugar,
returning to his desk to write for another hour or two, putting off
the breakfast his housekeeper prepared for him, postponing the
glass of nerve-steadying gin until after lunch, sometimes into the

evening. He stored the bottles, full or empty, in the drawers of his bedroom dresser.

For more than a week now he had been scheming how to break the news to Sheilah. In a few days he would travel to North Carolina to check Zelda out of the hospital and take her on vacation to Cuba, just the two of them, husband and wife, headed somewhere warm and new and within reach. He had promised the trip as far back as November. Zelda was counting on it; his plans could not be altered. Of course, Zelda herself knew nothing about his lover Sheilah Graham, the beautiful young Hollywood gossip columnist with whom he had been living for over a year. Last spring Sheilah had wrested him from his apartment at the Garden of Allah, a compound overrun with everyday temptations packaged as old friends—Dorothy Parker, Don Ogden Stewart, Robert Benchley, all of whom were writing for the studios and still going hard at it, pursuing thrills on which he too had once so capably depended, refusing to give up on bourbon, easy acquaintance, late-night revelry. He might have backslid into carnivalesque gaiety and tumult if not for Sheilah, who found him a cottage outside the orb of the industry. In the San Fernando Valley, in the anonymous town of Encino, on an estate called Belly Acres, the name so ridiculous he almost refused to sign the lease, he lived in tranquil exile from his own life. (Years later Sheilah would recall Scott's dismay over the estate's name. "How can I tell anyone," she remembered him protesting, "I live at 'Belly Acres'?") During the winter it was ten degrees warmer here than on the coast, and the temperate, dry air was good for his tuberculosis, which had been flaring on and off for much of the past year. Sometimes Scott would stand on his porch, inhaling the breath of the valley, believing he could taste desert behind it, and he would think then of Sheilah, overcome with gratitude for this woman who so often did what was best for him before he'd thought to do it for himself.

Sheilah retained an apartment in the city, near the studio lots, and he often stayed there during the week. After years of turmoil, after the paralyzing fear that he might never write again, or never again write well, she helped dispel the sense of anonymity and purposelessness into which he had been ready to subside. She was even adept at cauterizing psychic wounds—when, for instance, he was introduced to a director, producer, or some Hollywood nobody who started on hearing his name. "F. Scott Fitzgerald?" a young screenwriter once asked on being introduced, studying him a minute, trying to decide if it was all a ruse, before declaring, "I had it from a reliable source you were dead."

"Nobody who has written the books you've written," Sheilah consoled him later that night, "will ever be dead."

Much though he relied on Sheilah, it did nothing to alter his devotion to Zelda. These were the hard facts of his life. He had been brought to this end by circumstances, a man capable not only of loving two women at once, but of needing each to sustain his dented, almost shattered ego. He convinced himself he must do nothing to devastate Zelda's spirit. The staff at the sanitarium assured him she wasn't able to cope with unpleasant news. She relied primitively on hopes of imminent escape to get through each day, the vision of a return to her old life the only future she could construct for herself. Her belief in Scott's faithfulness—he was, after all, faithful to her in the most important ways, paying her bills, writing frequent letters, visiting whenever he could—was at the center of the fragile yet intricate equilibrium she had achieved for herself. For this reason he instructed Scottie, now a student at Vassar College, as well as the few friends still in touch with Zelda, never to speak with her about his life in California.

Zelda had been in residence three years at the Highland Hospital in Asheville, North Carolina, under the care of Dr.

Robert Carroll, who believed in fighting diseases of the mind such as schizophrenia with avant-garde medicines and the tried and true solace of recreational therapy. He was fond of citing the ancient adage, *"Mens sana in corpore sano,"* while counseling patients and their families not to be mystified by medical jargon. *Insanity:* the very word struck fear in all who experienced it in themselves or in the souls of people they loved. But Carroll summed up his approach in a peculiarly literal translation of that same Roman adage. "A sane mind in a sane body," he insisted, ordering the days of his patients in constant activity: outdoor gymnastics, five-mile walks, hill-climbing, tennis, tossing the medicine ball, games of volleyball, painting and dance lessons. In the spring of 1936—when Zelda left Sheppard Pratt outside of Baltimore, her fourth institution in seven years—she had been a waif of ninety pounds. Under Carroll's regimen she gained back twenty pounds in the first year, reclaiming her muscular dancer's figure as well as her robust, handsome face, able to believe for the first time in ages that there was nothing that could keep her from retrieving her health.

The Highland arranged day trips and as many as half a dozen vacations per year, mostly to picturesque destinations. The excursions were expensive, over and above the regular cost of room, board, and medical care. This past January, Scott had given his permission for a trip to Havana. As he scavenged for cash to pay for it, he suffered pangs of regret over *Fidelity,* his labor of love for much of the past year, an artful script nurtured for months by Metro-Goldwyn-Mayer, then left to wither on the vine, yet another casualty of Hollywood's moribund fear of censors, one more example of his own hard luck. When he couldn't raise the money for her travel, Zelda, in that mercurial way she had of overlooking the infinite setbacks of the past decade and surrendering herself again to optimism, told him she couldn't have enjoyed spending such a large sum of money without him. They had always only been extravagant together. He heard the invitation creep into her letters even before she declared offhandedly, weeks later, "We can go to Cuba ourselves, as far as that goes." He pulled together the funds for her to spend the month of February in Florida under supervision of the hospital. From the bone-white sands of the Sarasota beaches she wrote thanking him, wishing he could have been there to share the sun and warm water with her. In steady beckons she began calling him to her side, her one reliable resource against the world's severity.

He imagined that the right moment would announce itself, so he put her off, promising to come for her as soon as he could, certainly by the end of May. Here it was the middle of April and he still hadn't chosen a date or said anything to Sheilah about the trip because there were only so many ways the conversation could go, none of them cheerful, none all that different from the last time he'd left her behind to go on holiday with Zelda.

"How do I know you haven't been fucking her the entire time?"

"Sheilah, I've always told you the truth," he had sworn a few months earlier.

"I can't trust you. You know why I can't trust you. After all this while, and you keep running back to her."

"It was a promise I made."

"When? What part?" she asked, having resisted for as long as she could because it was humiliating to compete with a sick woman. "Are we talking about wedding vows, Scott? Because that was a long time ago and though it's chivalrous of you, even the Catholic Church might give you a pass on this one. After all, your wife has gone ins—"

"Don't speak of her. You don't know anything about Zelda, don't you ever say a word against her."

"The only thing that is sacred to you, that's what she is. Not me, I'm not worth it. I'll break off an engagement for you, but where's the value in that compared to the ordeal of Zelda, for whom you've waged a war against the gods and fate, the two of you struggling for your place in the sun, finding it denied and so fighting tooth and claw with each other? Who knows, as long as we're being honest, how much all that fighting contributed to her going crazy!"

"Now I am leaving," he shouted.

"You need the excuse first? Sheilah is a bitch, so now I'm free to go. Well, I won't be here waiting for you."

She was, though, as she must have known she would be, biding her time, waiting on his return if only so as to give utterance to her outrage. He found her in the afternoon at her apartment, a couple of weeks after his return from New York City. He was not averse to hearing what she needed to say. It was her right, she deserved no less. First, though, he had to tell her about the trip, spilling the news of yet another disastrous outing with Zelda, racing through it, trying to keep pace with the rapid-fire memories all jumbled and out of sync, his voice hoarse and sharp, the adrenaline and exhaustion surging through him like a compulsion, the many bristling thoughts of the wrong Zelda had done him yet again. There was no one else to whom he could say any of it. This time he really was finished, he raged. Of all the things Zelda had ever done, none could compare to this latest. She had attempted to have him committed—how was that for irony? On the last morning of the trip Scott awakened to find Zelda and his pants missing, called downstairs to the manager, who answered in soothing tones, "Please stay calm, Mr. Fitzgerald. Your wife will be back shortly with someone from the hospital to escort you home." Scott rushed to the door, dressed in bow tie and jacket but pantless, his irritation mounting toward panic (for Zelda was capable of harming herself) as he discovered two bellboys stationed outside his room. She had fed the hotel manager some tale in which she played the part of long-suffering wife, he the madman who could be checked out of his asylum every once in a while for a weekend in Manhattan. It took Scott ten minutes to persuade the manager that the spouse who was actually insane was even then roaming the streets of New York City, another ten to get him to send the guards at his door in pursuit, so that they might overtake her in Central Park, digging a hole in the ground in which to bury his pants.

He recounted the story for Sheilah, knowing that his fury and stupor made him sound just as crazy as his wife. He promised to break with Zelda so that the two of them—Sheilah Graham, his beloved infidel, and Scott Fitzgerald, her faithful paramour—could be married. He would find a lawyer, see the divorce through, he meant it this time. He would divorce Zelda. He uttered the words aloud like a vow and watched the eagerness for confrontation leave Sheilah's eyes as sympathy took up residence where minutes earlier there had been only anger. What made the confession worse in hindsight was that Sheilah never once called him on those promises of a future they might yet spend together.

It had been six short months since New York and here he was ready to depart for Cuba within the week, and he still hadn't mentioned it to Sheilah. Maybe that was how the fight started. Whenever he let himself sink into the alcohol he pushed her away, but she could sense that Zelda was again on his mind, inspiring his demands for privacy, time, and space. Sheilah had stopped by late morning and within minutes launched into a search of the cottage.

"What is this?" she asked, holding up an empty gin bottle pulled from the bottom drawer of his bureau, playing the part of innocence deceived all over again.

"Nothin' that concernz you," he said. "Now please shu' the drawer."

"Why? Because if I can't see the bottles, I won't know what's going on?"

"No, because you have no right tuh be going through my drezz'r and my perz'nal—"

"Pronounce the words correctly, Scott," she said. "Make a little effort, will you? How blind do you think I am?"

Really, how blind could she be? He wanted to throw the words back in her face. He resented her spells of indifference as much as her interferences. The tuberculosis active again in his lungs, he was hurtling toward collapse—how could she have failed to notice the signs?

"Did you think I wouldn't notice you slurring words? Tell me, I'd like to understand how you live this duplicity. How much of it do you expect to keep secret, how much do you hope I'll find out? What's the fine ratio in your head? When am I overstepping my bounds and when am I acting as someone who loves you and wants to make sure you live, let's be modest in our hopes, through the middle of this summer? Or is it all for the sake of form? Poor Sheilo, stowed by her mother in a London orphanage at age six, without even faint memories of a consumptive, dead father, witness thereafter to the degradations of poverty, alcoholic misery, and East End squalor—let's pretend for her sake I'm not destroying myself."

"Your powers of perception are truly stun—"

"You think I had to open this dresser to guess what was in here?"

"Then you won't mind goddamned shutting it." He started toward her, his hand balled in a fist.

"Go to hell, then," she shouted, turning her back to him, heading for the door. "I'm sure you can find it without me."

His plans with Sheilah aborted, nothing on his schedule for the week ahead, he was tempted to stay the course until he left for North Carolina in a few days, then maybe try to patch things up on his return. His day passed in misery, too many drinks. He tried alternating beer and Coca-Colas with the glasses of gin, but he had drained half a bottle by mid-afternoon, unable to work at all. Several times he almost got in his Ford coupe to drive himself to the airport, but he could no longer pretend his drinking was under control, and it would be reckless of him to visit Zelda in his present state. She was so superstitious about alcohol, about the scent of wine or beer on his breath. He'd have to straighten out before he left.

Sometime after midnight, after squandering the night on alcohol and indecision, he placed a call to a nurse he'd used several times before, and she agreed to arrive first thing in the morning. "Mr. Fitzgerald," she said before hanging up, "how about a show of good faith? Put down the bottle for the night, maybe get yourself halfway to sober before I arrive." So he brewed a pot of coffee and poured himself cup after cup, lacing each with sugar and cocoa, pacing the captain's deck at the front of his cottage and smoking cigarettes as he stared off into the desert-cool night. Above the magnolias, firs, and birches to his west he concentrated on a shiftless moon, bobbing on the crown canopy of distant forest. After a while he went inside to check the time. Counting down the hours, the first part of any cure. Except when he looked at the clock, less than an hour had elapsed. He'd never make it until morning.

Fixing a second pot of coffee, nibbling on chocolate from the icebox, he endured another hour. Then he called Sheilah. She picked up, her voice sluggish yet responsive, sounding those rare notes that were only for him. "Scott, what is it? Are you all right? What time—"

"I'm sorry for the way I've behaved these past few weeks."

"Sorry for what exactly?" She intended to make him say it, if only so she might know where she stood.

"About the drinking, of course. About the way I've treated you, with mistrust, with anger, resenting your interferences when you were only—"

"Okay, that's enough," she said. "What's next?"

"I've called the nurse and she's coming in the morning. I need to sober up because I've acted badly, quite badly."

"And you probably won't let me see you," she said.

The fight with his body, the pain and convulsions, the days of constant retching, the sweat and stink—none of it would be pretty. He had grappled with all of this before and he preferred for Sheilah not to see him when he was drying out and in such sorry shape.

"Well, you could visit me tonight," he offered.

"When?" she asked. "Tonight is just shy of over."

"I don't suppose I could talk you into coming to me now?"

It was more than a twenty-minute drive from the city to the valley. A lot to ask, especially at this hour.

He waited on her reply.

"Do you need me?" she asked.

"I promised the nurse I'd make it 'til morning without a drink and I'd really like to keep my promise, but the night lingers, and my will is rather debilitated."

"Okay, I'll be there within the half hour. You can hold on that long, can't you?"

* * *

On the deck, dwelling on his dishonesty and his dread of telling Sheilah about Cuba, he was so overcome by remorse that he hardly registered the sound of her car pulling into the drive.

"How are you faring?" she called from the walkway, not yet his girl, the resistance still strong in her voice. He doubted he could win her back in time, or that he had the right to do so.

"The deck is the best feature of this cottage, don't you think?" he asked. "I almost forget myself when I'm standing here beneath the tapestry of California night, the sky to our west like the last frontier of the American imagination, or so I tell myself—Hollywood, the place to which you come to die all the while believing you're about to be born again."

"Scott, we can't have that kind of talk," she said, "I simply won't listen tonight to . . . ," her voice tapering off as she slipped between the rose-covered trellises onto the porch.

Once inside the cottage, she refused to join him on the deck. The business for which she'd come pertained to what went on inside these walls, to the confinement soon to follow, to the sordid rebirth of a soul from the detritus of its own ugliness. Long days of darkness, cruelty, and torpor had transformed him into a person who shared little in common with the Scott she loved. The man before her was someone who could emerge only after weeks and weeks of drinking had warped both vision and memory. So she treated him with clinical coolness, making no decisions about the future.

"How many bottles will I find?" Sheilah asked, returning to the bureau where she'd made her stand earlier that day.

"Oh, let's not bother with any of that. It's a history of which I'm not proud, of which we'll soon be free. Please, Sheilo," he said, peering again into the graying light of the predawn sky, gesturing for her to join him outside. "Can we not think about that right now?"

"Why am I here?" she asked.

From where he stood he could make out a convex of light inside the door, Sheilah positioned within the recessed darkness, her silhouette just visible, the expression on her face illegible. She tugged at the chain on the freestanding lamp next to the dresser, then knelt down and jostled the bottom drawer, already ajar, widening the opening so she could run her hands through T-shirts and underwear, over the empty bottles, rattling and rolling together in a musical, hollow tinking. In the next drawer too, she took stock of how far he had descended into that part of him that wished never to be returned to the world. Her hands stayed longest in the top drawer, digging beneath handkerchiefs and socks until she must have felt the cold hard metal, most likely wrapping her fingers onto its grooved cylinders, knowing right away what it was.

"What are you doing?" Scott stepped inside. "Get away from there this instant."

"What is it, Scott? What's here that I'm not allowed to see?"

She pulled the object from the drawer and held it in her palm, thumb resting on its handle, fingers relaxed under the trigger guard.

"Sheilah, goddamnit, that's not yours. It has nothing to do with you."

"Like hell it doesn't," she said. "I want to know, I want you to tell me why you have it."

He didn't owe her an explanation, not for the gun anyway. The conversation they were supposed to be having was about Cuba. Her eyes shone with self-righteous indignation, only her mouth giving her away, her lower lip unable to hold its naturally gallant shape.

"Hand it over," he said. "I'll only ask once."

"Fine, see if I give a goddamn," she said, and threw the gun at his head. He ducked and the gun crashed against the wall behind him. "At least it would be efficient. You don't want to change, you're in love with your own ruin. I'm leaving. The nurse will be here before long and I don't care anymore. What happens to you is none of my concern, I think you've made that perfectly clear."

She waited to see what he would do next. When he said nothing, when he didn't budge an inch, she walked out of the bedroom. Seconds later he was listening to the fall of her even, unhesitant steps on the stairs, the front door of the cottage opening, the lock rattling as she slammed it shut behind her.

By the time the car disappeared down the lane, he was again on the deck, surprised by his contentedness. By leaving him twice in the same day, Sheilah had absolved him of duplicity. For better or worse he was Zelda's husband again; he could go to Asheville and rescue her from a loneliness that, if not identical to his, was so parallel as to be at times indistinguishable from it.

He would leave today, he told himself. He laid a suitcase on the floor and began reaching for clothing in his closet. Havana, he imagined, would be similar in climate to Southern California, and as someone who suffered chills even on seventy-degree Hollywood winter days, he packed four sport jackets and four pairs of heavy cloth pants, fistfuls of underwear and socks, the suitcase overflowing until he returned half of the clothing to the closet. The gun lay on the floor beside the bed, so he wrapped it in a pair of BVDs, burrowing it deep in the suitcase, explaining to Sheilah in some far-off future, "But darling, the gun was loaded," wondering if that made a difference, if it justified anything.

By the clock on the night table he saw that it was nearly five. He could leave for the airport, attempt to board a postdawn flight. Then he remembered the nurse. Too late to call. He couldn't strand her at the door of an empty cottage. He would have to postpone his departure for the airport until she arrived. He felt his spine slacken, his courage leaking from his pores as he succumbed to lightheadedness, vertigo, nausea. He would never make it through the day without sleep. He lay back on the bed and closed his eyes. The nurse, of course, would recommend he put off the trip, see the cure through, and make plans from the other side. But surrender to the regimen of drying out meant weeks as an invalid, and afterward he would need to call in favors across the city to see if he could pick up freelance work. All the while Zelda would be planted evenings in the foyer of the Highland, sitting quietly, reading, imploring him for as long as spring should last to be true to his promise to come for her.

The knocking from below—a steady pounding by the time he heard it—woke him. He made his way down the stairs and caught a whiff of his own alcoholic stench, disgusted on the nurse's behalf. He unlocked the front door without so much as a hello, retreating to the second-floor bathroom, hearing her greeting while still on the stairs, "Mr. Fitzgerald? You all right?" Turning the faucet on, he removed the T-shirt and pajama trousers he had been wearing under his robe, lathering chest, armpits, groin, then toweling himself off. Next he doused his hair with water and cologne, scrubbed his face with soap, splashing water freely, squeezing toothpaste into his mouth, searching in vain for his toothbrush, then sawing each side of his mouth upper and lower with his finger, tasting the cologne in the toothpaste, spitting out the froth; and only after he'd done all of this did he swing open the bathroom door to answer the nurse.

Mrs. Carmichael chattered to him from the kitchen, cleaning the overflow of dirty dishes. "I'll make you some breakfast. Get your strength up for the long battle. Were you sleeping? Jesus, Mary, and Joseph, you was out, Mr. Fitzgerald."

He was annoyed by her maternally hovering presence.

"Mrs. Carmichael," he called from the bedroom, trying to be heard above a boiling kettle. "My calendar's changed. An appointment this morning, a matter of some urgency, it can't be helped."

"I'm sorry, did you say something, Mr. Fitzgerald?" She climbed the stairs and entered the bedroom doorway just as he was removing his underwear from beneath the robe, though, fortunately, with his back turned to her. Securing the robe in front, tucking the underwear in a pocket, he pivoted on his heels.

"I was saying I have to leave town this afternoon. Planning to return in a week or so. Headed for New York, can't be—"

"Mr. Fitzgerald, you sure? Last night you sounded like the prodigal child who knows he better turn back or he'll soon be knocking on death's door."

"Alcohol makes one melodramatic."

"Alcohol makes one a lot of things, none of them very good, but I don't know how many second chances we get in life. You've already had your fair share."

It couldn't be helped, he told her again, trying not to let her see how badly he was hurting, his hands shaky with the d.t.'s, nerves tensed in one long scream whose only solace was the dose of alcohol he would allow himself once he was out of her presence.

"I'm not nearly so bad off as I sounded, but I may want your help on my return."

"Tell you what I thought this morning when you didn't come to the door. I was pounding for better than ten minutes, readying myself to go for the police."

"Guess I woke in the nick of time."

"You mightn't have."

"It's possible," he said, hesitating. If she meant to frighten him, she was doing a fairly good job of it.

Informing her less than an hour later that he had to run to the studio but would be back in the evening, he left with suitcase in hand (just in case, he told Mrs. Carmichael, knowing he wouldn't return). During the drive he thought of Sheilah, how she accepted the symptoms of being in a relationship with him but not quite the facts of it. As long as Zelda remained a tragic ghost, Sheilah could cope with the marriage, doing her best not to interfere. But any sign of Zelda creeping back into his life to lay claim to even a portion of what was rightfully hers and there was trouble. Only last week Sheilah had discovered a letter from Zelda.

"Oh, Scott, she is still so in love with you. What do you say to her? She is waiting every day for you to come and rescue her. Why don't you go and be with her? She'll take you back, she will always take you back."

As if any of that were an option.

"I didn't mean to read the letter," Sheilah said afterward. "It was just sitting there among a stack of books in the living room, her dramatic penmanship, her untamed spirit, so much to admire in her. I only read enough to hurt me." Scott was almost certain he'd stored the letter with the others, in a folder he kept in his dresser, but he didn't press the issue.

At the studio he flashed his identification badge for the guard and drove beyond the heavily wired perimeter to park his Ford coupe in the commoners' lot. Crossing the campus he felt his chest tighten in the humidity and pulled out a handkerchief to wipe his brow. A trickle of sweat gathered in the small of his back and he couldn't wait to get upstairs to his office. On the stairs he remembered again the letter snatched last week from Sheilah, which he'd stowed in the breast pocket of his finely threaded tweed jacket, the same one in which he was now profusely sweating in the midmorning sun. He reached inside the pocket for the letter and, sure enough, it was there.

He pulled the scented green stationery out of the envelope, surveying Zelda's undated, amorous scrawl.

Monsieur mon cher,

Spring awakens in me memories of all the happiness that awaits us, and at times it presses on me like a pain in the heart the size of memory itself. I believe so much in your writing and your talent and your oh so handsome face, and I do not see how they can continue to postpone your much-deserved good fortune in Hollywood. Cannot they see what is right there in front of them? Shall I write a note to your boss, Mr. Goldwyn, conveying my outrage about their infidelity to your wonderful ode to adultery, the Fidelity that wasn't to be? Well, only if you promise to spend your carnal appetites (assured always of my indulgences and special dispensations) in humble doses and on women who are not nearly so pretty as I once was.

Do you suppose you could ever again find me beautiful? I have my doubts. Some days I drown in regret over missed chances, our missed chances, and I become so bitter I am not fit company even for myself. But always I decide to be happy and hopeful for your sake, won't you be so also for mine? I'm sure you'll remember how charming I can be and how my hair once bobbed still pleases, how I too may be pleasing if you'll please visit me soon. Regret seems frivolous. Who are we to question the fates? All things incline toward tragedy, we know this better than anyone. It is the way of the world not to value what you and I have fought to achieve. Scott, I know you have been sorry and unhappy, but you were once my religion, or the dream of us was like religion to me, and I cannot altogether believe that faith doesn't bear fruit. I read the Bible at night and tell myself that prayer still works. Can you feel it? Shall I recite for you the Song of Songs, our favorite passages, all the dirty parts?

If you come for me, I will succumb to any and all forms of transportation. Oh, this newly discovered fear of flying! Another weakness of constitution, another missing piece in my inadequate psychic armor—how can you ever have loved such a woefully in-adequate girl? But with you I am always brave and if the plane plunges into the ocean and you are there are at my side, well, you see how my imagination runs.

Devotedly, as ever, Zelda

Though no longer under contract with the studio, Scott retained a desk there, in a high-ceilinged office shared with several other writers. The office was empty, the air stifling. None of the fans running. No mail in his box. All in all, an extraordinarily useless errand. Nobody looking for him, his life unaccounted for. Still, he would leave a note, just in case someone should try to reach him. He dug a pad out of the desk and wiped his brow with his handkerchief. In big block letters he scrawled across the sheet of paper *"GONE TO CUBA,"* then signed it *"FSF,"* placing the note on his desk, where it was likely to raise more questions than it answered. Still, he liked the style of his reticence. Why tell the bastards anything?

He sat at the desk studying the note, then picked up the phone. Soon he was making arrangements for a plane that would deliver him on Zelda's doorstep that very afternoon, and a second to take them to Miami, so they might leave for Havana the next morning.

And now he descended into the festive, superficial light of Los Angeles, pausing under a row of date palms at the far end of the studio lot, shading his eyes from an unreal sun situated atop the mountains, the late morning sky so blue and pristine as to pro-voke belief in nature's regenerative power. The past twenty-four hours had simplified his life considerably. If Sheilah was gone for good, he would suffer for it, but he had lived so long and on such intimate terms with grief that it was no threat to him. He felt vital and self-sufficient, free to do whatever he chose, perhaps nothing at all. For just a second he entertained the thought of not traveling all the way to North Carolina, not running again to Zelda's rescue. He could leave town and go almost anywhere, alone, accountable to no one. Except he could picture Zelda in the foyer of that sanitarium, seated there evenings, feeling important because her husband was coming (as if they were just any leisure-class couple) to take her on holiday.

What he needed was a drink to brace him against the requirements of conscience. Spotting a bar across the street, he decided he had time enough for one beer before heading to the airport to catch his flight—always pursuing the path of past promises, always returning to Zelda. He was all she had in the world, the ironclad law of his life. There was no other way of seeing it. Duty was the form his love for Zelda had assumed, this loyalty to a woman he'd always loved the one last truth to which he held firm.

2

AT THE FAR END OF THE PIER THE FLYING BOATS OF PAN AMERICAN
Airways rested like dormant leviathans, their fat bellies
dependent in the water. She looked up ahead to the
planes, then behind her toward the white stucco terminal building,
so many times that Scott said, "Zelda, please stop that, you're making me dizzy." Most likely they were being followed. She couldn't
say who it was or what he wanted, maybe a private eye hired by
the Highland to keep tabs on them. A bad report to Dr. Carroll
might bring an end to these trips with her husband, who despite
his many flaws was her only company in the world.

"I was checking to see how many people will be on our flight
to Havana."

"Well, stop turning your head."

"Okay, Scott," she said, feigning childlike submissiveness, all
the while thinking that with his petulant, nervous impatience it
was he who was childlike.

A stewardess passed them, walking briskly toward the plane,
and Scott touched her elbow. "How much longer 'til we board?"
he asked.

"Don't bother the nice girl, Scott," Zelda said, smiling into the woman's vacant yet comely face, appeasing her. In all likelihood Scott had stolen a drink before they left the hotel, perhaps during the early morning errand he ran shortly before seven, without explanation, saying only that he would be back in twenty minutes. She was dressed by the time he reappeared, moving out of his way as he dashed into the bathroom, far enough to the side that even if she had been trying to smell his breath, and she wasn't, she couldn't have done so. He emerged from the bathroom primped, a blue silk cravat-shaped tie knotted in a neat square, the white shirt collar framing his freshened face, only his eyes showing signs of weariness. Not twenty minutes later he had them arriving at the Pan American Terminal at Dinner Key well ahead of schedule, too early for his own good. He had been going at this clip since yesterday at the sanitarium, where he was hasty and abrupt, speaking few words to the attending nurse, insisting there was no need to call a doctor and then escorting Zelda through the lobby with such haste you might have thought he was abducting his wife rather than taking her on holiday. It seemed to Zelda that if he slowed even a little, his body would give out. She hated traveling with him in this condition, not simply because it was in violation of hospital rules—she could hear the doctors warning her, "His drinking is not good for you"—but because Scott might prove incapable in an emergency.

"He's been traveling for two days straight," she told the stewardess, explaining his impatience. "He's a writer in Hollywood and he's very tired."

"Not long now, sir," the stewardess answered. "Would I know any of your pictures?"

"Did you see *Three Comrades*?" Zelda asked.

"No, I'm afraid I never heard of it."

"It was an important film last year and won several awards," Zelda told her. "Look for *Gone with the Wind* later this year."

"Did you work on that also?" the stewardess asked Scott. "I think I've—"

"Yes, he—," Zelda started to say.

"Not really," Scott said simultaneously.

"He's quite modest," Zelda explained.

"That's a refreshing quality in a famous person." The stewardess smiled, then moved on.

"Why did you do that?" Scott snapped.

"What did I do?"

"You made me the author of a script I worked on for three weeks, without permission to insert a single sentence that wasn't already in Margaret Mitchell's execrably mediocre novel, a script from which as far as I know all traces of my input have by now been excised, every one of my lines rewritten."

"Scott, it makes no difference," Zelda said. "She didn't know the other film and I thought it might make her feel important when she's out with her beau this summer to be able to say, 'I met the screenwriter of this film on a flight to Havana.'"

"You could have told her about something I actually wrote."

"Like what?"

"Like *The Great Gatsby,* for instance, because everybody— oh, never mind."

"If she hadn't heard of *Three Comrades,* she's not likely to have read *Gatsby.*"

"I don't see why you had to humiliate me."

"Don't be silly," she said. "You're a wonderful writer, but that doesn't mean people have heard of you. If you were less wonderful, perhaps *more* people would have heard of you."

"And the *Saturday Evening Post?*"

"Yes, I'm sure she's seen the *Saturday Evening Post* and maybe even our glamorous picture on it when she was a little girl, but I've learned the hard way not to mention—"

"Well, never mind," he said. "Just don't ever again advertise me as a third-rate writer on a third-rate film I'm not even going to get a screen credit for."

Soon they were boarding, crossing the tarmac and filing down the pier to ascend a moveable staircase positioned against the aircraft, into which the people up ahead in line were disappearing, one by one. Zelda said in an offhanded manner, "Into the belly of the whale, each his own Jonah," and Scott was scratching something in his notebook, probably her phrase.

Within minutes of taking his seat he fell asleep, and she slanted close to his wilting head, close enough to discern the bouquet of his breath beneath the Lucky Tiger Bay Rum aftershave, but whether the traces of alcohol were from this morning or yesterday or the day before she couldn't tell. The engines revved, the rapid-fire slapping of the propellers churning the air, and she could feel the waters beneath them become choppy, rocking the aircraft in a cradlelike motion. For several seconds she doubted she would be able to master her fear and she squeezed Scott's forearm with the thought of waking him, but no, that would be selfish. Only wake him if you really need him, she scolded herself, adding in a faint whisper, "Don't be foolish, Zelda," then conjuring the things Scott might say to console her, running through a list of commonplace assurances. He had flown dozens and dozens of times. It was perfectly safe. Nothing could happen on a plane that couldn't happen by any other mode of travel, say, while driving a car. *Except plummeting into the depths of the ocean.* She laughed at the recklessness of her imagination, at the part of her that would not submit to etiquette, even to an etiquette she herself had invented.

From her seat by the window she could feel the cyclonic whir of a nearby propeller. Lifting her eyes, then lowering them again, she tried to focus on an individual blade and keep distinct its peculiar oblong shape before it finally spun free, dissolving into the blur of its own speed. As the aircraft drifted out into Biscayne Bay, she pictured its nose pointed toward the ocean and again looked at Scott, still asleep, oblivious to the danger of takeoff. Soon the flying boat was heaving its pregnant belly into flight and she could feel the fingers of water gripping the sides of the aircraft, not wanting to let go, until in an instant it tore free, wobbling and bobbing on the Atlantic winds as it climbed the sky, every now and then slipping and falling back so that there was a hollow sensation in her stomach and she clutched Scott's forearm. But even as she fought back the nausea, the plane steadied itself on the contrary winds and she allowed a simple, exhilarated thought: they were on vacation, Scott and she, on a flying clipper headed for Havana.

Contented, she closed her eyes and let her mind wander. She was twenty-two again and famous. She graced the covers of magazines, an icon of style quoted for her witticisms, and she said to Scott without melancholy, "This is as happy as we'll ever be." His stories in demand everywhere, his name on the tip of everyone's tongue, the voice of a generation. As yet no envy: somehow she too would find her place in the sun, Scott would help her get there. On a lark she wrote a review of *The Beautiful and Damned* accusing Scott of plagiarizing her diaries, but she hadn't meant anything by it. She tried to remember what it felt like to live in the glory of his achievement and his even greater potential, with no ambitions of her own, at least none she had announced. Then she saw them in the spring of 1924: on an ocean liner, headed for France, husband and wife eager to shed their younger selves. "America is the eternal present," Scott said, adding with biblical solemnity, "the land of mother's milk and money." It was harder in the States than anywhere else, he speculated, to cast off the glamour of being young and beautiful and carefree. So they fled to Europe. To grow up and live economically and put frivolity behind them, maybe stay several years if France could hold their interest. Scott had much of *Gatsby* on the page, the rest of it in him, ready to be written, though he kept calling the book by another name, what was it he had wanted to call it, she couldn't remember—well, it didn't matter.

Next to her Scott fidgeted in his seat but slept on. Outside, the even rows of white clouds folded like crests of waves on the empyreal blue. She wanted to pause memory where it had taken her, stay there without moving forward, so as not to arrive at her summer's flirtation with the French aviator Edouard Jozan, to which Scott would respond so punishingly, their intimacy poisoned thereafter by his aversion to her charisma, artistry, and uninhibited sexuality, by her aversion to his freedom, talent, and stature. Envy, the beginning of a new era in their lives. In the spring of 1924, though, there was as yet no real division. She wished to stay within those long weeks in Paris when they were always together, implausibly happy. Stay entirely within that spring so as to fall in love again with Sara and Gerald Murphy, Zelda and Scott's elegant doppelgängers—all of them so enchanting. Paris was like a gala every night, one at which Zelda always struck a figure, her performance sometimes histrionic but never boring. She experienced again the charge of her body when she danced in clubs, how she held the attention of so many men, moving with athletic knowingness, always pushing at the limits. Scott, in a sour mood, might come and wrap his jacket around her on the dance floor, especially when she started pulling her skirt up, but he was titillated by her antics and never remained angry long.

She didn't believe in the adoration of the public, but that didn't make her any less aggressive about seeking it. She took baths at parties, causing guests to line up to use the toilets and knock and then crack the door as she hailed them, saying, "I'm bathing," and they might ask how long, and what was she doing anyway bathing in the middle of a party. Some of the desperate souls would beg to be allowed in to use the toilets, men and women alike. The women coming forward to sit on the rim of the tub and peer into the water to witness the shape of her splendorous naked body beneath soapy bubbles. The men pretending not to look at her as they asked teasingly if there were other American girls like her, and would she mind letting them know ahead of time which parties she was planning to attend. More than once a gentleman offered to scrub her back and she leaned forward, breasts skimming the surface as she folded her chest to her knees and let him work the brush along her spine, as far down as he could reach.

"I'm braver than the others," she said aloud in a whisper.

Scott, stirring in the seat beside her, asked in a mutter if she had been speaking to him.

"I see the way the world is," she said in a low voice, "and refuse to look away."

She ordered a ginger ale from the stewardess and asked how long until they landed, surprised to learn they were almost there. Scott opened his eyes and sat up.

"Oh, hello, did you have a good nap?" She was doing her best to sound like an ordinary wife, concerned only about the little things that bound them in the day to day.

"You're in a good mood," he answered, as if he'd been uncertain of what to expect.

"But why shouldn't I be?"

Perhaps he suspected she had gone and made herself young again. For whenever she came all the way into the present tense, embracing the possibility of the world before her and what might still be done in it, he grew nervous.

"Right, why shouldn't you be?"

"All I meant," she said, "was that my talented and handsome and supremely beneficent husband has traveled thousands of miles to take me on an adventure." She heard the theatricality in her voice, worrying for a second she would be unable to carry it off, until she realized she meant everything she was saying.

"I'd still like to take care of you," she added, sensing that deep down he remained hers, though he couldn't trust the part of himself that was devoted to her. "Of course, I'm not sure how much I can help, or if you even want my help anymore."

Well then, he proposed, let them try to take care of each other as best they could, day by day, starting small, starting with tonight, moving on from there.

It was the end of the dry season in Cuba and the road from the airport crossed through the heavily cultivated plains of the *campo,* the American-made cars up ahead trailing clouds of red dust so that the windows of their car had to be kept up despite the stifling heat. Below them were the harvested fields of sugarcane and tobacco, here and there a hacienda embedded in a grove of trees, its colonnaded portico steeped in shadows. They passed hovels set close to the road where dirty, naked children played in yards full of dilapidated farm machinery and rusted tools. It reminded her of the South of her childhood, the aristocratic decadence of an Old World culture disdaining yet nonetheless dependent on the degrading poverty that everywhere surrounded it, but she felt no nostalgia for a style of life amid which she'd once shown so splendidly. One day last year after suffering a bout of eczema, she had looked into a bathroom mirror at the Highland Hospital and glimpsed a person unrecognizable to anyone who'd known her as the Judge's rare

jewel of a daughter, whose talent for fusing nobility and exper-
imentalism only added to her allure among the staid Montgomery girls. As she ran her fingers over tormented skin, she
envisioned herself slipping off to reside among the rural poor,
forever disdaining what she'd once been for an existence based
on the body's most basic capabilities. But what of Scott? she
had asked herself even at the time. She was his last reason to
live, his excuse for failure but also his remnant purpose in the
world. She could imagine him roaming the countryside in
search of her, inquiring after his flapper-bride at every inn and
farm in the Asheville area, until one day he encountered a peasant midwife with mildly pocked skin and a voice hinting of forgotten hardships, so charmed by her way of speaking that he
stopped to take notes, unable to recognize the midwife as his
missing wife.

She didn't realize she was crying until Scott reached across
the seat and brushed her cheek with his handkerchief. How
long since he had touched her face, how presumptuous of him.
Make me yours again, she said to herself, but he was always so
careful.

Scott had given the driver their destination, a fine establishment in the Old City just off the Plaza de Armas—at the heart of
everything, near several of the most famous squares, along one
of the central shopping thoroughfares, not far from the fine
restaurants and jazz clubs, the sorts of places the two of them
loved so much. There was something so gallant about the way
he described it that she pictured him as he'd been twenty years
ago, a young man with an overinflated sense of his prospects
and a tendency to boast of them if only to mask his insecurities.
He was far more dignified now—except in his drunken fits, of
course—and she wished she could make him believe it. Age
hadn't ruined him.

When they pulled up to the Hotel Ambos Mundos, he told her to wait in the car.

"But Scott," she said, "after all this time I'm simply famished."

"Of course," he said. "I'll stash the luggage and we can check in later."

It was a hot and humid day, with lazy rain clouds sweeping the sky, and as she and Scott descended Calle Obispo several vendors shouted after them and a mulatto shoeshine boy back-pedaled in front of Scott while repeatedly clapping brushes and pointing at his shoes. She was conscious of perspiring beneath her dress, worried lest spots become visible on the fabric. It was the hour of the siesta, hardly anybody loitering in the streets, three or four older couples promenading on the plaza, delivery-men and messengers cooling themselves in the long shadowed arcades that framed the square. Leaving the plaza, they passed a hotel restaurant at which the custodial staff wiped down tables, mopped floors, and opened shutters to air out the rooms for the dinner crowds. Eventually they found a table at a restaurant renowned for its seafood, Scott asking the waiter if it was possible to order something other than sea delicacies. Gershwin's "Someone to Watch Over Me" could be heard from a café down the street, the music an invitation sent anonymously into the world. She and Scott were the only patrons in the restaurant except for a pair of old men in the far corner huddled over a game of dominos and a neatly dressed upper-class, fair-skinned Cuban of Scott's age, who sat with his gray linen slacks pressed against a young bronzed girl who looked no older than fifteen.

"We have decided, *gracias,*" Scott said, then awkwardly pronounced each of the dishes in Spanish. Soon the waiter returned with a ginger ale for her, a bottle of Coca-Cola and a brown bottle of beer for Scott, who restated his intention not to drink before dinner. It always struck her as funny that he did not count beer as alcohol.

"I like this city," she said. "I like the indolence of places where the sun is so heavy it drives people indoors to their beds. I like thinking of all the people lying naked on clean white sheets, leaving the cafés and restaurants to those of us in need of food or drink or conversation."

Scott seemed lost in thought and she decided he must be worried about his career. It was altogether possible that while here in Cuba he would be unable to let go of his Hollywood misfortunes and his anxieties about the novel he was starting.

"Scott," she said, sipping at the ginger ale, "it's going to change for you. I believe that deep in my heart."

He was a forgotten novelist, he told her grimly. It was two years since his last story in the *Saturday Evening Post*. Even worse, he feared Hollywood had turned him into a hack.

"Don't be ridiculous, you could never be a hack. It's not in you."

Morosely, he imagined bookstores across the country filled with novels on every shelf, none of them his.

"What did you say to the bellhop?" she asked, trying to turn his mind to practical matters. "About our room? Don't we have a reservation?"

"It will be all right," he assured her. "The concierge himself told me there were many first-rate rooms left, not to worry."

When the waiter set the dishes before them—a plate of *Moros y Cristianos* to share, *huevos* with plantains for Zelda, a plate of *ropa vieja* for Scott—Zelda determined that his was the better of the two. When he reminded her she'd asked for eggs because she hadn't eaten breakfast, she said, "But I've changed my mind, now I want your flank steak."

Too weary to protest, he passed his dish to her.

"Oh, not if you're going to be a martyr about it," she said.

Scott pulled the eggs to his side of the table, scooping some of the *Moros y Cristianos* onto his plate, asking if she wanted some also.

"What is it again?" she asked, already cutting into the sinews of tomato-doused meat, taking a bite. "I mean other than beans and rice."

Zelda poked with her fork at the beans and rice, prepared with pepper, garlic, tomato, and bacon, and took a small bite. "Oh, it's quite good. Yes, please serve me some Moors and Christians. I suppose I can guess which ones are the Moors."

In fact Scott wasn't all that hungry. He told her she could help herself to the eggs he hadn't ordered and anything else on his plate.

"It's only a lull," she assured him, greedily consuming a second helping of beans and rice, and then half his serving of plantains. "I have a good feeling about this year." She was getting better and better—she could always discern the onset of sanity ahead of time, what it felt like to be determined and unconquerable. She was going to be like that again soon. "And when I'm like that, I'm always good for you."

Talk of reunion made Scott uneasy, talk of the future, period, made him uneasy.

"It used to be," she continued, refusing to be cowed, "I was resentful about being so much less important than make-believe, but I don't feel that way anymore. It's only for a while, I tell myself. This time I'll be self-sufficient for as long as it takes you to get the book right."

Scott smiled, indulging her.

"Scott, you know I'm always right about these things," she said. "Remember how I sent you away and refused to marry you until you finished your novel and became famous? I wouldn't have done that if I didn't believe in you. I'm not cruel, just practical when I have to be."

"Practical and visionary, how rare," he said. "A lucky combination to find in a wife."

"That's what I've been trying to tell you."

Scott laughed, charmed by her ebullience, by her inexhaustible ability to spin narratives that weaved the past into a tapestry of eternal romance.

The waiter asked whether they wanted anything else. She sensed Scott's hesitation, remembering his vow of moderation.

"You can have one more beer," she said, telling herself that if she established this precedent, he might listen to her later on when she said enough already. "I'll be your conscience. I'm having such a nice time talking to you. Go ahead and have another beer and we'll sit here in the shade and comment on the people passing on the street."

Scott raised one finger. *"Una cerveza, por favor."*

Zelda studied his profile adumbrated by afternoon light, his classically flared nostrils. A slow-moving donkey dragged a wooden cart loaded with fruit toward the harbor as a bell from a nearby church chimed flawlessly in the Caribbean sky. She could smell her own perfumed skin, ripened by heat, hinting of a leisure that had long eluded her.

Her reverie was interrupted when a young boy bawled at Scott in Spanish, one hand on the rail separating the restaurant from the street, the other on a wooden box camera that he aimed at them, saying, *"¿Les gustaría que les tome una fotografía?"* Scott put his arm around her shoulder, but she pulled away on instinct, not from Scott, but from the boy and the camera.

"Please," she said, "I'm tired and I'll dislike the picture intensely and I don't want you to waste our money. Maybe after I've been in the sun for three days and we've slept twelve hours each night. I do wish to be terribly lazy, the two of us sleeping off our exhaustion until we're young and beautiful again; maybe then we can take a picture. Besides, I'm getting nervous that they'll give our hotel rooms away."

"Oh, for crying out loud," Scott barked, waving off the boy, who took one step backward, still aiming the camera at them, then propping it on a three-legged wood stand and burying his head in the hood attached to it and before they could say anything else depressing the shutter, waiting several seconds, then pulling the box from the case, announcing, "Handsome Americans, *es una buena fotografía,* very best photograph, you buy from me." Zelda started to protest, "We asked you not to take our picture, please go," flipping her hand up and away from her, but Scott put his palm on her knee and said he would take care of everything.

The boy, lapsing into Spanish and raising his voice, appealed to *el Señor* or some godly notion of *justicia,* wishing to make it clear that he knew only a few phrases in English and any misunderstanding about the photograph must be laid at the feet of the foreigners to whom he'd offered his services. Scott slid his chair back, rose, then strode off the patio, disappearing behind a pillar near the entrance so as to negotiate with the boy on the street, but she could hear the boy naming his price as Scott approached, "Pay me, *señor, por favor.*"

Already she saw what Scott would do and she was opposed to it. "Scott," she called after him, "don't let the boy trick you into buying that photograph. We didn't ask for it, I don't want it, I don't want to see it." Angry with the young boy, she didn't believe it had been a mistake at all. For several seconds she even considered that somebody might have sent him to spy on her. What right did the boy have to come and take their picture without permission, intruding on her privacy, ruining what until then had been a happy start to the holiday? If Scott gave in to this extortion, she wouldn't soon forgive him.

Sure enough, he returned to the table minutes later, holding the photograph by its corner, saying, "It's really not half bad, if you—"

"Please, don't. I told you I didn't want my picture taken, that boy had no right to take it, and you had no business rewarding him for his treachery."

"We'll throw it away then," he said. "First, though, we must rush down the street to the front desk to find out if there's still room at the inn."

Scott held out his hand to guide her from the restaurant, crisis averted just like that, and for the first time in years she believed he might set things right in her world. Only as they entered the Ambos Mundos, the porter holding the door for them, did she remember to ask about the photograph.

"What have you done with it?"

Why, he'd left it on the table as she'd asked, so they might pretend it had never been taken.

"But it was taken, Scott."

And he'd paid for it, then discarded it.

"You can't erase the past by pretending it didn't happen. We have to go back."

"What about securing the room you're so worried about?"

She released his arm and stood clear of him, the porter pretending not to listen to their mild squabble. Scott stiffened in surprise, eyeing her, his mouth contorted in a grimace.

"First things first," she said. "It can't be helped."

By the time she reached the table at the restaurant, the tip was still there, but no photograph.

Oh, they have found us already, she said to herself.

"The boy must have come back for it," she said to Scott, who now caught up with her, panting heavily.

"I'm sure there's another explanation. Stay here, let me find out."

Deep inside the restaurant, he leaned forward onto the bar as he spoke to the owner, hands gesticulating toward their table. Shortly thereafter he opened his jacket and accepted an item from the man, tucking it into an inner pocket.

"Problem solved," he said, his face broadening into a smile as he came jaunting toward her. "A man saw we'd left the photo and gave it to the bartender, predicting we'd return for it."

"That makes no sense. Why didn't he run after us?"

Scott, pulling the flap of the jacket away from him, reached inside to extract the photograph.

"I said I didn't want to see it," she cried. "It's just odd that he didn't run after us."

"I don't pretend," he said coolly, "to understand the etiquette of Cubans."

"I wonder if they'll intuit our arrival right away," she said under her breath as they crossed the lobby, scouting for familiar faces. How many days until they were tracked down? There was no place they could run where they wouldn't eventually be found.

Scott handed a ticket to the bellhop, requesting their luggage before asking her to repeat what she'd said. All she wanted to talk about, though, was whether there would still be rooms available. Just two couples ahead of them in the check-in line. She shuffled her feet in place, and when at last it was Scott's turn, the clerk informed him that the hotel did have rooms, exactly two of which were side-by-side: at the front of the hotel, overlooking Calle Obispo, very nice rooms. He named a price, which Scott, failing to barter, paid in full. She was sure he spent more on the rooms than they could afford, but she was relieved nonetheless.

What can you remember of Cuba? She put herself through the exercise after Scott had deposited her in her room and gone next door to his. In the country but a few hours, and already she was committing roadside palms to memory, retracing the route from the airport, the highway plunging in and out of fields and trees, the Caribbean sky reappearing in pools of blue by which she kept her bearings. Also the clean washed marble of the pillared porticoes, the gold and rose-colored estates, their windows and doorways shadowed in layers of carbon and opal that refused insight into interiors. It didn't take much to imagine what was behind those doors, all that plantation history, the backyard slavery and obscured suffering.

"What are you thinking, Zelda?" Scott asked, standing in the doorway of her room.

"Scott, please knock." Her words sounded harsher than she meant them to be.

"I only came to see if there was anything else you needed."

"It's just you scared me."

"Zelda, am I that strange to you after all these months?" He was regretful, oddly formal, a man who had taken his secrets and hidden them away in a vault so as to pretend there was nothing to hide. You are not mine anymore, she said to herself. Still, she managed to lift her head, reminding herself to be grateful for the trip, folding her mouth into the image of some happier time, say, a photo taken years ago in Cannes on their first visit.

Scott gravitated to the curtained windows and pulled back the heavy folds of fabric so that arrows of light shot into the room, elongating fuselike across the carpet.

"Scott, please!"

He was about to parry with awful words, but at that moment the bellhop entered with their luggage.

"Leave the large trunk here, please, also those two valises," Scott commanded, handing American dollars to the bellhop.

When the bellhop left, Scott turned to her. "That was unnecessary."

"I didn't mean it that way."

"How, then?"

"I only meant," but she stopped herself, not sure she could make him understand her desire to memorize the lovely neoclassical houses along the Prado or the vistas on the Plaza de Armas, her effort to retain this vacation piece by piece. Call it intuition, call it clairvoyance, but something was telling her, in spite of her hopes to the contrary, that her imminent liberation from the Highland was far from guaranteed, that there might not be many more of these trips to be counted on. Each holiday she and Scott took was costly, in all senses of the word: they were down to two per year, and some ended catastrophically, dissolving in bitter quarrels. On returning to Asheville she would try to figure how and where things had gone awry, blaming her own judgment, discovering flaws in Scott's character further and further back into their marriage, sometimes tracing the damage and misunderstanding to the very beginning, her memory chewing up the scraps of joy little by little, year by year. With so many places lost already, she needed Havana to last. But if she said any of that, he might believe it a sign that she was going crazy again, when nothing could be further from the truth. So she improvised. "Scott, I'm sorry. The light, it's a fuse, if it so much as touches—"

"Why didn't you tell me you had a headache?"

He walked over to the trunk, which had been set on a stand near the dresser. What she needed right now was to be alone, the wish for privacy so intense she could hear it shrieking inside her. But better to let Scott feel useful, believing again in his own kindness.

"See if you can't find that yellow silk nightgown you gave me that I love so much. I'm almost certain I packed it."

His search of the trunk was inefficient, impatient, confused, as he turned up dresses, undergarments, and shoes, sighed, then dug into recesses of clothes that kept sliding back like dirt into a poorly excavated hole. She would have found the gown by now, without the mess. What's more, she would need to repack the entire trunk after waking from her siesta. At last he extracted the gown, rubbing its fine silk between his fingers, perhaps remembering it on her body, remembering the reams of expensive clothing he'd bought for her over the years.

She walked across the brightly polished wood floor, placing a hand on his shoulder.

"You found it, thank you. You were always so devoted whenever—"

"Was I?" he asked. Honestly, he couldn't remember most days what he used to be like.

"Can't you remember how you were when we first married?" she asked him.

Assured that her headache would dissipate once she lay down, he left her to herself, promising to call in time for dinner. A single day in his presence, and already she could feel herself taking on his anxieties and displeasures. She was surprised by how much she relaxed once the man she loved was no longer in the room. Within minutes she lay undressed and supine, spent from the effort of stripping herself, the nightgown on the bed seeming far away, too much effort to reach for it.

3

T HE LOBBY OF THE HOTEL AMBOS MUNDOS WRAPPED ITSELF AROUND
the bar, in front of which sat dark rattan couches with gold
cushions for well-to-do Cubans and foreigners, wood tables
and chairs off to the side for those opting to sit less conspicuously.
The ceiling fans whirred quietly in the heat. A half dozen towering
wood-shuttered windows on the north wall opened onto the persistent buzz of Calle Obispo. Seated at the bar, early in the
evening, counting drinks, Scott alternated the hard stuff with
Coca-Colas. Their second day in Havana had been passed mostly
in and around the hotel, he and Zelda strolling down to the harbor once in the afternoon. Just now Zelda was again catching up
on sleep, and he suspected he ought to be doing the same. Twice
he had asked the bartender to save his stool so that he might run
upstairs and check on her, but she hadn't responded to his knocking on her door either time. Returning to the lobby, he reclaimed
his seat only to be approached by a handsome Cuban he'd noticed
earlier sitting with a cocoa-skinned girl on a sofa beneath one of
the windows, its dark wood shutters thrown back.

"My friend, you are American," the Cuban said in impeccable English, his Latin accent softly infecting his n's, rolling his vowels.

Often distrustful when inebriated, Scott could be just as suspicious en route. But he took an immediate liking to this Cuban who had been educated at Columbia University in the late 1920s. On learning that Scott hailed from Princeton, Señor Matéo Cardoña insisted on buying him a drink and fondly toasting the United States. Next he led him across the lobby to join the long-legged girl who sat alone on the gold sofa, distracting herself by tilting her head to listen with apparent rapture to a nearby piano. Scott installed himself in a chair to the left of the sofa, the piano at his back yielding amicable jazz as he peered over the girl's bare shoulder at the streetcars, automobiles, and horse-drawn carriages passing with regularity.

He paced his drinking by his companion, persuading himself that he was only showing respect for the customs of Havana. So far the strategy was working: the alcohol hadn't gone to his head. Maybe it was the humidity of the Caribbean night. For he was sweating beneath the collar of the blue pinstriped Arrow shirt he wore under a Scottish tweed sport coat, his new acquaintance remarking on his stylish wardrobe, from the jacket to the shoes to the hat, worrying nevertheless that Scott must be warm in such attire. He is flattering me, Scott thought, conscious of the decade-old tweed of the sport coat, slightly worn at the elbows. He now and then wiped his brow with a paisley silk handkerchief, the thought of removing the jacket increasing his self-consciousness about how much he was sweating, which of course made him sweat all the more. But he didn't wish to succumb to a bout of those chills that often emanated from deep within his body. Even on the warmest of days they plagued him, only Sheilah knew how badly, harbingers (so he feared) of the final onslaught of tuberculosis that would draw him under. For months now, through a

California winter as mild and dry as anyone could remember, he had felt a tickling in his chest, his breathing often difficult, and he couldn't keep warm except when burrowed inside his cottage, wrapped in an extra layer of clothing, a blanket over his shoulders, a stiff drink in hand.

Several times the *Habanero* raised his glass to *"nuevas amistades,"* Scott grateful for these easy hours in a foreign place, relishing the elation of unearned intimacy that was alcohol's greatest gift. He made the choice to trust it for as long as it should last, wishing he could know how long that might be, but of course that was the one thing you couldn't know. Matéo asked what Scott did, translating the answer for the girl, his voice full of respect when he used the term *un escritor* and next asked for Scott's surname. He rocked back in his chair, tilting his jaw, hesitating as he chose his words, before inquiring if by chance the American author before him bore any relation to the writer who had invented the flapper, whose *Saturday Evening Post* stories were once read by all of New York, whose novels Matéo believed he might also have read. Scott didn't ask him to name titles.

Matéo prodded Scott to help him remember what it was like to stroll beneath the skyscrapers of New York City, or take the ferry from Manhattan to Brooklyn, or comb the beaches of Rockaway, or walk into one of those many speakeasies filled to capacity with people whose "good time" was sought in relaxed defiance of prohibition. Matéo hadn't visited New York since the end of 1930, and Scott's own returns to the city over the past decade had been infrequent, chaotic, or worse, so the two men toured the city together in their minds, revisiting nights passed at the Cotton Club or at 21, deciding they must surely have become drunk together, unknowingly, in the same Manhattan joint, on the very same night. It was like the crush of first love, the thrill Scott once felt on being introduced to his classmates Bunny Wilson and John

Peale Bishop on the Princeton lawn, squandering time with spendthrift eagerness in lofty conversations about novels, poetry, Broadway. It was like the charge of first eyeing a young Zelda at a military ball in Montgomery, intuiting what she would someday mean to him.

His thoughts turned to Ernest, who might be here in this city, in this very hotel, ready to walk through the door in the next few minutes. Weeks ago Scott had left word with his editor Maxwell Perkins, asking where Ernest stayed when in Havana, receiving a wire the same afternoon with the name and address of the Ambos Mundos. The last time he'd seen Ernest? At a Hollywood screening of a film about the Spanish Civil War that Ernest had narrated, Scott attending the event in the company of the playwright Lillian Hellman. Taking Ernest aside, he offered hasty congratulations as reporters clamored for words from the icon who was Hemingway. As Ernest walked into the throng of photographers and journalists, putting himself at the beck and call of those for whom his propaganda was intended, he yelled out, "You look well, Scott, better than I expected."

When Max had cabled Scott, he mentioned that Ernest might be in residence in Havana during the spring, even asked whether he should relay a message, advising the first of his prized writers, "You and Ernest have suffered different miseries these last few years, Scott, but you should stay in touch. The only thing I can offer either of you is the recommendation to guard your friendship!"—the gesture, though well-intended, as unrealistic as it was sentimental. Max knew full well the difficulties between the two writers. Scott sent a wire in return, judicious in its understatement:

DEAR MAX THANKS FOR OFFER TO PUT ME IN TOUCH WITH EH BUT HAVE TO ANSWER PROBABLY NOT STOP

TOUCHED BY NOTION BUT MOST LIKELY ZELDA AND I
WONT HAVE TIME STOP SHE WILL HAVE AN ITINERARY
REPLETE WITH BEACHES AND HORSEBACKRIDING AND
PHYSICAL ENDURANCE AND TRIP IS ALL FOR HER STOP SO
IT MUST REMAIN STOP EVER FONDLY SCOTT

Scott could expect Max to sniff out the allusion to Zelda's old
animosity to Ernest, reason enough in itself not to make contact.
Still, the irony wasn't lost on Scott that if he truly wished to avoid
Hemingway he might have visited any Havana hotel other than
the one in which his former friend regularly stayed.

"Our memories of New York do not bring you pleasure,"
Matéo said, breaking Scott's train of thought.

"Memories often do not," Scott said.

"Then we must think of something else altogether."

The charismatic Cuban was distinctively Mediterranean in appearance, with thick, dark hair, eyes brown-black and piercing
like those of some magnificent bird of prey, and a long, rugged,
lightly tanned face, his sloping nose set symmetrically like a
pitched tent above a paintbrush mustache and two quarter-moon
lips. In a beige linen suit, a white shirt, and brown and red striped
tie that accentuated the lines of his lean body, he wore the last
throes of youth well. He hailed from a traditional Catholic family
that owned a tobacco plantation outside the city of Santiago de
Cuba and openly professed loyalty to the Spanish crown. Since
the mid-nineteenth century any man who didn't join the family
business went on to become an architect, lawyer, engineer, or
government administrator, their contributions as citizens demon-
strable in the buildings, roads, statutes, and policies of their
beloved city. When Matéo chose to study in the United States, he
broke with tradition and cast himself as the family's black sheep,
further alienating himself by later supporting the now

defeated Republican cause in Spain as well as a succession of failed progressive reforms here at home. So fierce were the disagreements with his family that on returning from New York to his homeland, he had emigrated within his own country, from the east up to Havana.

His memories of New York City were bittersweet, since he looked back on those years as the best of his life. He had thrived in that cosmopolitan city, on the easy exposure to new ideas in arts and letters, in the commercial and social sectors. In winding up a story about an evening at the Algonquin, he reached out to touch Scott's jacket, saying, "Listen to this," as if to impart a secret of great significance, except each sentence that followed proved no less generic and predictable than those that had come before. His stories about New York were twice-told stories, constructed over the course of a decade to account for his time among the *yanquis*. When he spoke of the crash, Matéo talked as if it were a distinctly perceptible event, as if the market when it came down made a sound like a building collapsing and everyone rushed into the street to see what was happening, the loss of investments and savings and stored-up dreams instantaneous, the resulting suicides occurring all at once, people tumbling out of windows everywhere, littering the streets and sidewalks like corpses on a battlefield.

"Where were you in October 1929, *mi compañero?*" Matéo asked him. "What did you see?"

"On a camel's back, most likely," Scott said.

Matéo translated his words and the girl laughed, spitting out a bit of her drink.

"It's no joke," Scott said, "though I thank you for laughing all the same. I seem to recall that I was in Morocco with my wife."

"I think to myself," the woman explained, "there are no *camellos* in New York, and the picture is *muy raro,* how you say—"

"Bizarre," Matéo interjected.

"We were ignorant of what had happened for several days," Scott said, "catching only echoes of the event in the international papers."

"And it is no joking matter, of course," Matéo said to the girl, reprimanding her for her irreverence. "I must walk over several suicides as they lay dying in the streets, their spines shattered, no reason to hang on anymore."

But it wasn't like that, Scott wanted to protest. Even war wasn't like that most of the time.

Just then he felt a wave of dizziness wash over him. Staring at his shoes, he tried to remember where and when he had purchased them. The room was revolving like a carnival ride, the lobby populated in its corners by soft, shadowy black forms, everything in the foreground out of focus.

"I have to be off."

"*Mi compañero,* we are enjoying your company, you cannot leave. Besides—"

"I must see to my wife's dinner," Scott said, aware that he was being rude, but knowing from experience that if he did not get food in his stomach soon, he would lose hold of the night.

"Besides, it is uncivilized to eat before nine," Matéo declared. "I miss much about your America to the north, except your dinner hour. This I could never bring myself to accept."

"We only arrived yesterday, we haven't made the transition. My wife is still catching up on sleep," Scott said, "and she will—"

"I will tell you what we shall do," Matéo said, refusing to relinquish his new friend. He proposed that they walk to the end of Calle Obispo and enjoy a drink at La Floridita, renowned for its daiquiris and seafood. Scott yielded to the friendly coercion because he thought the open air might do him good, postponing thoughts of Zelda and dinner until he regained his equilibrium.

His equilibrium, however, was in no hurry to return. They walked several blocks into the flow of automobile and pedestrian traffic on the Calle Obispo, under awnings that cast nighttime shadows folding one over the next. The tourist crowds thinned and soon the people passing were mulatto or dark skinned and spoke only in Spanish. The girl, silent for much of the night, attempted to describe an event of some sort, at first in broken English, next in Spanish, then lapsing into pantomime. She gestured at the steps of nearby buildings and the natives assembled there, turning to Scott, asking, *"Entiendes?,"* fearing he hadn't and so repeating her phrases, mentioning *Americanos* and *Cuba libre* and maybe also the sufferings of friends and family in the wake of the depression and the country's many internal military conflicts. He couldn't remember her name, only that it was a thick Spanish word beginning with a Y or a yielding J, and his inability to do so troubled him. He asked Matéo how many blocks until they reached the Floridita.

Not far, the Cuban promised, motioning up the street into the dark.

At the next corner Scott still couldn't make out any likely destinations.

"It's too far."

"My friend, it is not far at all," Matéo said, guiding him by the elbow. "We will soon be there."

The girl, still gesticulating, pleaded with him to follow.

"What is she saying?"

"Only that she wishes you to join us, she is sure you will like La Floridita, she has many friends who drink there regularly."

"Tell her that it is kind of her, kind of both of you, but I can't, not tonight. Zelda will soon come downstairs looking for me and she will be alarmed when she can't find me."

Earlier in the evening Matéo had explained what he did here in Havana, and if only Scott had been paying closer attention, he might have recalled more than the word *liaison* and a vague account of recruiting American investors. Was it possible that the past three hours were part of a Saturday evening con to draw a lone American down a forlorn urban street?

"We will escort you to your hotel," Matéo announced, turning on his heels. "If you wish to enjoy our company, we will join you for dinner at a restaurant on the Plaza de San Francisco near the harbor, but perhaps you and your wife will be eager to dine alone."

When the familiar pale rose building of the Ambos Mundos came into sight, the street again populated by people speaking multiple languages, Spanish, English, but also French, German, and Portuguese, Scott remembered his hunger and felt torn about what to do next. The places Matéo had proposed along the harbor seemed far away, but in a spirit of compromise Scott allowed himself to be led to the rooftop restaurant of his own hotel.

"You are worried about Mrs. Zelda Fitzgerald, perhaps?" Matéo asked once they were seated, and for a second Scott couldn't remember having used his wife's name. His companion offered to run downstairs and leave a message for her. Only tell him which room. Before Scott could think better of it, he had given out Zelda's room number, realizing as Matéo walked away that it would have been more circumspect to write a note to his wife and leave it with one of the bellhops at the front desk.

Seated alone with the girl, Scott studied her closely. He wouldn't have put her at more than seventeen, the age of his daughter Scottie. Experimenting with English phrases, she inevitably lapsed into Spanish, frustrated to discover from his earnest but puzzled expression that he couldn't understand a word she was saying. So she took to giving him language lessons. *"Tenedor,"* she said, lifting her fork as Scott nodded. A band played a sauntering style of local music, and she began to identify their instruments for him by opening her hand in a soft sweep. *Bajo de pie. Guitarra. Maracas.* After what seemed a longer than necessary interval, Matéo rejoined them, reporting that he had run into a friend in the elevator but nevertheless completed Scott's errand.

"Not long until nine o'clock," he said with evident satisfaction at having spared his guest the mistake of eating at an uncivilized hour.

"And where would you go," Scott asked, "for a late-night cocktail on a Saturday night in Havana?"

Matéo named several clubs and bars—the bar at the Plaza Hotel, the Two Brothers Bar near the docks, the Pan American Club. "I will show you any of these, or I will escort you to places off the beaten track, in honor of Manhattan speakeasies."

The waiter brought the first course, and Scott placed an order for a chicken dish and a side of *Moros y Cristianos* for Zelda, trying to imagine how he would take the food from the restaurant when the time came to leave. He sampled the vegetables course, *yuca* and *chayote,* the latter a kind of squash, and was enjoying a hearty yellow soup when all of a sudden there was a terrific two-beat carom of metal on metal like the sound of two large trucks colliding at high speed or a sharp thunderclap heard from the center of a storm. Scott surveyed the restaurant, then the street, looking for calamity, for violence, for panic. The waiters hadn't dropped their plates. The customers conversed with one another as they had moments earlier. Only the behavior of the girl at his side was altered. Her tongue rolling in rapid Spanish, she demanded Scott's attention as Matéo repeated her name again, so that this time Scott caught it, memorizing it by saying it several times in his head: *Yonaidys, Yonaidys.* Now translating her sentences into English, Matéo managed to keep pace with the zealous outpouring of words.

"That sound just now," she explained, "it is the cannon that goes off each night at nine across the harbor at Morro Castle." She couldn't say exactly how old the tradition was, older than herself, older than Matéo or Scott, older than anyone she knew. When she was a child her mother would say to her, "As soon as the *cañonaso a las nueve* sounds, *los niños* must go to sleep." It was a custom, so someone once told her, started perhaps by the British when they wrested control of this great city from the Spanish, the signal by which they closed the harbor each night. Over the years in a country where there were not so many clocks, not so many watches, not so many whatever, it became a way of telling everybody, it is now nine o'clock. An everyday threshold for the people of this city—the end of day, beginning of night.

"So you might enjoy that," Matéo was saying on behalf of the girl, "if you go to the castle, they have a ceremony around that issue, soldiers who form and march and ignite the cannon." In pomp and majesty the custom was observed each night.

"We will be sure to visit the castle," Scott said. He was imagining his wife sitting up in bed, staring into the darkness of a strange room, groggy and disoriented, jolted from sleep by the blast of the cannon.

What the girl remembered most of all, well, what she meant to tell him, she could remember saying, "No, *Madre,* I cannot sleep yet, it hasn't sounded, you know, *el cañonaso* hasn't sounded." She didn't know what else to say. It was in their memory, every night, all who were born or made their home in this city.

The waiter brought the main course, a filet mignon, setting the plates before them, and Scott stood up to take him aside, asking if he might bring the extra plate of food as soon as possible.

"I must go and check on my wife," he announced as he reclaimed his seat.

Matéo looked surprised. "It is just a loud noise. She will have slept through it, either that or she will go back to sleep."

"But she will be up and about, expecting me to take her to dinner. She needed the rest yesterday, but she will wish to see Havana tonight," Scott replied, resenting that he had to explain anything to a man he hardly knew. "I'll tell you what, I'll see if she'd like for us to meet you later for a cocktail."

"Muy bien," Yonaidys said agreeably, alert to the growing tension.

"Eat and we will discuss many things," Matéo said, and Scott had the sense he was being bullied.

He could stomach hardly any of the meal. He took small bites, trying to look as though he were savoring each, spreading the rice and plantains across his plate, nibbling at pieces of steak, the food settling high in his stomach, ballooned from all those drinks. The waiter returned with the check and Scott saw that the bill was given in pesos. He had forgotten about the need to change money. He calculated the exchange rate in his head, adding several dollars to the standard tip, the extra money meant to appease someone or maybe just to allow for the possibility that his math was poor. "This should cover it," he said, putting the money on the table. "Will they accept American dollars?"

"It is no problem, my friend, but you were to be our guest."

"Another night," Scott said, worrying about his impulse toward generosity. Always this habit, even while in debt, even when he couldn't predict next month's income: the worst part of the past ten years was having to hear that damned voice in his head—

You can't afford this, let someone else pay—every time he went to pick up a check.

Yonaidys rose from her seat, folding her arms around Scott's shoulders, tilting her chin so that he might graze her cheeks with his lips.

"Please, if Mrs. Fitzgerald is not too tired," Matéo said, also standing but not yet embracing Scott, "we will be here for at least a few more hours."

"I'll do my best to persuade her."

"If we have left and you wish to find us—"

"You can leave a note for me at the front desk," Scott said, uncertain whether he was brushing his host off or making plans to enjoy his company another time. He wouldn't know anything for certain until he had returned to the room and made sure Zelda was safe.

Once he was free of his dinner companions, Scott's affection for them returned. He believed again in his talent for spotting the "good ones" at any party or bar: those people there to be looked at—because, after all, who wasn't?—who also delved beneath the surface, seeking the beauty from every gathering because memory of it might be all there was to keep you afloat years later when the tribulations came.

The arrow of the brass dial above the doors indicated that the elevator was on the bottom floor. Too impatient to wait, he made for the gray marble staircase, his dread returning as he envisioned his wife waiting for him, alone and afraid. Taking the stairs in a hurry, he found that he was short of breath after a single flight, annoyed by the fact that he could be winded from descending stairs, but refusing to slow down. Halfway down the next flight, the dizziness set in and he reached a hand to one of the railings as he watched the caged iron elevator ascending, empty except for the operator. By the time he reached their floor, he was panting, having to rest his hands on his knees to catch his breath. He had been pushing himself too hard, for weeks now. Not just the drink, but the worry over Zelda's and Scottie's expenses, the constant trolling for work in the wake of his expired contract at MGM, trying to land on a picture, any picture, not caring how good or how promising it was; all he needed was a job that paid well enough to keep his head above water while he made room for his real work, the kind that mostly didn't pay well, not for him, not anymore. He needed time to immerse himself in the new novel about Hollywood, for which he had already prepared copious notes. It was doubtful he would get much rest on this vacation, most of his hours to be spent worrying whether Zelda was happy, making sure she didn't slip back. He couldn't let that happen, he had to bring her back to Asheville intact.

"Where were you?" Zelda said as he entered the room.

"Zelda, you're up at last."

"Where were you?"

When it appeared she might sleep through the night, he'd gone for food, figuring she would be hungry when she awakened.

He held the plate of food in front of him, but as soon as it came within range she slapped at it, connecting with a blow strong enough to have toppled the warm dinner onto the bed if he hadn't been ready for just such a response.

"I don't want your food," she said. All her fear converted to choler, she was imperious, impassive, prepared to put everything on him, her eyes the color of granite, her skin ashen. "I want to know where you were."

She held his gaze without flinching, her expression radiating a fierce indifference. She was waiting for him to say the wrong thing, to make the mistake that would allow her to detach from him and everyone else.

"Have you been drinking?"

Maybe a drink or two with dinner. After all, she had been asleep a long time.

"Where were you?" she asked again.

She sat erect, stiff backed, sheets pulled up to her neck, her fingers clenched so hard on the white cotton that the blood had gone out of them. Also she was shaking, either from the cool night air or from her muscles relaxing now that he was here at her side and she didn't have to fight the terror all by herself.

He had stopped in to check on her several times.

"Scott, there was someone at my door."

She must have heard the cannon, that's all, it was a custom of the city.

"I know what I heard. There was someone at the door and you weren't here."

Again he tried to explain about the cannon, which went off at nine each night to mark the closing of the bay. Most likely the carom of the blast had penetrated her dreams.

"No, there was someone at the door, knocking over and over. I heard voices in the hall. They knocked at my door and they might have gotten in, but you were nowhere to be found."

The old, pure pity for her overtook him. He knew what to do when she was like this, how to handle her, if only she would let him. All he had to do was walk to the bed and sit beside her, reach his palm onto her shoulder, his moves methodical and understated as if he were appeasing a vigilant watchdog awakened in the night that recognized his smell from years ago but couldn't yet place him. Slowly he let his hand drop, gliding it over her well-defined arms until he was cupping the opposite shoulder, now kneading his thumb into the tautness of her neck.

But she jerked away, her torso unbending as she tilted to the side, rolling from him like an ocean buoy toppled by the rise of a wave.

"Don't," she said. "I want an answer. Tell me where you were, why you left me alone while someone was trying to break into my room."

He hadn't been gone long, he assured her, realizing he would have to play the bluff all the way through. "I stopped to check on you not an hour ago, Zelda. I cracked the door, you were sound asleep, perfectly safe the entire time. I was never more than a few minutes away."

She was almost ready to believe him, he could see it in her eyes.

"It was only the cannon, which sounds, well, it sounds like a huge gun, the crash and echo. I'm sure it startled you and then you heard the knocking in your dream."

"But it was so real."

He wrapped his arm around her, pulling her close, maybe too close, because she abruptly jerked free, head cocked to the side.

"You were with him just now, weren't you? Or did he visit last night while I rested?"

Now it comes, Scott thought.

"He's here in this city, maybe at this very hotel. I knew it, you arranged it all."

He wouldn't listen to any more of her nonsense.

"I want you to take me downstairs. I'll bet he's down there waiting for you."

Did she know how unreasonable she sounded? She was just saying whatever came to mind, with no thought as to whether she believed it or not.

"Prove to me he's not here," she said, throwing back the covers. "Take me downstairs." She stood before him without a stitch of clothing on, without so much as a pang of modesty. Despite all her sufferings this past decade, despite the troubles inflicted on face and skin by her broken, patched, and several times refurbished mind, her body was as shapely as ever, her breasts fecund, muscles toned and vital, everything about her charged with sex.

All right, he said, suffering stabs of lust for her but banishing them. "Whatever you want, that's what we'll do." He was happy enough to go downstairs. First, though, she had to eat a few bites of the dinner he'd gone to so much trouble to fetch for her.

"Why didn't you just wake me in an hour like we planned?" she asked, walking onto the shallow balcony where she might be observed by almost anyone, letting the cool night air into the room, then turning and sauntering toward him, her nipples newly alert. "It's Saturday night, maybe our only Saturday night in Cuba, and now I've slept so long and it's so late."

"But Zelda, you know it's early yet for Havana."

Rounding the corner of the bed still stark naked, then folding her toes over his leather shoes, she stood like that for several seconds, her body gently radiant, each of her movements supple and trained. On her left leg she executed a half-pirouette, with the right held out from her as she fell back into a sitting position on the bed, bouncing once before coming to rest, her legs opened and her pelvis arched as she folded the right leg into her body.

"Okay," she said, in a voice airy with mischief, "you may feed me."

All at once she had let go of anger.

"Zelda, you can't eat like that."

"Why not? Nothing you haven't seen before."

"Aren't you cold?" he said, laughing, already giving in.

He unwrapped the plate, realizing only then that he had failed to bring any damned utensils. How could he forget such a simple thing?

"Oh, it doesn't matter," she said. So Scott picked up the leg of chicken and lowered it to her lips, instructing her to take a bite. Zelda laughed like a spoiled child and said, "All right, daddykins," sinking her teeth into the chicken but then having trouble tearing it, saying with mouth half full, "Schotth, you hath to hold it shtill," as he pulled the leg back until the meat tore free. He opened a ginger ale, held it to her lips, and tilted it until she raised her index finger, his cue to lower the bottle as a trickle of gold liquid dribbled from the corner of her mouth. She smiled at him, and again he held the chicken to her mouth so she might take another bite, and she was like a wonderful, stupendously naked, and sexy child, but also his own thirty-eight-year-old wife with a long history of reinventing herself, again preparing to become brand new, someone trusting and ready to hope. She laughed that exultant, devilish laughter of hers, so different from the laugh she put on in public when trying to imitate the happiness of other people— no, this laugh was truly her own, the kind that couldn't be faked. It came up dark, eager, and destructive from within her. Here was the Zelda no one else knew, his reckless companion of the bedroom, the eternally youthful spirit she revealed only for him. Holding her palm out, she waved the chicken away, turning her head to the right and left as she struck herself between the breasts, pointing at the bottle and rolling her hand toward her chin, still laughing as Scott raised it to her lips and she touched the drink to steady it, inhaling the liquid until she could free the chunk of chicken lodged in her throat. When she finally stopped laughing, she could breathe again.

"I was choking," she gasped.

"I saw," he said. "That's what you get for eating in the nude."

"Well, I've eaten all I'm going to eat. I'm simply not that hungry and I do so wish to see Havana at night. I'm much happier now that I know something awful hasn't happened to you and you were checking on me the entire time, now that you've stood before me like my very own valet while I sat naked on the bed eating my dinner, my own dear Dodo taking care of me."

God, how he hated that nickname. He tried to remember when she'd come up with it. Probably after her first collapse, maybe early fall of 1930 when she was writing letters to him from Prangins, flooding them with affectionate, imploring epithets, Dearest One, D.O., next Deo and Dearest D.O., next Dudu and Doo-do, giving rein to her imagination as revenge against reality, letting it take on the properties of an indulged child. Sometimes she would use pet names in the bedroom, while kissing him below the waist or while he was preparing to put himself into her, and if his penis went suddenly soft, she would remark, "Don't you want me?" or "Did you have too much to drink?," never surmising that her words were to blame.

Within minutes she was dressed and ready to go, wearing a lavender cloche above a pale-ivory silk dress with short sleeves showing off her still lovely, if slightly too muscular, arms. Whenever healthy, Zelda put on muscle. The nap had been good for her. The glow had come back into her face, her skin like the surface of calmed seawaters, buoyant, lush, reflective.

"What's that?" she asked.

"Nothing," he said, stooping as he opened the door to pick up and pocket the note left by Matéo. "It was supposed to go under my door. It's from the concierge, a question I posed about their dining hours."

On the stairs it occurred to him that even now his new friends might be waiting for them in the lobby. Sure enough, as Zelda and he cleared the small crowd of guests waiting at the base of the stairs, he spotted the *Habanero* and his girl Yonaidys seated on the gold sofas, deep in conversation with two new gentlemen.

"Let's make our way across the Plaza de Armas down to the seaside promenade," he said.

"Do you know where you're going? Did you ask the concierge for recommendations?"

"There's a place called Sloppy Joe's where all the Americans go," he said, improvising, having no idea where it was, planning to ask an American on the street how to get there, calculating his chances of slipping Zelda out the door before his Cuban friends saw them. "I inquired earlier, we'll be fine, we'll stay within shouting distance of—"

"Please ask the concierge," Zelda said, rotating toward the lobby, then wheeling around in the next instant. "Scott, why is that woman waving at you?"

When he looked up, he saw that Yonaidys was indeed waving at him; there was no one else in the vicinity.

"Oh, yes, well, I had a pleasant chat with her companion while I sat in the lobby waiting for you to wake up."

"Do you want to join them?"

"Let's go for a walk before it gets too late. You slept so much today. We've hardly had a minute to ourselves."

"Scott, aren't you being rude?" Zelda asked, but she allowed herself to be led out the door as he waved at Yonaidys. "What's your opinion of them? The man is certainly handsome, if somewhat swarthy in complexion. What does he do?"

"He was educated at Columbia University; he's quite Americanized, an investor of some sort."

The foot traffic on the Calle Obispo had thinned at this late hour, music from an invisible jukebox sounding somewhere up the road, tinny and desolate. An old Model T drove directly toward them on the narrow cobblestone street, as Scott hoisted Zelda by the waist onto a ridiculously narrow sidewalk. Two taxis straddled corner curbs on opposite sides of the street, and the driver of a green-colored Plymouth parked beneath an American flag hailed them. On the Plaza de Armas they strolled inside the columns of the City Hall's magnificent arcade, which stretched the length of the square, the shadows here in the tunneled recesses spooking Zelda so that she touched his chin and asked again, "Do you know where you're going?" A lonely horse-drawn carriage, an empty two-seater with a driver up front, crossed the plaza where those walking at this hour did so mostly in pairs. Splendid elms highlighted by electric street lamps cast silhouettes along the walkways. Beneath the bronze statue of a Cuban patriot and several towering royal palms, Scott saluted and tipped a bongo player and guitarist for playing an American jazz tune he vaguely recognized. On the harbor side of the square, he found the Templete, explaining to his wife that the silk-cotton tree beside it had been grafted from a ceiba tree beneath which the first Mass in Cuba had been celebrated.

"Where did you learn all this?" she asked.

"You were asleep a long while," he said. "The Cuban gentleman in the lobby recited endless stories about the Old City for me. I've taken copious notes in my journal. Follow me, I must show you the fort to the north of the plaza."

They reached an ancient wall of gray coral from behind which rose a Moorish fort with a silolike watchtower, and Scott told her how the famed explorer Hernando de Soto built this fortress, the most secure in all of sixteenth-century Spanish America, in order to make sure his wife Isabel was safe while he set out for Florida to conquer the North American continent.

"For more than four years she waited for him, the New World's very own Penelope," he said.

"I know how this ends," Zelda muttered under her breath.

"Each morning contemplating the sea for hours, searching for clues to his fate."

"Oh, Scott," she said, interrupting him, "please."

But he found the tale irresistible. He couldn't keep himself from reporting how de Soto surveyed North America for years, the first European to explore the continent as far west as modern-day Texas, before succumbing to fever on a stray bank of the Mississippi River.

"No doubt she pined for him the entire time," Zelda said, and only then did Scott regret telling the story. He suggested they walk on.

The city's magnificent promenade curved along the harbor, up and about the face of the northern coast where Gulf waves splaying themselves against a ragged shoreline of coral boulders cast a pleasant mist over the pedestrians. The number of people following the seawall at this hour of the night was astonishing, and Scott noticed many foreigners among them. All the same he instructed Zelda to stick close to his side.

"Is it not safe?" she asked. "What did the concierge say about this promenade at night? Should we get a cab? Let's either take our time and enjoy the walk or, if it's not safe enough to be out walking, let's hail a cab."

"It's perfectly safe," he said, scanning the street for criminal elements, because whenever she fretted about her safety, he started to believe the worst really might happen.

4

THE WINDS, STRONGER BY THE MINUTE, BLEW OUT ONTO THE GULF. Several times Zelda reached up to secure the lavender cloche atop her head, its floral bow tossed frantically by the gusts. Scott walked to her left, near the curb, her gloved hand resting on the cuff of his coat, their conversation aimless yet stilted. Despite the constant flow of correspondence between them these past few years, he existed now on the perimeter of her everyday life, and sometimes he wondered whether he had the right to be admitted to the inner workings of her mind.

"Tell me again," he said, "about the painting lessons in Florida, the time with Dr. Carroll."

Two months ago while in Sarasota under the hospital's care, she'd taken a life drawing class at the Ringling School of Art, another in costume design.

"Dr. Carroll thought it odd that I could be such an accomplished painter, his words not mine," she said, "someone who has held exhibitions, sold paintings, and been reviewed in the *New York Times,* without the benefit of any real training."

"Some people are born with natural talent."

"That's what Dr. Carroll said, but I know better. So many of my talents went untrained for so long. My natural creativity is highly undisciplined."

It was an unmistakable reference to her thwarted career as a dancer, for which she'd started too late, for which in an effort to compensate for her belatedness she'd trained too fast and frantically. Scott didn't wish to take up the topic.

"Some of the women from the Highland must have strolled here early evenings in January when they visited," she said, alluding to the trip for which this vacation was a substitute.

"Do you wish you'd come with them," he said, "instead of coming with me?"

"Scott, don't ask that. You know I'd rather be with you than with anyone."

She stopped to rest against the seawall, leaning onto its wide-girthed bulk and into a purpling sky, the winds warm off the ocean, the moon and the city lights sparkling along the water far out into the straits where everything disappeared into black. She listened to the break of the waves, slapping on coastal rocks, then receding in a gentle wash.

"I feel sorry for the other women sometimes," she said. "They must do everything for themselves, must make sense of small things such as a walk on a promenade entirely on their own. I always have you to help me sift through my thoughts and memories."

She rarely spoke of her fellow patients as individuals. She spoke of exercises executed in groups, of her superiority to the women in sporting activities, of their prevailing opinions on films and books, but she cited none of them singularly as you might speak of a friend. Whenever he imagined her participating in some activity, she was stolid and alone. Always she had preferred men to women, and on the occasions when she broke from this basic pattern, her affections turned to crushes, passionate in their intensity. Madame Egorova, her former ballet instructor, was only the most illustrative, catastrophic example. Zelda's obsessive desire to please her had led to the ascetic diet, the unceasing practices, and the insomnia that precipitated her first breakdown.

"You think that's petty of me," Zelda asked.

"What?"

"You think it petty, or perhaps egoistical, of me."

"They're hardly the same thing."

"Do you think it egoistical of me to see myself as better than the other patients?"

"I didn't take you to be saying that at all."

It was odd how easily they fell into familiarity, and yet there was so much that went unsaid, so much of everyday worry they no longer shared. She asked about Hollywood, when his contract was up for renewal, when he would be assigned to a new film, and he said to himself, She's like a bloodhound, always on the scent of my troubles. He avoided any mention of his failure to be renewed by Metro-Goldwyn-Mayer, promising there was no need to worry, work would soon come his way, downplaying the drama of his circumstances because, after all, there was nothing she could do to help and her worries only compounded his own. There was no one in whom he might more naturally have confided the cumulative injustice of this past year's string of professional heartbreaks, and yet he couldn't risk it for fear of damaging her fragile psyche. Also, he had entrusted that privilege to another woman. Sheilah, in the role of confidante and booster, was entitled to hear his grievances, his increasingly humbler hopes. As someone who trafficked in the industry's secrets, sharing them with the public in her syndicated "Hollywood Today" column, she could offer consolations based on practical knowledge of his trade. And he was sometimes able to return the favor, repaying her with writerly advice, helping her work out an idea for a column.

"Are you thinking of her?"

"Excuse me," he said, stumbling, trying to remember where he'd left off. "Weren't we talking about Dr. Carroll?"

"That was a long time ago."

"Also about the women at the hospital, whether you were petty?"

"Well, I don't care to repeat myself just now."

"If you were trying to bring up our daughter—"

"I wasn't."

"I wouldn't mind speaking about our need to form a united front in conveying to Scottie the seriousness of her situation. How she must make her way in the world after Vassar, without resources to fall back on. How she must prepare to live on her own and for herself, realistically, beginning now while there's time."

"So she doesn't end up a young fool without a plan, much like her mother?"

"Or her father," he said equably.

"Scott, you must remember she's only a child, seventeen."

"She doesn't have much of a safety net."

"Don't make me worry for her," Zelda said with a hint of panic in her voice. "Not here, not now, not yet."

Clearly, Zelda had intuited his reason for changing the topic. Her pride, however, would keep her from pursuing the original question. It was altogether possible she had never heard the name Sheilah Graham voiced by another person, but still Zelda could be counted on to sense when there was someone new in his life, some usurper eager to take up as much room as his imagination would allow her.

Ahead of them the promenade opened onto a plaza, people huddled along the seawall. "How marvelous," Zelda exclaimed.

"If I lived in this city, I would come here every night." A shabbily dressed young man with neatly cropped, kinked hair drew near. "You are *Americanos,* no?" He walked beside them, slowing their pace, soon joined by a woman as he explained, *"Es mi madre,"* repeating the phrase several times, though Scott couldn't figure out why a young man in his early twenties was accompanied by his mother at this hour of the night. He spoke of the United States, mixing English and Spanish, dashing off complex sentences in his native tongue. Whenever they tried to negotiate a difficult phrase, Scott cringing at his own incompetence in Spanish, Zelda took the lead in contriving pacts of compromised knowledge by picking up Latin roots in ways he couldn't. Or by repeating cognates with the syllables accented in the wrong place, à la the rhythms of French. Or, still more crudely, by pantomiming objects to match the words. The system had its limits, but through it they figured out that the young man and his mother resided in one of the barrios within the Old City. Infinitely patient in his desire to be understood, he proposed many places the Americans might visit, then issued an invitation that neither Scott nor Zelda could decipher, though, clearly, it involved listening to music.

"He wants to take you out on the town, presumably at your expense," a man interjected. Scott turned to find himself face to face with Matéo Cardoña, the girl Yonaidys at his side. He didn't believe for a second that the meeting was by chance.

"Scott, it is good to see you," Matéo said, looking from him to his wife. "Zelda Fitzgerald, I hope you enjoyed your dinner."

Zelda started at the mention of her name, leaning in to whisper something Scott couldn't hear, even as he replied, automatically, under his breath, "It's okay, Zelda."

"Señora Fitzgerald," the girl now chimed in, "we believe you, how you say, *sueño*—"

"Sleep," Matéo said.

"Yes, sleep," Yonaidys said, echoing Matéo, "until there was no night? No time for revel, revel, what is—"

"Revels," Scott said.

"*Si,*" said the young girl, whom Scott now saw through Zelda's eyes: the hem of her dress hanging slightly, her white shoes scuffed with dirt. She seemed woefully deficient by contrast to the elegantly dressed man at her side.

The young man, perceiving that he and his mother were being supplanted by this new couple, said his goodbyes, but not before inviting the Fitzgeralds to visit his home, rolling his finger several times before his mouth in an effort to encourage Matéo to translate as he explained that the Americans had expressed interest in joining him for dinner.

Scott asked, "Was he inviting us to visit him?"

"Very good," Matéo said easily. "I've made a mental note of the directions and would be happy to escort you tomorrow or another day, if you wish to see how the other half lives. But I recommend visiting during the daytime."

"I hadn't made up my mind one way or the other," Scott said, resenting Matéo's paternalistic tone, "but I certainly wouldn't have taken my wife to an unknown, most likely impoverished section of the city at night."

"That is wise," Matéo congratulated him. "So will you join us on our walk? I am far better suited to introduce you to our fashionable city and its history and culture."

Scott understood there was no easy way to extricate himself a second time from Matéo's company.

"We're headed for a drink," Scott said.

"Where?"

"Maybe Sloppy Joe's."

"*¡No lo permita Dios!*" Yonaidys cried.

"She is offended on behalf of God and Cuba," Matéo explained. "That place is strictly for Americans. Let us escort you to a worthy Cuban establishment."

So they followed the charismatic Cuban, who kept two steps ahead at all times, walking sideways now and then to direct Zelda's attention to vistas of the city. He stopped them before a monument to the *USS Maine,* sunk in 1898, then turned them toward the center of town, the salt air thinning, the sound of waves against the seawall receding. They walked the Prado, a tree-lined, terrazzo-floored promenade dense with restaurants, hotels, galleries, and music halls, but also with musicians, dancers, prostitutes, and street peddlers of all stripes.

"Ignore them, that is all." Señor Cardoña referred generally to the undesirables.

"So you will know what you are missing," he said moments later, cupping Zelda's arm, directing her vision down the block to the crowds overflowing from under the arcade of an Italianate three-storied building, its flattened arches and distinctive cornice shining coral pink in the nighttime sky. "It is the place we must avoid, the famous Sloppy Joe's."

"En éste dirección, por favor," the girl said cheerfully, ending her long silence, motioning with her hand as if to hurry their escape from the tourists assembled there, and soon they bypassed several raucous bars packed with Cubans and foreigners.

Beyond the last of these their hosts turned them onto a narrow lane, halting before an establishment from which throbbed the sounds of rhythmic African music.

The girl began to chatter in Spanish and Zelda was exasperated. Who were these people? How could Scott know anything about them from an hour's conversation in a hotel lobby? Had he given any thought to where they were, whether it was safe? Inside the bar there wasn't a foreigner in sight. Matéo led them to a table with a view of the band, an eight-person ensemble—guitarist, four percussionists, two guys on horns, and singer—pumping out a sultry but high-energy modern music on a makeshift stage in the far corner, the song paced by the layered percussion. She felt summoned by the brightly clicking claves and steady two-tone beat of the woodblocks, by the diffuse shimmer of the large gourd keeping time with the rippling beat of a washboardlike wooden instrument. All around them blacks, mulattos, and a very few fair-skinned Spanish Cubans swayed and tapped their feet without paying attention to the band.

It was a juke joint, for all practical purposes, like one of the many seedy establishments strewn across her own Deep South and patronized exclusively by blacks, at which on any given night the pulsing music inspired dance, sultry liaisons, lovers' quarrels, sometimes quarrels between rivals over the same lover. From the time she was a girl of twelve Zelda had been up for any adventure. She relished the jazz bars she and Scott had visited in Harlem in the early years after their marriage, but she never managed to get herself inside a Southern juke joint. It just wasn't something white people did. Thrilled by the idea of listening to this Cuban cousin of jazz blues in an establishment her genteel parents would never have set foot in, thrilled also by the sensual progression of the song, she let the pulsingly metrical music roll through her like nervous excitement, listening for space within the melody, deep within the beat, attempting to squeeze her way inside the song as if it were a crowded room.

"Your wife understands music," Matéo said to Scott, but Zelda did not look up.

"She was once an accomplished dancer," Scott said, and she heard her own thoughts, unvoiced, Until my art disrupted the routine of your writer's life and you put a stop to it, but even as she phrased the words, she realized she could no longer feel the bitterness they once inspired. Enjoying the music, she instructed herself: He has done his best and fought battles for you, losing many, but never casually.

Matéo bought drinks for the group and Zelda absently sipped hers without tasting it, not wanting to lose the thread of the song. Scott was saying something, but she waved him off. Her body in motion on the inside, she could project images of herself that corresponded to the music. For every arrangement of notes built on intervals and rhythm there is a motion through which the body might objectify it in dance. In listening for that form, Zelda released herself from the strictures of social etiquette, let go of the night, her rough sleep, and the distress of traveling with an alcohol-wearied Scott. Let go also of waking alone in a hotel room, not knowing where he was or how long he'd been away or if he would return. Music is healing, she might have said under her breath, knowing she would give anything, after all it had cost her, for one last chance at the ballet. So what if devotion to her art unfit her for the world. Once you knew what it was to live inside a song, and allow your body to become its instrument, everything else in life was disappointing.

"Zelda," Scott was whispering to her, "you're being antisocial. Are you angry with me?"

"I'm having a good time," she said, charmed by the song's percussive drive, "and I know you'll watch out for me, I have absolute confidence in you."

How strange it was that she of all people had married a man with no ear for music. If she were to stop and ask Scott to describe how it made him feel, whether he could hear the intervals, the structure of memory and anticipation by which any song lived, he would look at her with admiring annoyance. He might dismiss her as a mystic, worse yet a Dionysian. And so what if she was. Did he think his the only true art? He couldn't hear what she heard in song, the echo of meaninglessness, the place inside it where we all become nothing. About music he was merely sentimental, the way he was also about women. All he heard were the lyrics in their scant ephemerality, how they scuttled like mice across the surface of the song, extrapolating on the rhythm. He couldn't understand that the words were beats and syllabic notes and varying lengths of breath, and if she were to jumble them in a babble of consonants and vowels, all that really mattered was that she could unscramble them well enough to find usable vowels through which to hold open the notes, also some punchy consonants with which to scat and propel the melody forward so it didn't succumb to the ecstatic drive of the percussion.

She moved closer to Scott, wrapping her palm on his forearm, squeezing it. She listened closely to the song, how different this relentlessly percussive music was from jazz. Scott, listening only to Matéo, nevertheless tilted his head to smile at her.

Could he hear it too? she asked in a whisper, and Scott rotated to stare at her as though reproving an eccentric child.

"Speak plainly, Zelda. We can't afford mystery this time around. It's too risky."

"I wasn't being mysterious, only musical."

From across the table she could feel Matéo, pretending to look away but listening to every word, studying the two of them out of the corner of his eye.

"Is this about your dancing?" Scott asked.

"Oh, never mind," she said, "and don't start accusing me of bringing up things I've long ago stopped bringing up. Not my fault if you still feel guilty about squelching my dance amb—"

"Zelda, stop," he said. "Not while we're out with people."

"We don't know these people," she sighed, "and, besides, I'm done now. As a matter of fact, I have to use the bathroom. Can you ask them where it is?"

Matéo proposed that Yonaidys escort Zelda. To which Zelda replied, without so much as glancing at the Cuban, "Scott, I don't expect to be treated like some patient in an asylum, watched at every minute."

"No hay problema," Yonaidys said. *"Yo también,* I have need also of *el cuarto de baño."*

"Zelda," Scott scolded, "she is only being courteous."

So Zelda waited as Matéo stood clear of the table to let Yonaidys pass, and soon the lithe young woman was escorting her to the rear of the bar, beyond the band, now driving the song to its end with cadent harmonies layered over the percussion, the crescendo rolling forward into the crowd like a storm front until even the portion of the room it hadn't yet reached was sweltering, stifling, and Zelda suddenly wished she were headed out of this bar rather than into its bowels.

"She is nervous, no?" Matéo asked. "Your wife is made nervous by this place to which we have escorted her?"

Scott shifted uneasily. He could no longer see Zelda through the throngs at the rear of the room.

Matéo was preparing himself to make a pitch of some sort, everything he said inclining toward greater consequence. Wending through banal chatter, he told Scott about his acquaintance with the bartender, about the bar's reputation for playing the best African music in the city, about his practice of bringing here only those Americans who could appreciate cultures other than their own. He'd known Scott for such a person right away. Scott rested an elbow on the edge of the table, propping his chin on his thumb and caressing the thin two-day stubble along his jawline.

Matéo, his intentions seemingly as aimless as his manner, asked for Scott's opinions on baseball, wondering whether he was a fanatic of the great American sport, also the national pastime of Cuba. Matéo had attended games of the New York Giants and Brooklyn Dodgers, he had witnessed firsthand the impressive feats of the New York Yankees, but he believed in the prowess of his own countrymen. The best among the Cuban baseballers, men such as José de la Caridad Méndez, Joseíto Muñoz, and Cristóbal Torriente, were as grand as Cobb, Ruth, and Gehrig. Though no expert on the sport, Scott had spent countless hours in the company of famed sportswriter Ring Lardner, long evenings squandered on Ring's porch in Great Neck, lapping up his booze and his stories about the greatest of pastimes, many of which ended with his drinking ballplayers under the table while instructing them on the art of a game they played expertly but appreciated far less than he. Ring had bestowed on Scott enough knowledge to make him capable of comparing Matéo's present chatter, for instance, to the tactics of a clever pitcher working a batter with off-speed junk, tossing slow curves and change-ups early in the count in order to sneak the fastball by a few pitches later.

Shifting gears, Matéo made mention of a new project in development, a hotel here in Havana. The developer was a friend. If Scott had ever thought of investing in Cuba, now was an ideal time to do so. Matéo could personally assure him that Americans were making money hand over fist in Cuban real estate, in hotels, in bars and jazz speakeasies, in beach properties. Scott should think about it. Matéo would be happy to set up a meeting any time over the next few days, an informal talk with the magnate, or one of his associates, so that Scott might assess such a nice opportunity. Scott smiled grimly. Inside him was an echo of laughter, sturdy and nihilistic. He thinks I have money, Scott said to himself. He thinks because I was on the cover of a few magazines and he can remember my novels, probably owned *This Side of Paradise* without reading it, because I should have saved and invested or because my books and stories will have continued to sell or because my wife so far as he knows never broke down and spent the last decade in expensive institutions, draining the dregs of her desperate soul, costing every last penny we had and then some, so much that I had to go to Hollywood and whore myself; he thinks because I will have stored up against the prospect of just such a terrible future and not spent money liberally in my youth; he thinks for all these reasons—and because I'm here with my fine American wife in Havana, mingling with the well-to-do—that I have the funds to invest in some cockamamy Caribbean venture of which I have no way of assessing the legitimacy.

Scott didn't answer Matéo. Several minutes of conversational calm ensued, each man pretending to listen to the band while scanning the rear of the establishment for his companion.

Just then Scott spotted Zelda dashing into the crowd, something awry in her expression as she leaned a forearm into the back of one person after another. Men and women alike wheeled about, prepared to protest but mostly failing to do so, maybe because they recognized the desperation on her face, maybe because they made allowances for esoteric behavior from a lily-white foreigner so obviously out of place. Yonaidys followed in Zelda's wake, slowing to speak with people she had jostled, offering excuses for the American. "Is something wrong?" Matéo asked, as if Scott could read his wife's mind from across the room. It was possible someone had threatened her, or leered at her, or made unwelcome advances. It could have been almost anything. Halfway to him, Zelda stalled in the densest portion of the crowd, the band no longer playing, the club's patrons amassed in a thick swarm between the stage and the bar as she tried to shove through them. A mulatto nearly as fair as Matéo, who wore dark hair streaked with brilliantine and a light-blue jacket, whirled in place shouting curses above the milling masses. He dropped his voice somewhat when he saw that he had been denouncing a woman but nevertheless continued his tirade for the benefit of those immediately surrounding him.

Matéo caught the attention of a dark-skinned man at a nearby table, indicating with a slight nod that he should intervene. The young man, who wore a white guayabera with a camp collar and stood several feet beyond Zelda, shouldered the two men who were in her path, and again she slanted toward Scott, slipping through the clustered people at the center of the bar. The next thing he knew, Zelda stood beside him, whispering into the side of his head, teeth clenched, voice gruff, her sentences impossible to hear. All he could make out was a phrase or two about her being unable to use the toilet. Meanwhile, he kept his eyes on the scene unfolding in her wake, whole sections of the crowd tossing one way, then another, as those siding with the man who'd cursed Zelda stole forward and those backing the black man who'd liberated her drove them back.

"Why, you ask," she said. "Well, for one thing, it wasn't clean enough." She wanted him to ask what the second or third thing was, but he said nothing because he was studying the escalating violence and because he dreaded what she would say next; and if he could have put it off until later, he would have done so. Zelda's ash-colored eyes bored into him. She was going to speak her mind whether he felt like hearing it or not. "And for another," she said, "that crazy girl pulled a knife on me as we entered the bathroom."

At first Scott didn't believe her.

"You don't believe me," she said, then tried to explain, but still it didn't make any sense, the details all jumbled. For a moment he feared she had come unhinged. Only later, as they lay awake in each other's arms at the hotel in the early morning, did the source of her panic resolve itself into something like linear narrative, as he arranged the component parts neatly enough to see Matéo's girl guiding Zelda into the bathroom and announcing, "I'll stand guard," or some such well-intended phrase that Zelda couldn't hear for what it was, concentrated as she was on the fine steel blade the girl extracted from a case strapped to a garter inside her thigh. "She was offering to protect you, I am sure of it," Scott told his wife by the gray morning light, and Zelda could no longer disagree. But that hadn't seemed a likely explanation as she stepped into a stall with a flimsy door and broken clasp, her pelvis tightening, her bladder though full unable to release a drop of urine. No time for hindsight or clearheadedness, not while crouching in such a vulnerable pose, with a stranger outside your stall holding a long, thin blade. She had risen from the seat and rushed back to the table, shoving her way through the crowd, oblivious to the ire she provoked, to the curses, even to the handsome black man who had chivalrously thrown himself at her maligners—she must find Scott and tell him what had happened.

Amid the commotion of the bar he had tried to calm her, still not quite believing her, not finding any cause for alarm in Yonaidys's actions in the bathroom, even if what his wife said was true. He praised the band, vowed that the bar was safe even as he shot nervous glances at Matéo, who surveyed the ongoing ruckus, which was gradually rolling forward, spilling into their corner of the establishment. Scott draped his arm over his wife's shoulders, protectively, keeping her attention averted from the wildly tossing, listing swarm she had incited. Eventually, though, she must have heard the shouts and threats, or felt the pressure of Scott's forearm holding her in place, because she shrugged her shoulders free of his hold and spun around and into the glint of a second knife, this one held less than a foot from her cheek by the black man in the guayabera. He was turned sideways in a defensive posture, his flank toward her, his right arm raised high and held away from his body, the blade dancing in his hand. The mulatto in the light-blue jacket who'd cursed her had squared off with the black man, also with knife in hand, the crowd spreading out in all directions, opening a circle around them.

It was impossible to say how long she stood in harm's way. Scott, dulled by drink, reacted more slowly than he should have. Matéo stepped between Zelda and the melee even as the knife-wielding man nearest her lost his footing and tried to interrupt his fall with the hand in which he held the knife, whereupon the man in the blue jacket seized the opportunity to plunge a blade twice into the prone man's chest, the white guayabera flowering like a rose as his body rolled toward Zelda and Matéo, blood splashing onto her dress.

She was still fixed on the injured man's bleeding shirt when Scott pulled her stare to his own, her pupils empty and dilated. He cupped her clenched jaw in his hand so that she couldn't peer down at the splatters on her pale-ivory dress, while Matéo, grasping her at the wrist, dragged them from the scene. She was whispering loudly under her breath, "I could kill you for this, I could just kill you," and in case Scott hadn't heard her the first time, "I could kill you for exposing me to this," the tremolo of her voice succumbing to thoughts beyond her control.

5

ON THE OUTSKIRTS OF THE CITY THEY TOURED A DERELICT bullfighting ring, hardly recognizable as such, the high sun-bleached walls framing an arena long over-run with grass, the sport having disappeared from Cuba forty years ago under pressure from the United States. Their guide was an elderly man with sunburned skin, dark mustache set against a silver mane of hair, and a milky left eye, and he had never recovered from the death of his country's once-beloved pastime. He could still conjure the bulls as they entered the ring, hides glistening like dark burnished wood in the sun, their tall-shouldered, majestically sculpted bodies arched and readied for battle, an entire stadium hanging on the grace of their incensed charge. Scott mentioned the bullfights in Morocco, attempting to introduce his experiences into the conversation, but the guide was too lost in his own longing for that which he would never again witness to hear his guest's words.

"Scott, this is boring, I'm bored," Zelda said. "I keep expecting Ernest to sprint round the corner in a cape, chasing a mythical bull, sticking it in the ass, saying, 'I will overstand you, bull, or I am not the man.'"

"*¿No explíco correctamente?*" the guide asked, fearing he had erred in some way. "You and the *señora* wish me to explain again?"

"Zelda," Scott said with exasperation.

"I don't care, I'm awfully bored."

"I understand English, *señora*," the guide said, hurt by her rudeness. "I have been talking to you in English all day."

"Yes, and mostly boring me in English all day."

Scott grimaced, flashing her a look of gentle reproof.

"If he would only speak in Spanish," she said, "I might imagine centuries of recondite history beneath his words, the dark Catholic soul of the Romance languages, all those monks mysteriously transcribing the thoughts of God in illuminated texts, taking dictation from Jews and other heretics stretched on the rack, the torture of bulls some kind of metaphor for—"

"Zelda, this must stop."

He was not altogether against the humiliation of the guide, who was a surprise gift from Matéo Cardoña and also something of a pompous ass. They'd come downstairs from Sunday brunch on the rooftop restaurant to find themselves summoned across the cavernous lobby, and at first Scott thought it must have something to do with the previous night, the end to which he began to replay in his head. First, the panicked urgency of getting Zelda out of the bar—he could remember saying as much to Matéo, in those very words, "I have to get her out of here," and Matéo accepted Scott's petition as though he were used to solving problems under circumstances more hazardous than these: "It is easily done. I will slip your wife out before the police arrive, here like this." Scott hadn't yet given any thought to the police, but no matter, Matéo took hold of Zelda's wrist, beckoning Scott to follow, expertly guiding his guests through the huddling patrons and the onslaught of newcomers gathered at the entrance by the rumors of blood, most having been nowhere near the violence when it occurred. As yet no police. In this way, Matéo remarked, the Havana police were reliable. Nevertheless, they would soon arrive to comb the crowd for witnesses, some of whom might well remember a white American woman with high cheekbones and piercing eyes who stood only inches from the slain man, his blood splattered on her dress. Only then did it occur to Scott that Zelda was a material witness to a crime. Who knew what Cuban law called for, what the duties of a witness were in this city?

Might the police detain her for hours or days, demanding that she remain in the country until the trial? He foresaw the hassle, the need to borrow money, and if so, from whom? Over the past three years he'd paid down his debts but only at the cost of exhausting the goodwill of all his creditors: Max Perkins and Scribner's; his agent Harold Ober; maybe even reliable Arnold Gingrich at *Esquire*. He could never turn to Sheilah for money, not after the way they'd parted. Of course, worse than any material debt was the possible cost to Zelda—who knew what toll reliving the crime over and over again might take on her?

They had slalomed through nighttime revelers on narrow streets, turning often, wending through a barrio ripe with the sweet, sickly smell of excrement and trash. Eventually Matéo drew them across an unevenly cobblestoned plaza at the far end of which stood a baroque cathedral in gray limestone with oddly asymmetrical bell towers. Along the colonnaded porticoes of the government buildings that flanked the square to the north and south, vagrants clustered around barrels of fire, their voices not quite carrying to the center of the plaza. "It is best to keep moving," said Matéo, making sure Scott understood what was being done for him. At the far end of a street branching perpendicularly off the square, he could make out several men in uniforms, either soldiers or police, and immediately scanned his memory for details he had accumulated about this city's recent history of coups, military dictatorships, and rogue paramilitary armies. "We must part here," Matéo said, instructing Scott to continue three blocks down this same road past the uniformed men, until he reached Calle Obispo, there to take a left. Another four blocks, and the hotel would come into view. "Excuse me," Scott interrupted. "Are those soldiers or policemen?" If stopped, Scott was to say he and his wife were returning from a romantic stroll along the Malecón. "Where?" Scott asked, and Matéo explained, "El Malecón, the seaside promenade on which I found you earlier. Tourists cannot get enough of it. And remember you enjoyed the ocean air, you lost track of the time, cutting back by way of Cathedral Square. You did not stop anywhere else. *Entiendes?*" Scott replied that he did and shook hands with his new friend, wondering how he could ever repay Matéo's solicitude, worrying that his favors came at a price still to be named. Then he and Zelda walked hand in hand into the night, circumnavigating the soldiers who wore rifles slung halfway down their arms and inspected tourists through white clouds of cigar smoke without saying anything.

Being met this morning in the lobby of the Ambos Mundos by a guide they hadn't hired, before they'd even decided what to do with their day, had made Scott uneasy. It felt too much like being spied on. But it wasn't this fact alone that inspired his resentment of the silver-maned Cuban guide, who was, after all, hardly to be blamed for his paid-for meddlesomeness. No, it was the guide's alternately officious and sycophantic manner. One minute he was bragging in petty bourgeois terms of hiring himself out to the highest bidder, the next slandering the Europeans who paid for his words but were indifferent to the wells of historical truth he could tap, preferring to be told nonsense (the guide used the word *burradas,* then translated it) about the passion of the Caribbean soul. Such were the results, he said, of a national economy dependent on the production of sugar, tobacco, and rum, on sweets and sin, on *Americanos* for whom Havana was an around-the-clock carnival; such, the wages of endless corruption. He spoke contemptuously of foreigners and his fellow countrymen alike.

Not only did he deserve to be put down for his airs, but maybe his cynicism merited a client such as Zelda. Still, it wasn't wise to let go of the reins on her spite for too long.

"Zelda," he said again, "please get yourself under control. Señor Famosa García will complete the tour and then we will—"

"I do not wish to subject the *señora,*" the guide said, interrupting Scott, "to my observations if they do not please her, if they are too boring for her ears."

"Well, that can't be helped," Scott said. In her unkindness Zelda was a picador, pricking the hide, enervating the soul, weakening the guide's will to go on. "You've been paid well, and I'll tip you later for having to put up with my wife's cruel if precise wit. So let's move on. Where to now?"

Already this morning the guide had driven them along the famous seaside promenade he judged an acceptable consequence of the brief American occupation of his country three decades ago, stopping at the far less acceptable monument erected in the 1920s to commemorate the sinking of the *Maine,* presuming they would wish to pay homage to their countrymen and the event that provoked the United States to declare war on Spain. He talked them through a visit to the Catedral San Cristóbal de la Habana, which they'd briefly glimpsed the previous night, entertaining them with stories about the rivalry between Havana and

Santo Domingo over two sets of bones, each reputed to be those of Christopher Columbus himself.

"It is up to you," the guide said politely. "I am here to provide for you, of course."

"One of the haciendas, then?" Scott suggested. "What other remnants of Spanish barbarism might we find entertaining, perhaps the defunct slaves' quarters at one of the sugar mills?"

His refusal to soothe the guide's vanity won Zelda's gratitude, he could tell from the way she held herself, and it pleased him to be able to read her body language.

"Was I awful before?" she whispered when they were in the backseat of the car.

"No," he said, only then pivoting to look at her, understanding that she meant much earlier—as in, the night before, when she hadn't spoken as Scott pulled her gaze from the skirts of her dress, not a word of gratitude or curiosity as she was dragged through dank, shadowed streets by Matéo, not a whisper to Scott as he avoided the cigar-toting soldiers and delivered her to the lobby of the Ambos Mundos, riding the elevator to regain the safety of her room.

"You were frightened, that's all. I've seen you far worse," he said.

Even today she couldn't remember anything of what had happened after the knife plunged into the man's chest, the blood bright and effervescent on his white shirt. She asked her husband to tell her how they'd escaped the bar and made it back to the hotel, and as Scott described their exit remarked, "Oh, yes, I remember someone pulling at my arm."

"We arrive at the hacienda of one of the great sugar mills of the old regime in Cuba in five minutes," the guide said to them. All morning he had been estimating the time it took to go from one place to the next, and always it took longer than he said.

"Do you think anyone noticed anything?" Zelda whispered.

"Maybe they could see the shadow of the crime, the way it clung to us, maybe they could see it my eyes. Do you think they will come for me?"

She spoke as though she didn't want him to give her an honest answer. Sometimes he would have liked to ask her, "What are you capable of hearing today?" His impulse even after all these years was to confide in her, but he could never be certain whether she was up to the challenge of assessing her own well-being.

"For all they know, I could be the person who stabbed the man."

"Don't be preposterous, Zelda," Scott said, reminding her again that they had done nothing wrong.

"Oh, I know," she said. "Besides, I probably couldn't tell them anything. I don't remember looking at the man's face, and if I did—"

Scott asked her to lower her voice.

"If I did, I hardly remember the color of his skin or the slope of his nose or the angle of his jaw. Still, do you think it's right that we left without saying anything?"

In her mind she was a fugitive from last night's violence, calculating how long she might have to stay on the run.

"We did nothing wrong," Scott said again. Wrong place at the wrong time, that was all, but they were safe now.

She laid her left wrist on his lap, palm open and up, a gesture of invitation, and he stared down at her hand for a brief while, then clasped it in his, intertwining his fingers in hers.

"I didn't mean what I said," she whispered.

At first he couldn't figure out what she was talking about.

"It's a powerful feeling, I really can't control it," she said. The guide tossed off phrases from the front seat, but Scott ignored him. "It accumulates in me like bile, and I have to get it out of my system—you understand, don't you? It doesn't mean anything, not really. They were just words and you were in the way of them. I'm sorry you're so often the one who is in the way of them."

Now he understood and he heard the words again, fresh and sharp as if she'd just spoken them, *I could kill you for this,* suffering their malice for the first time.

"It's only because you're so good and loyal, and what's your reward?" she said. "You always come back for me, even when no one else will. Even if everybody else is content to let me rot my days away in a madhouse."

"Zelda, don't."

"Not you, you always come back."

Not an insignificant portion of Matéo Cardoña's Sabbath had been devoted to making inquiries on behalf of his new acquaintances from the United States. He started by visiting the police station, letting it be known he was at the bar last night when the incident took place, since he was certain to be placed there sooner or later.

"Tell me, Mr. Cardoña, what did you see?" asked the detective, who was well aware of the prestige of the Cardoña name and whose courtesies were so exaggerated it might have been reasonable to infer hostility beneath them.

"If only I'd caught a better glimpse," he replied. "It would make things simpler."

"Indeed it would," the detective said.

On any other night Matéo might have remained on the scene and taken charge, paying the two largest men he could find to seize the assailant and obtain the weapon. Of course, it all depended on the man—whether Matéo owed favors to any of his acquaintances or might procure their favor on credit. Matéo Cardoña was by all accounts a pragmatic man. Even now, if the police were to apprehend a suspect and it was someone he agreed to identify, his reputation in the city was such that a prosecutor would have little trouble obtaining a conviction on his word alone. But then the assailant might remember seeing Matéo in the company of the two Americans who had riled him in the first place, and Scott had made it clear he didn't want his wife involved. For the time being, there was more to be gained in covering for the Fitzgeralds.

What was it that made his actions from last night suspicious to the detective? Well, for one thing there was the mistake of leaving the scene, his judgment warped by the Americans, by his own inscrutable desire for the woman with her languorous eyes and thick pouting lips, also her amply curved figure, more like that of a *Cubana* than an *Americana*. Even today the image of her slow swaying inside the music pursued him, her motions sensual yet precise; and when he'd spotted the knife in the air, so close to Zelda's face, the animal terror in her eyes, the color draining from her cheeks, he had known he must act. So he seized hold of her wrist as the man nearer Zelda slipped, his rival's knife plunging into his chest as Scott rushed forward to obstruct her view while the wounded man writhed on the floor. The sensible thing to do was to stay and report what they had seen to the police. Not much could be made of Zelda's role in the affair. Who would care if some white woman out of her element became claustrophobic and tried to shove her way through a crowd? Nevertheless, when Scott said, "We have to get her out of here," Matéo took it as a command.

"Any Americans in the bar, by chance?"

Matéo ignored the question.

"So you didn't see anything?"

"Nothing that can be of much use."

"Then why are you here?"

"Duties of a citizen."

"That would be a first," the detective joked. It was impossible to tell whether he meant to accuse all of Havana's citizens of a lax sense of duty or only the one sitting before him.

"Well, I am also an acquaintance of the victim's family and of course I feel someone must pay for what happened. How is the victim this morning?"

"The family has not told you?"

"I have not spoken to his family since last night," Matéo said.

"Let's only say," the detective replied, hesitating, most likely revealing less than he knew, "he has not regained consciousness."

The detective asked in whose company Matéo spent the previous night.

"Only a girl," Matéo replied, and the two men laughed.

"No foreigners in your party?"

"I believe you just asked me that, yes?" He couldn't decide if the detective was merely fishing. "Why do you ask, my friend?"

Matéo had to be careful. The detective knew more than he was letting on; perhaps someone had mentioned seeing Matéo in the company of the *yanquis,* buying them drinks. He was a man known for mixing business and leisure, the two modes hardly separable for him. None of which was truly compromising, so long as he didn't get caught in a lie.

"One witness reported seeing foreigners in the club," the detective said. "I wondered if you met them, maybe spent time or some friendly cash on them."

"What good would foreigners be to your case? They were not part of the fight, this much I can be sure of. What are the chances they witnessed anything in so large a crowd of people?"

"Well, Americans often make the best witnesses," the detective said. "They are cooperative, they wish to see justice move swiftly so they can get on with their lives. Our judges find them reliable. We have a society that puts its trust in Europeans of all stripes, no sense pretending otherwise."

The detective himself was a mulatto with a long jaw, a thin smile, an even thinner mustache, and cobalt eyes. When he spoke he showed no teeth, curling his lip so that one of his nostrils flared even as the thin mustache tented, then fell. It was hard to determine whether there was any bitterness in what he said. Matéo had known all along why the police and lawyers might be interested in tracking down Scott and Zelda. It was true, Americans were good for clearing cases. Even if Zelda had seen nothing, the police might persuade her to identify a suspect who resembled the blurred image of her memory, and whatever she said, the prosecutors could make it stick.

"In your opinion, the victim will recover, yes?"

"Of course this makes all the difference." The detective smiled wryly. "If he recovers, it's a petty squabble over some girl that got out of hand, American, Cuban, it does not matter. Two gamecocks preening for a female. We have all been subject to such fits on occasion."

"Yes," Matéo said, "a spontaneous crime, the passion of jealousy, hard to say which of the two was to blame."

"Except one has not regained consciousness," the detective said.

"And, of course, the assailant stabbed the man after he stumbled," Matéo replied. "He must be held accountable. Intentions do not always matter under the law. I will keep my ear to the ground and maybe I will stumble across your Americans."

"You'll let me know if you hear from them, is that what you're saying, sir?"

"Duties of a citizen," Matéo replied, and rose to take his leave.

He walked out of the office convinced that the detective was holding out on him. It would take some maneuvering, but he could track down the necessary information—was the wounded man dead or alive, and if hospitalized, what were his chances?—before the day was done. He might as well start at the top: General Benítez, chief of police. Matéo had made Benítez money several times over on a string of investments. Benítez would tell him what he needed to know.

In the afternoon Matéo kept a reporter at the *Havana Post* from running a story about the Fitzgeralds' visit to the Old City in the society pages. Or perhaps it would be more accurate to say he bought himself and the Fitzgeralds some time by promising to get together with the reporter the next afternoon. Matéo's motives in protecting the American couple weren't entirely mercenary. Something about Scott reminded him of his younger brother. Of course, Matéo's break with his family in Santiago had strained his relationship with his brother, whose politics were as twisted and reactionary as those of the rest of the family, but nevertheless every now and then Hector traveled to Havana and they met for dinner, drinks, and conversation about their favorite baseball players over Por Larrañaga cigars. During his youth, Hector had been a hard drinker always in trouble with their father, and the only one who stuck up for him was Matéo. Scott too had the habits of the hard drinker and the kindly soul often at odds with authority, and from his days in New York City, Matéo remembered such men of talent fondly, tolerant of their bohemian, sometimes squalid tendencies. Everything had been so aimless in the Village in the twenties, the parties so free and licentious; some men never righted themselves afterward.

But what was Scott's story? There was an air of irrepressible poise about him, the style of someone who'd made a success in the world but now exuded whiffs of intermittent hard luck. If he was writing for Hollywood, he must be doing pretty well.

They visited an old church on the hacienda, the doors still open for Sabbath devotions, several local women lingering to light candles and recite rosaries in the pews nearest the altar. Zelda redeemed herself in the eyes of their guide when she too insisted on lighting a candle.

"Your wife is religious," he said to Scott as he observed her crouching low in one of the pews, genuflecting as she dropped to her knees. Scott, while apparently studying the altar, wondered what Matéo had intended in procuring this guide for them. Was it a way of keeping track of them? And if so, for what purpose? "My wife, *Dios la bendiga,*" the guide continued, "was also a holy woman all her life. Now she is dead, sometimes I tell my friends, who is to look out for my soul? All the women of Cuba, they are religious. This is a country in which God matters, the women look after us."

Mentored throughout his teen years by an avuncular priest whom he had loved as a father, Scott had lost his feeling for God in his early twenties, but he couldn't enter a church without awakening the rhythm of belief, if only in the echoes of his love for that kindly, cultured man. On dipping fingers in a font of holy water, crossing himself and murmuring a prayer without consciously thinking about the words, he felt a calm flow through him. It was like returning to a place where he belonged, his wanderings completed, as though life were a journey on the order of the prodigal son's, your greatest ambition to get back to where you started.

So Zelda prayed while he and the guide toured the church, Famosa García deciphering some of the finer details of the stations of the cross, revealing demons crouched in the corner of a stained glass window that displayed Jesus scourged. He said mysteriously, "Are sacred places not worth fighting to preserve? You would agree, yes, churches cannot be desecrated, men and women of God should not be forsaken?"; and Scott understood him to be speaking in code of Spain and the victorious alliance of royalists, clergy, and nationalists. The afternoon sun slanted through the windows above the chancel, suffusing the marble in an arrow of colored light that folded over the altar rail, casting shadows into the nearby pews. Those at the back of the church where Zelda knelt were darker still. It was time to leave, so he slid into the pew beside his wife, her eyes shut tight, lips fixed in beatific contentment. He tapped her on the shoulder several times. She smiled as she lifted her head to see him sitting next to her, as if she were used to him at last. They exited the church in silence.

"I wasn't unbearably rude earlier, I don't think," she said to Scott as she drank wine over a late lunch. She probably shouldn't be drinking wine—how many times had the doctors taken him aside to remind him that alcohol wasn't good for her and he must avoid drinking in her company? But he was exhausted from the sightseeing, eyes heavy from lack of sleep, simply too weary to police her choices.

"Scott, didn't you sleep well? You have bags," she said, running her finger into the bone-sore sockets above his cheekbones. He wondered if she had no memory of asking him last night to watch over her while she slept or of his combing her temples with his fingers as she purred gratitude. Not until she was all the way under, more than an hour later, was it safe to leave her, and still he lay at her side, waiting until sunlight was leaking beneath the curtains to slip next door to his own bed.

"You didn't answer my question, whether you thought I was terrible to the guide earlier."

"I thought it was a statement."

"You think he's forgiven me, then?"

The table at which they sat, in a café in a small fishing village along the northern coast, faced the Gulf of Mexico. From its stilted wood deck they looked out over a harbor where small to mid-sized ramshackle fishing boats, some no bigger than dinghies, docked along two weather-beaten piers that jutted out into the expanse of ocean beyond. The boggy seawater, full of reeds and cattails closer to shore, ran up to and beneath the deck of the café. Not much of a breeze today, but the coastal air was cool, pleasing in its briny stench. Flies settled on the pink meat of the guava slices set before them. The waiter returned with bowls of mussels, fish, and lobster in a red broth. Scott ordered another rum and a bottle of Pepsi-Cola. The waiter, when he wasn't tending to Zelda and Scott, talked with their guide at the bar, the restaurant otherwise empty at the siesta hour. "We keep eating when we should be sleeping," Zelda remarked midway through her bowl of soup. All he had a taste for was the guava, though the thickening flies (he waved them off every now and then) discouraged his enthusiasm for the tart, pasty fruit. Several times Zelda looked up from her bowl to suggest Scott try the soup, and for God's sake stop waving at the flies, there was nothing to be done about them, but he continued to sip his cola, occasionally flapping his hand, his chair pulled out from under the table's umbrella into sunlight because it was too cool in the shadows.

"I feel rather bad for the poor man now," Zelda was saying. "He held up bravely under my derision, in his own servile way."

"He's making a living, Zelda. Just getting by, like the rest of us."

A copy of yesterday's *Havana Post,* an English-language daily, lay on the table next to them and she retrieved it, flipping absent-mindedly through its pages.

"But he's forgiven me," she said, trying to find a headline that grabbed her. "I can tell. What did he say again about his wife?"

On the fifth page, as if she had been searching for it, she discovered under the headline *"Wings Over Cuba"* their names in print: *"Arrivals from Miami by plane yesterday were F. Scott Fitzgerald, novelist writer from Hollywood, Calif., and Mrs. Fitzgerald."* She was his spouse, nothing more, but to the world at large they were still a couple of note, the writer and his wife.

"When you were praying in the church," Scott was saying, "Señor Famosa García told me that you reminded him of his wife."

"And she's dead?"

"For several years."

"Then he's definitely forgiven me," Zelda said, folding shut the newspaper. "We'll make it up to him by asking if we can take a picture with him. Does he know who you are?"

"I'm sure it would mean nothing to him."

From the beach below came a rush of angry voices in Spanish, and as Zelda darted to the rail of the deck, Scott rose slowly, tired of alarm. Two young boys had been fishing with hand lines from the shore, and one of them had hooked a sizable fish, fighting it by backing up the beach in order to wear it out. In his distracted state, he had walked his own line straight into that of the other boy. At the rail Scott heard the explosion of the fish breaking the surface maybe twenty yards from shore, magnificently iridescent in the sun as it slapped sideways on the water and disappeared again. The boy who had hooked the fish became all the more frantic. He let out line from his stick as the fish ran, let the stick on which the line was wrapped rotate like a motor in his palms so as to avoid slicing his fingers, and when the fish no longer ate up line, he again backpedaled up and away from the shoreline, tugging at the hopelessly tangled lines and shouting in Spanish at the other boy who followed him only because he had to. The owner of the café descended a wood staircase to the beach, striding across the blanched sand to settle the dispute. As soon as he reached the two boys, each plunged into his version of events, gesticulating fiercely, now and then pointing to where the fish had jumped. When it again broke the surface, the owner of the café pulled out a knife, biting its leather handle to hold it between his teeth as he assumed possession of the two sticks on which the lines were wrapped.

"He'll have to cut the lines," announced Famosa García as he came forward to perch his forearms on the rail. "It's only the one with the fish on it that matters, of course."

"He seems to be gathering a lot of line," Zelda remarked as the café owner cautiously wrapped the lines together around the conjoined sticks.

"That's no way to catch a fish as strong as the one the boy has hooked. My friend is letting the eager one down easy, would you say; he is doing everything to pretend they will catch the fish. *Cuando el pez huye de nuevo,* when it makes its run, the boys will comprehend necessity. The fish is too far out. Without a proper reel, it will take all day, hours and hours, to pull it in."

"And the sharks will claim it before then," Scott said.

"This could be true," the guide replied.

He seized this opportunity to hand Scott an envelope on which were written the words *"To Zelda and F. Scott Fitzgerald,"* and for a second Scott imagined the note might be from Ernest, who'd learned somehow (Max might have told him, after all) that Scott was in the country. Scott tore it open, but when he didn't recognize the handwriting, he glanced down at the signature. In the note Matéo Cardoña inquired after Zelda and expressed his hopes that the Fitzgeralds were enjoying the expertise of one of

Havana's finest guides. He closed with an invitation to join him for drinks and dinner at La Floridita tomorrow, the restaurant for which Scott, Matéo, and the girl had started only last night. "Arrive by eight," Matéo instructed. "I will meet you there and report on what I will have learned for you."

"What does it say?" Zelda asked, sidling up next to Scott and the guide, resting her forearms on the rail, which suddenly bowed forward, not just a few inches as if testing the groove in the newel but rather a full foot or more, bending like the string of an archer's bow, even as Zelda's trained instincts as a ballerina took over. It was as though she'd thrown herself too far forward during a performance, catching herself before anyone could detect the wobble, already recovering by the time Scott caught her dress at the waistband and wrapped his hand around her waist and brought her to him until they were posed in a travesty of the ballet's "*poisson* position," or "fish dive," the woman with head tucked, dipping beneath the horizontal plane of the man's hold. The guide hadn't been so lucky. With no one to catch him, he pushed at the rail in an effort to right himself, but when the beam failed, popping free of the newel on one end and crashing to the deck, he could only fall to his knees, throw his legs into a baseball slide, and let his shins eat splinters as Zelda burst into laughter.

"Why are you laughing?" Scott asked. "You might have been seriously hurt."

The guide, from his knees, was spewing a torrent of Spanish profanity.

"I tell my *amigo* how many times, it is necessary to fix the rail," he said, rising to his feet, gaping at the strangely laughing woman.

"You two are awful bores," she said. To the guide she added, "If only you could have seen your face as you lost balance."

"You wouldn't be laughing if you'd plunged into the water," Scott said.

"Maybe, maybe not," she said. "But comedy is all about what hasn't happened to you. And it's funnier when it could have been you, but it's somebody else instead."

They could hear the café owner's sandals on the staircase. He had sprinted across the beach as soon as he heard the crashing beam, relieved now to find that everyone was all right, unwilling to surmise how many times he'd asked the village carpenter to look at that post. Zelda wandered to a darkened corner of the café. "Does this work?" she called to the owner, drawing every-one's attention to a camera on a shelf loaded with plates and pitchers, its stand propped against the wall beneath the shelf.

It did in fact work, though the owner wasn't sure there was any film in it just now.

"Then you must find some film," Zelda said. "We'll pay, of course. We want a picture with your friend, our guide for the day, who has been so lovely and patient with us."

The guide might have been angered by Zelda's fit of laughter, but her talent for finessing people prevailed. Once he realized she was asking to have her picture taken with him, he took on the role of intercessor, negotiating with the owner as to where they might find film and how much it would cost, the owner now hastening away in search of the film. In his absence, the boys from the beach climbed halfway up the stairs, complaining that the café owner had cut their lines and allowed their fish to get away. It was clear they felt that something was owed them for their loss, and they appealed to Scott, asking him if he spoke Spanish, until Famosa García came to the top of the staircase, rec-ommending that they renew their labors. *"Debe pescar otro pez,"* he shouted, waving them away. Another fish, that was the answer. *"Eso es todo lo que se puedes hacer ahora."*

The café owner returned with a pad of film, and Zelda told him exactly where to set up the camera. Minutes later she was traipsing across the sandy lot toward the black Plymouth sedan, the photograph wedged between the pages of a book, the negative in her hand.

The unhappy boys loitered near the car, again drawing near to Scott to see if he would compensate them for their loss, again chased off by Señor Famosa García, less kindly the second time around.

"They are unfortunate today," the guide said with a sigh, "and wish to blame somebody."

"You are a handsome man," Zelda told the guide, entranced by the photograph, talking to his image rather than the man himself. "And you liked having your picture taken with us."

In the backseat she was distracted, her mirth quieted by the shock of studying herself, the crooked smile, her face gaunter than she remembered it. She recognized the roundness in her cheeks, flushed and healthy from the day's activities, but she couldn't quite place the eyes, so small, stealthy, and averted. She was never sure how she would photograph, her responses to her image ranging from alienation to full-on disgust to the despairing conviction "That's not me." Even in the prime of youth, when the camera had liked her as much as anyone she knew, friends used to remark that she never took the same picture twice.

It was true, you could run through photo albums, through the pictures in magazines, and there was Zelda in shots taken within minutes of one another, often by the very same photographer, yet she appeared as two entirely different women. More peculiar than how it portrayed her eyes, though, were two facts about the picture in her hand: first, it showed Scott and her together, after all these years still resembling a couple; and, second, it depicted the guide's face as oddly familiar, the graying black mustache and strong chin underneath a straw hat wrapped in a black band.

It took her a minute, but then she understood. "You remind me of an old friend of ours," she said to the guide as they rode into town, waving the photograph in front of Scott's nose, asking if he too could discern the resemblance.

6

"SCOTT, SCOTT, YOU'RE NOT AWAKE, ARE YOU?"

He didn't answer, but she continued whispering to him, rehearsing a conversation they would need to have sooner rather than later. The days passed so quickly on their holidays. It was Monday already, the weekend having come and gone. She couldn't let this trip lapse—he still hadn't said how long they were to stay in Cuba—without addressing the question of whether or not they planned to forge a future together.

"Once I thought, if I went away, I could create myself again—for you, Scott, it was all for you. I could remake myself, never without cost, never without doubts, and I thought, how long will he wait until I am new?" He didn't stir, but she was restive, wishing to be out on the streets of the Old City, so she swung open the window, inclining into the low balcony wall, the chill of its stone entering her thighs as she let the street noises climb the evening air. Breathing deeply, she dipped into a plié, up and down several times, and then, as if her yearning were at one with the movement, rose on the balls of her feet, pressing her toes into the ground as though en pointe, imitating old habits, wishing she could feel the platform of her Capezio pointe shoes as she leaned out over the balcony, testing her balance, thinking to herself, It would be so easy to fall.

Beneath her, the Calle Obispo was lively with music, chatter, traffic whistles, and impatient horns, with cries of vendors and the squeal and grind of trolleys—the evening's bustle preparing to give way to the sordidness of night. She could hear someone playing a variation on ragtime, the spangled shimmer of ivory. She withdrew from the window. At the desk, Scott's sport jacket was folded over the chair, his Florsheim shoes tucked beneath it. He was still so fastidious, she liked that about him. Reaching inside his jacket, she found the journal where she expected to find it, knowing she shouldn't pull it from the coat or snoop in its pages.

Still she ran her thumb along its spine, resisting temptation, satisfied merely to be touching an object that Scott held daily in his hands, remembering his habit of jotting down ideas day by day, keeping a ledger of characters, dialogue, paragraphs or scenes he'd written, sketches for new plots. A spike of jealousy pierced her, not resentment of the secret contents of the journal per se, but of his arrogant belief in his right to so much secrecy. "I have to trust him," she chanted under her breath. "If he's going to come back to me, I have to trust him." But she couldn't bring herself to return the journal to his jacket. She remembered a technique of divination taught to her by a psychic she had visited in Asheville. First, you stood a book of sacred import, say, the Bible or the Koran, upright on its spine on a desk or flat surface. It was hard getting the soft leather binding of the Moleskine to stand upright, it wouldn't balance on its own, so she placed a finger atop the spine. She heard the raspy hum of snoring behind her, Scott murmuring and stirring in the bed, but when she turned to check on him he rolled onto his side to stop himself from making the noise that was interrupting his sleep.

How did the technique work again? You let the book fall forward, the pages splaying on the surface of the desk, as you slid your finger beneath the folded-open book with eyes shut and then flipped it, running your hands over the surface of the page as if reading braille until your index finger stopped. That's all she would read, nothing else, no matter how awful or mysterious those few words might prove to be. Just the sentence on which her finger came to rest, enough also of the surrounding passage to make sense of it. Then she would close the journal and become his obedient wife, respecting those sacrosanct boundaries he was always so worried about. She let the journal fall onto the desktop, inserting her finger into the tented space beneath the binding to turn it right-side up, eyes still shut, gliding her hand along the provident page. When her finger paused, she worried she was on the wrong passage, so inched it downward, but then, not wanting to second-guess herself, slid it up to the original location. After a few seconds she opened her eyes. *Reconstituted.* Her finger had come to rest on that word. She read from the beginning of the sentence: *To go back to her and be reconstituted—that was what he wanted today as on so many previous days, the wanting of it like a nagging injury, a hole at the center of his being. After a few drinks he was able to make the desire subside, grateful for the dulling of memory, but always he could recall, even after the sensation itself was gone, what it felt like to want her again.*

"Where are you?" Scott asked from the bed.

Those few words from his journal could only refer to her, maybe some fictive version of her, but they were about her nevertheless. She must not let Scott see what she had been doing. Quietly she folded shut the journal, dangling it behind her over the desk, craning her neck toward him.

"I've given myself a chill," she said. "I woke up a while ago and stood too long by the window in the evening air. So I came over here to put your coat on, you don't mind, it smells like you and I like the feeling of being wrapped in you."

She lifted the jacket onto her shoulders, arms crossed over her chest as she tugged at the lapels from inside, then reached a hand beneath to stash the Moleskine in the inner pocket. The jacket really did smell like Scott as she poked her nose inside the collar, detecting the traces of Bay Rum, also the spicy scent of cinnamon, chocolate, and cigarettes, and an earthy odor she associated with the back of his head. She heard rustling and when she lifted her chin again he had tossed off the sheets, thrown his lanky white legs to the floor, pausing to catch his breath.

"Are you all right?" she asked. He did not appear to be rested from the nap, the side of his face ruddy, irritated from the pillow.

"You're probably hungry by now," he said.

"How did you guess? Am I always so hungry when we travel? I really can't remember, but it seems to me it's been a long time since I had such an appetite."

"Only when you're happy," he started to say.

"I suppose it's because I'm happy," she said, answering her own question, laughing at the happy coincidence of their words, then splashing onto the bed beside him, soon caressing the high tense muscles of his neck and running fingers through the mossy thin hair at the back of his head. Even as her fingers combed the hair, she was thinking two opposite things at once: He is a stranger, his life is full of strangers, and, I know this person better than anyone in the world.

"When I'm miserable," she said aloud, "I never want to eat at all. You remember how pinched and cadaverous I was only three or was it five years ago in New York when I had to stay at the, what was the name of that institution, oh, let's not dwell on such things. Right now all I am is happy—for the two of us, for our days in Cuba, for this time out of time."

"And, doubtless, you'll appropriate my dinner again," he said.

"Not if you're going to be so ornery about it, memorizing and then listing all my trespasses," she said. "Although I can't see how it matters, since you hardly ever finish your meals. It's my duty to eat for both of us."

"Well, maybe if I had half a ch, ch—," he started to say, breaking off in laughter that dissolved into a fit of coughing, in which she could hear the customary wheezing of the disease tunneling deeper into his lungs, the hollow barking of his badly bruised brachia.

"I don't like the sound of that cough," she said. "Are you sure you're taking care of yourself in California?"

"It's nothing," he said. "I've beaten worse. You should know better than anybody the wonder of my recuperative powers. I'll rest up and be better in no time."

"Yes, and I'll make sure you eat something more than chocolate for dinner tonight. Of course, you won't be able to keep up with me, but can you imagine how much I might eat if we ever again have a run of good luck—I might become as big as one of those Goya women."

Outside the hotel she took his arm and he walked to her left, stepping now and then off the narrow sidewalks into the street thick with pedestrians, cars, and horse-drawn carriages, sheltering her from its dirt, exhaust, manure, smears of discarded food, all the refuse from a day on Calle Obispo. The foot traffic parted only for street trolleys, their bells angrily clanking as they rattled along tracks that protruded abruptly from the street, the drivers slowing but never fully stopping to release passengers or take on new ones. In the wake of the trolleys, the automobiles would make a run of half a block, swerving around potholes only to bog down again among the people crossing indiscriminately from one narrow walk to the other. Repeatedly a bright red Packard raced ahead of them, and then slowly they reeled it in.

"Tonight is too early," she whispered, keeping herself from leaping ahead, from plunging straight into years of pent-up desire.

Wading through the crowds that funneled in either direction down the narrow street, she stepped up onto the sidewalk, then down into the street, careful not to snag her heel on the broken, crumbling curb, her wide-heeled shoes catching on an exposed iron rod, but Scott was there to prevent her stumble. Vendors tried to draw them into shops whose bright window displays featured flowers, fine dresses, shoes, and everywhere the colorful banners of the lottery, the numbers in bold display. "Americans, come here, please," the shopkeepers called, walking alongside Scott, wares in hand. Again she and Scott caught up to the red Packard and she stared down at the well-dressed passengers, immersed in pleasant conversation, unfazed by their sluggish pace.

Out of nowhere a girl with bare feet, sporting streaks of dirt on her nose and jaw and a soiled beige jumper, appeared at Zelda's side. Uttering words in Spanish that Zelda could not understand, the girl petitioned the *señora,* taking hold of her wrist with softly supplicating words. *"Bonita mujer Americana,"* she said and inserted her small, soft, clammy palm into Zelda's, directing her attention across the street, but at what it was impossible to say.

"What is she saying, Scott?" Zelda asked, smiling at the child, flattered but also rendered uneasy by her pleas. "I think she wants us to follow her. Do you suppose something's wrong?" The girl tugged at Zelda's arm with ever-greater urgency.

"Zelda, we have to be at the Floridita in a few minutes."

This was the first she'd heard about a schedule, and it

annoyed her that Scott hadn't said anything until now. She had a right to be kept apprised of their plans.

"Well, what do you want me to do?"

"Let go of her hand."

"Give her some money, Scott. I'm sure that's all she wants."

He started to take out his billfold, peeling off a five-dollar bill, but the little girl waved her head from side to side, motioning with her free hand for Zelda to follow her, saying, *"No, no, de ésta manera no, por favor; me siguen,"* jerking almost violently at Zelda's arm now that she detected reluctance.

Angling across Calle Obispo, led by the girl, they headed down a side street and Zelda, briefly overwhelmed by the rotting-eggs stench of sewage from nearby drains, felt queasy as a woman with an infant in her arms greeted them. Even before the woman spoke, it was clear what she would say. Indicating the infant bundled against her chest, holding out an empty palm, she informed them that she was without food for her family.

"No tengo comida para el bebé," she said, repeating herself several times. *"El bebé,"* she said, extending the child in her arms, as if the wants of an emaciated child need never be translated. She scraped together enough English to say, "You come, please."

"Zelda, we have to be going," Scott said without resolve, and she looked at him with helplessness, shrugging her shoulders, tipping her head sideways to indicate the girl still clamped to her wrist. At a store doubling as grocer and pharmacy, they approached a window that opened onto the street, where a slight, round-faced Chinese man had already prepared a sack of groceries for the woman.

"You pay money, yes," the woman announced. The man behind the counter passed the sack to the woman, then looked up at Scott, naming a price in excess of what he expected.

Money matters made him irritable. He could recall years when he'd thought nothing of throwing ten-dollar bills at waifs, friends, strangers met in a bar, the doormen at the Waldorf or the Algonquin, Zelda all but indifferent to how they squandered money as long as enough of it was spent on her. It was her simple belief that he would always provide more. Even now she couldn't understand that the sum he was giving away, if doubled just twice, might make the difference between seven days in Cuba and five.

"Zelda," he said, forking over the money to the clerk, hearing the sharp treble of the Western United States creep into his rebuke, as the woman with the infant in her arms and her beggar child at her side waved goodbye, retreating down a narrow lane on which the yellow, pink, and green buildings so closely fronted the sidewalks that the awnings and white iron balconies above seemed to form an arbor here in the middle of the city.

"We can't afford," he said carefully, "to pay for the upkeep of every waif we encounter."

Back on Calle Obispo he checked his watch, wondering how Cubans interpreted late arrivals, whether they took them for granted much as the Spaniards did. La Floridita came into view, the building framed in gold frieze and folding around the corner of Obispo and Bernaza, its shuttered doors thrown open so that the street and restaurant were continuous, some of the patrons standing above friends seated at dark wood tables whose bowing legs crawled crablike onto the sidewalks, the actual entry to the club seeming a mere formality. Scott led them under an awning, where a host greeted them, inquiring if they were here for drinks or dinner. "We're meeting Mr. Matéo Cardoña," Scott said, and the host waved him through, saying, "Of course." Beyond a refrigerated seafood display case emanating cold air and the ocean-heavy scent of mackerel, shrimp, stone crabs, and lobster, he guided Zelda to an open spot along the bar, where a bartender measured rum and maraschino liqueur in arcing splashes into a silver-plated shaker, adding shaved ice, then tossing the concoction, before pouring the drink into long-necked martini glasses.

"Two of those," Scott said in clumsy Spanish.

"How did you know about this place?" she asked. It was reminiscent of cafés they used to visit along the Riviera before it was overrun by Americans.

"Señor Cardoña is meeting us here," he said.

Scott didn't mention that he'd also heard Ernest speak of La Floridita last year in California, nor that Max had reminded him by cable that, whether or not he looked Ernest up, he ought to try the daiquiris there. Nothing complicated about Max's motives, and though Scott wasn't altogether against a rapprochement with his old friend, he knew the fates were set against it. It was never just the two of them in a room anymore—all the history of unwanted advice tossed back and forth, the omnivorous ego of Ernest to be grappled with, and of course the dreadful combination of Scott's failures and Ernest's constant climb.

The bartender slid the daiquiris along the bar, and Scott peeled off a few bills from his roll of pesos. Drinks were cheap, at least someone in this country wasn't gouging him. He looked around the bar. Matéo was nowhere in sight, which meant they weren't late, which meant Scott could relax, enjoy his drink, and feel the knot inside his stomach release.

So far it had been one of those days squandered on trivialities: a fruitless follow-up to yesterday's visit with the detective succeeded by an errand to the bank, a dispute over the sum in his account, then the hassle of wiring payment to a lawyer in New York City for paperwork he was executing on behalf of an American investor (the lawyer kept billing him for additional petty costs). His reporter friend from the *Havana Post* was to arrive shortly after the siesta hours, no specified time, but it was growing late. Annoyed by the fact that he still hadn't received a reply on his query to the chief of police, Matéo kept busy in the meantime. Displacing papers on his desk, he moved items from one stack to another while drafting a list of potential investors in a new casino near the Hotel Nacional, a list filled with local citizens but also Europeans and Americans who were regular or part-time residents of Havana. Appetite began to kick in and he decided the reporter wasn't coming. He snatched his sport coat from a rack by the door, preparing to set out for La Floridita early, when he heard the buzzer. Pulling on his white linen jacket, he met the reporter outside, remarking, "Almost left without you," before leading him along San Pedro, the noisome harbor to their right, ships running in and out at this time of day, belching smoke, releasing the flatulence of burnt oil and gas from their engines, horns blaring so that the skiffs and smaller boats would steer clear.

"Did you know the wife went crazy a decade ago?" the reporter asked.

"Mrs. Zelda Fitzgerald, are you sure?" Matéo asked. Scott hadn't mentioned anything about mental illness, but of course one wouldn't talk about such matters, not even with close friends, never mind new acquaintances. "In what way?"

"Not many details, I got it off the wire from a colleague at the *New York Evening Post*," the reporter said, preening for Matéo, trying to come off as more important than he was.

"But you are too canny to have learned nothing."

"My colleague tells me Scott has disappeared into Hollywood, never publishes anything of note, while she spends most of her time in asylums."

"None of which you would mention, I hope," Matéo said.

"No, my angle is that they were the most glamorous couple

of New York in the twenties, also in Paris for a while, he a front-page writer for the *Saturday Evening Post,* his wife the celebrated flapper. I'd like to find out what they're doing in Cuba, if he's researching a script for Hollywood, that kind of thing."

If the story came out and it brought the Fitzgeralds unwanted attention, they might flee the country before Matéo had secured Scott's trust, and he wanted to make sure that didn't happen. So as he entered the café at Hotel Santa Isabel, Matéo reminded the reporter that he was to be his guest.

"What is of passing interest in the Old City this week?" he asked the reporter after a first drink. He didn't quite trust the reporter—after all, gossip was just that, something whispered, not worth saying aloud. He rather hated the society pages of newspapers, having been featured there himself one too many times, his name popping up in association with various women found on his arm, sometimes winning him a note of reproof from his otherwise noncommunicative mother in Santiago.

"It is a service, like any other," said the reporter, who like many a soft journalist before him still harbored serious ambitions. He had started working for the *Post*'s *"Activities in the Social World"* page three years ago on the rationale that it might open doors. It was hard for him to accept the fact that his secondary status in life appeared to be a permanent track. Keeping company with Matéo was one of his tricks for maintaining a high opinion of himself.

"You offer the public a view from the ground, without filter, the rumors of the street," Matéo said, indulging his old associate. "What is the latest covert political news?"

"So you recall that I was among the first to track Falangist activities in our country?"

The two men ordered a second round of mojitos as the waiter brought a plate of prawns.

"Months ago when it became clear Franco must win, did I not say that Antonio Avendaño and Alfonso Serrano Vilariño would begin to feel confident in their cause?" The men he mentioned were closely monitored proponents of Franco's Falangist alliance, who sought a Fascistic solution to Havana's notoriously unstable politics.

"And you were not wrong," Matéo said, his voice hushed. His friend the gossip columnist was far too brash and boastful to make a good journalist.

"I did much research, you know," the reporter said, heaving the ignominy of neglect into his chest. "*Collier's* was to run all that I found as a feature article, but instead turned the information over to the FBI of the Americans."

"A tough break," Matéo conceded. "But your information tightened international security, and these men you talk of, what do they matter now?"

The reporter still believed the article in question would have made his name, and the memory of it stirred bitterness in him. Matéo had served as a source for the story. Since the Cardoñas were among those old families that put their faith in the Church as a beacon for national life, he fed his associate tidbits about where one might find Fascist sympathizers in Havana, among, for example, the staunchest of Fulgencio Batista's supporters, all on the tacit condition that the reporter would point the finger away from the Cardoñas—away from, for instance, his beloved brother, Hector, celebrated in some circles, maligned in others, for spending the past two years in the mountains north and west of Barcelona among the Falangists as they advanced on that great city. It wasn't just family Matéo protected, though. He did business with proto-Fascists, several of whom he gladly named for the reporter, others whose identities he labored to conceal, even though the ones he kept secret leaned just as eagerly toward Fascism as the others—all of them encouraging Batista to take his cues from Franco and to protect Cuba's Hispanic heritage, and bask in the Church's guiding light, and curtail American influences. To this day Matéo was divided in his opinion about whether Cuba's interests and those of the United States coincided, and for that reason could not entirely endorse his associate's rabidly anti-Fascist views. Officially Cuba would side with the Americans in the war to come, this was only proper, but still he remained ambivalent about how much advance work Cubans ought to do for their neighbors to the north.

"In this very hotel," the reporter said, "there are Germans who should not be here."

"Let the authorities follow the leads, you did what you could," Matéo said, checking his watch, pulling his seat back from the table. "Please, the bill is paid, finish your meal, though I must be off. And on that other matter we discussed, you will give me a few days."

"Sure, why not," the reporter said magnanimously. "Let us give Mr. and Mrs. Fitzgerald their privacy for now, let them enjoy our great city. It is hardly breaking news, but you will help me get the interview with them, and will not let them slip away?"

"Not a chance," Matéo said.

Zelda poked him in the ribs, her head listing to the side, until he too turned to peer down the bar where a row of women dressed in garish clothing leaned against it at the far end.

"It's nothing we haven't seen before," he said, keeping his eyes below the gaze of the prostitutes to avoid misunderstandings.

"That's not what I mean," she said. "Look at the one third from the end."

He lifted his eyes to the mirror at the back of the bar, and when he saw that the woman in question was waving at them, he immediately said, "Zelda, please don't overreact."

"What was her name?"

"It doesn't matter."

"He presented her as his girl, didn't he?"

"I can't remember. What difference does it make?"

"You really think it makes no difference?" she asked. "You take me out on the town with such a woman, and it's not supposed to bother me? What did you think would happen?"

"She had nothing to do with what happened."

"What about the knife, I forgot all about the knife until now, what about the knife she pulled on me?"

Scott reached into his coat, trying to remember something he'd written in his journal Saturday night after they returned to the hotel, but the Moleskine wasn't in the pocket above his heart where he kept it. He felt down along the side of the jacket. Nothing there either. Panic swept over him as Zelda clamored for attention and he reached his hands to his chest, patting himself down, two hands at once, discovering a square bulge in the other breast pocket, the wrong one, but at least the journal wasn't lost. As he reached for it, however, he could no longer remember what it was he'd wanted to check.

The girl from Saturday night beckoned for them to join her.

"Now we must say hello, Scott," Zelda said.

"This is neither the time nor place for renewing acquaintances of that sort, Mrs. Fitzgerald," a man said, intercepting them.

It was, of course, Matéo Cardoña, who uttered his command while firmly gripping Scott's shoulder, then bowed forward to graze Zelda's cheek with a kiss.

"We were only going to say hello," Zelda protested. "She was good enough to be on your arm last night."

"Our table seems to be ready," Matéo said, offering no further explanation, refusing even to glance at the girl as they passed within a foot of her at the bar. Another man was seated at their table and he now stood to pull out a chair for Zelda.

"May I present General Ernesto Menéndez," Matéo said, obviously expecting his friends to intuit the honor of being in the presence of such a man. He explained briefly that the general was a hero of Cuba's war for independence.

"The Spanish-American War?" asked Scott, his curiosity piqued, since he had long been a student of military history. "Which battles, if you don't mind my asking?"

"That is your name for the war for *Cuba libre*," the general said. "For you *Americanos,* a Spanish-American war includes all battles to be rid of the Spanish presence in the Americas, while collecting as much of the leftovers for yourselves as is possible."

Scott questioned the general's interpretation of history, saying he had always understood his nation's intentions in Cuba to coincide with the course of self-determination on which the country continued to this day. He mentioned Teddy Roosevelt and the Rough Riders, the Battle of San Juan Hill, the sinking of the *Maine.*

"Perhaps it is not so simple as that," the general replied amicably. Still, he had met Roosevelt; he had friends from the United States who fought among the *Brigadas Internacionales* in Spain, in defense of democracy, in the effort to prevent Spain from falling into the wrong hands.

"Only now it has fallen," Scott said.

The general was immaculately dressed, in cream-colored jacket and pants, the jacket with a double-breasted lapel, the tapered trousers drawing a fine line toward his tan loafers. His neatly cropped white hair set off a square face, his skin fair, though of a pearl rather than pinkish hue. An old friend of the Cardoña family, he was on display, maybe only so that Matéo might impress upon his guests that he was not a misfit among his own people.

"My friend, however, is a diplomat always," the general said to Scott, who hadn't been paying close attention. "I am no *compañero* of the Communists, but they rally to our cause, it seems to me."

Zelda had missed a piece of the conversation and asked Scott whether it was important. Was the general giving his views on the war in Spain?

"What war? It is over. What hope to defend democracy if the great democracies will not defend her? In your opinion," the old general said, again facing Scott, trying to mask his disgust, "should not the United States intervene? Was this not a war for them?"

It was, Scott assured him. Unfortunately, not all saw it that way.

"Unfortunately."

Scott was tempted to mention his friend Ernest Hemingway and his work on the film *The Spanish Earth,* a piece of propaganda for the Republicans, also the screening of the film at a fundraiser Scott had attended only last year in California. He might have named others among his circle who had taken up arms or pens in defense of Spain. He was tempted to expound on his own hatred of the Fascists, but thoughts of war in Europe made him recall his time as an enlisted man during World War I, when he had failed to cross the Atlantic; and under the sway of neglectful history, he suffered once more pangs of irrelevance.

Zelda was asking Matéo about the man from last night, and Scott could hear him saying, "Most likely he will recover, so please do not concern yourself, Mrs. Fitzgerald."

All seated at the table had spent time along the Côte d'Azur in France, enchanted by the white splendor of its beaches and the translucent Mediterranean waters. Charting their travels as a couple, Zelda spoke cheerfully of Antibes, of the villa at St. Raphaël, of trips to Monte Carlo—all of this, she asked them to remember, before anyone had discovered summers along the coast. She took long swims in the sea and danced at the beachside bistros, she relished the private salons in the casino at Monte Carlo, asking Scott to corroborate her memory on this point or that. It was as though she now recited pages from her 1924 affair while omitting mention of the French flyboy with whom she'd fallen in love, recalling the year in which she betrayed her husband as a time of complete unity between them—and yet she meant every word of it. Scott could see no reason to steal that year back from her when there were so many since with which her imagination could do so little.

At one point the general took Scott aside to say that Matéo had mentioned his interest in investing in one of Havana's new hotels or casinos.

"Your friend must have misunderstood the state of my fortunes," Scott said with a laugh.

"You're very thoughtful about your finances," the general said. "This is exactly what I myself look for in an investor."

So the general and Matéo were in business together. It annoyed Scott to have been dragged to this bar under false pretenses.

"This is why I recommend, my friend, that we present some options to you," the general said.

Scott had respect for the man's elegance, for the nonchalance of his sales pitch. It was beneath his dignity to become importunate or pushy. The matters of which he spoke were affairs among gentlemen.

Assured of the general's good will, and reaffirmed in his confidence in Matéo by the company he kept, Scott began regaling the two men with stories, told with deadpan panache, about the exploits of Zelda and Scott as a foolhardy young couple. He told them about being photographed running through a fountain outside the Plaza Hotel.

"What was the point of your actions?" the general asked.

"But that's just it," Zelda jumped in. "There wasn't any. Why not just be glad that you were beautiful and oh so young and able to drink for several days, dance every night, even in fountains, or go for a swim in the Hudson River in your finest clothes."

Matéo seconded their careless view of life in the twenties in New York City, and also in Paris, which he had visited only once, and though the general was a man inclined to order, he was a drinker who believed in catharsis, as he put it, as long as it was not a perpetual state of existence.

Testing the old man's tolerance, Scott told him about the time he had passed out behind the wheel of an automobile on their way home from a soiree in the French Alps, Zelda in the passenger seat, the car stalled at the edge of a precipice, the two of them sleeping off the glimmering daze of several consecutive nights of revelry, unaware that for hours on end they were no more than two feet from rolling into a gorge.

"In the night I got up to relieve myself," Scott said, "and I found a bush of some sort, most likely some thistle running along the precipice, and somehow I returned to the car without stumbling over the edge, apparently without ever noticing where I was."

"Like a man who sleepwalks in a minefield," the general said.

"It was not until morning," Zelda remarked, "when I awoke and opened my door to find that if I took one small step at a time, *pas de bourrée* as they say in ballet, I might patter tiptoed back up the ledge, alongside the car, walking uphill—"

"*Couru, couru,*" the general said, showing himself to be an aficionado of her forsaken art.

"But if I took merely two graceless forward steps, like any crude pedestrian, I would have plummeted to my death. Only then did we back that beaten-up jalopy off the precipice."

"That's magnificent," Matéo said.

"It was a fine sports car," Scott said, "a coupe of some sort. Zelda has no memory for such things."

"I thought we were just telling tall tales," she said. "What do the details matter?"

"And they are mostly true, yes?" Matéo interjected.

"Fair enough," Scott said. "I have always enjoyed my wife's flair for adding color to our history." They both knew he might speak of the time she grabbed the wheel and attempted to steer them over the edge of a cliff, but he wouldn't say such things, not unless prompted by her jealous, impassioned denunciations of him, not until years of pain and alcohol and remorse were again all at once coursing through his system.

"In the real story," he said, "but honestly I can't remember, didn't the French police come and wake us up and warn us how close we were to the cliff?"

"It's more exciting the way I tell it," she said, turning again to their hosts. "Isn't it, gentlemen?"

"For all my action in the field, I have been so close to death few times in my life," the general said. "Your adventures, Scott and Zelda Fitzgerald, are battles in their own right."

The waiter brought another round of daiquiris and Scott took a swig of his drink. He no longer felt defeated by the misadventures of this past year, or by the follies of his youth, but somehow better for them. He asked if his Cuban hosts wanted to know what making movies was like, what it was really like, and the two men responded, "Hear, hear," and he could tell they found Hollywood far more interesting than the life of an ordinary author, even one who had formerly dominated the pages of the *Saturday Evening*

Post. He excused himself to use the bathroom and as he passed the bar, lips set in a neutral if friendly smile, he stared down the row of prostitutes and observed with some relief that Yonaidys was no longer among them.

"Do you know big-name stars?" Matéo asked as he returned to the table.

"So many," Zelda said, bragging for him.

"Not so many," he said, "but more than a few."

"Oh, do tell them about Joan Crawford," she said, pleased that they were taking pleasure in each other's company, in shared history, in stories of his life and hers volleyed back and forth. "Tell them about her marvelous weakness. Someday my husband must write an exposé, he is so satiric and gentle and yet full of terrifying insights about the superlative egos of the glamorous. You would read such a book, wouldn't you, Mr. Cardoña?"

"If written by Mr. Fitzgerald, why, of course."

"Will you tell us the story, Scott?" Zelda said, trying to get a read on him, begging ever so sweetly. He was flattered by her flirtations, no matter how transparent.

"I begin with the sad part," Scott said. "It is about a wonderful film I wrote for Joan Crawford that has been put on hold, as so many great projects in Hollywood are. It was perhaps a little too spicy for the censors, since it featured a story of adultery in which the sinners don't end up groveling for mercy from the gods. Of course, everybody knew the risk going in, it would have been groundbreaking, the celluloid *Madame Bovary,* an honest, hard-hitting look at passion and betrayal and their consequences without easy moralizing. Just people as they really are, suffering for their mistakes, not all that regretful about them. No one was more eager for the story than Joan herself."

"Well, after all," Zelda said, "you might have been writing her biography. First, that horrible, abusive marriage the papers paid so much attention to, then the affair with Clark Gable, so steamy and notorious the studios had to put a stop to it."

"When she heard I was to write the script," Scott said, "she approached me at a party and said, 'Write hard, Mr. Fitzgerald, write hard.' I told her writing is always hard, but I would exert all my talent and time and energy to produce a script she could be proud of. She was convinced, of course, that the very idea of writing for her ought to be enough to make me write well."

"I should think so," said the general.

"And why do you think this?" Scott asked. "Because she is such a special talent?"

"Well, a great beauty certainly," the general said. "Do not all Americans revere their Joan Crawford? I have it on authority from my nephew who fights for liberty in Spain that a band of *yanquis* quarrel many weeks for the right to name their battalion after Joan Crawford, the marvelous actress whom they all revere, but it was not allowed. She is a very good actress also, I think, no?"

Zelda began to laugh, anticipating the punch line of a story she knew in all its versions, relishing any anecdote about the vapid personalities of Hollywood.

"Well, no, not exactly," Scott said. "I'll speak in candor if all present swear a pact not to pass my story on. It's not the best of strategies for obtaining work in Hollywood to run down the stars you write for. So do I have your word, gentlemen, lady?"

"Of course," Matéo's friend said.

"Swear," Scott said.

"I swear, I swear," Zelda chimed.

But Matéo hesitated. "I am insulted that you ask me such a thing." Alluding to the events of the weekend, he added, "I am a model of discretion. Is this not clear by now?"

"Never in question," Scott said, reaching for the Cuban's forearm, feeling in his element, master of the situation. "It was a mere formality, a pact to illustrate my point. I don't share these stories with just anyone."

Matéo acknowledged the gesture, extending his hand over Scott's, clasping the knuckles, then releasing them to say, "Now you must continue. You were about to tell us that Joan Crawford, named by *LIFE* magazine as queen of the movies, is less than talented."

"Well, as your friend and mine reminds us," Scott said, pausing, nodding respectfully at the general, "she is beautiful, but as for talent—"

"Oh, never mind about her beauty," Zelda interrupted. "I'm not entirely sure why bug eyes have become all the rage."

"Because of Joan Crawford," the general said with sincere detachment.

In the late twenties while Joan Crawford's star was on the rise and Scott still the voice of the Jazz Age, he had declared her in an interview the supreme flapper, smartly dressed, dancing at clubs until the daylight hours, eyes larger than life, larger even than the fast life she was taking in all at once; and the remark stung Zelda. It was during the years of their long falling off that he came to see how cruel it was to have said what he said. To strip Zelda of her title as the quintessential flapper, a title he bestowed on her but she had procured by rights as model for all those brave, reckless, winning heroines he wrote of. To take what was Zelda's and give it away to a Hollywood actress—that ranked high among his crimes against her.

"Well, fair enough," Scott said, raising his glass. "To Joan Crawford, the champion of the stunned, wondrous, eye-popping gaze. Let me tell you something, though. She is interpersonally charming, charismatic, and some of that quality is what translates onto the screen, but I find her beauty forced." He did not look at his wife, but he was certain she delighted in what he was saying.

"Never mind, though, because we were talking about talent. So when I realized Joan was to star in the film I was writing, I made a study of her past performances, watching her in almost everything, asking the studio to screen them for me day after day, films such as *Possessed, Grand Hotel, Chained, Forsaking All Others*."

"Fine work if you can get it," the general said. "I would not be sorry to be paid to watch Joan Crawford movies."

"Writing for the movies is hard work," Scott replied. "It's good to know whether an actress can carry off the lines you write for her. So I studied Joan's films and soon realized that she has one glaring weakness. She can't change emotion mid-scene. In every movie, every scene, she's all one thing, then she's altogether something else. No in-between. No gradations. Ask her to change emotion over the course of a scene, ask her to shift gears, and she freezes, strains, puts a hand up to her face like a mime and runs it down from forehead to chin so as to wipe away the old expression and put on a new one."

"Oh, she struggles so sincerely as she moves from sadness to mirth to wrath," Zelda joined in, "that it's impossible not to overhear her thinking, 'Now I'm supposed to be blasé' and 'Now I'm supposed to be stunned by terror.'"

"Or she turns her face from the camera, on the supposition that the present emotion is too much for her," Scott said, smirking as the picture became clearer in his mind, "and she looks up and there's the new expression, she found it somewhere down by her shoes."

"Surely you exaggerate," Matéo said.

"Possibly," Scott replied. "But go back and watch her films sometime and you'll start to see what I mean. Of course, directors and cameramen have all kinds of tricks to distract you, moving another actor into the foreground, panning the camera away for a few seconds, but if Joan has to carry the scene on her own, and there are two emotions to be enacted in relatively short order, well, all I'm saying is, in that scenario, I'll take the mime."

"So what good does it do for a writer to know such things about an actress?" the general asked. "I would think you would find it paralyzing. What am I to do with such limits?"

"That's quite perceptive of you, General," Scott said. "But in reality a writer can help out a director quite a bit if he understands the actor's strengths and limits. Use minor characters to push her through transitions. Make sure much of the emotion occurs—as Aristotle recommended one should always do with violence—off-stage. The strength of film as a medium is sometimes also its weakness. We want to read everything on the character's face, but just as in real life, there are so many ways to see a face and not see what is happening there."

7

FROM THE PORT BEYOND MORRO CASTLE, WHERE THE FERRY DOCKED shortly after dawn, Zelda and Scott traveled by car through the countryside up along the northern face of the island into the province named for the seaside city of Matanzas. For anyone else in her condition, the adversity of the last two days might have proven too much, but that was the thing about Zelda. All who met her at her best spoke of this quality—the quickness of mind, almost too quick, her way of racing ahead to the next adventure until you could feel it pressing down on you like an already existing event, as though the future were written in advance, needing only to be deciphered. Always this eagerness to conquer life, this resilience with which she met adversity: she was inexhaustible, buoyant, expectant.

The morning so far had passed in a blur. First, the knock at the door in the middle of the night, jolting her from sleep as she cried out, "Scott, Scott," fearing he'd gone back to his room and left her alone, except he hadn't, he was there, in pajamas and bathrobe in bed next to her, already awake in the dark. "It's nothing, Zelda," he said. "Probably the bellboy with that Coca-Cola I asked for hours ago." Of course, it wasn't the bellboy, not at that hour, and she could hear the whispering as Scott cracked the door, the heaviness of the man's voice in the hallway, heavier for the fact that he was whispering. Almost certainly it was Matéo Cardoña, his bass tones mixing English and Spanish, his use of cognates making the excitable phrases easier to understand. *"Traigo noticias del incidente."* He had news of some sort. Scott pulled the door shut behind him and she could hear footsteps in the corridor, trailing off. Now and then, over the rhythmic whisper of the ceiling fan, with her ear pressed close to the doorjamb, she detected the interplay of voices in disagreement down the hall, and after a while footsteps walking toward the room, someone turning the knob, the door cracked in a rusty breath.

"Would it not be simpler," Scott was asking, "to go to the police, explain what we saw?"

"Except it will not change anything, except we do not know what others think they saw or what they will say, for example, about how the fight started."

"Well, I appreciate all you've done for us, I do, and I'm glad for the bulletin."

"Then you will do as I advise."

"If you think there's no reason to go to the police," Scott said, "we won't."

"And I will call on you tomorrow evening," said Cardoña, his voice penetrating into the hotel room. Zelda studied her husband's profile as he closed the door, his robed chest and pensive chin silhouetted by light from the hallway.

"What did he want? I don't understand why he keeps bothering us. It isn't over, is it? It's never over, everything always catches up with us."

"Zelda, please don't talk that way," he said, pacing the room. "Of course it's over. It has nothing to do with us. Matéo just wanted to tell me what he's learned about the investigation into the events from the other night."

"You're handling me," she said. "You were always the only person who could calm me. Once I told you that, but you were insulted."

He halted, as if hunting down a memory in his head. "Not insulted," he said. "Maybe, though, there are things one would rather be called by one's lover, other than 'calming,' I mean."

Scott stood with shoulder pressed against the drapes, staring into the night, retreating from the window after a while to rest on the writing desk.

"What are you thinking?" she asked, but he was distracted. Soon he was scratching notes to himself in his journal and she knew better than to interrupt him.

When at last he walked to the bed and laid the notebook on the night table, she ran her palm inside the smooth folded lapel of his robe onto the hardy cotton flannel pajamas, thinking to herself, He is always so cold. Her fingers teased his pectoral muscle through the flannel, sliding down to and encircling the nipple, wandering up over the edge of the collar onto naked skin so that she might nestle her palm against his clavicle and let her nails play dapplingly on his neck. She was not thinking about the day ahead or how much longer they might stay in Havana. Let Scott take care of their itinerary, when they awoke, what they ate and when, what they saw—he loved to be in the world and in control. She would follow his lead, except maybe when it was the two of them alone in a bedroom, where for a while she might take charge, trading parts in the dance, tantalizing him with the qualities he liked so much in a woman: daring, whimsy, forwardness. When things worked well between them, he relished the low rumble of her voice, seductive, wanting what it wanted, the way she took her pleasure on his body. "Would you like to?" she would say, unbuttoning the pajama shirt before plunging her hand down over the smooth skin of his stomach, beneath the elastic waistband of his pants.

Before them on the road the sky now brightened. Off to their left, groves of trees rose and fell and rose again, then tumbled downhill like bowling pins into the Gulf. The car rode up high over a clearing, only grass and low brush between them and the coast, the shallow skin of greenish blue along the sea's surface dissipating into thin bands of morning light. Observing trees strung with red flowers Zelda aligned them in rows of garlands, as if there were a pattern in everything she saw.

"I find it so exhilarating when you take care of things," she said, "when you know exactly what we should do next."

"I'll always look out for you, Zelda."

"Isn't it a wonderful thing," she said as if speaking to someone other than Scott, a stranger or perhaps the driver of the car, "to be a man and to know your own mind?"

Not more than three hours ago they lay in a hotel bed, her hands inside his pajamas, but he was stirred without being aroused, too tired or drunk or maybe too agitated by Señor Cardoña's interruption at their door to concentrate on what she was doing. "I'm sorry," he said, excusing himself for the fact that he wasn't ready to return to her yet. It was okay, she assured him, there was time. But she worried it was false comfort: what if the news from Cardoña was bad, what if they had to leave town? In the next instant Scott announced, "We're departing for the beach this morning." She didn't question him as he threw off the covers and changed into street clothes, pulling his jacket on, the hour still shy of four. "I'll go downstairs to see about a car." Minutes later he was bursting through the door, his energy having the inverse effect on her, making her head sink into the pillow.

"I've ordered a driver to come for us in an hour," he said. "It will take us to a ferry that leaves for the other side of the harbor at dawn."

Now she really was irritated. In an hour? Why hadn't he asked her first?

"Scott, I'm so tired, what's the sudden hurry?" she asked. "Is there something you're not telling me?"

A small V-shaped inlet revealed bungalows with burnt-sienna roofs in a Mediterranean style. They rode through sleepy towns where children kicked footballs at the side of the road, the curtains of the bungalows drawn, here and there a man in a doorway staring out into the street as if searching for an event that would tell him to start his day. Zelda asked how long the drive to the resort would take and Scott promised to have them checked into the Club Kawama by early afternoon. He instructed the driver to pull over at the next filling station so that he could use the bathroom. As they drew up to the pump, Scott snatched a bag at his feet, and when she asked what was in it, he said it was nothing to worry about, just something he'd meant to throw away back at the Ambos Mundos. She could tell he was lying. Maybe he planned to sneak a drink while in the toilet, but that didn't make sense of the bag, which was too light and in the wrong shape to contain a bottle. It hung from his arm, bulging at the bottom like the mouth of a bell, a scrap of ivory fabric peeking out from the top. When he returned to the car, he no longer carried the bag.

"Part of me resents myself for being happy when you take care of things, it's so very Southern of me," she said as they resumed the drive. "But I'm not going to think that way on this vacation, no zealous modern women in this car. I've decided to let myself be appreciative that my own Deo is watching over me again, protecting me should anything go wrong."

She sat close to him in the backseat, inside his personal space, in the way of a woman wishing to send out the signal that she is receptive, her scent, energy, and entire being part of the signal.

"I still consider you my best friend," he said.

"I always let you help me."

They were in different places, caught up in different rhythms of thought.

She resolved not to be saddened by the dashed dreams of recent years. Several times she had declared, "Scott, I can feel it, I'm almost well. The doctors say I'm making progress and I'm stronger than I've been in years, mentally, physically, emotionally, as happy as I've been since the early days of our marriage." But the business of getting him to take a chance on her, a full-time chance, of persuading him to let her move to California so the two of them might start over, well, that was an altogether daunting proposition. It required a perfect trip, several days to drain the stored-up acrimony, bile, and censure, days in which they might learn how to be good for each other again. Everything fell on her shoulders because she was the one who, while persuading him to let her back into his life, was at the same time begging for her freedom. She had to be careful not to slip up, so damned careful.

He placed his hand on the back of her head as he sometimes did when she was sleeping. She could remember the gesture from years past, waking to the soft pressure of his hand, then closing her eyes again.

"You've held up brilliantly," he said. He was thanking her, in code, for not making a fuss about their hasty departure from the hotel. While she dressed he had packed her bags and composed a note for Matéo Cardoña. "I'll just leave my address at MGM, don't you think?" he called out while she was in the bathroom, and she suggested the address at Scribner's would serve just as well. "It all depends," she said. "I can't decide whether we're trying to give him the slip or whether you really want to see him again." She walked to the threshold of the bathroom to see if her words stirred anything, but Scott was all business, head tucked low, pen to the page, shouting over his shoulder, not seeing how near she stood, "Five minutes." On their way out of the hotel room, at the last minute, she discovered his journal on the night table by the bed. He might have left it, the entire vacation a casualty to that one mistake. She slipped it into her own bag, wanting credit for its recovery, vowing to return it only once he realized it was missing.

"Scott, I need you to be honest," she said, sliding across the leather seat to separate from him. "I know you love me and you're loyal to a fault, more loyal than anyone has ever been."

He was looking over the driver's shoulder ahead of them at the road, trying to judge the treachery of the terrain. *"Despacio,"* he muttered once or twice, loud enough that the driver might have heard but casually enough that it was just as likely he hadn't.

"Once not many years ago," she said, starting again, "we traded bitter words about divorce, oh, when was that, it seems ages since, but I don't feel that way anymore."

"I know you don't."

"I can only recall all that barbaric hate and resentment in the abstract."

"We can let it go," he said. "It takes discipline, not to let ourselves return there."

"Still, maybe you've decided you're better off without me. It's okay if in the end that's what you decide, Scott, but you should just say it—I'll grieve the loss of you, but I'll pull through somehow, you know I will, look at everything I've survived."

"Zelda," he said, "please don't talk that way. I'll never aban-don you."

"I know that, Scott," she said. "But please listen to me, you're missing my point. If you can't live with me again, in my presence, in the same house, if too much has happened and we're too much for each other, you need to tell me so I can begin to make plans for how to live my life after the Highland without you."

He was silent as she stared over his shoulder at the splashes of water and sky.

"Let's not be sad, Scott," she said, pressing her cheek to his, brushing her lips on the corner of his mouth, and then he turned and cupped her chin in his fingers, crushing her mouth in a kiss as though determined to keep her.

"I'm still your future, Zelda," he said. "You're still mine."

Those were the words she'd come all this way to hear, but having won them so easily she couldn't trust their meaning. She was tired of the conditions placed on his promises: if she contin-ued on the course she was on, if only some director bought his next script so that he could buy time for the new novel, if her doctors said this or her doctors said that, then maybe, and only then, could they resume planning a life together. She could recall promises after a trip to South Carolina, in letter after letter, prom-ises running back to the year he was holed up in Asheville and broke his shoulder on the diving board showing off for that nurse, oh, what was her name, Scott recklessly making promises to his wife about resuming their life together while falling for one friv-olous, mentally unsound Southern belle after another, all of them mere shadows of her former self. Really, the folly of it—Scott play-ing the bachelor, acting with impunity because he was wretchedly tubercular and drunk and she so sick at the time he imagined she would never find out. Still she forgave him, and on each trip they took thereafter she imagined a future they might yet spend together, but it always ended with Scott again putting everything on hold. Chunks of each year passed, without the doctors signing her release, without Scott forcing their hand, God only knew how he could afford the payments for the Highland. It was all so extravagant, his endless worry; maybe he could never be free of the memory of what she was like when broken.

"Let's not take two rooms at the resort," she said as the car banked into a curve and rode within inches of a tall rock outcrop built into a hill to which the skeletal roots of a tree and a portion of trunk clung; and Scott sucked air asthmatically as she was thrown into him, pressing against his ribs, not wanting to straighten herself even after the car righted itself on the road.

"We really can't afford two rooms anyway," she said, "and I always feel so much better when you're in the room with me, in the bed next to mine."

"Yes, that would be fine," he said, a hint of formality in his reply, maybe also shyness.

"Only if you want to."

As a young girl she had been tomboyish, up for any adventure, undeterred by taunts or challenges, unable to tell the difference between them. In Zelda there was a daring that went beyond bravery and teetered on the edge of recklessness. She possessed more innate verve than most men of her generation, never mind women. Throughout her childhood she was known for an indefatigable tongue. She could talk for hours on end to anyone who would listen, sometimes at the age of four wandering off her family's property to find a neighboring mother to regale with thoughts about everything from the proper way to soothe an angry dog to the best among hundreds of possible names for a box turtle. Her deeds, though, soon caught up with her words. Her friends used to say to her, "Zelda, you should have been born a boy." Scott would later recall on her behalf tales told by Sara Haardt and Sara Mayfield, her companions in adolescent mayhem—a story, for instance, about Zelda racing downhill on roller skates from Montgomery's Court Square, straight down the middle of Perry Street, weaving among pedestrians, forcing the horse-drawn carriages to pull up, causing Model Ts to brake and choke and often stall, and if no one followed her example, she would bolt to the top of the hill and repeat the act until at least one of the other girls, or a timid boy watching from a distance, worked up enough courage to imitate her. She would assemble parties for expeditions to the Alabama River on the edge of town. Disrobing among the elm trees that lined the river until all she wore was the sheerest of undergarments, she would climb to the highest rock in half-naked splendor, before jumping off without so much as a glance below—even the boys looked before they leapt, but not Zelda, she cast her body out, arms and legs on the air, plummeting with such abandon that her admiring friends would conclude years later that she had been bent on self-destruction even then. All the proof they required was that image of her waiting to the last minute to tuck into a dive or a mock-fetal ball before hitting water.

She carried that lack of inhibition into her debutante days in Montgomery, dancing provocatively at galas, hastening suitors with teasing notes when they were a step slow in getting to her doorstep, doing her best to maim what was left of the stodgy mating rites of the Deep South. One night she drove herself and a friend to the outskirts of town to shine the headlights on their male classmates as they exited a local brothel.

Now, under the boundless skies of Varadero, on this strip of land jutting out into the Gulf, from which Florida could be glimpsed on a clear day by the naked eye, Zelda felt it would require little effort to change herself once more. She was cut off from as much of the past as she wished, in a foreign land, in salt winds with the palm leaves quivering above her. It was up to her to choose what to be. Instinctively she chose again, before they were even checked into the resort: that girl of eighteen from Montgomery who could have had any man she desired, but what she wanted, desperately, expansively, was a blond-haired Yankee soldier from Princeton, possessed of a chiseled but also somehow effete profile, and (when viewed from the front) a soft chin, and deep-set, gently sullen eyes.

The entire resort consisted of a central building, a few beach-side cabins, and a square, two-storied stone villa for guests. Scott arranged for transport into town for the evening, and the porter led them to their room through one of the villa's dank archways, into a sunlit courtyard of mottled cobblestone at the center of which was a fountain, water falling down over the edges of several increasingly widening concentric basins, cascading until it reached a pool in which plants danced slowly if fretfully, in tight loops, every now and then breaking free from the conventions of centripetal motion. In a first floor guest room two maids tended to linen and towels, sweeping the floor, airing out the bathroom and beds. The porter led Scott and Zelda up a staircase at the top of which a waist-high bronze-railed balustrade wrapped the entire second floor.

Their room at the front of the building was small but airy, beaming with light, its French doors thrown open to a balcony furnished with a view of the ocean obstructed only by several co-conut palms. Zelda believed in this anonymous place. Just two options on the immediate horizon: siesta or a dip in the ocean. Scott, in favor of the former, tumbled onto the bed as soon the porter shut the door. He hadn't slept more than an hour or two the previous night.

"Don't drowse off on me now," she said.

She wanted him to follow her onto the balcony and share the exhilaration of the nearby ocean, the white sands stretching for miles along the coast, the water layered and thick like colors in a terrarium, cerulean folded onto jade onto emerald, each shade a current of buried history. Scattered along the beach were umbrellas with chairs beneath them, lily pads on a pond blown apart by wind, their occupants stranded in relative isolation.

"Oh, it's not a social beach at all," she called from the balcony. "You can't make me go out there alone."

"Lie down beside me first," he said. A quick nap, then he'd be up for anything.

"But you can sleep on the beach." She strode into the room, ransacked her portmanteau in search of a bathing suit. While searching her belongings she talked at him. "Dearest Deo, have you seen my dress from the other night? We must have left it in the wardrobe at the Ambos Mundos." He started to answer, but she immediately interrupted him. "Perhaps you could telephone the concierge," she said, pressing on his knee with her hand as she headed for the bathroom. Leaving the door ajar as she peeled off her dress, she stood at such an angle that (if he wanted to) he might see her from the bed, the curved lines of her breasts, her round hips. By the time she reentered the room wearing her old one-piece maroon bathing suit with the slender white shoulder straps, his eyes were shut.

"Scott," she said, "Scott, please, don't fall asleep. I'll find your bathing suit and set it out for you, then I'll run ahead and find us a spot on the beach." She refused to take no for an answer, singing his name until he opened his eyes, his long-lashed lids quivering. She indicated the swimwear draped on the chair by the desk, also a robe, then gathered everything else into her arms: blanket, towels, two novels, bathing oil, sunglasses. All he had to do was drag his lazy self to the beach.

"No broken promises," she said. "Let's make this the trip on which we keep all our promises, starting now, starting with your promise to meet me at the beach in five minutes."

"Five minutes," he said, eyes curtained in sleep.

She pulled the door shut behind her, refusing to look back, believing in her power to conjure him. She crossed the courtyard in a straight line and followed a cobblestone walk that gave way to fresh lawns, after that to white sands, the granules grinding under heel against the soles of her sandals. It took longer than expected to procure an empty umbrella. Several of those she visited first revealed traces of people if not the people themselves: a straw hat on a chaise longue, a blue plaid shirt strewn over the back of a chair, sometimes nothing more than a stray towel discarded on the shaded sand. But she didn't want to take chances, not on someone returning from lunch once she and Scott were settled. So she wandered the beach until she found an umbrella with a single empty chair, the sand beneath furrowed from the prongs of a rake. She spread the blanket on the sand, the upper third in shade, then pulled the base of a folding wood chair onto one of the corners. No need to search for a second chair—it didn't make a difference, Scott could have the blanket or chair, whichever he preferred, she would take the other, or they might lie side by side on the blanket.

Up the beach toward the hotel a cluster of fashionable young people volleyed English and Spanish phrases as portions of their party played a game of volleyball, the women standing to the side and cheering, their joyous shouts whipped on the wind. Nearer to Zelda two bathers, a man and woman, now stood up, folding their towels and blanket, the woman's face shadowed by a large beach hat as she pulled at the base of her bathing suit, releasing the sand trapped there.

She turned to Zelda, only her lips visible beneath the brim of the hat as she nodded up the beach. "The wedding party, from this past weekend, what's left of it anyway."

"Oh, isn't that supposed to be good luck?" Zelda remarked, aware that she was inventing freely. "To share a beach with newlyweds?"

"Not if your cabin is next to theirs and they've been celebrating for three days straight," the man said sourly, without turning, his back to Zelda the entire time. She tried to place his accent: maybe Ohio or Indiana.

"It's the daughter of Colonel Silva, the owner of Club Kawama," the woman said sheepishly, hoisting her bag onto her shoulder. "She married a prominent young man from New York here at the club this past weekend. Well, enjoy your stay. We're leaving the resort this evening."

"I'm not going into the water 'til he arrives," Zelda said once the couple was gone, addressing the eager ocean.

For some reason she felt the need to have Scott's eyes on her at all times. She was a strong swimmer, stronger than Scott had ever been, even in good health, but she wanted him to watch her as she swam far out, wanted his witness if she were to go missing from the world. She could taste the fresh, briny scent of the water, inviting her. Gulls cawed nervously overhead. She began to doubt his arrival. Maybe he hadn't been awake when he made his promise. Maybe she should run back to the room.

Just then she saw a pale figure walking toward her in the sun, wearing far too much clothing for a beach, a jacket over his navy swimwear, shoes and socks on his feet, on his head a proper tweed hat. His hand perched on top of the hat, he ducked under two or three umbrellas, already wearied as he righted himself and gawked at the water and forlorn beach. She waved, but he headed off in the opposite direction, hooding his eyes with his hand to peer under someone else's umbrella, hesitantly, infirmly, seeming much older than she'd ever allowed herself to imagine he might become. He was middle-aged, not a specimen of robust middle age—there were some men who grew stronger and stronger late into life—but rather of its decadent variety. He was one of those whose bodies had begun to betray them, the tubercular poets. She thought of Keats and all the sickly young literati, even the brave ones like Byron who wanted to be revolutionaries but instead died of pneumonia while espousing some lost cause.

At last Scott spun around and caught sight of her waving at him and she could relax her arm as he dragged himself up the beach, lips parted wryly as he came into view, his face happy with recognition of her, his smile still so youthful.

"What took so long?" she asked. "I felt certain you'd abandoned me for slumber."

The smile fell from his face, however, as he hauled his body onto the blanket.

"I lost my journal," he announced. "Several weeks of dialogue, scenes, sentences, paragraphs, also character sketches, observations to be used in the new novel."

"Oh, but you haven't," she said from the chair above him, worrying that she had kept her secret too long.

"Zelda," he said sharply, "I ought to know when I've lost my own goddamned notebook. I keep it in the breast pocket of this jacket and I always put it back here when I'm done with it, but I've checked my suitcase, also the pants I wore yesterday—"

"If you'd let me finish," she said, knowing she would have to tell him now or he would spend all afternoon brooding. "What I was trying to say is I found it."

He jerked his chin over his shoulder, tilting it upward, his distant agate eyes fixed on her. She felt the sting of ancient distrust.

"You left it on the night table at the Ambos Mundos and I

only happened to notice, lucky for us, as we were leaving the hotel room."

Relief rippled across his face, mixed nevertheless with irritation.

"Why didn't you say any—"

"Scott, can't you just be glad I found your journal, that your work isn't lost, can't you say thank you and be grateful I was watching out for you, as I always am?"

He reached an apologetic hand behind him, wrapping it onto her calf, but she refused to acknowledge him.

"Well, I'm going for a swim. Will you join me?"

"Maybe later," he said. "I'm beat from the trip."

"Scott, really, you must learn to relax. You might as well have been driving the car the way you kept looking over the driver's shoulder. You can't control everything. Sometimes that's a good thing."

"Not in my experience."

"Well," she said, her tone lightening, "would you at least take off your clothes, those shoes and socks, the jacket, you do look rather ridiculous."

"You know I have a hard time keeping warm," he said sheepishly, smiling in shameful solidarity, infected by her mirth.

"What were you thinking just now? Was it witty?"

"I look like a caricaturist's notion of Paddy the Irishman at a beach, don't I? Is this the way you imagine Thurber would draw James Joyce stretching his limbs on the Riviera?"

They laughed together as his jacket came off and he untied his shoes. Scott hated the appearance of his own feet and rarely removed shoes or socks. For years he'd slept with socks on, like a soldier on alert.

"I wish I had a camera, I'd send your photo to old Jim Thurber for inspiration, maybe with a caption, 'A puritan in the tropics,'" she said. "You really should come into the water, Scott. Strip down to your bathing suit and follow me because it will be good for you."

"Not now," he said, leaving hope he might join her later. "I need that nap you promised me, now that we're newly set on keeping our promises to one another."

"Yes, and we have so far," she said with satisfaction. "We're all the way up to two. Before you fall asleep, though, I want you to watch me walk to the water and observe my lazy crawl into the tides. While I toss in the current, you in the sun, let's think each of the other the whole time. Later you can tell me whether my body still pleases you."

At the water's edge she accepted the warm lapping of the waves, her toes sinking into the claylike sand, which molded itself to her feet. She tugged on her bather's cap, tucking stray curls of hair up over her ears, pulling the plastic flaps taut over the lobes. The afternoon was brilliant along the surface of the water as she squinted, looking out over the straits, several small sailboats on the horizon, a freighter or some kind of navy ship farther out. Someone had told her that German U-boats had been discovered in these waters. She did not look behind her to check if Scott was watching but instead lifted her legs to hold her soles, one foot at a time, on top of the warm, thick water, depressing them into a tide so gentle there was almost no break. Waves ebbed into her knees, rolling on past her toward the shore.

She walked still farther out, water swelling up her thighs into the crease of her bathing suit, dolloping her groin like a patient lover's tongue. Now raising hands above her head, she threw herself into a dive, and there was the pleasure of lying supine on the salty ocean, arms folding and unfolding, a mere seal's kick to keep herself afloat, easeful, rocking in the waves' slow rhythm, then torquing her torso also like a seal to twist and roll onto her back, her mind as empty as the sky above her, striated here and there in thin bands of white.

"Oh, I want to dive off of something," she said, standing over him, dripping onto the blanket, shaking her body and sprinkling his forearms before bending for a towel.

"Zelda," he said, floundering away from her, flopping onto his side with displeasure.

"Okay, I'll be quiet. It's just I thought you would be awake by now. I swam all the way out to a boat and flirted with several sailors and kicked my tail at them as I swam away."

"That's nice," he said. "I hope they were on our side of the war."

"We're not at war, Scott."

"Not yet," he said, "but wait until Hitler takes a country we care about, such as France."

"Well, my soldiers were Americans," she said, and laid her body beside him on the blanket, her wet suit skimming his leg so that he jerked away reflexively. "At least that's what they told me. Aren't you even a little bit jealous?"

"Were they real?"

"No."

"I didn't think so. In which case, yes, I'm very jealous. I find imaginary rivals so much more intimidating, since I always endow them ahead of time with such wonderful capabilities."

"In a manner of speaking they were real," she said. "You see it was a military ship with an American flag and I swam out toward it, but it was miles away and it was going to take such a long time to get there and I had to turn back because I didn't want to leave you all alone getting sunburned on the beach. Would you have been jealous if real soldiers had flirted with me?"

"I was trying to sleep here," he said.

"I know, but do you think you could wake up and solve the problem of finding something for me to dive off?"

"What if we save that pleasure for tomorrow? We'll find a beach that has a promontory where the water is deep enough for you to throw yourself off and risk breaking your neck, as you're so fond of doing."

Now she drew the tote bag to her, looking through it for something to read, warning Scott that his legs—the only part of his body exposed to the sun—were turning red and perhaps he should sit in the chair for a while. She found her copy of Rachel Field's novel *All This, and Heaven Too,* one of last year's biggest sellers, folding it open to the page where she'd left off. Scott sat up and moved to the chair as instructed, casting his shadow over the book.

"Does that mean you disapprove?"

"About the diving?" he said. "Would it make you happier if I disapproved?"

"Oh, probably. But I meant this novel. You sat down and there was a mini-eclipse and it was hard to see the words."

She began to explain the plot of the book to him. Bedlam, she maintained, couldn't get enough of stories about people who are insane. Everyone at the Highland was in a tumult about the imminent release of *Wuthering Heights* starring Merle Oberon and Laurence Olivier as Catherine and Heathcliff. It was likely she would return to a house full of hubbub about the film, but no matter, half of the women would be up for seeing it again. As for Field's novel, it featured an insanely menacing duchess who plagues her duke until, poor man, he must confide his miseries to his children's governess. "That movie actress with whom you had an affair years ago, what was her name, Lois Moran, the once-aspiring homewrecker, she might be perfect for the part, if only they'd made a movie of this book while she was still young and attractive enough." Scott ignored the taunt, failing to defend his old lover as he might have in years past. Even Zelda couldn't feel the prick of her own words, that original betrayal no longer hurting as it once had, the newer, fresher ones (women whose names she didn't even know) stinging less still. None of his infidelities could reach her here in Cuba. Even after a history of fights, threats, and fallings out, she still felt her advantage over every rival for Scott's affection.

In the novel the duchess turns up dead, Zelda continued, and naturally the dupe of a duke is accused of the murder.

"Did he do it, did he bump her off?"

"Of course not, or at least I don't think so, but he's in the midst of committing suicide in vague, ineffectual remorse," Zelda said. "I'm sure it was the governess, and what's worse, she'll get away with it and live the rest of her life pretending to be innocent."

"I'm not sure why you read such tripe." Scott sounded genuinely offended by his wife's fondness for pulp novels about the insane.

"And why do you care so much that I do?"

He sighed. When she read a book just because everybody was reading it—they'd been over this before, did she really want him to repeat himself?—it was an insult to every writer who tried to make a name for himself by writing well.

"Pardon me, but didn't we live off of what everybody was reading for a while?"

He said nothing.

"Scott, my tastes aren't to blame for the poor reception of your tender novel about an insane heroine who just happens to have lived much of my history. Sometimes people read books to distract themselves. I too once wrote a serious novel on insanity, and believe me, I can sniff out fraudulence." Here she held the novel by Field over her head, finger between its pages as she waved it like a flag, saying, "Fraudulent, fraudulent." Maybe that was why she read such books, in order to figure out how it was possible that easy clichés about madwomen who cling unjustly to husbands they don't deserve were so popular.

"You see," he said, "that's exactly what I mean by tripe. I don't wish for you to become bothered by stupid popular notions that don't help with your recuperation."

"Always looking out for me."

Well, she could read what she wanted, he said, whenever she wanted. What had she brought for him?

For Scott she'd chosen their old friend Joseph Hergesheimer, the novel *Java Head* from 1919, still his most acclaimed. The exoticism of the prose, the splash of the Orient dousing puritanical New England, the lurid approach to miscegenation and its consequences—all of Joe's old Anglo anxieties made for good beach reading. Secretly, she chose Hergesheimer because she knew Scott had a hard time reading anyone whose star was on the rise. In Hergesheimer, her husband could enjoy the company of another literary light precipitously fallen from on high. Once the most popular writer in America—only a decade ago still outselling everybody, except possibly Sinclair Lewis—Hergesheimer, like Scott, hadn't published a novel since 1934.

From the west end of the beach a couple approached, walking along the perimeter of damp sand onto which the thin milky foam of dying waves reached with ever greater frequency, the weak tide rolling in. With the sun at their backs, most likely guests at the resort, they showed no sign of breaking stride or turning in toward the row of stone cabins, instead continuing on up the beach and passing maybe ten feet in front of Scott and Zelda. *"Tout ne tourne pas autour de toi,"* the woman was saying in perfect French, and the man, attempting to placate her, asked what she thought they should do. Zelda studied the two of them, the woman especially, her thin, spry mouth, the wilting jawline and long slant nose, her slender body sporting a cream one-piece, shoulders draped in a wrap of reds and oranges, her sorrel-brown hair knotted in a scarf. The man, whose face Zelda caught in profile, angling evenly from forehead to the knobbed tip of his nose, was darker in complexion. He was square, sturdy. He reminded her of a foot soldier among the Catalans of Spain, someone whose body testified to its capacity for bearing hardship without speaking of it. "I would like to know both of you," Zelda said under her breath, surprised by her response to them. Unless Zelda misunderstood—parts of their conversation were in French, parts in Spanish—the woman was arguing her right to accompany him to a cockfight.

"He's not disciplined enough," Scott was saying, "our old friend Joe. Still, he's really not a bad writer at all. It's a disgrace that the public has turned its back on him so absolutely. There are so many fine sentences in this book. He has a talent—sometimes used as a crutch—for measuring people by their eccentricities. I do hate it, though, that he and I are mention—"

"How would you describe the couple that just passed us?"

Scott admitted he hadn't paid them any attention.

"Well, I'm glad about our search for high places tomorrow," Zelda said. "That and the swim have made this a perfect first day of our vacation. Only now that we've found a beach does the vacation really begin, in case you're logging days. And that counted as a promise, yes?"

"Which part?"

"The promontory, the diving tomorrow."

"Sure, I promised we would look, though I don't know the geography of this peninsula."

"That's enough for me," she said. He was silent again, eyes lowered to the page but waiting (she could tell) for what else she might say.

"I just need there to be a next chapter. I'm someone who needs to look forward to things."

8

I T WAS THEIR BEST DINNER IN CUBA SO FAR. SHE HAD ENJOYED THE *PARGO frito,* a blue snapper indigenous to Cuban waters, garnished with mango and scallops and served with a creamed plantain soup, while Scott managed to swallow a few oysters and to pick unambitiously at the large crab on his plate. The town was small, not a great many dining options, but she delighted in this quiet restaurant overlooking a lagoon, several dunes and a nearby bank of trees separating them from the ocean, the surf audible whenever the winds relented and a hush fell over the otherwise chattering pines and palms.

"What are the chances? I wish you would invite them to join us for a drink when they finish their meal."

"Are you still talking about those two Europeans?"

"I didn't question your taste in friends back in Havana." He was about to challenge this assertion when she amended the statement: "At least not until I'd given them a chance." Then also added: "And I've said nothing about the Saturday trouble those friends got us into."

"What does that have to do with anything?"

"It's my turn, that's all."

At the table nearest to them sat the very couple she'd spotted earlier on the beach. As the waiter cleared plates, Scott glanced at her to assess whether her heart was truly set on this latest whim.

"It is, Scott," she said. "Let me plot this little piece of our adventure."

"We'll order another round while I think about it," he said, but she could always tell when he was going to give in. It had been a good day overall. He hadn't taken a drink until they sat down to dine. Their conversations had been even and cooperative, neither of them allowing a desperate pitch to enter their repartee. He appreciated the ocean almost as much as she, its soothing effect.

"But don't think about it too much, Scott. The worst that can happen is they say no."

"And you're sure it won't bother you, that you won't feel rejected?"

He raised his hand to catch the waiter's attention so that he might order another rum over mint leaves and sugar, a Cuban specialty neatly suited to his insatiable appetite for liquor and sweetness. The waiter offered to replenish Zelda's half-full glass of wine from the carafe in front of her, but she lifted her hand to say no.

"Also, *por favor*," Scott said as the man turned to leave, "we would like to buy the couple at the next table a bottle of wine. Your house favorite."

Zelda rested her fingertips on Scott's forearm, applying gentle pressure.

"Don't you love the smell of this place," she said. "Don't you love how modest and unassuming everything here is. It's like Cap d'Antibes all over again, right after the Murphys discovered it and invited us for the summer—nothing's gone wrong yet, no crazy people, no dead children. Poor Patrick, I wept so long for Gerald and Sara when I heard. The losses of those two lovely children are always with me and I pray for them almost every night."

Scott expressed dutiful sympathy, but he didn't like to talk about the death of children, especially poor Patrick, who had lost an eight-year battle with tuberculosis.

"Excuse me," the man from the next table interrupted, addressing Scott. "Right now for me is very, very nice feeling, this gift you bring us, and I wish somehow to say thank you."

"Oh, please." Zelda rolled forward in her chair, twisting to face the stranger. He was even more striking now that she saw him up close, with a strong equine jaw and deeply inset brown-black eyes. "You must come sit with us and tell us all about yourselves."

"It's not required," Scott said. "It's merely an invitation. You're free to keep the wine either way. But my wife would like to meet you, if you're in no hurry to be off for the night. She thinks you make a handsome couple."

"No, nothing secret, nothing magic," the Spaniard said. "I will implore my wife."

The couple, Scott and Zelda soon learned, were newlyweds on honeymoon at the resort, but after a glass or two of wine they admitted to being exiles, he a refugee by necessity, she by choice, her choice predicated on love for him. The man was in his late thirties, the wife roughly a decade younger. He had fought in the Spanish Civil War, wounded above the knee in battle, already knowing that his unit of *gudari* must soon surrender to the Italians, he among the first wave of refugees to cross into France even as his fellow Republicans fought well into the present year, refusing to lay down arms until this past month. But for him the war had ended long before that. Detained on French soil, in Camp Vernet in the Pyrenees, imprisoned for weeks in squalid conditions, he remembered a distant cousin near Lyon whom he'd met only once before while she was still a child and he a young man touring Europe, visiting relatives en route to Paris, aware even at the time of the impression he made on an altogether impressionable girl. In letters mixing Spanish and French, he invoked the memory of his long ago visit and chronicled his forsaken revolutionary aspirations, his love of his country, and the squalid conditions of the camp. Appealing to her fine sensibility and good-heartedness—she was known as a nurse and a humanitarian throughout the extended family—he asked if her parents might vouch for him and get him released into their custody in France. It was too risky to return to Basque territory, he wrote in sincere French, and she memorized his words—*"Ce n'est pas prudent pour moi de retourner dans ma patrie"*—rightly intuiting that his life was in danger.

Since hers was not a wealthy family, nor one with contacts in government, she made the only move left to make, all for a man she'd met once in her entire life. Already working in Lyon as a Red Cross nurse, she petitioned to get herself assigned to Camp Vernet.

"This was a big fortune for me," said Aurelio Lopez. "I feel all pain in my leg, but I don't know what is the problem yet. Seems like it was in the muscle first, then in the bone, which means I was pushing hard when I walked and always it gets worse and worse; so I was able to continue, but it will depend, I tell myself, on whether *cualquiera de los santos,* if just one of the many saints, you understand me, watches out for me."

"Instead it was me," Maryvonne said modestly.

"Better than a saint," he said, smiling.

Zelda sipped her glass of wine, newly poured from the bottle Scott had purchased for the couple, her own carafe still three-quarters full, as she studied her husband, pleased to find that he was entranced by the tale.

"Tell me about the conditions of the camp," he said.

"Il n'y a pas de mots pour ça," Maryvonne replied. Simply beyond words. Men slept in the open, without tents, huddled in small circles around fires, only their blanket capes to cover them. They ate carrion, they ate dead mules, once in a while they ate a rabbit someone caught or a smuggled-in chicken to stretch their meager rations of canned food. All of them far too thin, worn down to the bone. The trees on the rocky hills long ago ravaged of leaves and branches for use in bonfires. It was a landscape not unlike Armageddon.

"Of course, she never see the wars," Aurelio said, interrupting. "If it rains, if the rain is there and the day is cloudy, and then it rains many more days without stopping, the hills turn to mud and there is no place to sleep. Everything is water, everything is mud. This is life in the hills, this is life in the camps often also, only no more bombs tearing up the countryside. Now it is only hunger and disease and injuries that will never heal. Sometimes it is very bad, but I am thankful not to be in the war. We lose this war and I lose my country, this breaks my heart, but also I do not wish to fight anymore. If this is the will of God, I cannot say what is wrong or right. I do not have nothing against him. It was nothing against him."

"Perdón, lamento interrumpir," the waiter was saying. *"El restauranté está cerrado."*

"Oh, that's impossible," Zelda cried. "We're not even done with the bottle of wine."

"You must come back to our bungalow," Maryvonne proposed. "For a nightcap, yes?"

Scott and Aurelio rose from the table to settle the bills, Aurelio insisting that the waiter allow them to purchase a bottle of wine to take with them. Rejoining the women, the Spaniard seized the unfinished bottle and motioned for Maryvonne to pilfer the carafe and glasses as she wrapped the contents of the bread basket in a napkin to stow it in her bag.

"It is not a long walk," Aurelio informed them, so the two couples took to the shore, where the waves rolled in under a sky bright with stars that made them feel strong and safe.

Trailing the European couple whose habits were those of refugees, salvaging always what they could, unwilling to relinquish new friends or a night's revelries, Zelda considered that she and Scott had once fallen into many of these same habits, albeit for different reasons. The Frenchwoman, easily annoyed by their every attempt to deploy their rusted cosmopolitanism, responded in English to the queries posed in her native tongue. The only French they could elicit from her was the rather ill-tempered command to switch to a language everyone could speak: *"Mais je ne comprends pas, s'il vous plaît le répète, en anglais."* It never occurred to her that they might likewise complain of her use of their native language, her vowels so curled and elided that the lag between her pronouncing a phrase in English and their making sense of it was considerable.

"I made a resolution at the restaurant," Zelda whispered to Scott as they plodded through the sand. "I promised myself to adore this couple, they are so lovely and have so much potential, but her superiority is testing my resolve."

"I thought by now," Scott quipped, "you would be used to the tyranny of the French."

Overhearing those words but misunderstanding the reference, Aurelio lamented, "Well, what you say is true, now France is also a dictatorship."

He condemned a recent vote by the French National Assembly to cede all powers of state—the right to build up the military and air force and leverage the funds to do so; the right to engage in preemptive tactics in anticipation of German aggressions; the right to wage war against Hitler on all fronts when the time came—to Prime Minister Daladier.

"Such a decision is *momentané*," Maryvonne said in defense of her homeland. "We face enemies without scruples, who do not keep their word from some month to the next. I do not see what decision, that my country had a choice, Hitler takes away our choices."

"Yes, the French now prepare to do what is necessary," Aurelio said, "but what if that time has passed already?"

"After the Great War," Scott remarked, "I set myself against all wars. No more war in my lifetime. But Fascism is not politics, it is a mode of perpetual warfare against the vulnerable, Jews, Czechs, the Basque people—"

"Politics as war by other means," Aurelio said.

"It can only be defeated," Scott continued, "by armed opponents, I'm afraid."

"I do not see how you are going to be so critical of my country," Maryvonne said, addressing herself to her husband, nationalist pride creeping into her voice, "a country that have provided you refuge when, without refuge, you surely will be dead."

"I find fault with the French government," he answered diplomatically, "but not her people. To me the French people are you, faultless, generous, someone to whom I owe my entire life."

Zelda wanted to hear more of their story, what had happened after Maryvonne found her handsome cousin near death in a refugee camp.

"I wrote letters to my government lamenting conditions," she said, but it was unclear whether she was addressing her husband's criticisms or moving on to speak of his escape. "So many letters, without ever a reply."

It was up to Aurelio to explain how Maryvonne had nursed him back to health, never letting on to her superiors why she dogged the overworked doctors to make sure they tended to an anonymous Spanish soldier. Her brother helped her smuggle provisions into the camp, for Aurelio as well as several other soldiers in dire condition: rainproofed tents, deloused blankets, fresh dressings for wounds, tea, cigarettes, rations of sardines. Already the authorities were relocating Jews and Communists to camps farther inside of France, repatriating Basque farmers who were less than deeply committed Communists under a guarantee from Franco that after being reeducated they might return to their homes. But Maryvonne knew that her cousin could never pass for an ignorant Basque farmer. For men such as him, the prospects were dismal. They had nowhere to be except on that barren borderland. Still, guards could be bribed, if you had money and means, some help from the other side of the barbed wire, maybe also the know-how to embed yourself, once you were inside mother France, in the country's interior.

She arranged it all, exhausting her paltry savings, bribing a guard to look the other way while her brother smuggled Aurelio out of the camp in a supply truck and escorted him to her family's modest farm outside Lyon. Only days later she resigned from the Red Cross and joined her cousin. Every member of the family, including her brother, assumed she would never have gone to such lengths, even for a cousin, unless she were also in love with him. So after a week of prodding innuendo from her mother, sisters, and brother, she approached Aurelio and said, "Since everyone believes we are to be married, I propose that you marry me"; and marry her he did, in a modest ceremony in the village, allowing him to elude notice of the ever increasing, rabid minority in France who were hostile to all resident aliens.

"Oh, stop here," Maryvonne exclaimed as they neared a row of spaciously set-apart stone cabins ensconced in a grove of Australian pines that abutted the silver-sanded beach. She directed attention to the moon, lying low on calm ocean waters, the lights out in all the cabins except one, so that it was impossible to tell whether they housed sleeping guests or revelers who hadn't yet returned home. It was just shy of midnight, not especially late for a country participating in the rites of siesta and the recalibrated inner clock that followed from the introduction of second sleep into everyday existence.

Maryvonne pulled the radio as close as possible to the small patio door, spinning the dial for a station, while Aurelio dragged chairs from the cabin so his guests could enjoy the sultry ocean air. The announcer now and then peppered his comments with English, reading an advertisement for cigarettes before introducing a song that Zelda recognized right away. *Pack up your troubles in your old kit bag, and smile, smile, smile. While you've a Lucifer to light your fag, smile, boys, that's the style.* It was from a war movie made this past year starring Jimmy Stewart and Margaret Sullavan, in which she played a Broadway singer whose soldier husband gets killed in battle, and after receiving news of his demise, she must take the stage and sing this cheering song.

"I love this song," Maryvonne said. Zelda doubted a Red Cross nurse from France could be aware of its association with the movie, since, in that case, the lyrics would surely have troubled her more. "Everybody must dance to this song."

Maryvonne walked over to Scott instead of her husband.

"Mr. Fitzgerald, you would be so kind?"

Before Zelda could search Scott for his reaction—he might be flattered, he might be irascible, it all depended on how his lungs felt, whether the drinks had restored or drained his strength —she felt a man's grip on her elbow, as firm as his voice: "We have marching orders." Zelda allowed herself to be lifted from the chair, the glass of wine extracted from her hand and placed on the ground as the Spaniard pulled her into his arms.

Swaying to the jaunty, marching, military pomp of the song, she gazed over the Spaniard's shoulder at her husband, who though slow on the uptake had accepted the Frenchwoman's invitation without protest and now stylishly pulled her through lush, tight waltzing squares. Zelda, chin resting on another man's shoulder, took simple pleasure in the song. *What's the use of worrying?* Sullavan sang with warbling steadfastness, her voice milking the contrast between what the words recommended and what she must really be feeling. *It never was worthwhile, so pack up your troubles in your old kit bag, and smile, smile, smile.*

When the song finished, Aurelio escorted Zelda to her chair, topped off her glass of wine, and offered a cigarette, which he then lit for her, asking where she had learned to dance so well.

Maryvonne complained about the cool night air and Zelda suspected that Scott had put her up to it. So the couples pulled the chairs inside, where they resumed drinking and smoking, dancing now and then to someone's favorite song, the room muggy and claustrophobic. Aurelio hung at Zelda's side, doting on her, and she felt suddenly self-conscious—about lost youth and lapsed social skills, about the roughened texture of her face— unable to receive his stare without glancing away. It occurred to her for the first time that the European couple (theirs was a marriage of convenience, after all) might be in earnest about swapping partners. She watched Scott enjoying the young woman's flirtatious banter, when suddenly Maryvonne shot to her feet and fled the room.

Aurelio asked Zelda to dance again and she accepted, so the Spaniard guided her through a form of native Cuban dance he himself had only recently mastered. The swift, neat movements, always in a radius of a few feet, the constant retreading of the same ground, intensified the dance's air of intimacy. Scott stared at them in silence from his chair, perhaps winded from the dancing, perhaps dizzied by alcohol or his weak heart.

"Explain to me," Aurelio called to him, apprehending the duties of host even as he danced with a guest's wife, "since we have talked of dictators, explain why is Franco attractive to Americans, also Mussolini—why so many Americans affectionate for Fascists."

"Not all Americans are soft," Scott responded irritably, and Zelda feared he might get testy, obsessed as he was by perceived insults, always prepared to defend his maligned honor in fistfights he could not possibly win. "I consider myself to be vehemently anti-Fascist."

"I mean no disrespect," Aurelio said.

"Excuse me," Zelda interrupted, finding it odd that no one had said anything about Maryvonne's departure. "Is she all right?"

"Why didn't you try to get back into Spain?" Scott asked. Weren't there ways to continue resisting Franco from within, just as the Germans must now fight Hitler from within their country? How else would Fascism ever fall?

"I am almost certain to be executed," Aurelio reported with sangfroid. To go back to Franco's Spain meant certain death before a firing squad.

"It is in here," Maryvonne announced, entering the room again and holding up a recent copy of *LIFE*, "a small glimpse of what my Aurelio suffers." On the cover a girl in straight blond bangs and ribboned ponytails bore a dour expression, a doll in similar blond bangs and ponytail positioned to her right, making it seem as though the girl stood erect, her arm loosely, even reluctantly enfolding a lifeless replica of herself. To reinforce the effect—Zelda found the photograph discomfiting—the doll and girl wore matching jumpers: short rounded collar, diagonal striping in the style of a cravat except that it was flat and sewn into the dress, a thin waistband in the same diagonal striping. Aurelio tried to spin Zelda through a lift in the song, but she pulled free of him, as Maryvonne flipped through the pages of *LIFE,* arriving at stark photographs of a camp for Republican refugees such as the one she'd found her cousin in.

"It is not Camp Vernet. What you see in this picture is bad but not horrible," she said, rolling r's, elongating her i's, her accent pulling the word into French. "How would you say *effroyable?*"

"Outrageous, dreadful," Scott suggested.

"Yes, it is not full of dread," Maryvonne replied. "The men do not look as though they are fearing for death."

She flipped the magazine shut, handing it to Zelda, saying she was welcome to take it home with her.

"Where would you stop your life if you could?" Zelda said à propos of nothing, addressing the young woman. "I mean, if you could stop it, and then keep living at that age, having gained enough wisdom, know-how, and talent to make good use of yourself, enough happiness to stare down adversity—"

Aurelio said he thought he understood what she meant: if you could go on living forever, without aging, without losing will, what Schopenhauer called the "will to life."

"At thirty-five," Zelda said, "on my birthday. That's when I'd stop time."

"Do not forget to blow out the candle, then," her dance partner said with a sportive lilt in his voice, "and maybe you will get your wish."

But there was something artificial in his flattery. He didn't believe she was shy of thirty-five. True, she had stayed young for so long, far longer than most people were able to manage, indulging only her appetite for experience, indifferent to the taxes imposed on pleasure. No longer, though—too many bouts of eczema and insanity, too many starvation performances that weren't even meant as such. Now she looked her age, several years past thirty-five.

"On my birthday, three years ago," the Frenchwoman said. "Before that war," she added, lowering her voice to a hush.

"It has already begun," Aurelio said, taking Maryvonne in his arms, dipping her in a mock dance, naming her as his raison d'être. "All the world does not know it, but even three years ago, the war, it commences already." Spinning in his arms this distant cousin who was also his wife, who somewhere along the way must have fallen in love with him, he began to kiss her immodestly, the two of them standing in the middle of the room, grinding into each other as if trying to crush some sadness wedged between them. "Besides," he said, "you would not know me then."

There was a pounding at the front door and Aurelio disappeared into the small foyer, only to be greeted by a boisterous man scolding in Spanish who forced his way inside. The hotel's on-duty manager stood in the center of the living room. *"Los invitados no pueden dormir aquí!"* While waving two fingers at Scott, he spoke only to Aurelio. "You cannot sleep here, he say, unless you pay for your own room." Aurelio's translation was unnecessary. Both Zelda and Scott understood the manager well enough. On the trail of raucous behavior, immorality, maybe just pleasure itself, the man spent part of every night policing noise. It was not an easy aspect of his job, but it was his job all the same.

"We're staying in the main villa, second floor," Scott said, interrupting.

"Excuse me, *señor.*"

"Hardly the freeloaders you've mistaken us for," Scott said.

Zelda had the feeling that the manager wasn't there to prevent freeloaders so much as to break up an imminent orgy.

"Perdón, mi error," the manager said automatically, but he held his ground, suggesting it might be best if they returned to their room. Other guests had lodged complaints about the noise.

"Which guests?" Scott asked. "I would like their names." He hated having authority of any kind wielded over him. It made him irate, violent, rash.

"Lo que me pide es imposible," the night manager said, before switching to English. "Impossible, I can give no names; I can violate the privacy of the guests never, not at any time."

"It is late in any case," Maryvonne said. Zelda looked across at Aurelio, but he seemed ready to join Scott in the quarrel.

"Well, we'd like our privacy now," Scott said to the night manager. "You may wait outside, please."

The manager, perhaps regretting having labeled guests of the resort trespassers, capitulated and stepped outside. The two couples said their goodbyes, Aurelio pleased by Scott's performance, Maryvonne professing her pleasure in the night and insisting on meeting again.

The night manager stood under a bull-horn acacia tree, waiting on them, humbler now in manner, oddly contrite about having to break up their party, but it was true, other guests had complained about the noise. It made no difference to him, personally.

"Recent troubles notwithstanding," Zelda said as they walked across grass and fallen palm fronds, "I enjoyed them, and they're clearly more appropriate company for us."

"You're a snob, Zelda," Scott said. "Besides, Matéo is from older money than any three of tonight's party combined, yourself included."

"True enough," she said. "On the whole I liked him too. But you can't blame me for worrying about his judgment."

"What he did for us cannot be denied."

She let the remark pass. Enough of that, no bickering, she wanted to talk about how much she had enjoyed tonight, how charming and knowledgeable Scott could be, how calmly he'd put that manager in his place. Did he think it likely the girl Maryvonne had a crush on him? Scott said she was hardly a girl, and he hadn't noticed anything except Aurelio's doting on Zelda. "But his wife's so much younger than I am, what could he see in me?" Maryvonne was in her late twenties, Scott said, pushing thirty, hardly a young girl anymore. It felt like a huge divide to Zelda—a decade was such a long time in a woman's life.

"I like it when we do things," she said as they followed the path back to the villa. "We don't go on outings often enough, maybe that's why we forget how good we can be together."

She didn't mean it as criticism. To make this clear, she pressed herself against his flank, inspiring him to wrap his arm around her waist. She hardly noticed the ocean, never more than thirty yards away during their homeward stroll, but she could taste the salt air going into her lungs.

Inside their room he sat next to her on the bed. "Why did you choose that date, of all years? It was such a bad year, the year you turned thirty-five; you suffered so, you were so far gone and I wasn't sure you—"

"You were still mine," she said.

He grew quiet.

"It was the last time I truly believed, that is, when I was well enough to think or believe anything—"

"But you believe in so many—"

"It was the last time I believed—your promises were so

earnest, desperate, mostly you were saying what I needed to hear—but still it was the last time I felt sure we would get there."

"Maybe we're here now," he said, slanting forward to kiss her as she fell back on the bed to receive the sturdy weight of a man's body on top of her, his hands stroking her face, her shoulders, her breasts and neck, fingers gliding along the satiny surface of her dress, his movements gentle but purposeful. Shivering to his touch, she anticipated where his hands would go next, as delighted when she was wrong as when she was right, waiting, waiting, enjoying the wait and the way it filled up everything. She wanted his hands on her skin. At last he was unzipping her dress, saying, "Hold on to my neck," so he could lift her torso off the bed and peel the elegant charmeuse gown from her shoulders, as far down as her waist. She rolled sideways on the bed, throwing her legs out until she was standing beside him on the floor, his cue, which he took immediately, to pull the dress down over her hips.

There were times, especially in recent years, when their lovemaking was halting, bungled, clumsy, always one or the other of them on the verge of feeling wronged. On more than one occasion she had accused him of being unskillful. Alcohol got in the way, also her prickly nature, also her expectation that he should know without any prompting what pleased her. It was a mode of magical thinking, the belief that men were supposed to be naturally skillful, able to intuit a lover's every desire. She had a hard time forgiving him when they fell out of sync, fearing that it was some kind of comment on their basic incompatibility. But not tonight, tonight his moves coincided with hers, what he wanted to do next aligned with what she also desired. She was naked, only her hat still on, pinned to her hair for a bit longer anyway, and he stripped himself while continuing to caress her. Soon all he wore were his socks, which she slipped off with her feet. She felt his penis, firm, unambivalent. "Oh, you feel so nice," she said, sighing, arching her back on a pillow, rolling her hips upward to press into him, curling her fingers up and over the helmeted tip of him, applying pressure on it and rocking into it until in one swift, straight motion she pulled him inside.

When they were done she rolled from the bed, walking into the bathroom to wash her face. And after that, without understanding what she was doing or why, she began to pace the room while Scott, worn out on the bed, now and then coughing in his groggy sleep, made vague inquiries into the dark as to whether she was all right, whether she was coming back to bed soon.

"I'm just so happy," she said, still pacing. "It will be fine, I'll calm down, I'll come back in a minute."

In the morning she woke him with breakfast and a gift, throwing herself beside him on the bed, announcing that she had been up for hours and found a market in town—in fact she'd run into the Frenchwoman from last night, Maryvonne, and they had talked and shopped together. Before Scott could open his gift, he had to eat something. Either the fresh guava or one of the baguettes she had purchased. Either a red banana or one of those whose surface was mottled like a snake's skin. Last but not least, there was a Hershey's chocolate bar. Knowing how he craved chocolate, she held it out as a reward, so that he would take at least one bite of each item of real food, which was exactly what he did, one bite of each kind of banana, one bite of a baguette, maybe two or three bites of the guava, before devouring the chocolate bar.

Now it was time for her presentation.

Zelda was in the habit of interpreting the presents she gave to people. It enhanced the pleasure of gift-giving, the opportunity to explain the thought she put into the choice of an item, why it was exactly what Scott, Scottie, or her mother needed. She told him how she had borrowed pesos from his wallet for the food, but the gift was purchased—she watched him unwrap it and, oh, she was so sure he was going to like it—with money put aside from her discretionary fund at the Highland, saved specially for this trip so she could purchase a few items for loved ones.

What Scott held in his hand was a small silver medallion, a religious icon.

"It's Saint Lazarus, dearest Dodo, do you remember him?"

"Of course I remember Lazarus." Scott said. "What is he, the patron saint of coming back from the dead? Did you think he might bump start my career?"

"Be serious, please," she said. "He takes care of the sick, and you need to remember that your lungs and heart and overall health are more precious to some of us who walk this earth than they are to yourself. Since you won't look after you, I found some-one who will. Soon we'll find a chain, and as you wear it you'll think, I must take better care of myself. Meantime we can attach it to this piece of hand-braided twine so you can get used to it."

"Zelda, you can be so sweet," he said leaning forward so that she could drape it over his neck. "Is there anyone as sweet as you?"

She laid her head on the pillow next to him, staring into his eyes, their noses inches apart.

"Will you remember this, Scott? If I die tomorrow, say you'll remember and write about it, because I don't want them saying I was a narcissistic person. I know sometimes I've been hard on you, but tell me you remember all the kindnesses too."

"Of course," he said. "I always do, but Zelda, no one's—"

"You promise?" She jerked her head up off the pillow, propping herself up by her elbows to stare down into his eyes. "Do you promise, Scott?"

"What's this about?"

"Nothing, really, I just need you to remember. I had a dream last night, it's silly."

In her sleep she had suffered a vision of how she might be seen—how literary men and biographers would talk about her. She knew what Ernest said about her already, even to common friends such as Gerald and Sara. She knew what John Dos Passos and John Peale Bishop thought. And there were others, of course. She wasn't blind, she wasn't deaf. Now that she had spent all these years in sanitariums and hospitals, unable to procure her freedom, the naysayers would have all the proof they needed. What was everybody else to think? She would always be "poor Zelda" to the masses; maybe Scott himself took comfort in the arms of lovers while referring to her as his "poor Zelda," but she didn't want their pity. She wanted to be remembered for the things she had done for him, for the joy he obtained simply from being in love with her. She was special, she wasn't like other people, he was lucky to have known her.

"I've never said otherwise."

"Then we're agreed," she said. Because she had made plans for them while he slept, and, yes, it involved their friends from last night, but that was all she would say for now. Did he approve? They were to leave in an hour. When he raised no objections, she began to talk again of the gift.

"Do you see the two dogs at his feet? It's from a story in the Bible, about the beggar Lazarus eating with the dogs. He's always depicted that way, since the Middle Ages, the old woman at the market told me. But here in Cuba he is special for the Africans also because he resembles an old Yoruban god, Babalú-Ayé, I think he's called, who tends to the wounded, who heals the chronically ill, who oversees health in the family. I want you to wear this medallion, and your lungs will get better and no harm will come to you."

Scott extended his palm to clasp her by the neck so that he might pull her lips to his, but she jerked away.

"Say you'll remember," she said.

9

THE WOMAN TOEING THE EDGE OF THE PROMONTORY WAS HIS WIFE, her posture balletic, back held erect in a line with her heels. From this distance she seemed supple, lithe, as irrepressible as in the days when she had trained for dance with steadfast indifference to body and mind. In the gusting of a coastal wind, he put a hand to his hat, then allowed his eyes once more to climb and behold Zelda's crimson-suited body framed by empty sky, hair blowing, face turned into the wind, waiting until it should subside so that she might plunge into the ocean. She was brave, maybe even foolhardy, and he swelled with admiration for her.

"Are you sure this is safe?" the Frenchwoman asked, standing beside him as his wife rotated away from the water, spotted him below on the beach, and raised her arm in a stilted motion not unlike a salute. She was thrilled at having found this high place, eager as always to show off for him, but for a split second—instantly he beat back the thought—it was as if she were waving goodbye. Several feet behind her stood the Spaniard, his naked skin almost pale in the sunlight. He too was prepared to dive into the ocean, but only after Zelda had taken her turn and brought the arc of the morning's chase to its rightful end.

It had started in the hotel room after she gave him the St. Lazarus medallion and announced that she needed to borrow more of their vacation money because surprises were so very expensive. Not to worry, in the days to come she would prove herself frugal, only let her have today. When he gave in, she let out a squeal of excitement.

"Oh, you'll see, it will be such fun. You'll keep an open mind and remember we're on holiday and in the end you always like the things I find for us to do."

Did he, was she so certain?

"Oh, yes, you do, you will, you always do, I'm sure of it."

Her enthusiasm was like a primitive grace ravaging everything in its path. So he handed over the pesos in his possession, and she said, please, sir, more, and he gave her another wad of bills. In the courtyard half an hour later he crossed in front of the fountain misting in his face and through the archway of funneled wind to emerge squinting into the speckled light. No sign of his wife at the reception desk. No sign of the Frenchwoman or her refugee cousin.

"Señor Fitzgerald," the man behind the desk called, holding up a slip of paper, *"ésto llegó hace poco para usted."*

It was a cable, and Scott rested his forearms on the reception desk to read it, first surveying the lobby with its spare yet handsome furniture, several benches and chairs and a long bureau, all carved from a wood so dark it was almost black. It didn't surprise him that Matéo Cardoña had managed to track him to this resort on the peninsula, even though he couldn't recall ever mentioning their next destination. In the hallway of the Ambos Mundos,

Matéo had spoken of Saturday night's event as "under control" and yet "far from settled," Scott wondering how it could be both things at once. "The wounded man has died, Scott," Matéo said. Under circumstances such as these, the police were inclined to use any means necessary to acquire a verdict. Someone might remember, even if it wasn't the entire truth, that Zelda had provoked the fight by rushing through the crowd and crashing into the man who'd cursed her. "Let me take care of this for you," Matéo had insisted.

As Scott now skimmed the contents of the cable, he took in key phrases—"*several matters unresolved,*" "*not informed of your plans,*" "*next steps to be considered*"—and he understood that Matéo was unhappy with him for leaving Havana without notice. The cable concluded with news that a messenger would be dispatched to Varadero, maybe tomorrow morning, maybe this evening, Scott should remain on the lookout.

"Too bad we'll be gone all day," Scott said to himself. Still, he jotted down Matéo's telephone number and address in his Moleskine, just in case, then tore the cable in half, sliding it across the dark granite surface toward the clerk.

"*Entiendo, señor,*" the clerk said. "*A la basura.*" He made a motion with his arm as though tossing an item into a basket, and Scott nodded his assent.

No sign of Zelda in front of the building, so Scott exited at the rear through French doors that opened onto a dirt and cinder pathway winding through coconut palms toward the beach, his breathing raspy, his stomach queasy, though he wasn't as bad off as he might have been. Too much food in his system for this hour of the day, but he couldn't have refused Zelda's impromptu banquet. In the pockets of his light tweed jacket was enough Benzedrine and chocolate to keep three men awake for several days, and he promised himself to use the medicine sparingly. Fingers plunged into an outside pocket, he broke off a chunk of a Baker's German's sweet chocolate bar, lifting the rectangle to his nose to detect its malty fragrance before folding it in one sharp snap into his mouth, letting the chocolate sit on his tongue.

Halfway to the beach he spotted her, perched on a knoll that rose like a burial mound amid a small cluster of columnar palms, at her side Maryvonne, Aurelio, and several horses.

"Can you guess what the surprise is now?" she asked.

"Let me see," he said, holding a thumb and two fingers to his forehead in imitation of a clairvoyant, "you and I are going to watch Maryvonne and Aurelio race horses along the beach?"

"So you've already noticed the horses?"

"Hard to miss them."

"How did you know they were ours? You didn't think for a second they might belong to someone else?"

"Well, Aurelio is holding the reins."

"This is the plan of your wife and mine also," Aurelio said, as if he wished to go on record ahead of time as a neutral party.

"There are only three horses," Scott remarked.

"It is all that is 'vailable," Maryvonne said, the last word pronounced as if she were mimicking the term *valuable*.

But Zelda had thought of everything, deciding they would rotate seating throughout the day so that each woman might take turns riding with each man.

"Some horses do not like to carry two people at once," Aurelio protested.

"That is why we have the large saddle," Zelda said, annoyed by the Spaniard's prosaic imagination. "Scott and I will share a horse for the first rotation."

One of the horses was a bay gelding thoroughbred, the other two of no particular breed, including the medium-sized palomino with an ivory mane that he and Zelda were to mount.

"He's the docile but hardy one," Zelda said. "The owner often rides him with his young daughter seated on the saddle before him."

"That is not the same thing," Aurelio insisted.

"It will be fine," Maryvonne interjected. "Zelda and I are small, like children."

Scott walked toward the animal, wishing his wife might have consulted him about the horseback riding, and that he in turn might have put her off a day or two, until he was sturdier. Still running short on sleep, hands jittery from weeks of hard drinking, he inserted his left foot in the stirrup, reached his hand to the pommel, then swung himself up onto the saddle. His chest tightened, and he could feel the pinch in his lungs as though someone were thumbing an internal bruise. He didn't like heights of any kind, not airplanes, not diving boards, not even horses. In defiance of his fears he sometimes performed reckless acts, such as that ill-advised Olympic-style swan dive off a fifteen-foot diving board in Asheville a few years ago, inspired by (what else) a woman, resulting (no surprise here either) in a shattered clavicle and months of drunken convalescence. He let his thoughts race ahead to a full day of riding in the sun, in search of beaches and high places over the water, dreading the hours during which he would have to put up a brave front. Fortunately—if not for this provision, he might have despaired in advance—he had stowed a flask of Martell's in the breast pocket of his sport coat.

"Well done, Scott," Aurelio said, praising his new friend's mount as he held the second horse, a black mare, still for Maryvonne, then scaled the bay gelding in one swift motion without provoking so much as a flinch.

"Hold her still, Scott," Zelda said as the palomino took a step back. Scott clenched the reins to calm the horse, now lowering his free arm so that Zelda might grab hold and hoist herself into the air in a dancer's leap. In an instant she sat in the saddle, preposterously facing him, her orange and white muslin dress bunched over the pommel, her crotch snug against his.

"Zelda, we can't ride like this."

She peered hard into his eyes as if assessing his élan vital, sniffing out symptoms of alcoholic or tubercular deterioration, then playfully she licked the corner of his lip.

"Sweet chocolate," she remarked. Had he brought any to share?

"Of course."

"Nevertheless we're stopping at a market for picnic items." She and Maryvonne had already purchased two bottles of wine from the hotel and stored them in Aurelio's saddlebag.

"You've accounted for everything except how I'm supposed to direct this horse with my wife riding in my lap."

"You're not," she said, then told him he would have to dismount so she could turn around in the saddle.

"But Zelda, that makes no sense," he muttered. "Why did I get in the saddle first?"

"I was wondering that myself," she said.

He could tell that she was in a buoyant and willful mood, and it was useless to argue with her, so he draped the reins over her forearm, slipping his feet out of the stirrups to dismount the horse. The horse skittered forward, expressing its displeasure, but Scott retrieved the reins from Zelda to still the horse. He watched his wife place her hands between her thighs, then lift the flaps of her dress so that she might swing her left leg out from the horse, rotating her body by moving hand over hand in the center of the saddle, her weight balanced on those well-developed dancer's triceps as she made the 180-degree turn. "Are you pleased?" she whispered midmotion. About the horses, she meant, he wasn't angry that she'd gone ahead and arranged everything without him. Soon she had ensconced herself face-forward in the saddle, inviting him to remount the horse, posting in the saddle as he settled in behind her and then lowering herself, her derriere pressing against his mildly stirred genitalia, her neck craning to ask her question again.

"It's a nice surprise," he said. "I want you to do what brings you pleasure."

"I know you don't love riding the way I do, so we'll ride gently at first."

Dressed in snug canvas trousers, boots, and a bright red shirt, Aurelio rode the gelding with skill, directing them up the beach into the winds, swinging his outside leg back and prodding the horse with his heel, urging it into a canter. Maryvonne, also dressed appropriately in black riding pants and a loose white blouse, could not get her mare up to speed. After pressing the mare with her heel, she snapped the reins against the withers repeatedly, but without result. Only Scott was overdressed for the outing, and he regretted that he hadn't insisted on running back to the room for a change of clothes.

"He rides well, don't you think? He trained for the cavalry," Zelda said, and Scott tried to remember whether he had read anywhere about the Republicans assembling a cavalry.

Zelda crouched forward, one hand on the reins while she ran the other forward over the horse's silky golden neck, stretching her leg over Scott's in an effort to prod the horse's haunches. The jolt of acceleration caused Scott to lose balance, swaying to the side, so that he had to right himself by inching forward in the saddle and wrapping a forearm around his wife's waist, struggling to find the horse's center of gravity.

Zelda let out a laugh, whinnying and zestful. She loved speed in a way he did not; she loved any occasion to test her body and her nerve. She rode with a destination in mind, one she would not share despite several queries from him. For the moment she concentrated only on passing Maryvonne, after that on catching up with Aurelio, who rode the bay gelding with manly elegance, the horse's hooves kicking up sand, the beach ahead resplendent in sunlight, empty of sunbathers. Zelda guided their horse close to the water where the sand was damp and firm, and soon she was shouting to Aurelio as they drew near, "Do you remember where we turn?"

"Any one of the dirt roads," he called back.

"Zelda, where are we going?" Scott shouted into the wind.

"Why are you against surprises?" She laughed as she overtook Aurelio and the slowing gelding, and next she turned their horse with a single snap of the reins onto a dirt path to ride between modest stone bungalows and cottages with thatched roofs into the center of a small village. Aurelio, somewhere back where the beach met the dirt road, waited on Maryvonne.

Scott discerned the small church with its modified mission front as they cleared an open-air market that consisted of several huts side by side, the posts of one hut all but indistinguishable from those of the next, a long row of them running up into the straw and frond ceilings, beneath which merchants stood hawking everything from fruit and live chickens to pottery, colorfully embroidered peasant shirts, and silver jewelry.

"I think we should buy you a proper hat," Zelda said. "In that silly tweed you resemble an English lord taking survey of the manor."

For a second Scott's thoughts ran across a continent to Sheilah, his girl from England, marooned in California with her great secret. Zelda's remark made him think of Sheilah's elaborate cover story, the illustriously invented ancestry backed by the picture she'd once showed him of an English lord propped on a horse who was supposed to be her uncle, how after weeks of his poking for details she'd broken down and let him in on the enigmatic truth: she had been reared in a British orphanage, a Jewish waif forsaken for eight years by a mother too destitute to raise the child herself. She was a self-made woman in every sense of the term, including the fantastic lineage concocted to procure a place on the London stage, later a husband (whom she quickly divorced), and still later work as a Hollywood gossip columnist. No one else knew, not her ex-husband, not the real British lord with whom she had months ago broken off an engagement to become Scott's full-time mistress. Some honor, he thought, and now *I've left her*. But he couldn't think of her just now—that was over, most likely.

"A lord pompously propped on his fine pony," Zelda said, "while he checks on the good-for-nothing Irish serfs."

"Your point is that the serfs or the indigenous populace might be less likely to resent me if I buy one of their hats?"

"Honestly, Scott, I'm worried that your stodgy old cap won't shield you from the cruel sun, but it's simply more efficient to appeal to your vanity than to your health."

"Tell me about the church," he said.

"Well, it's on the scale of chapel more than church, don't you think," she said, informing him that she had scouted it earlier this morning. "It was built only this past year, funded by the du Pont family, if I understand correctly, Irénée du Pont, who has a place here on the peninsula."

The facade of the church, constructed of large rectangular stones, had battered sides rising to a gable, on top of which there was a small altarlike form encasing the bell.

After the European couple caught up with them and all four tourists dismounted their horses and tied them up, Aurelio refused to enter the sacred building. A priest emerged from behind the church, one of the villagers having run off to inform him of the arrival of guests, and he smiled for the tourists, speaking in blunt provincial Spanish, Maryvonne translating.

"He would like to show us the inside," she said.

"Oh, yes, *gracias, monsieur.* Wait," Zelda said, mixing Spanish and French. *"Excusez-moi, gracias, Padre."*

The priest guided the women past the diminutive buttresses toward an entrance on the side of the church near a cubic stone chapter house connected to the back of the church, Scott trailing them, observing Aurelio still planted, stiff backed, not far from the horses.

"Zelda," Scott called, "I'll catch up with you in a minute."

His words drew the priest's attention to the two men, and as the duly appointed liaison between God and men, even perhaps between men and their own souls, he issued a second invitation.

"Dios y yo," Aurelio called out, *"hemos elegido sendas distintas."*

The priest flinched at the staunch rejection of God's hospitality, looking around him for local villagers, obviously embarrassed.

"Él nunca te abandonará, cualquiera sea tu senda," the priest said, bowing respectfully, then extending his arms to either side of him to lead the women inside the church.

"As you wish to believe, Padre," Aurelio answered curtly.

"Aurelio," Zelda called, intervening, "remember, you must go to the market to obtain the items for our picnic."

"Gladly, Mrs. Zelda Sayre Fitzgerald."

"Why did you tell him you had rejected God?" Scott asked his companion once the priest and the women were out of hearing distance.

"Your Spanish is not very good, my friend," Aurelio said. "Not what I said, though it is true enough. Perhaps I would be more precise if I say, God, he has rejected my people."

"I get it," Scott said, thinking of the lost war in Spain. "You've a quarrel with the Church."

"Not personal," Aurelio said. "The *pelea,* perhaps you say complaint, it belong to all of Spain. You are faithful man, *piadoso*—if so, if I insult you, for this I am sorry, truly."

"Not religious, not insulted," Scott said. He pulled the flask of Martell's from his jacket, looking over his shoulder to ascertain that Zelda had in fact entered the church and could no longer see him, then extended the flask to Aurelio. After the Spaniard took a polite sip and handed it back, Scott tilted his chin for a slow, pleasurable swig.

"Well, I must check on them," Scott said, half-inclined to visit the market with Aurelio and stand in solidarity against the Catholic Church for having thrown in with Fascists, but instead he entered the small church where Zelda knelt at the altar as though she were a communicant waiting on the host. It caught him by surprise every time, his wife's newfound piety. Studying her face, her chin burrowed in her breast, he witnessed someone longing for a peace that refused to overtake her. Scott envisioned thousands of mothers and wives kneeling on prie-dieux, whispering in pews across Spain, petitioning for the return of husbands, sons, and fathers they knew to be lost, silently pleading that an entire three years of ruthless violence might be undone.

Before they could leave, Zelda insisted on lighting several votive candles. They stood beneath the church's exposed-timber ceiling, reminiscent of colonial missions, and as she implored him in front of the priest to make a donation, he tried to remember when her modes of prayer had become so Catholic. As a young couple they used to attend services together, visiting St. Patrick's Cathedral in New York, where they had been married, later appreciating the High Mass at Notre Dame, which despite her Protestant upbringing she relished for its pomp and majesty. Still, prayer was something they rarely discussed. They were acolytes of a post-religious era, in flight from the strictures of the Catholic and Protestant God, all those teetotalers, prohibitionists, anti-petting prudes, the generally puritanical populace—it was hard to imagine they might ever look back.

Aurelio, with his arm full of groceries, met them in the shade where they had tied up the horses.

"Why is that old woman staring at me?" Zelda asked, and Scott looked across the road at a woman in a frock and kerchiefed head, who, with her dark, sun-wrinkled skin and broadly bridged nose, might have hailed from any sunny climate from almost any period in history.

"She believe with all her heart it is something she must say to you," Aurelio said.

"How do you mean?" Scott said, as Zelda asked simultaneously, "What can she have to say to me?"

"We have right to disobey her," Aurelio proposed reasonably.

"Doubtless she's a fortuneteller of some sort," Scott said. "On the prowl for customers."

"I know that, Scott," Zelda snapped, addressing herself again to Aurelio. "Why do you say *must?*"

"Her words, not mine," Aurelio said. " *'Tengo que hablar con la doña elegante,'* she say. It is very important. Scott is right. Is the way of women who speak to the spirit world, it is true. Always some message must be translated, if you pay, only if you pay them."

"Perhaps she meant me," Maryvonne laughed. "I am also elegant."

Scott was grateful for Maryvonne's courteous instincts, for the effort to distract Zelda—as a trained nurse, the Frenchwoman could detect the symptoms of an obsessive personality—but Aurelio wouldn't eat his words.

"She mean Zelda, I am sure."

Scott looked across the street and saw the old woman's hand held open before her, several fingers curled in a gesture of invitation, neither the hand nor fingers in motion. How long had she been doing that?

"I won't speak with her," Zelda said, the peace she had achieved minutes ago inside the church already evaporating.

"Zelda is right. It is best to speak to the spirit world," Maryvonne suggested, "only in God's house."

Aurelio untied the horses.

"I have watered horses," he said.

Scott and Zelda were to ride solo for the next leg of the trip. Immediately she seized the reins of the bay gelding from Aurelio. The Spaniard claimed the palomino for Maryvonne and himself, handing Scott the reins of the third horse, reasoning that since the mare was the weakest, someone should always ride her solo.

"That way there is better chance to keep up," he explained.

Zelda nicknamed Scott's horse "the old nag" and the name stuck the rest of the day. For as long as he rode the mare, Scott sympathized with her, perhaps detecting something of his own ragged state in her plight, though he wouldn't have put it that way. What he told himself was simpler: he was far from a skillful rider and didn't require a good horse, so why not this tired black mare?

Zelda took the lead, enjoying the lively athleticism of the gelding, and Aurelio kept pace for a while, then dropped behind to see how Scott was faring.

"Does she have any idea where she's headed?" Scott asked.

"*Le prêtre,* he give us instructions," Maryvonne said.

"That was kind of him," Scott replied, "but where to, exactly?"

"Zelda, she ask about a place for diving," Maryvonne said. "The father just smile, then say, *'Je sais l'endroit ideal,'* so perhaps it is a blessed and blissful place."

The Europeans tried to engage Scott in conversation about his wife, her derring-do, her skill on horses and prowess at dancing, but it alarmed him to learn she'd spoken to them about the ballet, and he was deaf to their words as he strained to keep track of Zelda up ahead. The Europeans did manage to extract one story from him. It was of a young Zelda, still a girl of eighteen, during the era of their multiply broken, narrowly repaired engagements (the European couple interrupted, asking for details about the engagements, but Scott put them off). Again he saw the beautiful Zelda Sayre, red-gold hair to her neck sweeping outward in bold wings, her round cheeks flushed pink, the most pink-white girl imaginable. The incident he recited for them? Zelda, flouting Montgomery customs with customary zeal, accused of lewd behavior at a holiday ball, maybe for close dancing, maybe for showing more than a little leg, he couldn't remember what exactly. Pulled from the dance floor a fourth or fifth time, she found a sprig of mistletoe, attached it to her skirt tails, and for her last dance waved her rear end at the chaperones like a peacock, letting them know, please excuse his French, what part of her precious person they could kiss.

From time to time Zelda raced back on the gelding to check on them, inquiring, "How's the old nag holding up?" She made sure no one second-guessed her command of the expedition, declaring, "It's not far now," then sprinted ahead until she and her horse were one faint image on the horizon.

Ultimately, she deposited them on a stretch of beach at the far end of the peninsula just shy of Hicacos Point, the priest having promised her it was secluded, the promontory good for diving, the water deep enough and without rocks. She had dismounted and tied her horse to a tree, already disrobed by the time they approached, in the midst of donning her crimson bathing suit under a date palm, her dimpled lower back visible as she pulled the suit over her waist and the straps onto her shoulders. She announced that she was headed to the top of the cliff.

They should test the water first, Scott suggested.

The father, she said in French, had promised it was safe.

How could she be sure they'd found the right spot?

"Faith," she assured him as she marched off.

He might have run after her, but there was little chance of changing her mind. He might have stripped and swum far out into the water beneath the promontory to assess the depth, checking for boulders, but he hadn't taken a swim in two years.

"I will accompany her, my friend," Aurelio said, beginning to undress beneath the tree to which he'd tied the palomino.

Scott felt remiss in the face of the Spaniard's chivalry, but also exasperated by Zelda's impulsiveness, by the effort entailed in merely keeping pace with her. So he let her climb the steep back of the crag until she was out of sight, with the naked Spaniard chasing after her. All that was left for Scott to do was to stand on the beach and murmur a small petition on his wife's behalf to some saint in whom he no longer believed, wondering if the Lazarus he wore about his neck held province here, worried lest catastrophe once more befall a woman he'd watched ruin herself, repeatedly, for over a decade. The two figures eventually emerged atop the promontory.

The day was bright blue and warm and the wind carried the ocean rushing through you, vigorous, salty, but also entirely fresh because this far out on the peninsula everything swept from one narrow strip of beach to the opposite, a terse Atlantic wind whipping across dunes, beach brush, and tall grasses out onto the Caribbean. No fetid pools of backwater, nothing of the land to be gathered up and carried on the breeze—the wind was ocean and sky, nothing else.

"The sky is always so blue on our vacations," she said, falling beside him, panting from her sprint across the beach, her wet body spraying him as she collapsed on the sand. Maybe thirty yards on, Maryvonne stood, shoes off, a pair of men's shorts over her arm, her riding pants pulled up off her knees as she waded through the white-foamed scum of splintered waves to greet her husband when he emerged from the water.

"I'm surprised to find you sitting in the sun, and, look, I forgot all about the hat we were going to buy you earlier, you'll be sunburnt by now, let me see." Zelda rested her wet hand against his chin, depressing her thumb on his forehead and cheeks. "It's all my fault."

"Nonsense," he said. "You look lovely and sun-kissed and happier than I've seen you in a long time."

"You forget, that's all," she said, "how charming I can be, how much you like being with me when I'm happy and you're all mine and nothing could ever make me happier than that you're all mine and it is right now. Maybe you should take your pen out and write it down in that surly Moleskine. I worry about it, that you only retain the sufferings, never the joy, where's the joy, Scott, there was also always so much joy, most of the time anyway."

"I remember both in equal portions," he said.

"Now you're just being an ornerykins for no reason," she said. "Why do you want to spoil everything? Tell me, did you watch me the whole time? Would you like to grade my form, and were you jealous thinking of me in the water naked with that handsome man?"

"You weren't naked."

"How can you be so sure? I might have been, I wanted to be, I love swimming naked in the water."

"With strange, handsome men?"

"Don't forget naked."

"I noticed."

"And why not?" she said. "He's no threat to you. If I didn't love you, he might be, but I do love you so, and haven't any interest in men like him. Tell me, have you found my note yet?"

What on earth could she be talking about? He stopped himself, making sure not to let ire creep into his voice.

"Zelda, your mind's too quick for me just now. Please slow down. Did you write me a note, and if so, when? While we were in the church? Are you aware that you never gave it to me?"

She laughed, twisting her head so that he could see the pleasure she took in his confused ignorance. She was eager for questions. This appetite for mystery or whatever it was alarmed him.

"Now that we're on a beach discovered by me, ready to have a picnic lunch, we really are living so idyllically, don't you think." She was trying to get everything back at once. "There's no reason for it to change, unless, of course, you spoil my day by not remembering the note."

"Zelda, you never gave me a note."

"How can you be so sure?"

Then he understood—she had passed the note to him in secret somehow. He began to search the outer pockets of his sport coat, rifling through the torn wrappers of chocolate bars, fumbling through pills, moving the search to inside pockets, plumbing his fingers down along the sides of the flask, unable to extract it for fear Zelda might notice, almost certain, though, that there was nothing else in the pocket. When he started in on his trousers, she let out a wicked laugh and he began to retrace his steps. His journal, of course. He pulled the Moleskine from the opposite breast pocket, cracking the binding to the most recent entry, where he discovered a piece of green stationery neatly creased in squares. He unfolded the stationery—her Salud de Schiaparelli floating up, that fragrance she'd asked him to procure for her only last year—to reveal a bold, unruly script, the rolling loveliness of the alphabet under her sway.

"Not here," she said, and he looked up to see Maryvonne and Aurelio striding up the beach toward them, the Spaniard still nude. "Please, Scott," she implored him, "you can't read it in my presence—have you no sense of etiquette?"

"Apparently not," he said. "Otherwise I'd most certainly be naked by now."

"That would be delightful," she said. "But don't say anything to make him self-conscious."

Aurelio stood before them, dangling his shorts from his fingers, lamenting that they had forgotten towels. Maryvonne ran back to one of the horses to grab the blanket, asking where she should spread it for the picnic.

"Near the trees," Zelda said. "We could use some shade after all the riding."

Scott wished the Spaniard would put some godforsaken clothes on. His skin was grayish white in the sunlight, his wine-blue veins running like dark rivulets beneath the surface of his fine limbs. Scott couldn't help but lower his eyes to the man's privates, the stem thick, purplish, and dormant, dangling over testicles that rounded into a bulbous pouch, the genitalia resembling nothing so much as a heart and an aorta, the body's most essential muscle exposed. He couldn't look away—that is, until he noticed the mangled right thigh, the bone-white, ridged lines where the shrapnel had torn into flesh and muscle, the scar in the shape of a country such as Chile, widening in the middle but narrowing again at the tips. Only when Aurelio detected Scott gaping at the scar did he turn away and walk up the beach; and, thankfully, by the time he rejoined the party on the blanket under the tree, he wore shorts that mostly covered his wound.

They lunched on salt-cured olives and baguettes onto which Zelda and Maryvonne laid slices of chorizo or cured Cuban ham, topped with a pungent local cheese. Scott could stomach no more than a few bites of his sandwich. No surprise there. He could rarely eat anything until evening. He was grateful, though, for the wine. It was a Torres dry white, which Aurelio retrieved from the shaded rivulet where he'd stashed the bottles on arrival, the wine cool and crisp, fruity and apple-heavy, its texture soft on the palate. Apparently, it was the only Spanish wine worthy of mention, the owner of the winery loyal to the Republican Army. Both Aurelio and Zelda praised the sandwiches, Aurelio devouring a second made for him by his wife, Zelda picking at Scott's after finishing her own. When the Spaniard fell asleep on the blanket, Maryvonne expressed the desire to take a stroll along the beach and explore the crag, asking if Zelda or Scott cared to join her.

"You go ahead, Scott," Zelda said. "I've seen it and will only want to dive off again."

"What will you do?"

"Sit in the sun and read my novel."

So he walked up the white-sanded beach with the taciturn Frenchwoman, feeling Zelda's eyes on him, fearful lest she get it in her head that he'd planned for any of this.

"You and your wife are lovers still, yes, no, sometimes?" the young woman asked in French. He found the question strange but did not let on. It was only that sometimes, she explained, he and Zelda acted like strangers or newlyweds, not like people who'd known each other a long time. He became winded during the ascent, felt his heart aching, a hollow pain in the center of his chest, and she studied him with a concern steeped in the knowledge of illness.

"Ah, the Caribbean Sea," she exclaimed, stopping short to

take in the view to the south, letting him rest. It was magnificent, she said, the first time ever she had laid eyes on it.

When they started again she lost her footing and he caught her elbow, preventing her from falling.

"You are a man loved by many women," she said.

He couldn't figure out why she said it, but he remembered another woman uttering that same phrase—not Zelda, not Sheilah, who was it who'd spoken those very words to him?

"So you and your wife are lovers, yes?"

Again, there was more to the question than the simple if wildly inappropriate interest in how often he had sex with his wife.

"She is everything to me," he said in clean, pithy French.

"Le monde entier," she said, repeating his phrase. "But of course, this is never in doubt." She returned to French for emphasis. *"Cela n'a jamais eté en doute."*

Now they were on the tip of the promontory, and as the wind rose and fell he removed his hat. When it was up, the wind whipped her words out to sea, and all he could hear was the flap of her blouse or his jacket lapels. Wisps of his thin hair fell into his eyes, and the young woman flushed above the line of her narrow, elegant jaw, her eyes tearing and bright, the color of the sky itself. He hadn't realized until that moment that he was attracted to her.

"It is pride," she was saying, à propos of nothing, referring to Aurelio's conduct earlier. "The wound is *una vergüenza,"* she continued. "In French the feeling is not so strong as in Spanish. What does English say for this? Dishonor?"

"Shame," Scott suggested.

"It is also a strong word?"

"It can be pretty strong," Scott said.

"And what must one do to become free of shame?"

"It is a losing battle," Scott said.

He looked into her eyes, full of understanding, and believed she was someone he might take into his confidence, as he'd done with any number of women over the past decade, always in intense episodes, in liaisons dependent on drink, charisma, confession. She too would fall for him if he let her, the nurses always did, always trained nurses and actresses. He couldn't remember why he grouped them, but in his experience women from either profession found his story hard to resist: invalid on the mend, sinner in remission, someone fearless in the face of indignity. With nurses, he supposed, it was that having seen men so often in distress, the facade of manliness crumbling, they were drawn to vulnerability again and again.

As they headed back along the shoreline for the blanket, he worried that Zelda might detect a change in him. He kept watch on his wife in her broad-rimmed straw hat as she pretended to be lost in the pages of a novel, now and then lifting her chin to glance up the beach toward Scott and Maryvonne, whose hand rested on his forearm.

"You were gone a long time," she said, eyes on the page, too immersed in what she was reading to extricate herself just yet.

"He sleeps the entire time?" Maryvonne asked, eyeing her husband.

"Unless he's faking," Zelda said.

"I am awake," Aurelio said from the blanket, his hat pulled down over his brow and nose so that the brim danced ever so slightly on his lips as he spoke.

"I had no idea," Zelda proclaimed, springing to her feet, recoiling from the blanket. "Were you awake the whole time?"

It was impossible to gauge how disturbed she was by the idea of his lying there feigning sleep while she read. She drew close to Scott, resting her hand flat against his chest.

"Dearest Dodo," she whispered to him, "was the walk invigorating?"

"The wind was strong on the promontory, but otherwise it was quite relaxing."

"She's good company," Zelda said softly, gesturing toward the Frenchwoman. "Don't I choose well? May I borrow her for a few minutes?"

"I didn't know we were rationing."

"Don't be that way," Zelda said, her breath heavy on his cheek as she hooked Maryvonne by the arm while still addressing Scott. "Do you remember the interview you granted that newspaper in Kentucky oh so many years ago, the first to tag me the original for your flappers, what you told the journalist when he asked you to describe me?"

"That you were charming, the most charming person I'd ever met."

"It's true," she said, brushing a leaf slowly from the front of Maryvonne's blouse. "That's what he said, and yet when the journalist asked my husband to continue, when I said go ahead and tell the readers what you really think of me, he wouldn't say anything else. He couldn't list any examples of my reputed charms. Imagine that—if somebody's supposed to be the most charming person in the world, you'd think you could name a few of her charming traits."

"Not everybody finds the same things are charming," Maryvonne reasoned. "Perhaps your husband, he finds you charming no matter what you do."

"Didn't I tell you we would like her, Scott," Zelda boasted, turning now to confide in Maryvonne. "Scott is hard and slow to please, but I can see from the way you two were promenading, arms interlinked, that we'll all soon be fast friends. Let's you and I walk in a direction no one else has gone."

By the time Maryvonne and Zelda returned from the walk, something had been decided. Zelda spoke of the day's itinerary as incomplete. Next she claimed the gelding for herself, announcing that Maryvonne would ride with her, a change in the rotation.

If that's all there is to the secret, Scott said to himself, I'll consider myself fortunate.

"The only question is who takes the old nag this time," Zelda said.

"Stop calling her that, would you?" Scott said, rubbing the nose of the black mare, aware that he sounded annoyed and was in fact annoyed, though not so much about the horse.

"It's decided, then," she said, handing the reins of the palomino to Aurelio. "My husband is incurably romantic, always taking the side of the downtrodden."

Immediately Zelda and Maryvonne rode ahead, prodding the gelding into a full trot.

"Should we chase them?" Aurelio asked.

"They won't get far."

"Are you sure?"

"One is never sure with Zelda, which is how she prefers it."

Most likely Aurelio wanted to see if he could get the palomino to outrun the gelding, but was holding back to be polite.

"I do not know that I have met a woman so daring. She would daunt many soldiers beside which I fight in Spain."

From time to time the bay gelding would gallop toward them, its triangular head bobbing in perfect syncopation, the small heads of the two women tucked low behind it, Maryvonne peering over Zelda's shoulder so she too might enjoy the rush of wind, the horse pulling up in a din of snorts and hoofbeats, Zelda looking down at Scott from the taller horse.

"Remember the wisteria in Montgomery? How you said it always reminded you of me wherever you were, also the sycamores and the gothic willows by the river, the one which drooped so low with branches and foliage thick like stage curtains? I suggested we might spend a whole day inside there kissing and doing whatever we wanted and no one would ever find us, but still it was exciting to think they might, if they tried hard enough."

"I was enchanted," Scott said.

She rode off and when next she returned she brought up one of her thousand witticisms. Though it was difficult to remember her own words exactly, she could summarize the basic idea. It involved an especially stunning riposte offered to John Peale Bishop or Edmund Wilson.

"I believe that's already in a story," he replied.

"Oh, yes, well, I'll think of others."

He was still trying to track the first episode of which she spoke. For the life of him he couldn't remember when it had taken place. It stirred in him a desire to kiss her beneath a willow tree. Most likely she had wished for it to stir in him the desire to kiss her beneath a willow tree.

His wife turned the gelding sharply and Maryvonne yelped involuntarily, but Zelda steadied the horse without event, again heading off down the beach, this time with Aurelio giving chase. Zelda cocked her head over her shoulder, light glancing off her auburn hair as she crouched low to welcome the competition. Scott made a few halfhearted attempts to get the mare to pick up her pace, but she wasn't in a hurry and neither was he, in all honesty, so he settled for keeping the others in view.

After they disappeared on the horizon, he began to lose track of time. The beach stretched monotonously before him. His head swayed from too much alcohol and activity, his thoughts heavy like the rhythmic footfalls of the horse, the sand beneath him dizzying as it ran uphill into palms, brush, and timid forest. He let the mare wander down to a dune sprouting grass, and only after she stooped to feed for several minutes did he jerk the reins to lead the horse along the shoreline and enjoy the splash of kick-back as she trod through softly rolling peaks of breaking tide.

After a while he came upon a mansion in the Spanish Colo-nial style so popular in the Caribbean basin, with high white stucco walls and green-tiled roofs, their extended eaves creating shadowed overhangs. The molding above the main floor served as the balustrade of a balcony decorated with symmetrically rounded forms reminiscent of an old mission. It was straight out of the sudden proliferation of architectural styles along the Great Neck waterfront during the 1920s boom, the exact kind of estate in which his Gatsby (if only he were still alive, or real, for that matter) would choose to live. Scott couldn't remember having passed the building earlier. From Hicacos Point to Club Kawama was more or less a direct line, there was no way to have gone so far astray, and yet somehow he'd done just that.

His head was swimming: how was this possible, goddamnit?

The very thought of pivoting and trekking back in search of his mistake exhausted him. Sweating in the sun, he could feel beads trickling along his chest and belly, his vision bleary. He sim-mered with low-order rage at Zelda. Why did she always have to turn everything into an adventure? He pulled the reins taut, riding on for several minutes, preparing to turn the mare around and re-trace his route, when he caught sight of the palomino underneath a date palm a few hundred yards on, the Frenchwoman alone in the saddle. Why was she on the palomino instead of her spouse? And where were Zelda and the bay gelding?

He dug his heels into the mare's ribs, pulling up on the reins at the same time, and she neighed and reared, but when he instead slapped the reins on the withers, she fell into a gallop for the first time all day, Scott now sprinting toward the emergency that was always awaiting him, the latest episode in a long history of catastrophes. Maryvonne called to him across the beach and he knew what she would say, that Zelda had been careless and injured herself, that she had wildly attempted to clear a hurdle of some sort and been thrown forward off the gelding as it jumped, crashing to the ground and breaking her neck. Except if that were true, why was Maryvonne unharmed? He tried to fit the pieces together, factoring in Zelda's talent for soliciting her own ruin. Meanwhile, a Frenchwoman he'd met only yesterday, with whom he'd flirted during a walk on the beach earlier this afternoon, was shouting at him, her voice like orchestral timpani above the percussive trollop of hooves so that at first he couldn't make the words out. Those sibilant, strung-together sentences sounding like mere babble, until he realized that she was calling to him— "Slow down," she cried in French. "Scott, slow your horse," she exclaimed. "No need for urgency, there's no misfortune here. Zelda is fine."

10

WITH HER ALMOND-SHAPED EYES NARROWED, HER WIDE, SEN-
suous mouth wearing an expression of concern,
Maryvonne asked, "She is unwell?" He was glad it was
she who used that word, not him, still shamed by the panic of seeing
this strange woman alone under the date palm as he rode toward
her on the black mare.

Zelda and Aurelio had gone ahead into the village in search
of the old gypsy woman, Maryvonne choosing to wait on Scott in
case he couldn't locate the road from the beach, though Zelda assured her it was unnecessary. Her husband would know where
to find her. He was like a bloodhound, she couldn't shake him if
she tried. Still, Maryvonne decided, if she were on a slow horse,
left behind by her party, she would want someone on the lookout
for her.

Riding beside this handsome man with his wispy golden locks
splayed on a sun-reddened face, with his thin lips and diamond-
shaped jaw, their horses funneling between the low cabins and
thatched-roof cottages, she didn't pry into his dread thoughts, but
asked only, "How long?"

"Since the first breakdown? Ten years."

"It is difficult on you."

"The costs you mean? Not insurmountable," he said, downplaying the history of illness, finding composure in his gravity. "It's put a strain on our livelihood, but I could never place her in less than capable hands. Once she asked me to stow her in a public asylum because she was afraid she was ruining everything she touched, myself, our daughter, our future but also our past—it was one of those periods when she couldn't fight the illness—but I got her out of hospitals in New York and Baltimore, away from doctors who were only making matters worse, and I found her the best care I could, down South, in warm weather where she could be outdoors year round. Sometimes over these last two years it has seemed as though we might win, as though she might come all the way back."

"You hold yourself responsible." Maryvonne spoke slowly in English, choosing her words carefully. "There are people who never forgive themselves for the misfortunes of loved ones."

"I should have read the signs earlier," he replied. His glinting steely eyes made him seem stubborn but not altogether hard. "Maybe then it wouldn't have been so bad."

"You have done much. Even I can see this from outside, from the way she speaks of you with gratitude. Also never forget how strong she is. It is the experience I have when I find Aurelio wounded."

Thankful for her kind words, he feared he was saying too much, his tongue loosened by sun and worry, but also by the exultation of having been spared the worst yet again. His self-accusations felt formulaic. He'd said these things too many times: to Bunny Wilson, Gerald Murphy, and others who could remember Zelda from better days. But such friends were few and far between, and he saw them rarely. Instead he confided in strangers, incanting for some woman who reminded him of Zelda the grim play-by-play of the past decade, typically over drinks, sometimes as a prelude to bedding her. The new woman might console him, her pity permissible, even desirable, but as soon as she started in on Zelda, saying, "Poor dear," or "It must be awful," barely skimming the surface of his wife's sufferings, he recoiled in disgust. He vowed a dozen times never to speak of it to anyone again, and when sober stuck admirably to his resolution, stiff lipped, withdrawn, stoical.

"Please, no more talk of our history," he said to Maryvonne. "Sometimes I think she could leave it all behind if there was no one to remind her of it."

"By which you mean yourself."

"Yes," he said, admiring her astuteness. "I suppose I do."

They held the horses in a trot, riding beyond the church into the small square where hours earlier there had been the bustle and squalor of a market, but now they encountered only lonely stalls, stray crates of produce stacked in the dirt lanes waiting to be loaded into the bin of a rusted pickup truck parked in the shade of a banyan tree. After dismounting the mare, he stood below Maryvonne, offering his shoulder. Her foot in the stirrup, she swung the other leg over the arch of the palomino's hindquarters, then shuffled her hand from the saddle to Scott's shoulder, freeing herself from the stirrup to swing pendulum-like into him as he caught her by the waist, her cheek brushing against his chin.

Zelda came running toward them.

"Isn't it exciting?" She pointed to Aurelio in front of a hut, towering over the small elderly woman from earlier that day. "She wants to read my cards, but here's the weird part. We rode into town straight for the church, and she was at this post calling to us that she knew I'd be passing at this hour. Isn't that wonderful?"

"It is what she might say," Maryvonne suggested, "even if she, how does one say—"

"Happened to be there by accident," Scott said.

"I expect this from you, Scott," Zelda said, before rotating in a dancer's quarter turn to cast reproach on the Frenchwoman. Now she inserted her arm into the nook of Maryvonne's folded elbow, the sleeve of her dress dragging so that the naked skin of their forearms touched. "But you and I agreed to this plan, Maryvonne."

"I am not disagreeing now," Maryvonne said amicably. "For all I know, it is a meeting with providence, *vraiment,* truly."

Like many lapsed Catholics, Scott was uneasy about the occult. In Asheville he had enjoyed the companionship of a palmist named Laura Guthrie. It was Laura whose words he had been remembering earlier, it now occurred to him, in response to Maryvonne's compliment, Laura, head wrapped in a turban, set up in a corner of the Grove Park Inn to read the fortunes of wealthy guests and predict the good things that lay ahead, declaring as she held his wrist and ran a finger along the lines of his palm, "It's true your adversities have been many, but I can assure you of this. There will always be women, many women drawn to you for years to come. It will sometimes be hard for you to choose." More flattery than divination, her words gave off the scent of practiced flirtation. Her inability to pick up on Zelda's illness or his devotion to her convinced him that Laura's otherworldly insights amounted to nothing more than parlor tricks, so he had returned in the evening to ask her to dine with him.

But the old Cuban woman was different. Her irises streaked yellow like Murano glass beads and the taut silver strands of hair pulled beneath a garish headscarf made him wonder if she could access a realm he didn't believe in and didn't especially wish to hear from.

"Zelda, this is silly," he said as they approached the hut, she on one forearm, Maryvonne on the other. At this angle his wife's face looked gaunt and austere and he could discern the gentle line of rippled scarring along her jaw from the eczema. She had that faraway look she used to get in Paris, then later at Ellerslie, when she set herself against the opponents of her desire. He was only the most obvious of them, for not believing in her talent for ballet, for not helping her chart a professional course while she was young, and the defeats yielding only slowly to growth might have been easier to bear. There were other opponents of her desire: her family, for underestimating her; any woman (actress, painter, writer) who might be perceived as competition, for presenting as more accomplished than she; lastly, the dance itself, for being alluring and so often beyond her.

And her willingness to beat up her body until every muscle in her legs was pulled, twisted, or deformed—her thighs reeking of the muscle oil she rubbed into them religiously, those thighs always in such pain that even while she slept her legs twitched and convulsed beside him in bed at night—well, how could you interpret that except as some way of paying him back for his doubts? She would exorcise all the demons of wasted youth at once, memories in which she was the spirit of an era incarnate, beautiful, frivolous, marvelously irresponsible, promiscuous yet loyal, experimental in action and opinion, always full of wit. She would sculpt her fine muscled body until it was an instrument of the dance and nothing else. Hardly sleeping, practicing six to eight hours a day, she spent the rest of her time worrying about mistakes made at rehearsal, what she needed to do to improve, whether improvement was even possible. The ballet not so much art as proving ground. All the many steps and maneuvers still beyond her, the heights she couldn't attain on her leaps, the latest loving reprimand from her taskmaster Madame Egorova, were obstacles to be surmounted. She talked endlessly about her limits, doubting she could overcome them; and he failed the test every time, saying it wasn't necessary to surpass any limits, she had no one to prove herself before, no one was watching. "You're just afraid I might actually have talent," she would cry out. "You want to harvest my brilliance, charms, and free-associative thoughts for yourself, so you can churn out stories about useless girls with potential, but God forbid one of us gets into the ring with you. Then you have to put me in my place. What you're really afraid of is that I might be as good as you are."

He had never believed in her, she would sometimes say. He had underestimated the diversity of her talents, for painting, for conversation and writing, for dance, riding, and sports of almost any kind. Every criticism he'd ever made of her, mostly while angry and provoked, was an excuse to do whatever the hell she wanted. No regard for his opinion. No worries about the cost to their love affair. Never a pang about the dereliction of her duties as mother or wife. Ballet was an opportunity to rebel against every choice made under the influence of her husband and their disaster of a marriage.

"Okay, let's get on with this," Scott said, distrusting the urgency of his wife's latest desire but seeing no way to deter her. "It's not real, though. It's just voodoo superstition mixed with effrontery, the bravado of performance."

"Then what are you so afraid of? Let me have my fun."

The levity of her tone made it seem that he was making too much of it. All she wanted, for Christ's sake, was to consult a palmist or tarot reader and have her fortune told.

"I go to a clairvoyant all the time in Asheville, as do several of the other women. I learn all sorts of things about you and your mysterious double life in Hollywood, since you're so hush-hush about which films you work on, how your new novel is coming, what you do at night with the women who fall in love with you."

Modestly, Maryvonne retreated one step, then another, before Scott caught her by the wrist, dragging her forward to demonstrate that he had nothing to hide.

"Ask her how much for two women," Scott instructed Aurelio, and the Spaniard, standing in the wings for much of the conversation, now took up negotiations, letting the clairvoyant name a price, then shaking his head.

"Scott, I wish to go alone," Zelda whispered, her face averted from the Frenchwoman.

"But I thought the idea was for the two of you to visit the clairvoyant together," he protested. "Wasn't that the great secret you were keeping on the beach?"

Zelda laughed in that way she had of finding her own antics preposterous yet amusing.

"I also wish," Maryvonne interjected, "for my fortune to be read."

"You can wait your turn and get a reading after me," Zelda said sharply. "I don't want anyone listening to my secrets."

"But your Spanish is not very good," Maryvonne said, "and this divining ancient woman will not speak English."

It was impossible to argue the point.

"Then we'll go together," Zelda sighed, "but only tell her what I tell you to tell her, and only ask questions when I say so."

Scott pulled out his wallet and Aurelio did the same, but Scott waved him off. "No, allow me. It's my wife's crazy idea, so the least I can do is shell out the cash."

"What if she says something I don't wish to hear, Scott?" Zelda asked suddenly.

"Well, that's easy enough to solve," he said, shooting her a severe look, trying to get a handle on her state of mind. "You don't have to go inside in the first place."

"Don't be a high hat, Scott, and don't be so cowardly. Perhaps my fortunes will have changed," she said lightly. "Besides, what hazard can a clairvoyant predict that we haven't already encountered? If she says anything unpleasant, I'll tell her to move on, a good strategy, don't you think—I won't let her say anything I don't want to hear."

Zelda parted the red serge curtains to slip into the old woman's lair, Maryvonne starting after her.

"Is it too much to ask you to keep an eye on her?" he said in a hushed voice.

Maryvonne didn't reply right away, her chin bowed.

"Don't worry yourself about it," he said, half taking back the request but not quite. "All you must do, please, if the old witch says anything ominous, water it down in translation."

"What is 'water down'?" Maryvonne asked.

"Tell a lie, *dire un mensonge*," he said, raising his thumb and index finger as if holding a delicate pearl between them. "A few small lies, kindnesses really."

Flipping through his billfold, he extracted a wad of American dollars, reminding himself of the exchange rate, knowing the amount he held was too large and trying to whittle it down. In the midst of his calculations, the old woman snatched the cash from his fingers.

"Sí, sí, el dinero americano es bueno," she said and their negotiations came to an end. The extra money, Scott decided, might motivate her to tell a kinder fortune.

Showing a full set of sandstone-colored teeth, the clairvoyant identified a ramshackle bodega beyond the market, saying *"Una hora"* several times amid a warble of Spanish words, alternately eyeing each man, then flapping her wrists out from the waist to chase them off.

"She say we can wait over there. The drinks are good, she promise us," Aurelio said, "and they will be on me."

The old woman put her hand on Maryvonne's waist, herding her into the hut.

Scott foresaw the tall glass of Bacardi rum waiting for him at the bodega. He was exhausted, as though he'd spent a long day under deadline on the studio lot, running between his office and that of some director who kept arbitrarily reversing course on a script. Only he wasn't at work, he was on holiday, and you weren't supposed to feel this worn out by the pursuit of leisure.

Not twenty feet down the road, Aurelio at his side, Scott heard the scuttle of footsteps behind them. Before he could turn she put her warm, soft hand to his neck, thanking him—for his patience, for doting on her impulses. "I know I'm taking advantage, but I'm having a lovely time and you're so tolerant. Scott, this year is going to be different," Zelda said. "It's going to be a good year for us, for money, for so many other things. I just need to hear the clairvoyant say it, then I'll know it's true."

"But Zelda, dear, don't put too much trust in—"

"That's not why I ran back, though," she said. "While riding on the beach earlier, while outracing everyone, I was flooded by memories and I almost forgot to tell you, it couldn't wait until after. About the dollhouse I made for Scottie that one Christmas, a perfect replica of our house at Ellerslie, curtains in all its windows sewn from the same fabric as the curtains hanging from the windows of that three-storied, high-ceilinged Greek Revival mansion we were living in, do you remember, also, the furniture carved from fine woods with seats wrapped and stapled in leather, the bookshelves in your tiny study made from oak, the perfect miniature of your writing desk, also the figurines for each of us, me, you, Scottie. Did you forget about that?"

"I hadn't thought of it in a long while," he admitted, looking to his left to gauge whether Aurelio was listening.

"You see," she said. "You never remember my charming qualities. But you won't forget that story again, will you, Scott?"

"Never," he said.

"Is it gone?"

He wasn't sure what she meant.

"The dollhouse? Is it gone?"

He thought it might be in storage in Baltimore. If she wished for him to do so, he would check someday soon.

She smiled, pleased to have their disagreement resolved so simply. She didn't want there to be any hard feelings between them, not when she was about to allow the old fisherwoman to trawl her soul and see what the future held.

Maryvonne wasn't sure what Scott's request required of her. Did he mean for her to betray Zelda's trust? She didn't think she could dupe this savvy woman even if she tried. Also, it felt like a favor you might ask of a friend of many years, not someone you had met a day ago. Slowly she had begun to reconsider her early impressions of this dazzling, presumptuous, and desperately isolated couple.

"If God came down and gave him the choice tomorrow," Zelda ruminated, expecting Maryvonne to translate, "which would my husband choose: a long life by my side in which we could finally make each other happy or a bestselling, Pulitzer Prize–winning—oh, never mind, I know the answer to that."

Maryvonne stopped mid-translation, holding a finger up to the divining woman, telling her to wait a minute, that wasn't what they wanted to ask after all.

"Zelda," she said in English, "you need to go slowly, please, and decide what you want to know. We are confusing her."

"Is she a gypsy?"

"You want me to ask her that?"

"I suppose not," Zelda said. "But what's your opinion?"

The woman handed Zelda the deck of cards and instructed her to shuffle them. Zelda cut the deck, nervously folding the two halves into each other until they merged, then splitting and joining them again, no longer chatting, no longer asking questions. Maryvonne took mental notes: the shifts in mood, the sudden lapsing from childish exuberance to dread. Receiving the deck from Zelda, the divining woman began to flip cards face up and lay them on the table, while Zelda, chattering nervously once more, also nibbling on her nails, strained to follow the hands of the old woman rather than the cards on the table, as though policing a poker player she suspected of dealing from the bottom of the deck. The old woman looked up and spoke sharply.

"She say the questions will come later," Maryvonne explained.

"Let her do it her way, then," Zelda said, "but I don't want to yield all control."

The divining woman flipped nine cards onto the table, structuring them in a V facing herself, a mountain peak from the perspective of Zelda and Maryvonne sitting opposite her.

"Is the card upside down according to whether it's facing me or her?" Zelda asked.

Maryvonne recognized the major arcana cards right away, the Fool in first position, the Death card reversed in the third position, the Hermit and the Lovers also reversed. Though no expert in tarot, she knew enough to discern that the minor arcana cards weren't much more promising. Zelda cursed the Fool. Also she didn't approve of the card in the far corner nearest to her, the shrouded figure, familiar from past readings. She always got dealt that card. No matter what she did, he shadowed her.

The old woman closed her eyes and moved her hands in the air over the deck. She demanded complete silence, and when she opened her lids halfway, you could see her eyes rolling from side to side like marbles in a confined space, until at last she began to incant the lessons of the spirits, her cadence monotonous and solemn like that of monks saying matins.

"She say you are far away from most people you care for and you have closed your heart. So much spirit and energy and confusion. It is for many years, all this confusion, she has rarely seen so much confusion in a deck. You have known great sorrow, sometimes greater joy, which you need to let come again because sorrow, she is winning."

"When can I ask questions?" Zelda whispered, but the woman did not lower her eyes, continuing in a steady drone.

"She say the cards speak of travel, many trips. Do you want me to interrupt her?"

"Not yet, I suppose."

"She says, the travel does not satisfy, it is not what you want. Your love is always running away from you."

"Ask her why the Fool came up first."

Maryvonne posed the question, but after falling silent for a few seconds, without ever lowering her eyes to them, the clairvoyant resumed her slow chant.

"New beginnings," Maryvonne said in French because she had fallen behind and could no longer retrieve English words quickly enough, "hope, your life without limits, you must leave something behind." Then in English: "What is behind you is hard to escape, but you are a decided woman."

"I need her to slow down," Zelda said. "It's too much, all at once."

The old woman, the yellow streaks of her irises set against burnt-sienna skin, the lines around her eyes channels of wisdom, punched out a phrase, *"Los demonios del pasado,"* as though re-buking a child for interrupting in class. Zelda's demons were real, the old woman insisted, and she must turn and face them. *"Usted siente que no puede escapar de ellos."*

"You fear the past and it chases you," Maryvonne summa-rized, again in French.

"What does that mean? Is she saying it's just my imagination?"

Maryvonne posed the question and the woman flipped three cards: the Star in reverse, the Moon, the High Priestess in reverse. Again the diviner stared at the deck in silence, this time looking up at Zelda with awe, before again shutting her eyes to prophesy.

"What did she say?" Zelda asked, and Maryvonne realized she hadn't yet translated.

"You are attuned to the spiritual world. You know things before you must know them. This frightens you, but it is only knowledge. You are stronger than those who tell you otherwise."

The old woman pressed on, her tone now chastising, now encouraging. A loved one, someone whose name was supposed to be large in the world, was self-destructive. Also perhaps quite ill. "This is not your worst moment, I'm sorry," Maryvonne said in numbed imitation. "A strong feeling here that all is not well, things are not as they appear, your life constructed of mirrors. You keep asking someone to reflect you, he asks the same of you, but why can not you trust yourself?"

Maryvonne decided to omit the part about a man who adores her but cannot love her as she deserves to be loved. She was try-ing to decide how much of the reading, if any, to share with Scott.

"You know each other intimately because of crisis," Maryvonne continued. "In the proximate future, you feel betrayed and old resentment returns, but this is where she cannot under-stand your choices. You need to be kind to yourself, not keep everyone far away."

Again the old woman spoke of a loved one who was ill and Maryvonne translated sparingly because she couldn't lie outright; the gravity of the diviner's tone gave too much away.

The diviner kept saying, "I am sorry to tell you this," and Maryvonne asked her to be precise, did she mean Zelda's husband, did she mean Scott?

"Who is it?" Zelda demanded, mustering all the authority she could. "One of you isn't telling me something."

"She say again you already know."

"If I already know," Zelda replied curtly, "what did I come here for?"

Outside the bodega two villagers prepped gamecocks, squaring them off so that the birds could preen and strut, wings pluming magnificently. The first of the villagers, his skin rough and grooved like tree bark, slashed a smile showing as many missing or broken-off teeth as whole ones; and the second, diminutive, stocky, with a round face and a pug nose, did not look up. The handlers hovered behind their birds as the adversaries stalked one another, the black gamecock now pressing its powerful neck as a lever onto the neck of the other, its rival now pushing off and raising its wings like a cape before lunging forward again, leading with its terrific talons. Each handler, allowing his bird to peck its opponent never more than once or twice, would then scoop it up from beneath with one hand, covering its eyes, shielding it from its rival. The birds' beaks were tied shut with string, and after taking the gamecock into his arms each handler would coddle his bird, primping feathers, stroking its clipped and stubbled comb, caressing its throat. Soon, though, the men had replaced the birds on the ground, squaring them off, not having to wait even a few seconds for the cocks' instinctive hatred of each other to kick in.

"Training exercises," Aurelio explained. Even a bird that had killed many opponents must be kept fresh. The handlers put him through exercises to make sure the reflexes stayed sharp, that the bird hadn't lost any of his braggadocio, his will to dominate, his impulse to kill. "I will tell you that the slick black one is veteran of many fights. Notice how he props his chest, how big he makes himself, how high off the ground he leaps. Is ready to strike, knowing already what damage he can do. This one," he pointed to the other bird, "is a *novicio*. It is difficult to tell—does he have talent for killing, does he not?"

Scott asked his friend how you could distinguish one type from the other, whether you could instill talent for the fights in all gamecocks.

The handler with the barklike skin shot a quick glance at Aurelio, addressing him in a swath of peasant Spanish from which Scott could make out few if any words. It was always so much harder to understand a foreign tongue as spoken by the lower classes.

"Any cock will fight," Aurelio said, answering Scott's question, "but many birds, they must die during the first fight, and maybe they are meant to die. It is not in them, the know-how to fight. It is true also with soldiers. Any man can die on a battlefield, brave man or coward, it make no difference. But some men, I can tell you which ones, must die in their first battle. In them the instincts are wrong."

"Let's have that drink," Scott said. The late afternoon sun was strong on his forehead, his back stiff from the riding.

"Los gallos de pelea son bellos," Aurelio congratulated the men, then to Scott, "Handsome birds, I tell them."

Aurelio, propping the door to the bodega ajar with his foot, turned to pose a question to the handlers. Apparently he'd won their trust, for the men answered at once, simultaneously, in a flurry of Spanish.

Inside the bodega a man behind the counter wore a wide-brimmed straw hat over stringy black hair and a poorly manicured beard that made his face resemble an unkempt shrub. Two rows of shelves stacked mostly sinful items, beer, wine, Bacardi rum, cigars, and dozens of varieties of cigarettes. They sat at the nearer of two tables in the establishment, nestled against a four-foot-high ledge running the length of a side wall on top of which a copper-colored oscillating Emerson fan, its aluminum blades in the shape of a yacht propeller, washed his cheek in cool splashes of air.

Aurelio ran through the information the two men had shared with him: who fought cocks on the peninsula, where the fights were held, how to procure an invitation to the fights tomorrow evening.

"You will join me," he said confidently to Scott.

When the Spaniard went to get drinks, Scott tried to distract himself from thinking about what the clairvoyant might even now be saying to his wife. He remembered Zelda's note, which she hadn't allowed him to look at earlier. Extracting the Moleskine from his sport coat, he found the note inside, hardly through the first sentence— *"Dearest Scott, I want you to know how much it means to me to hear you promise to take better care"*—when Aurelio returned.

"Ah, *un billet doux,*" Aurelio said as Scott covered the sheet of green stationery with his forearm, vowing to return to it as soon as he could. The Spaniard set four drinks on the table, two lagers and two Cuba libres, that cocktail of Bacardi, Coca-Cola, and lime named in honor of Cuba's throwing off the yoke of Spain and the United States. He carried two cigars, now biting off the end of his own and striking a match, which he held up to the thick wand of hand-rolled tobacco dangling from his lips. The Spaniard sucked on the near end until concentric rings of orange glowed inside the tip and several pungent clouds drifted across the table, then

he handed the other cigar and a book of matches to Scott. There
was no way to refuse the gift. Scott liked a cigar as much as the
next man, but he wasn't supposed to smoke anymore. Cigarettes
were hard to resist but, like beer, relatively inconsequential. Cigars
were a commitment, signifying everything he was supposed to
have given up by now. He struck the match, dragged on the end
of the cigar, then cupped his mouth into an O, releasing smoke,
feeling a tickle in his throat and a cough erupting from his ster-
num. Head turned to the wall, he held a fist sideways to his mouth
to quell the coughing and its slicing pains.

"Are we to speak of love or war?" Aurelio asked, drink in one
hand, his cigar stabbing at the green stationery on the table. Scott
folded the letter into squares and put it back in the Moleskine to
prevent an ash from scalding Zelda's words.

"War," Scott suggested. One of his favorite subjects. He had
been an officer, second lieutenant in the U.S. Army, during the
Great War, on the verge of being sent overseas when the armistice
was signed. That he never made it over was one of the great regrets of his life.

"A strange regret," Aurelio said.

Scott recalled the Spaniard's horrific-looking wound, his
scrape with death.

"I don't mean to suggest that war is anything less than
devastating," he said. "It's more like the way one feels about an
unpaid debt, and maybe too the writer in me believed it was
something I ought to have witnessed. A confession between you
and me—my publisher bought my first novel on the premise that
any day I was to be shipped out as fodder for the war machine,
one of the millions never to return amid that war's unprece-
dented rate of fatalities, another illustrative case of the might-
have-been."

"You are a writer, then?" Aurelio asked, and Scott realized too late that he had effectively avoided the topic of what he did until now.

"Let's not talk about that," Scott said. He was also a military buff, versed in everything there was to know about the American Civil War, about the strategies of the Great War, about the Battle of Verdun; he knew a great many European wars inside and out.

"It is melancholy to speak of such things," Aurelio admitted.

If he had it to do over again, would he enlist in the Republican cause?

"Of course," the Spaniard said. "This is never the question."

Was he one of the soldiers with correct instincts on a battlefield?

"It is true, you require luck," Aurelio explained, "especially in the beginning. But say a man, he is ready for battle. Well, in that case there are things he can do in the field that others cannot do, things that make him an asset to his battalion." He might prove to be a good shot, he might prove efficient in maneuvering away from a line of fire. During his first battle he might suffer four or five false deaths, those occasions on which without some luck he should have died. By his third battle, though, a man might greatly improve his odds. "Now he understands the game better," the Spaniard maintained. "Improved as a soldier, he moves easier on the field. Deaths surround him, it is true, his own death closes in, but he sees it coming, steps aside. Even when they try to catch him by surprise, he has a play left. To himself a veteran whispers, 'I know the battle so long and so well,' but this is dangerous way of thinking." The trick was to trust what you learned on the field and let the knowledge improve your odds of survival, while yet remaining cautious, never cowardly, but ever cautious.

"Don't believe your own propaganda, you mean?"

"Yes, I like this saying. Now I see why you are a writer."

"Let's not talk about that," Scott insisted, angry at himself for having said anything in the first place. It made the friendship so much less natural.

"Well, yes, then," Aurelio replied. "Never believe you know all there is to know because there is forever something new to learn about war."

Scott couldn't resist removing the Moleskine from his sport coat. Opening the journal, he jotted down Aurelio's phrase, about never trusting oneself too much, about always learning something new on a battlefield.

He took a sip of his drink, its cola sweetness an antidote to the remnant taste of bile at the back of his mouth. The drink's medicinal properties were rather limited. Instead of deadening the nerves, the alcohol fired his frenzied thoughts, making his pulse race, his head feel lighter and lighter. It was a matter of finding the right balance, of reaching the point where the alcohol would quell yesterday's long hangover, the cumulative toll of weeks and weeks of excess. There were days when the calm returned and you felt again in control, as though you no longer had to burrow ever deeper inside alcohol's wondrous alchemy, as though you might take or leave the next drink—but this wasn't one of those days.

He puffed dutifully on the cigar, inhaling the smoke without any enthusiasm for its fragrance. The tobacco mingled on his tongue with the sugar and alcohol, an imbroglio of scents, tastes, forsaken desires. He felt the cough coming in advance this time, pulled out a white monogrammed handkerchief, slightly frayed at the edges, hacking into the linen, feeling the phlegm dislodge in his chest, his cough hollow and barreled, subsiding only to give way to a second fit of violent spasms. When he lowered the handkerchief from his mouth, away from the Spaniard's line of vision, he saw the blood-spangled pattern, dots and splotches here and there. It had been stupid of him to accept the cigar.

"Your lungs are unwell?" Aurelio said with concern. "I am no nurse like my wife, but in a camp men cough day and night, some of them infected with *enfermedad de los pulmones,* tuberculosis, some of them no. You have seen the doctor?"

"Not recently," Scott admitted, not wanting to talk or think about his lungs. He was concerned instead by a man leaning his forearms on the counter near the front of the bodega who appeared to be staring at them. He remembered Zelda at the Pan American terminal in Miami, certain at every turn they were being spied on, and he beat back his own suspicions as implausible.

"Do you see that man there?" Aurelio asked.

Scott looked across the room as if for the first time.

"What about him?"

"He keeps watch on us, no?"

"We're under surveillance, you mean?" Scott said and Aurelio nodded. It occurred to Scott that the Spaniard had his own reasons for paranoia. How had he accounted for his escape from the camp again, his subsequent emigration from France? A contact here in Cuba had played a role, but was it possible Aurelio had entered the country illegally?

"I can't be sure," Scott started to say, when the man pushed off the counter and walked toward them. In an instant Scott recognized him, Señor Famosa García, the pompous yet handsome silver-haired guide hired by Matéo Cardoña to show him Havana. Delighted at first by the coincidence, he studied the elderly Cuban's evenly bronzed face and ghastly milky eye as though registering the features of an old acquaintance, but it wasn't coincidence, of course.

"How do you two know each other?" Aurelio asked.

Famosa García stood above the table, uninvited, Aurelio preparing to rise and chase the man off if Scott didn't want him here.

"May I join you for a minute, Señor Fitzgerald?" Famosa García asked.

"Why not," Scott said.

The dignified emissary took the chair next to Scott and leaned into him as he sat down, whispering into the side of his head that he had a message to convey from Señor Cardoña.

"Not now," Scott replied. "Maybe later at the hotel. We'll have to get you a drink because we're talking of Franco's Spain. What are your views on the triumph of the Fascists?"

Aurelio shifted in his chair uncomfortably.

"Don't worry," Scott said boisterously, perceiving humor in the situation but unable to lay hold of it. "May I introduce Famosa García, who is friends with Matéo Cardoña of the formidable Cardoña family of Santiago de Cuba, not all of whom are enemies of Fascism. But my friend Matéo is a champion of freedom, someone who hates Fascism as much as I do."

Famosa García stiffened at his remarks, maybe because he'd come here on an errand and had to report back to Havana soon and it wasn't his duty to have drinks with Scott, but maybe also because he hated the United States rather more than he hated Fascism.

"Shall we drink to Señor Cardoña and the demise of Fascism?" Scott said, tilting his glass to the messenger, who lifted empty hands to indicate he was in no position to toast friendships or causes.

"Señor Fitzgerald, I am here on specific matters only."

"It will have to wait."

"After all Señor Cardoña has done for you," Famosa García protested coolly, "he deserves this minute of your time, no?"

"No," Scott said. After all he's done for me? he wanted to say. You mean guiding me to an out-of-the-way bar where my wife nearly gets killed but instead watches a man knifed? Do you mean promising to make it go away afterward but then constantly hounding me to report that, well, sadly, it hasn't gone away yet and he must track me through Cuba to remind me of this fact? "Not this minute of time, anyway," Scott added, softening his position, realizing it would be unwise to send Famosa García away carrying such a harsh message.

"Señor Cardoña has done much on your behalf," Famosa García continued, turning again so that he spoke only to Scott. "There is more to say, about the police, about the investigation."

"For now, though," Scott blustered, including his friend Aurelio, "we talk of Spain."

Scott couldn't explain his own recklessness, but he wanted to elicit a confession from the silver-maned Cuban. If you admit your sympathies for the Falangists, he said silently to himself, then and only then will I let you deliver your message.

"Sometimes I am tired of talking of Spain," Aurelio said.

"This man fought and was wounded," Scott said, holding up his drink, tilting it slightly so that rum and soda spilled onto the table like a libation. He didn't require Aurelio to fight his battles for him. Rather he would stick up for his noble friend. "Nearly died in the fight to keep Spain a free republic. I'm sorry to say this in his presence, but he and his men never had a chance, and do you know why? You haven't told me any of this, Aurelio, but you will see that I understand why the war was lost. Let me tell you. Because the Germans and Italians, the united forces of Fascism, controlled the air, because every time a battalion of Republicans seized a strategic position, the planes manned by Mussolini's Blackshirts, all volunteers I'm assured—no violations of the Non-Intervention Pact as far as President Roosevelt could decide—bombarded the trenches until they were as rife with corpses as with able soldiers."

"What of the priests and nuns?" Famosa García asked.

"Excuse me," Aurelio said.

"The Communists killed many bishops, many priests and

monks, many nuns," Famosa García said angrily, announcing his loyalty to the Church and the Spanish crown, refusing to look at Aurelio but instead gazing across the table at Scott. "Did he kill priests and nuns?"

"Never nuns," Aurelio said.

"On land the Republicans might have won the war," Scott continued, suddenly out of his depth. He had suspected Famosa García of harboring Falangist sympathies, but this was more information than he had bargained for. "And in many ways they did win it battle by battle, but the bombing of Madrid, it went on and on, the bombing of children and women never ending. What do you think of the Falangists now?"

Scott glared at Famosa García, no subtlety left in his insinuations.

"Maybe the *yanquis*," Famosa García said after a long silence.

Scott wanted to ask this silver-haired Fascist to step outside, but the man was too old.

"Maybe the government of the United States of America," Famosa García continued evenly, "should have assisted the Spanish Republic as everyone expected them to do."

"Good enough," Scott said, reaching a hand across the table to clasp the shoulder of the refined man with the strong jaw and milky eye, warming to him, or pretending to do so. "Let's drink to that."

Famosa García made excuses to remove himself from the conversation, but Scott said, "Sit, you might learn something," then instructed Aurelio to take them through the logistics of a people's army, how the platoons and battalions worked, how ranks were assigned, who gave the orders.

"It is the same as any army," Aurelio assured him, except the men sometimes weighed in on battalion officers, sometimes rendered votes of no confidence in leadership. This was especially true of the Americans of the Lincoln Battalion, infamous for rotating their crop of leaders, some voted out, others stepping down because they couldn't follow a direct order, others killed in battle, sometimes from incompetence. It was a joke among the Spanish battalions and international brigades, "Who is in charge of the Americans today?"

"Tell us about the day of your injury," Scott said to Aurelio. Famosa García protested that he must be going, and this time Scott didn't prevent him. Only when Matéo's man had departed did the Spaniard ask whether it was wise to have provoked him so, but Scott dismissed the worry, saying it was nothing compared to what Zelda had put the poor man through three days ago.

"She is for sure very dramatic," Aurelio said and Scott pushed his chair back from the table, glowering at the Spaniard. He would fight even this man whom he admired very much, whom he could not possibly defeat, if Zelda's good name was at stake.

"Take it back," he glowered.

"Stay calm, *amigo*." Aurelio took a swig of beer. "I mean no offense. She is free in spirit, braver than most women. Is she stronger than you believe, perhaps stronger even than you?"

Other men might have felt threatened by such a statement, but not Scott. Pleased to hear Zelda receiving her due, he sat again in his chair.

He was trying hard to keep himself in line, but there was something he was afraid of and he didn't yet know what it was. Maybe it was just the damned letter.

"Couldn't you ever go back?" Scott asked, wishing to stop talking of Zelda. He felt awe for the Spaniard, this socialist and Basque nationalist who'd fought so bravely for a homeland to which he might never return.

"My country is lost," Aurelio said sternly.

What if the Americans entered the war against Fascism and defeated Mussolini first, Hitler next, wouldn't Franco fall in the aftermath?

"I give no thought to such matters," he insisted. He was fortunate that his cousin had found him in the camps and married him, otherwise he would not be here drinking with a new friend.

"You admire my wife, no?" Aurelio asked and Scott felt he was being accused of something.

Just then there was a commotion near the entrance, the game-cock handler with bark for skin calling for Aurelio by name, something about a woman outside. Apparently the establishment in which they were drinking wasn't a place for women, at least not proper European women. Maryvonne, defying the ban, bulled into the room as Aurelio sprang from his chair, rushing forward to escort her outside, but she slapped at her cousin's arms, uttering defiant words, sweeping toward the table, there for one reason and one reason only, to speak with Scott.

It was too soon for the clairvoyant's reading to be over and he intuited some dire news. She stumbled to recount what had happened, but he could envision it all too clearly: Zelda running off in the middle of the reading, without explanation, without indication of where she was headed. At first Maryvonne thought her new American friend must have stepped outside for fresh air, certain to return in a minute or two, so she had remained seated across the table from the diviner, the two women staring blankly at each other. It was the old woman who at last announced that the *Americana* wasn't coming back. Maryvonne rose from the table, upsetting the half-interpreted deck of cards, all but floating out the door into the late afternoon, stunned by the light and air. She remembered the bodega where Scott and Aurelio were waiting. Zelda would have gone in search of her husband.

"She did not come here, then?" Maryvonne said.

Aurelio, at a loss for what to say or do, sidled up to the table and clasped his rum drink, eventually lifting it to his lips.

"I am sorry, Scott," Maryvonne was saying. "I was sure she

only needed fresh air, I was sure she would search for you, she has only been missing a short time."

"There will be a simple explanation," Scott said, expert in putting people off the trail of his wife's madness. The task at hand: interrupt the conclusions toward which Maryvonne might be racing. The first rule of every crisis. Control the room, manage rumors, anticipate the things that might get whispered by acquaintances and strangers and make it back to friends, family, their literary circle, the general public at large. After all, it wasn't anyone else's business—this decade-old illness, longer still if you included its genealogy. What people saw, what they believed they saw, wasn't reality. Reality was what they could remember afterward.

He was so calm and convincing that as he watched the spell take hold of Maryvonne and felt her shoulders relax under the steadying pressure of his palms as if he were a priest executing the rite of absolution, he wondered whether he believed anything of what he said. "No need for alarm," he heard himself saying. "In all probability it is nothing."

The initial panic she felt on entering the bodega having lifted, Maryvonne studied Scott. Truly the man was a puzzle. On the beach earlier he had prodded the mare into a dash, worked himself into a state, fretting about what might have happened to his beloved Zelda when nothing had. Now that she'd really gone missing, he took everything in stride.

"This is not unusual," he assured his friends. As a nurse she understood codes of discretion, the sentiments people couldn't express residing inside the words they allowed themselves. "Zelda is an impulsive, spontaneous woman," Scott was saying. "Most likely she headed for the shore, where we'll find her walking barefoot in the runoff of the waves. Or she'll be at the hotel when we return, having gone for a swim. My wife doesn't follow other people's rules. The gypsy woman was an imperious sort and I could tell she would rub Zelda the wrong way."

They toured the deserted, dismantled market in haste, but found no traces of Zelda anywhere. They made inquiries with a few straggling townspeople: no signs of anyone fitting Zelda's description. Next they crossed the road to untie the horses and Scott proposed, reasonably, "We'll retrace our route from earlier, look for her along the beach." Aurelio hastened Maryvonne into the saddle of the palomino, then mounted the bay gelding, leaving Scott with the mare. When they reached the sands at the end of the dirt road, her cousin proposed heading up shore, in the direction of the afternoon's outing. He was obviously unsettled by the entire affair. One of his childhood friends had suffered from nerves in the war, and after a week of heavy bombardment by Mussolini's airplanes woke three consecutive nights in screams, endangering his entire company, which was entrenched a few hundred meters from the enemy. Though fine during the day, brave and business-like, capable of shooting straight and accurately, he lost hold of himself by night. Lack of sleep drained him, the nightmares unrelenting, ever fiercer, until one day the lieutenant in charge of the company ordered Aurelio's friend banished from the front lines. Aurelio didn't believe most of the propaganda about arbitrary executions for desertion, but he never heard from his friend again. Had he escaped from a hospital bed to wander the streets, clothed as a deserter, earning a deserter's cruel end? Had he been assassinated by the enemy or, worse yet, by one of his own comrades?

Aurelio, haunted by memories, needed to be on his own. So he led his horse up the beach on a private reconnaissance mission, leaving Maryvonne to ride beside Scott. Applying pressure to the palomino with her heel, she soon had it cantering to the shore, where the waves were higher and rougher, Scott keeping pace on the mare so that they might cross the sands to explore brush, palms, and thin pine forest, then slash down to the water again, combing the terrain for clues of any sort. The spindrift off the water moist and cool, the temperatures dropping, she examined the western sky, trying to guess how many hours until sunset. Below them a trail of gray-black clouds unfolded like the plume of a forest fire.

While they surveyed the empty beach, Scott interrogated her about what the old woman had said inside the hut, how Zelda had reacted to each cryptic statement. Maryvonne fastened on the last set of cards, trying to recall which three cards the diviner had laid down, in what order.

"The occult details," he said, "are irrelevant to the situation as far as I can see."

"Well, Scott," she replied in French, "your wife flees in the middle of the reading, after the diviner deals those exact cards. It seems it might be important."

"My apologies, I didn't mean to suggest you were unhelpful," he said, again full of gentlemanly charm. Amazing how he could turn it off and on. "Was I terribly rude? That wasn't my intention."

He asked Maryvonne to take him through everything Zelda had heard and seen, trying to figure out what had prompted her flight. So she recounted the denouement of the reading, Zelda asking, "Tell me about the man I have loved my whole life," Maryvonne tracking the unfolding prophecy for her. "Is he faithful?" Zelda asked in a guarded tone. She didn't care if he slept with other women. All she wanted to know was whether an alien affection had taken root in his heart. "He will always love you," Maryvonne said, translating, watering down the diviner's words about a man in the cards who loved two women, whereupon Zelda leveled her accusation: "She is evasive on purpose; she needs to tell me what the cards say." Then the diviner dealt the final three cards—the Devil, nine of cups reversed, the six of wands reversed—and Maryvonne muttered to herself, "Christ."

"Why?" Scott asked.

Well, she explained, a friend in the Red Cross read tarot and had talked to her about cards of illness, blight, and mortality. Those three were dark cards, especially in combination.

"Any other signs?" he asked. "How did she look?"

"One minute she is fine, the next she accelerates—rushes, no?—from the hut."

As he turned his horse away from hers to angle it up the beach, she heard him mutter, "Damnit, Zelda," seeming rather more angry with than worried for Zelda.

The line of stone cabins from the Club Kawama came into view, the beach populated with straw huts, sun umbrellas, and stray late afternoon bathers; and now Aurelio hailed them from behind, his horse advancing in a steady canter.

"No sign of your wife that way, my friend, and I see she is not in your company. Should we notify the authorities?"

Scott blanched at the suggestion, stammering for a second, then with majestic cool began to thank them for their help, assuring them he could handle things from here.

He is lying, Maryvonne thought.

"I've inconvenienced you enough," he said.

"Nonsense," she protested.

"Well, we can return the horses for you," Aurelio said. "One less matter for worrying, and I mean what I say about the cock-fights tomorrow; you must be my gues'."

"Guest," Maryvonne said, correcting her cousin because she was angry with him, hearing that she too failed to hit the *t* on the end of that word in English. Normally Aurelio would have defended himself, but he said nothing, accepting her reproof—first, for his indelicacy in looking forward to tomorrow's outing while Zelda was missing; second, for having made plans with Scott that didn't include her.

11

MOST LIKELY HE EXPERIENCED THE ABSENCE AS LONGER THAN IT was, so he approached the clerk at the front desk, resolving not to let his worry show.

"*Buenas tardes,* Señor Fitzgerald," the clerk greeted him.

"My wife hasn't left word for me?"

"No, *señor,* you are expecting a message?"

"You haven't seen her?"

"*¿Hay algún problema?* Something is wrong?"

"No, no," Scott said. "We must have got our wires crossed in town. I was supposed to meet her, I forget where."

"Mrs. Fitzgerald has not been here," the clerk said as he checked the empty mail slot.

On the cinder path that threaded among the bowing palms to the villa with its red-tiled roof, Scott replayed the past three days in his head, the mistakes, the opportunities for reprieve. He shouldn't have taken her to that bar Saturday night in Havana; he should have reacted more quickly when she was in danger. He should never have allowed Matéo to take charge of their safety. Also, he had been far too lax about the wine and cigarettes, neither of which Zelda was permitted at the Highland, neither of which he was to allow her while on holiday—but once they were out of town he could never enforce the rules set by her doctors. Normally, when she started breaking down, there were warning signs. He had time to catch on and reprimand her, speaking to her at times as to a child. Saying simply: "That's enough." Now and then seizing her (a full-on clash of wills might ensue, objects thrown, slaps exchanged) to lead her home. His gruff tactics drew the attention of their friends, especially in the years before most people had intuited the depths of her illness. Many of their acquaintances accused him of being boorish—you couldn't treat a grown woman that way—but Scott knew from experience that often nothing else worked. Outside the church this afternoon, after he had caught up with her to find her raving about providence, about the words of that damned yellow-eyed clairvoyant, he'd known what to do. But he couldn't bring himself to humiliate Zelda in front of new friends.

He climbed the courtyard stairs, pausing at the door to his room to catch his breath, the tightness in his chest like pangs of regret, the by-product of the afternoon's rush of activity. His brow soaked, he raised the handkerchief to it, blotting the sweat, remembering only afterward about the coughed-up blood. Lowering the handkerchief, he eyed the reddish smears on the linen, the orange-yellow halos that had formed above them. Inserting the key in the lock, he called her name in a circumspect whisper— "Zelda, Zelda, are you home?"—then cracked the door.

Quickly he cased the room, checking the bathroom, finding his watch on a shelf by the sink and sliding it onto his wrist without looking at the time. On the balcony he surveyed the grounds of the hotel. Beyond the line of scattered, seething palms, the surf pounded the sands, hungrily lapping up beach. She was a strong swimmer, but the white-capped waves were as high as he'd seen them—the Gulf current must be formidable by now.

Clearly, she hadn't been back to the room. He checked the sun on the horizon: maybe an hour and a half of daylight left. He felt the chill of encroaching rains, the moisture in his lungs. Where could she be? Only so many places to visit on this peninsula, only so many ways to get lost, even if you wandered straight into the wilds of its largely unsettled terrain. The forests weren't all that deep. He knew of marshes, some swamps, maybe also quicksand; he had heard tell of alligators, iguanas, and boa constrictors. Of more immediate concern, though, was the human element. It was a peninsula of impoverished fishermen and their families, only recently annexed as a leisure destination by rich *Habaneros,* by Americans and Europeans. He remembered the unsavory characters from this afternoon's bodega, the rules about where women were allowed, where they weren't. He could imagine how deep the locals' resentments of tourists must run, and Cuba wasn't the south of France. This was an island nation of gambling, speculation, and organized crime, a one-crop economy propped up by dictatorships and frequent coups, a country kept under thumb first by Spanish rule, now by American moneys and policies.

Pulling the French doors shut behind him, Scott shuffled past the bed to his suitcase set on the steel rack, rummaging through the clothing until he found the pair of BVDs in which he'd wrapped his handgun back in Encino. Too bad he hadn't thought to bring it with him Saturday night at the bar. He checked the cylinder to see that the gun was loaded and cocked the hammer, holding the Smith & Wesson aimed at the ground, peering down its barrel. Then he released the hammer with his thumb and eased the trigger out. In case I need it later, he told himself, wedging the gun into his belt under his jacket.

On the beach he listened to the rhythmic wash of waves, the predictable break and roll. He had lived regularly with the prospect of her death for a decade now. Only let her not suffer, , he said to himself. Here he was, a man who hadn't prayed for anything in years, rubbing a medallion between his fingertips, imploring a saint to whom he'd never given a moment's thought for help as he headed down shore toward the main island.

"Saint Lazarus," he whispered, "she needs looking after more than I do."

Into the sky's extravagance of color he strode, the luminous glow of orange, red, and fuchsia reflected on the sea's surface like parade banners, his eyes welling from the brilliant sun. Whenever he imagined her gone from the world, everything else melted away. What did squabbles and recriminations, rivalries and sexual infidelities matter? How could drunken brawls and shouting matches hold any importance in the face of disaster? She was his true passion, the one thing he could never get over. He thought of diving into the waves even now, hazarding all to save her, letting the water creep into his leaky lungs, but if she had in fact gone under, he didn't know where. He accused himself of not checking the boulders before she plunged from the crag earlier in the day. She must have registered his neglect, must have told herself, He cares more about preserving his precious lungs than about my splitting my head open on some rock.

"It's my fault," he said aloud. He was incurably selfish, even narcissistic. Maybe that was true of all artists. He drank too much and neglected her. She distracted him while he was working, sometimes only by sitting still and saying nothing at all, the mere possibility of disruption making him tense and irritable. He ordered her to leave hotel rooms in which they stayed so he could write for a few hours. Even in strange cities, even in cold weather. On countless occasions he sent her away, and once she had asked, in a broken, sincere whisper, "But where should I go? I don't have anything to do with myself," and yet he still shouted,

"Why is that always my problem? Anywhere but here, please. Can't you ever leave me alone for a few hours?" As soon as she was gone, though, he gave in to regret, spent the entire day worrying about her instead of working, fretting about what might happen to her alone on the streets of Paris, Baltimore, or New York. "Your problem," she once said, "is that you can't work when I'm in the room, sometimes even in the house, but you also can't stand it when I'm out on the town without you."

He could hear her voice, the familiar tones, that bizarre sense of humor about his neurotic need to put her out of mind. "Did you enjoy bumping me off?" she asked him once while she was marooned in Prangins, shoulders, breasts, and face plagued by rashes, her entire being afflicted by the itching and flaking of a psychosomatic disease that got worse with every hour spent in his company, until the doctors pronounced him a precipitating condition and banished him from the hospital. And what had he done in the face of her seemingly incurable distress? He'd written a story hypothetically killing off the cracked soul of his poor wife, easily one of the four or five best of his career.

"What was it like with me gone, once and for all?" she said after reading the story.

"Don't be silly. I wrote from my deepest fears, I exaggerated my wrongs and put them on trial, punishing the man for what he hadn't even meant to do in the first place."

"It's a beautiful story, Scott, one of your very best in my estimation," she said. "You can tell he loves her, especially now that she's dead. But you and I have read enough Freud to know that our deepest wishes and deepest fears are closely related. By the way, I liked the detail of his locking her out of the house; I imagine that part wasn't hard to come up with."

"He didn't do it on purpose."

"No, he was drunk and could hardly remember anything at

all," she said, smiling royally, luxuriating in her ability to forgive his flaws. "I'm told it's a common phenomenon with dipsomaniacs. Vague remorse wrapped up with innocence, outrage at the very deeds perpetrated by their secret souls." She had let the point sink in before kissing him on the cheek. "All the same, the story made me feel loved. I felt sorry for you without me. You got one thing right. When he imagines she wouldn't want him to be so alone—that's true, Scott; if I disappear on you for good, if ever I can't climb out of this hole in myself, I won't want you to be alone." She was capable of a thousand small kindnesses. He resented the doctors who diagnosed her as having a megalomaniacal personality. Though vicious and spiteful when wounded, she was kinder, more giving and bountiful, than anyone he'd ever known.

The beach narrowed at the far end, the sun slipping low in the sky, soon to sink into the waves, the air above it purplish and peach with a low plane of clouds running out from the fiery center in striated lines. He had walked a mile, maybe farther, so caught up by his obsession with finding Zelda that he only now detected the drop in temperature.

He remembered the letter, wondering if it might provide a clue to where she had gone. Pulling the perfumed green stationery from his journal—that sudden trace of her in the air sent a coarse sadness through him—he began to skim it: *"Dearest Scott, I want you to know how much it means to hear you promise to take better care of yourself."* He looked for phrases: *"Hearing you speak with hope"* and *"fills me with a belief in the future."* He skipped ahead: *"This may be hard for you to understand, as I myself am only now beginning to understand it."* Then further on: *"If you lose your moorings, I will too."* The letter was full of judgments about his fine character, how he might get it back. She spoke of his writing, his struggles to write, comparing him to his peers. *"You are a finer writer than any of them, in every way, and oh so much more my own favorite writer."* She begged him to think of what they'd built together, not only of what they'd foolishly torn down. *"You've been sad for such a long time."* Then she brought it back to herself: *"It makes it hard for me to go on when you speak of your life 'being over.'"* He skimmed the rest, nothing new here, nothing especially ominous. Except perhaps all that overbearing hope.

A warm slosh of water filled his shoes. Without realizing it, he had wandered to the ocean's edge straight into a wave rushing high onto the sands. The water squished unpleasantly in his socks, trapped in the arches of his shoes. He inspected the beach, unable to proceed much farther. Immediately ahead the tide swallowed the shore as whitecaps rolled over a small embankment of sand, on the other side of which grass and reeds and trees grew out into the salt marsh. The sulfurous stench of landlocked tidal currents greeted him and he could detect the percussive chatter of insects, here and there the flapping of a crane or a pelican as it skimmed low over the grasses. Sitting down to rest his lungs, he heard the cawing of a gull and watched as it plunged into the marsh and emerged seconds later from behind the tall grass, a fish held like a thick branch in its bill as it flew directly above him. Several other gulls cawed searchingly after it, gliding on the wind, wings spread like children's kites as they swooped slantingly, clamoring, until the first bird dropped its prey on the sand not far from him. The fish convulsed, flipping into the air, as four additional gulls congregated (when one flew off, another descended to replace it), all stabbing mercilessly at the dying fish with hook-like beaks.

He felt the odd desire to lie down. The terraced sands carved by the day's waves, caked by sun but soon to be swallowed by nighttime tides, looked inviting. But he couldn't rest as long as she was gone. Not a person in sight for as far as he could see—why not call out? Go ahead, he urged himself. Zelda, Zelda, he recited her name but couldn't bring himself to utter it aloud. If he spoke her name on this desolate beach where no one could hear his cries, if he listened to his fears in a call and response between himself and the sky—well, who knew what possibilities that might invite? He couldn't predict how he'd {re-spond to hearing his own desperate need for her to be safe echoed back to him.

It was time to ask for help.

The manager hesitated at first, doubtless recognizing Scott as the man he'd evicted from one of the cottages only last night. Scott explained that his wife spoke almost no Spanish, and that she suffered from mental illness, a patient in an asylum back in the United States. This news put the manager on alert, instilled in him a proper sense of urgency, though Scott resented having to leverage Zelda's illness to get him to do what he ought to have done simply and automatically. "I am a somewhat famous writer," he told the manager, wishing to see him squirm. "If my wife dies in an accident on your beach, it will be bad for the hotel's repu-tation." Of course, if Zelda learned about it later, what he'd said to provoke this man into action, how many people knew about her condition as a result, an entire hotel staff put on alert for a madwoman gone missing, she would be mortified. But she had left him no choice.

Maryvonne hastened from the restaurant as soon as she saw him, wending her way through small clusters of guests assembled on the patio to watch the sunset. "Have you found her?" she in-quired, as though she'd thought of nothing else for the past two hours, and perhaps that was true. "How can I help?"

There was nothing this woman could do for his wife, least of all if Zelda had already inflicted some awful, final fate on herself. Most often her suicide attempts were bits of theater executed in his presence: the time she jerked at the steering wheel attempting to plunge them off a cliff on the Riviera, or those occasional dashes for tracks when she spied a passing locomotive. He was always there to save her from herself. This time, though, she was roaming tropical terrain in a foreign land in the midst of a mild break, perhaps unable to find her way back or to ask directions to the hotel. Harm might descend from anywhere, from almost anyone.

"You have heard from her by now?" the Frenchwoman asked, as he escorted her to the perimeter of the patio, away from the other guests.

"She left a note," he told her. "She's off on yet another walk, it appears." Though he had just asked the hotel manager to dispatch several employees to comb the beach and make inquiries in the village after his wife, he nevertheless refused Maryvonne's kindnesses, maybe on instinct, maybe on the sad speculation that he didn't want her around if it all went south. It would be one thing if they found Zelda wandering the village, or swimming in strong waves, alive and well, waiting to be recovered, then escorted to the hotel so that everyone might pretend nothing had happened. Quite another if he got word from the hotel staff that local police had discovered a drowned woman.

"She will be fine, then?" Maryvonne asked, unconvinced.

He could tell from the tilt of her head and the tone of her voice that she didn't believe his feeble lies. Why should she? She was asking to be let inside his sorrow and he was saying no.

"Perhaps I will look for you later," he said. "Perhaps Zelda and I together will look for you later, if she's up to it."

"Would that not be lovely?"

"Will you be at the bar, here on the hotel patio, on the porch of your cottage?"

"One place or another," she said before retreating to the hotel restaurant where Aurelio sat waiting for her, waving once at Scott without rising.

He discovered Famosa García at a corner table in the hotel bar, reading a newspaper. The old Cuban looked up at Scott as if the two men had a scheduled appointment.

"Ah, Señor Fitzgerald, I am pleased to meet you."

Scott was anything but pleased. He didn't care to listen to news of any sort from Matéo's messenger, even if it meant the entire police force of Havana was about to descend on him without warning. Matéo was just using the threat of legal hassle to keep tabs on him. Scott wanted to have it out with Famosa García, tell him how lousy his timing was. For a split second, though, he paused, wondering how far Matéo's network reached, whether he was aware of today's events on Varadero, whether his skilled messenger might already know of Zelda's disappearance—a wild thought, so Scott put it out of mind.

"Have you nothing to say to Señor Cardoña?" Famosa García asked.

"Can you get a message to him?"

"Anything you like; I am only *enviado,* maybe you say, the reporter of news?"

"Envoy."

"An envoy, yes, at your service. So we drink first?"

The combination of the man's velvety voice and the milky eye that couldn't focus was appalling.

"I'll hold off on the drink," Scott said as the waiter approached. "*Una cerveza,* that's all for me, *gracias.*"

His head was spinning and he knew himself to be treading dangerous ground. Did he have the guts to say what he was about to say? The more he thought about it, the more he believed Matéo's kindness to be one long bluff, maybe not from the start— but somewhere early on during that long Saturday night, Scott had become a mark.

"Tell him I'm broke, won't you," Scott said, playing his hand more decorously than he intended. "I'm in no position to invest with him, wish I could, that I had some value, some net worth."

Famosa García ran his fingers through his mane of hair, his chin bent piously over his drink as though he had no stake in what was being said.

"I'm grateful for what he did for me back in Havana," Scott continued, feeling the old man's silence as leading, as though he was being given just enough rope. "Maybe he wants to broker an investment for me for the sake of fond memories we share of New York, and I appreciate all of this, I do, I enjoyed our two nights in Havana, I'm grateful for his company and his assistance—"

"He does not require your gratitude," Famosa García said. He was here to talk about the incident from the other night, the progress of the police investigation.

Scott couldn't believe what he was hearing. What more was there to say about the death of a peon in a juke joint, a death in which neither he nor Zelda had played any part?

"My employer, he finds another witness, this is no problem. Señor Cardoña always he have many ways of solving *problemas*."

Obviously, the witness in question was someone Matéo had coerced. None of it made any sense. Why did they need a false witness in the first place? But the customs of Cuban law were beyond Scott's grasp. He longed to protest, longed to shut down the conversation and shout, "Well, she's gone, the invaluable witness is gone, there's no need for machinations, let justice run its course."

"What is it?" Famosa García asked him. "You have something to say."

"What does that get us?" Scott finally asked.

"Excuse me," Famosa García said, as though Scott had directly challenged him.

"The trumped-up witness, how does that protect my wife?"

"The witness is the woman who the men fought over, she will say so."

"Well, convey my message, please," Scott said, "my sincere gratitude for his help. I wish I had some way to repay him just now, but I don't."

"It is done," Famosa García said, pushing his chair back from the table. "I am only envoy."

Scott felt that etiquette required some gesture of appreciation for the man's efforts.

"My wife kept the picture we took together," he said. "She was quite pleased with it."

"And how is Señora Fitzgerald?" Famosa García asked, his one good eye peering at Scott. Was it possible, he wondered again, that this man was behind Zelda's disappearance, all of today's events somehow orchestrated at Matéo's command?

"You know where she is, don't you?" Scott asked spontaneously, but it was just the long day of drink talking, maybe also the heat.

Famosa García stared at him without flinching, neither dumbfounded nor outraged. Either he knew nothing or he was a masterful actor. "She is in her room, tired from a day spent in the sun, no?"

"Sure, that's all I meant. She'll be sorry to have missed you," Scott said. "We were grateful for your guidance in Havana, and we also found a church here on the peninsula."

Of course, Scott said to himself, I should have thought of it sooner. He shook the hand of the Cuban, wishing him safe travels, even as he pictured Zelda in the pews of that small mission-style church, crouched beneath its exposed-timber ceiling and the modest holy glass windows while light drained from the sky.

That's where she had gone, the village church; he felt it with dread certainty. But would she still be there at this hour? He took a long, slow breath, ignoring the rasp in his chest, gathering himself, sipping at his beer slowly to slow his pulse. He was balancing two competing emotions: sudden relief from the insight into his wife's mind, this hope that the day might yet resolve itself peaceably, mixed with an undercurrent of terror. You haven't found her yet, he reminded himself. He needed to set out for the village right away, before night descended, except—the thought held him back, if only briefly—he was afraid of what he might find.

He pulled out his Moleskine, scanning its pages, pausing over a passage about Sheilah written days ago, in a stupor induced by alcohol or remorse, during that long night on which he'd vowed to go on the wagon, fighting off those middle-of-the-night dregs, then fighting with his mistress before fleeing to Asheville the same morning. *"It was altogether possible that Colman had pursued her so diligently, had stayed so long with her, for no better reason than this: she was someone who could keep a secret."* Lost in his own words, he gave in to regret over the way he'd parted with Sheilah, who had put up with so much from him these past two years. What if he never saw her again? *"He hadn't gone looking for that quality in her. It showed in her bearing, a sense of style mixed with decorum. She was among those whose ranks were thinning from generation to generation, a woman designed for privacy, that rarest of products in a herd-like society, the truly trustworthy person. If as a rule natural-born confidants didn't pursue work as gossip columnists, Colman had to admit it was perfect cover. In her bed he could unburden himself; there and there alone he was able to speak of matters which had plagued him for years, the secrets he knew about his wife—how damaged she was even in her finest moments, even at the peak of recovery—but could never reveal to the wide world."*

His instinct was to call Sheilah—why not?—she would want to know he was alive. She would apprehend the latest tumult into catastrophe without explanation. He trusted her discretion and judgment in all matters, so maybe she could tell him what to do next. He marched to the front desk and informed the clerk he needed to place a call, and for a minute, as he hovered over the piece of paper handed to him by the clerk, he was unable to remember the number, but then it came to him. The clerk indicated a phone by a dark wood bench where he could take the call once it had been placed. Thumbing through the Moleskine, he rehearsed what he would say to Sheilah. "Never let it be said there's no way down from disaster," he said and scribbled it in the notebook. He remembered the trip to Manhattan this past fall, the vows he had made to Sheilah afterward to divorce Zelda once and for all. It was selfish of him to want Sheilah's advice. He was too dependent on her sympathy.

The clerk caught his attention and shook his head to indicate that no one had picked up, and Scott nodded his appreciation, relieved that the decision had been made for him. He had no right to confide in her ever again. And yet there was no one else, other than perhaps Zelda herself in her periods of lucidity, who could begin to intuit how devastating the events of today might prove. "Zelda was gone, Zelda was dead." He experimented with the words, silently, chanting them so as to postpone their meaning.

He asked for escort into the village, but when told how long he would have to wait insisted on making the journey alone on foot, a plan frowned on by the night manager. This wasn't Havana, where all along the Prado the clubs and bars thickened until the morning hours with revelers, tourists, and, yes, thieves too, but also soldiers and policemen. The roads on the peninsula were treacherous at night, often washing out when the rains came. The night manager walked Scott onto the patio, made him listen for the low rumble of thunder rolling in from the Caribbean Sea below them. "You know about the alligators?" the manager asked, even as Scott felt inside his belt for his gun, answering cocksuredly, "Thank you, but I'll be fine." The manager handed his guest a lantern. "You will require this to find your way."

So, holding the lantern before him (rather like a figure he'd once seen depicted on a tarot card), Scott set out, tracking the dirt trail from the resort through the hum of the noisome roadside marsh, swatting at the insects perching on his neck, heeding the flop and fall of large fish or reptiles in the mucky waters behind the reeds on either side of the dirt lane, several of the splashes long and full enough to accommodate a gator. In the thin darkness, as he circumvented a bank of dunes covered in grass and sand brush that ran off into forest, he passed couples from the hotel returning from evening strolls. He hurried along a narrow partially paved road, past shacks where locals lingered on porches and children at play in the yards crawled out from behind trees like nosy nocturnal creatures. Now and then he stopped to ask someone in crude Spanish, *"¿Dónde la iglesia?"* and a native would skim his face for information before gesturing down the road, assuring him that it angled straight to the center of the village—no way to depart from it, no way to miss the church.

Soon the cottages and shacks fell away, and with them the people, as the air grew dark and heavy with moisture. He listened for the rumble of encroaching storms, but all he could hear was the drone of insects, the gurgling croak of frogs and lizards. He checked the kerosene in the lantern.

Dead on his feet by the time he reached the village, he welcomed the sight of the church set back from the road in an open field palely illuminated by the nighttime sky. As clouds rolled in shadows across the ground, they darkened patches of long grass, scrub, and thicket, and Scott muttered aloud, "What has become of her?" He walked under the freestanding arched gateway to jostle the front doors, locked, then walked round the side toward the square tower addition at the rear, attempting the door by which they'd entered the church this morning, rapping on the thick wood. Anyone inside, the priest or perhaps Zelda herself, would be certain to hear him. It made perfect sense. She had fled to this place to lock herself away from that which was chasing her, to take refuge from the bad tidings of the spirit world; but whatever had transpired in the hours since, she was no longer in the vicinity. No sound issued from inside the church. If the priest heard the knocking, he chose not to come forward into the night.

The modest chapter house connected to the church remained dark. Was there any point in knocking there too? What if the priest answered only to say, yes, he'd let Zelda inside the church to light a few candles but sent her away hours ago? Nevertheless, Scott approached the door, all other avenues exhausted. He rapped firmly if reluctantly: no answer.

So he retraced his steps through the thickened night, listening to peals of distant thunder, detecting the scent of this warm, muggy place for which he felt a strange affinity, not unlike what he felt for the Deep South. He was one of those who believed that the American South held the key to the nation's soul. For a long time he had intended to write the great novel of the Civil War, having often interrogated Zelda about the moods and texture of the land as it had inscribed itself on her being. Only months ago, while working on *Gone with the Wind,* he had pored through his ledger and her letters in search of sketches from Zelda's childhood, of anecdotes accumulated while stationed in Montgomery or while visiting her family, of lore gathered while living in recent years in towns such as Tryon and Asheville. Early in their marriage she used to stop him in the middle of a conversation to ask, "Are you writing that down?" or "Are you memorizing my words again?" She could think of nothing more amusing—that was how she put it—than to be someone's muse. He pretended, through his father's ancestry, that he too had the South in his soul, but he didn't, not really. Which was why he relished his wife's stories of her beloved yet horribly constrictive South, the stench of wisteria in springtime and the ache of the rain-drenched landscape, the history that came at you from all sides, filling up your imagination before you had time to exercise it on your own. As he walked through the thinly forested marshlands of Varadero, he felt he was tracking the scent of her childhood.

At the hotel he checked with the manager—still no news—returning the lantern, then escaping by a side entrance to follow the dunes out beyond the stone cabins to the shoreline, there to watch the roll of whitecaps as he roved moonlit sands for a long while, not really believing he would come across his wife.

"Everything is okay, I understand," Aurelio hailed him as he approached, and Scott smiled, saying, of course, why wouldn't it be?

Maryvonne and Aurelio had been drinking all night in the company of an American couple, an older man and a young bride whose names Scott didn't catch. Maryvonne presented Scott as a dear friend, only gently referring to his wife after he hinted that Zelda had elected to remain in her room. His European friends were nothing if not discreet, the sole allusion to today's outing to Hicacos Point occurring when Maryvonne reached under the table to capture and squeeze his hand in her fine, slender fingers.

It was probably well past midnight. Scott, in a black cast iron chair set before a black cast iron table, traded small talk and refused to glance at the watch on his wrist. Now and then he plundered a thinly picked over plate of cheese and fruit brought to the table before his arrival. He was ravenous but loath to admit it. His wife was dead for all he knew, and here he was craving food, the first time in weeks he'd had any appetite whatsoever.

"Do you mind?" he asked Maryvonne, helping himself to another chunk of the cheese.

"Scott, when was the last time you ate?"

He thought about it for a minute; the answer, of course, at the picnic this afternoon, and hardly anything then.

"No wonder you are hungry," she said.

Dying for a drink, he offered to buy a round.

"We have to be going," said the American man, who had tired eyes and a sallow jaw. He must have been in his early sixties, the wife still in the bloom of youth. She seemed reluctant to leave.

"Oh, don't spoil her fun," Scott said, but the man didn't appreciate misplaced gallantry.

Scott feared Aurelio and Maryvonne would follow the couple's lead and turn in. Over a long career as an owl and a drinker, he'd learned that even a single person's decision to call it a night could trigger a chain reaction, bringing the most vibrant of parties to an end. Among apes, someone once told him, most likely it was Ernest, yawning wasn't just contagious, it was communicative. When the head ape yawned, it was a cue—we're going to sleep, folks, whether you like it or not; and the other apes returned the yawn, submissively, suddenly tired themselves. From a young age Scott had quarreled with those inclined to quit on a good time before it was exhausted. He would sooner fall asleep on his feet (had done so on many an occasion) than leave a party early. Tonight, though, wasn't about extending pleasure. It was about postponing solitude for as long as possible.

The waiter returned with Cuba libres, and Maryvonne and Aurelio showed no signs of quitting on him.

"I never finished the story of my injury, about which you asked me earlier," Aurelio said. A crack of thunder hammered the sky, followed by lightning that illuminated the sand dunes and grove of pines behind them. The flames on the lanterns surrounding the patio bent low, nearly extinguished by a heavy wind, as the nearby palms and almond trees chattered nervously.

"What is this storm waiting for?" Maryvonne remarked.

"Sshh," Scott said, playfully putting a finger to her wine-stained lips. "If you don't acknowledge them, sometimes they pass right on by, like noisy drunks at a party."

"It was more difficult to accept I had the injury than anything," Aurelio said. "It is only until you are better, they say to me, confining me to a cot, only I was not prepared to fight again and try to have a good result. In the hospital I do not get better, do not get stronger." He could remember the morning when the staff came to impart the news that he would be sent away, the nurses checking on him more often than usual, promising the doctor would soon speak with him. In telling his tale Aurelio lingered over phrases, trying to find the right words in English, Maryvonne whispering to him in French or Spanish, helping him recall his own story, their voices tapering off in the wind, as palm fronds whispered above them.

Off to the north waves clapped heavily on the beach, sometimes supplemented by a long sigh of surf, the ruminations of the storm hanging on the wind. Scott let the Spaniard's voice wash over him, oddly comforted by this tale of woe that had nothing to do with his wife's sad story. He didn't have to pay close attention to the minor details because there was nothing at stake for him in them.

"Did we mention this part of our story last night at the cottage?" Maryvonne asked, worried lest her cousin prove tedious.

"I don't think so," Scott said. "Besides, Aurelio and I share an interest in the niceties and minutiae of warfare."

He imagined that the hotel bar would be closing before long and wondered if there was time for another round.

"You never want them to smile at you," Aurelio said, "with that face they put on for the dying, the maimed, the castrated." The sadness in his voice was curtailed only by the knowledge that his bright nurse of a cousin would soon rush to his side to see him through the valley of death. He could speak objectively of his own pain as a consequence of her intervention. He could report on what it was like to be a wounded, dying soldier stalked by a sedately smiling doctor, soon thereafter to be marooned in a refugee camp; and he could do so because, for all practical purposes, he spoke of another man's fate.

"I wish Miss Zelda were here to share this story too," Aurelio said, and the fact that the Spaniard was so ready to believe Zelda safe in her room made Scott think less of him. How could such a man have survived a war? But the Spaniard's affections were so simple and sincere that it was difficult to stay angry with him. "Please tell her I say that we miss her."

"Well, on that note," Scott said, "I must attend to her."

"And we attend *las peleas de gallos* tomorrow evening?"

"Of course," Scott replied, then turning to Maryvonne. "Will you be joining us?"

"Is not allowed," Aurelio said stiffly, and Maryvonne rose, her reddening face averted from her husband. In the French manner she pecked at each of Scott's cheeks, her lips moist on the corner of his mouth even as water simultaneously struck his forehead. The rains had come at last.

"Perhaps Zelda and I will discover," she said, pausing on that word she pronounced *dé-coovere,* then continuing as if for effect, "activities still more exciting."

"If she's up to it," Scott said, reminding himself that everything uttered over the past hour was more or less a lie. None of these plans—the cockfights, the renewal of friendship, the dinners— would come to pass.

Winding through the wildly tossing palms en route to the villa, he dawdled long enough to be sure the Europeans were out of sight, then doubled back to the reception area to find the night manager yawning, bracing his forearm against the counter.

"What are we to do next?" the manager asked. His narrow, rodentlike face was fearful, not a good sign.

"You've been in touch with the police already?" Scott asked, though he doubted the man had taken any initiative.

"I am waiting only for you, that is all," the night manager said. "We will call first thing this morning?"

"What," Scott cried, experiencing outrage even as he performed it, only too happy to pawn off his own negligence on this obse-quious, reproachful, slippery man. "But hadn't we agreed—if the search parties came up empty, you would call the police right away?"

"Señor Fitzgerald, I apologize, I do not understand, I thought you want me to wait."

"For what?"

The night manager shrugged his shoulders.

"Tell me what we could possibly be waiting on, for God to step in and find her himself?"

Scott wheeled about, started to walk away, head spinning with recriminations, for himself, for the night manager, for that damned clairvoyant and her cursed words.

"I should call the police?" the night manager called after him.

"Of course," Scott said, halting in his tracks, practically spitting the words.

"In the morning?"

"No, goddamnit, as soon as possible."

"They will ask to speak with you."

"So send them to my room. If I'm not there I'll be on the beach—"

"But the rains," the manager said with genuine concern, and the two men peered through the French doors that opened onto the patio, where nighttime staff were pulling down lanterns, stacking chairs, and securing tables with rope so they wouldn't get blown off in the fierce winds.

"At any rate, I'll be easy to find," Scott said, returning to the desk to make it up with the man. "Tell me what you think I should do next, Señor, but I'm sorry I've forgotten your name?"

"Señor Valdés," the night manager replied, then added gently, "You must sleep."

"I'll try, but you tell the police they needn't worry about waking me."

"I will call them, Señor Fitzgerald, they will find her, who knows, maybe the priest from the church, Padre Hijuelos, he find her a bed for the night—but *la policía* will know, they will know soon enough."

He had put off returning to his desolate hotel room, but he couldn't postpone it any longer. So he headed through the French doors into the lashing rains, the night manager whose name he'd already forgotten shouting after him, maybe starting forth with an umbrella, but not before Scott, assisted by the wind, slammed the door shut; and again he was on the cinder path, now pooling with water, having to hop from one patch of higher ground to another, weaving among the sudden ponds already inches deep. There was no way to continue the search in this storm. It was impossible to see even a few feet ahead of you—the villa, no more than fifteen yards away, nothing but a massive shadowy blur. He would wait out this round of storms, maybe try to close his eyes. If I lie down for half an hour, girding myself against the worst, he reasoned, I'll be better equipped to venture again into the night.

With the eave of the roof shielding him from everything but the ribbons of blown rain, he put his key in the door and stopped to look at his watch for the first time since slipping it on earlier in the night: 2:59, the witching hour, the setting for every dark night of the soul. He swung the door open, and as he stepped into the narrow corridor found his path dimly lit by a lamp from deep inside the room. Had the maids come to turn down the bed and left it on? Had someone, Famosa García or another of Matéo's minions, broken in and tossed the room? He felt for the handle of the gun in his belt and took two more steps, then saw her there, kneeling before the bed, her face pale in the artificial light, awash in dread. She scrambled to her feet. He couldn't fathom what had just happened. Nevertheless, relief surged through him, waves of it pounding his ribs from inside. She was all he'd ever wanted in life, he sometimes still believed that.

"Scott, I was worried about you," she said feebly, plaintively. "I didn't know where you were." But that couldn't change any of the basic facts concerning what she'd put him through these past twelve hours, which felt much longer than that, which felt like many episodes of disaster strung together and replayed before his eyes in unrelenting memory. She held her ground, though, demanding information. "Why did you stay out so late?"

12

WHAT SCOTT MUST HAVE FELT JUST THEN—ON WALKING INTO a hotel room to discover the wife he believed to be missing, possibly harmed, kneeling but now slowly rising from the foot of the bed, his own thoughts not quite accessible to him, the repertoire of grief playing out all at once. He must have experienced the euphoria of averted catastrophe even as the emotions rolled through him, tossing one against another, first joy, then fury, next despondency, next ardor, then joy again.

Zelda saw her opportunity. He'd spent the night fearing her death and he looked the worse for it. She needed to persuade him that the entire episode simply proved how necessary she was to him. Nevertheless, she didn't wish to explain herself, why and where she'd gone, what she prayed for, whether anyone answered.

"I'm okay," she promised him.

He couldn't believe she'd done this to him again.

"I needed to clear my head, but everything is fine now."

He'd been half certain she was dead.

"Well, you seem to have handled my demise rather riotously," she said, alluding to the alcohol on his breath, the late hour. The cruel glance he shot her hastened regret. "I didn't mean that," she said. "Can I take it back?"

The doors to the balcony had been cracked so that she might listen to the reliably pounding surf, the thunder rolling in while she prayed at the foot of the bed. Just then a gust of wind blew the doors open and she scampered forward, pushing them shut against the spitting winds, thankful for the chance to move out from under his stunned stare.

"Zelda, where were you?"

"It's not important," she said, facing him again, noticing he'd left the door to their room ajar, now striding forward also to close it and lock them in. "I can't remember all the places, in town, at the church—"

"I knew it," he said.

Then back to find the clairvoyant, after that mostly on the beach, in and out of the woods of the resort.

"We checked most of those places."

"I know you did, dearest Scott," she said. "Can we not talk about it just now? We need to take care of you, get you out of those clothes, into something dry and warm."

Under her coaxing, he seemed all at once to let go, the man before her no longer someone middle-aged, distinguished, handsomely graying at the temples, but instead a person on the verge of collapse, bags under his eyes, his posture slackened, exhaustion emanating from every fiber of his being. On cue he began to cough. It was a hacking, wet cough.

"Scott, let me draw you a bath."

"I need to let the front desk know you've come home."

"Later."

"They're looking for you."

"Not at this hour, they're not," she said. "Besides, I've already been found. I've been in this room for hours."

He tried to make calculations about the length of their separation, about the places searched, about his last visit to the room. She watched him doing the math in his head.

"Where did you go after the church?" he asked.

Having turned on the spigot, she ran her fingers under the stream, waiting for it to warm, no guarantee it would at this hour of the night, in the middle of a terrific thunderstorm. While the pipes clanked and water thrummed against the white porcelain basin of the tub, she exited the bathroom to undress her husband, peeling the sleeves of his jacket from his arms, fishing in the breast pocket for the Moleskine to discover it damp around the edges but otherwise undamaged. She placed it on the desk. Lifting her gaze, she saw the gun tucked in his belt and recoiled.

"Scott, where did you get that?"

His hand reached automatically for his hip, the place on his body where her eyes were fixed. "Oh," he said, "it's the old Smith and Wesson I bought years ago in Baltimore."

"Why do you have it on you? Have you been carrying it the entire time?"

"I thought you might be in danger," he said, extracting the gun from his belt, laying it on the desk beside the journal.

Though disconcerted, she resumed the loving chore of undressing him, remembering all the ways she'd stripped him of clothing in the past, trying to concentrate on the facts before them, wet clothing, wet skin, weariness, so as not to return to the events of the night. Off with the rumpled pinstriped shirt, also the T-shirt underneath, until he was bare chested and she could run her fingers through the ghostly blond-white wisps of hair on his well-defined pectorals, down along his muscled but alcohol-bloated stomach. "You have such nice skin," she said as she tugged at his belt and in one swift motion pulled his trousers to his ankles, realizing only then that she should have removed his shoes first. He shuffled to the bed and sank into it, coughing as he reclined, a fist held to his mouth to smother the hacking even as he raised his legs so she could unlace the Florsheims and free his feet, ripe from sweat and rain. Again she checked on the water running into the tub, lukewarm at best, but it would do.

He was lying on the bed, naked except for his BVDs, drowsing. She pulled him to his feet, saying, "Scott, let's get you washed, then we can sleep."

Afterward she walked him naked, rubbed dry, his pale skin flushed in splotches, only a bathrobe draped over his shoulders, the front hanging open to expose his *pene,* as the Cubans called it. Depositing him on the sheets, the covers pulled back, she burrowed in beside him.

At some point he must have passed out, he couldn't be sure for how long. She wore only a long sheer pink nightgown through which he could see the rise of her hips turned sideways, her body rotated into him, her groin warm against his. She nuzzled him, asking was he awake, and how long could they stay in Cuba. "Scott, Scott," she was saying as he listened to the wind-whipped torrents against the window. "Are we together again? I never know what any of this means." It was just like her to want everything put back together in an instant, always wanting back into the now, into her marriage, into the notion of family. She believed so desperately in the myth of normalcy, always fearing it had eluded her. *Normalcy:* he would have defined it, in the style of his friend H. L. Mencken, as the notion that somewhere someone who wasn't having a good life could still believe she was owed one. Through those long months of her first full breakdown, the institutionalization at Prangins and the tortures endured there in order to be readmitted to the world, the call to normalcy haunted her. Even when inside it, while living on the estate at Ellerslie, or vacationing with her husband and daughter in Charleston, or touring Cuba, she feared it was all just pretend and not how people who were really normal felt about being normal.

He dozed once more and then felt her stirring. She thought there might be somebody in the room. She wanted him to get up and check, then changed her mind. "Don't leave me, dearest." So he rolled onto his side to stare into the empty space between the bed and the balcony, assuring her no one was in the shadows. Heavy with exhaustion, listening to the rain, softer now as it prattled on the roof tiles above, he stroked her hair, but she was already asleep.

"I'm here," he whispered. "It's always just you and me."

When next he awoke it was quiet, only dripping drains, the sprinkle and shimmer of wind through drenched palm fronds. Their bodies were no longer touching, she on her side of the bed, he on his. As he drifted in and out of fitful sleep, he thought he heard her chanting in a prayerlike whisper, the murmur soothing as his head sunk heavy into the pillow. When he woke next he had dreamed of her standing by the bed, laying hands on him, running holy medallions and herbs and charms over his prone body, the old woman with the yellow feline eyes witnessing his nudity while guiding Zelda through some incantation. The image of the clairvoyant chanting over his naked body terrified him, and he jolted awake several times during the night, until he became aware of what was happening on the other side of the bed, feigning slumber so as to pretend not to hear his wife's words.

Eventually, though, he was peering through sleep-heavy lids at Zelda, propped against the headboard, eyes fixed on the air above as if listening to someone, then replying in a string of negation. "I am nothing, I am nothing, I am nothing," she chanted in a whisper, waiting a few seconds, then answering, "It doesn't matter, I am nothing."

"Zelda," he said softly.

"I'm all right," she said, gasping for air, on the verge of hyperventilating. "It was only pretend—I wondered what it was to be one of the devoutly possessed, you know, those virgin mystics who experience true union with God."

Gently he massaged her wrist, so that she would understand what was real, what wasn't, and she turned to him, tucking her nose into the crook of his neck, silent at first, but soon he could feel the warm trickle of tears pooling along his clavicle.

"Scott, I know something's wrong with me." She lifted her face, sniffling, unable to breath, her words nasal-noted from crying and congestion. "But I wasn't always like this, I don't care what you say."

On some level he had known all along how it would happen. So as the sun shone through the white muslin curtains, he held himself responsible. Silhouetted against the morning light, Zelda knelt in the foreground, arms tented in prayer on the brightly colored comforter, fingering the beads of a rosary, head bowed, eyes shut, lips moving rapidly in a simmer of mostly inaudible sound. Here was the reason why he hadn't slept with her on the trip to Manhattan last fall, even though she had tried several times to seduce him over wine at dinners. No sooner did she begin to envision what might be hers again than she rushed into the future, heedless of danger, without judgment, without temperance. "Is it because you don't find me attractive anymore?" she had asked in bed at the Algonquin on the last night of their stay in New York.

Why, then, if he'd known not to go down this road six months ago, had he behaved differently here in Cuba?

Well, for one thing, Zelda had seemed healthier, sturdier. He was always too quick to believe in her recovery, celebrating the

signs of her old self, the two of them embracing any chance whatsoever to unburden themselves of alienation and acrimony and
start over again.

"Did you say something?" she asked from the foot of the bed,
her voice hushed, and he remembered again the middle of the
night, wishing he had taken his own room as in Havana so that
he didn't have to see Zelda in such a state. In the gray night her
wide-open empty eyes had rolled up until nothing but the whites
remained visible, shocking, like the faces of zombies in photographs. And as she whispered words in a mantra of negation, "No,
no, no," he stirred, flopped, hoping to nudge her into a less hazardous dream, though he knew it wasn't a dream, but she shunted
him aside, her gaze fixed intently on the ceiling. "Who am I that
God should take account of me?" she had muttered. "Am I not
small enough yet? When I'm so small as to be hardly visible, when
I've emptied myself once and for all, will you leave me alone so
that I can be the nothing that comes of nothing?"

That memory belonged to the middle of the night. It was
dawn now and she had spoken lucidly, seeming to be herself
again, so he braced himself for the new day.

"I prayed for you and a clean feeling washed over me," Zelda
said brightly. "Do you have the charm I gave you? You didn't lose
it, did you? Let me see it."

He raised the twine round his neck to show the silver medallion of a limping Lazarus accompanied by loyal dogs.

"I think you should visit the church today and ask Father
Hijuelos to bless it."

"If I have time."

"You don't have anything better to do."

He remembered that he still hadn't checked in with the Club
Kawana's management to call off the search by the police. "Well,
I told Maryvonne and Aurelio," he said, focusing his thoughts else-

where, "that we might join them for an early dinner, and then Aurelio and I are going—"

"I don't think that's a good idea," she said and bowed her head in prayer again, not wishing to discuss the matter. But looking up from the bed a few minutes later, she asked, "Are you thinking of her?"

He thought she must mean Maryvonne.

"You want to go back to her, don't you?"

"What are you talking about?"

"Your girl in California, the one who probably resembles me, the way they all do in your mind."

He tried to pretend she was merely speculating, that she didn't mean a word she was saying.

"The one who stole you from me," she said. "You didn't think I'd find out? The old gypsy told me all about her, I know everything, you don't have to lie. If you would only be honest, I wouldn't hold it against you."

He wasn't going to have this conversation.

"She said you were living with someone, most of the time. Why do you keep secrets from me, Scott? I always find out."

Were these the revelations that had made her flee and take refuge in a church? Maryvonne hadn't mentioned anything about them. Had Zelda really returned, as she claimed last night, to visit the clairvoyant a second time?

"Scott, answer me," she said, angering. "I deserve to know the truth, I deserve to be respected. Why do you never talk about her?"

He was almost persuaded, remembering the times she had begged him to find someone else to take care of him so that she wouldn't have to worry about him alone in the world, working too hard, drinking too hard, no one to rein him in. Sometimes he wished to talk with her about Sheilah, this nobody who'd made a name for herself in Hollywood, how good she was for him, how kind and tolerant she was, how she consoled him when no one else could, helping him to believe in brief intervals that not everything (all his self-worth, all his future prospects) depended on the next novel.

"At any rate, I'm your wife, not her," Zelda was saying. "All this chivalry protecting the good name of your mistress. Doesn't she know you're married? And what do you tell her about me? Poor Zelda, to whom I'm loyal so long as I can keep her stowed away in a mansion for maniacs and not deal with her myself every day. Do you tell her all my secrets? I have a right to know."

"Zelda, I would never say anything against you," he said, but he was thinking how much easier it was without her, how much easier it was with Sheilah. It was a guilty thought. He had long prided himself on always being there for her. "I am loyal to us beyond your wildest imaginings."

"It's all just words now, words and memories. So what do you tell her? Do you say I'm crazy and you would like to be with me, but you can't, well, for reasons that are more obvious to you and my doctors than to me?"

"She has her own secrets," he said, aware that he'd crossed a threshold by alluding to Sheilah and admitting her into Zelda's life.

"Another sorrowful golden-haired woman, another replica of me?" Zelda came and sat next to him at the top of the bed, then surprisingly she nuzzled into him.

"Please let's talk about something else," he said.

"What's her name?"

"Zelda, please, let's talk about something else."

"Would you like to know what else the clairvoyant told me?"

"There's more?" he asked, again half-suspecting her of wild invention, and yet wishing to dig, if possible, for the root of yesterday's disappearance.

"She said we were like siblings, that's why we know each other so well, why we're bonded. We've known each other in many lives, and in a past life we were brother and sister."

Under different circumstances he might have pushed back on the revelations and asked in what era they had been siblings, whether they had gone ahead and married anyway. He might have asked whether it was possible to cheat on your sister.

"Don't you worry that you're taking advantage of her?" Zelda asked him. "What does she think of this trip we've taken? Or doesn't she know?"

She could never let go of anything. He walked onto the balcony, breathing in the late morning air, damp from last night's storm, his temples throbbing, his neck and limbs weary. He let himself remember again the thousand outrages of Zelda, how tense a few of her well-chosen words could make him, his back muscles clenching even now, but also how soothing and beatific—he was inclined to say, how necessary—it felt to be in her good graces.

"I can trust you with anything," she said, again behind him, resting her palm on his back, "you'll always come for me, won't you?"

"I'm going for a walk, Zelda," he said, stepping around her to get out of the sun.

She pretended not to have heard him. "Maybe you should come back to bed."

Suddenly there was a loud knocking, and she gasped, whispering to him, "Who is it?"

"Un momento," he called to the door, then turned to her. "We never called the front desk, remember, I told you last night we had to call the front desk." But he caught himself, adjusted his tone. "Zelda, stay here. I'll speak with them outside, I'll say I found you in the middle of the night during the storm, slightly before dawn, and I was dressing now to come and tell them to call off the search."

"You're just worried they'll think you're a hypochondriac who called in the cavalry when his wife went missing for a few hours."

"I'll say you're in a delicate state and you don't wish to talk with them."

"Why would I have to talk with them?"

"Because you went missing, because they might want to know where."

He dressed swiftly and stepped onto the landing, shoes still untied, to encounter a man he hadn't met before, a stalwart Cuban named Colonel Silva, owner of the resort, here to follow up on a report about the guest who had gone missing.

"Is there anyone you suspect?" he asked.

"What do you mean?"

"Your reason for asking us to call the police," Colonel Silva said. "I'll need to give our reasons."

Scott wanted to shout, "Because she is missing," but he caught himself, remembering that his wife was no longer missing. Still, it was infuriating: last night's manager had promised he would notify the police right away.

"I've found her on my own," Scott said.

"You should have called us."

"And the manager on duty last night should have called the police when I asked." Scott stopped himself, realizing he was working at cross-purposes to his present desire. The more he made of the disappearance, the longer this man would linger.

"We were preparing," Colonel Silva said, "to send our staff to look for her again."

"All taken care of," he said, entering the room. As he rounded the corner of the short foyer he saw Zelda seated on the bed, his revolver in her palm.

"What are you doing?"

"I was working up the nerve to come to your rescue."

"Zelda, put the gun down, you don't know how to handle it."

"Well, how hard can it be?" she asked, flipping it in her hand. "What did they want?"

"It was the hotel management, like I said it would be."

"Someone knocked earlier while you were sleeping."

He couldn't decide if she was making this up. "Since we didn't answer," he said, "I suppose we can't know who it was that knocked."

"Of course we do," she said. "It was Maryvonne, and maybe Aurelio too, inquiring about tonight."

Again he told her to lay the gun on the bed or hand it to him, barrel to the ground, handle forward.

"What are you planning?" she said, trying to find her way inside the next round of the quarrel. "Scott, I don't want you leaving the resort tonight, really I won't stand for it. It's not safe, the clairvoyant warned me."

"Now you're just wildly inventing, and, besides, it's not your decision."

He wondered why she had picked the gun up in the first place.

"Do you know what makes me angry," she demanded, "the only thing that still makes me angry?"

She flipped the gun absentmindedly from palm to palm, pointing it once at the ceiling, once in his direction, no idea what she was doing with that thing or whether it was even loaded.

"There's still time, lots of time for us," she continued, "life is long, Zelda, you would tell me, and I'd ask, Are you sure?"

"You're your own worst enemy," he said, trying to make himself stand down, experiencing the rush of memory, always so extravagant and expensive, as it pressed against the present, crowding out possibility with the knowledge of what had been lost, what they could never get back. His true feelings for Zelda were located elsewhere, he told himself, beyond the realm of mutual resentments, in a place where he had once seemed capable and marvelous to her, and she, in turn, the source of his ability. "You depend on niceties," he said, knowing better than to fight back yet unable to stop himself from doing so. "You depend on elegant vacations and fine clothing to cope with the asylum. You're used to the frills and bows, all my sweetly bought comforts, I've always indulged you, but do you know how often you write saying, I love you, Scott, and by the way we owe this to so-and-so, and could you scrape together money for my expense account because debts need to be paid at the tea shop in Asheville or at some boutique for a new dress? How am I supposed to save a dime? We've owed so much, Zelda, I've paid and caught up, fallen back and tried to catch up again—what more do you want from me?"

"My father was right."

"What are you talking about?"

"When the Judge first met you he said you were a man who would probably have trouble paying his taxes. That even when you had money, it would slip through your fingers.

"Why do you suppose you hate ballet so much?" she asked in a level, impartial voice. She had worked round to her favorite source of bitterness: his refusal to let her accept that role with a prestigious ballet company in Naples so long ago, her big break in dance. Apparently she couldn't be bothered to recall that the tentative offer from the company was hardly a major role, one she herself judged beneath her talent grade, or that it arrived while she was behaving erratically, weeks prior to her first schizophrenic break. Did she ever think what it might have been like if she'd lost control of herself on a stage in Naples in front of thousands of spectators?

"You can't ever admit that as a ballerina I fashioned myself into a true artist."

"Only at the cost of ruining yourself," he shouted.

In her opinion, he hated ballet because he couldn't stomach being in a room filled with accomplished dancers who were artists of a different order, who challenged the definition of art as he understood it.

"And your love of ballet? Well, it's about the quaint feeling of superiority you derive from immersing yourself in the only truly aristocratic art, no peons invited to the show. The Bolsheviks weren't wrong, you know," he said, reminding her how those enchanting exiles she loved so much, Madame Egorova and all the lovely Russian aristocrats displaced by the revolution to Paris, had perfected their art on the backs of the masses.

"Please, stop. Can we stop, please?" she pleaded. "Why are we talking about politics anyway? I didn't know you had decided to become a political writer, and I can't see how it will help us pay our bills."

She paced the room, wild with fresh grief, as if everything they were talking about had happened only yesterday. He recalled the hallucinations from last night, the chanting, the talking back to voices that only she could hear.

"Zelda," he said, "put the gun down and we'll get you some food."

"I'm not hungry, I'm too worked up. It's just that I'm losing hope, and I've never heard of two people in a bad place drawing each other out of it." She moved to the bed, poised on its corner, straddling it, her arm raised, the gun extended before her. "Scott, why do you have this?"

"Dearest, please," he said, trying to placate her, inching closer, halting a couple of feet shy of the bed. "Let's put the gun back where you found it and we'll forget the whole—"

"You're not always in charge," she said and he rushed her, shoved his weight against her body as if throwing himself into an opponent during a football training camp drill, toppling her so that her head dangled off the bed, her hair falling like a mop in her eyes as he seized the arm that held the gun, gripping the soft fingers wrapped on the handle.

"Scott, answer me."

"Who do you think you are?" he said, lying completely on top of her, attempting to pry her fingers loose. "It's just for protection. I bought it while we were living in the woods of Maryland, you remember."

"I don't remember a gun."

"Of course you do, now hand it over." He squeezed her forearm, digging his thumb into the grove of tendons beneath the wrist, and still she didn't let go.

He struck her torso with his free arm as she rolled away from him, the gun peeling from his palm, still in her possession, her dress riding up above the knees, her auburn hair splayed violently across her nose. In an instant he was suffused with regret, yet all the more angry with her for having pushed him to this precipice.

"Are you going to give me the gun," he said, standing again, "or am I going to have to fight you for it?"

Intentionally or not, she was pointing it at him, her index finger tapping the side of the trigger. She rose from the bed, straightened the folds of her dress, tidying her hair as he studied her expression.

"I can't do this anymore," he said.

"What do you mean, what are you saying?" Zelda asked, her voice cracking, full of dread. She replaced the gun on the desk where she'd found it. "I didn't know my holding it would upset you so."

Goodbye, Zelda, he whispered silently to himself, realizing

how. long he'd held on, never quite allowing himself to believe the day would come when he would give her up. "Goodbye," he said audibly now, aware that his eyes were welling. "It's over," he scolded himself. "Don't let her make you forget all the craziness and impossibility ever again."

"I didn't hear you. What are you saying?" she asked.

He didn't answer.

"Don't go," she said as he shuffled into his jacket. "When will you return? I told you I don't want you attending those cockfights because something bad is going to happen."

"I'm only going for a walk."

"And you won't go to the cockfights later?"

Again he didn't answer.

"When did you say you would be back?"

As he trod the frond-littered pathway that led to the beach, the lawns of the resort strewn with fallen branches, the ground flora still flattened by the rains, Maryvonne appeared from behind a knoll in a floral sundress. Her face flushed, eyes bright and sharp, she wore a look of invitation. Despite his almost desperate desire to be alone, he found himself welcoming her company.

"Scott," she cried, pressing two fingers to his chest as he stepped onto the beach. "You cannot wear those lovely shoes in the sand."

He glanced from her sandaled feet to his Florsheims.

"I have a cough coming on," he said. "Hardly the time to be going barefoot."

"The sand is warm," she replied, and after minimal protest he removed his shoes, leaving his socks on.

"She has returned," Maryvonne said as they strolled up the

beach, following the same route he'd pursued by himself the previous evening. "When you join us for drinks on the patio last
night, she still does not return, I sense this, but now she has. I
should be angry with you, for watering the truth, telling me gentle
lies, but I am not."

"I didn't want you to worry needlessly."

"It is your private life, no concern of mine," Maryvonne said
nonchalantly, as if putting distance between herself and a lover
but not throwing him over entirely. Though her lineage was anything but aristocratic, she was by instinct a rather sophisticated
woman. "Mostly I am glad to see you, *tu reprends*—resuming
yourself, would you say?"

"How can you tell?" he asked.

"By your smile, it is free. When you see me appear on the
path, you are happy, I can tell."

He tried to imagine how that could possibly be true, how he
could be caught smiling (if in fact he had been) after what had
just transpired in his hotel room.

"It is the only way."

"What?"

"It is the only way to tell about happiness," she explained.
"How you feel when you are not thinking about it. This is true
also of love, I think, also sadness perhaps."

She ran her fingers from his elbow down his forearm, her fingernails teasing the skin on top of his knuckles.

"Why could you and I not meet later?" she asked, halting,
cupping his hand in hers, pressing open the fingers and tickling
his palm softly with her nails.

"Zelda," he started to say, but how to explain that he had to
return to the room soon and make sure his wife hadn't harmed
herself, or that in states of manic paranoia she had an uncanny
talent for surmising when other women were attracted to him.

"Well, frankly, I'm not sure what we're doing, how long we're staying."

"You are here at least through tonight and you have an excursion with my husband."

"Also there is someone in Hollyw—"

"Yes, the second woman of the cards, I did not imagine it was I. So I know these things from the diviner, from our conversation, from my intuitions—but what is this to do with me?"

Hers was a highly European take on passion. It struck him as odd that he'd never had a truly sexual affair with a European woman. Two Brits, first Bijou O'Connor in the early thirties, and now Sheilah, but they didn't count. Europeans, especially the French and Italians, were so much more capable of duality, of grasping the divide between marital love and eros, between obligation and desire, without compromising one or the other. Americans, the Brits too, he supposed, were all so sincere and puritanical that even while committing adultery they tried to simplify their notion of fidelity. As soon as he took up with a new woman, she started plotting to steal him from Zelda, even after he made it clear—often stating the rules explicitly beforehand—that he could never desert her. Sheilah's tolerance for the duality of his attachment owed much to her own well-kept secrets, but once she'd shared the greatest of them, she became less cosmopolitan in her views, worrying about the depth of his affections, objecting to his use of declarations such as "my marvelous mistress" or "my beloved infidel" to inspire his lust for her. "Just once I'd like to hear you call me," she had said only this past winter, "the woman you would like someday to make your wife." Couldn't he give her that small satisfaction? Couldn't he tell her he wished it might be so? "You mean if Zelda had never existed, or if she had died during one of her bouts with insanity?" he had asked, and she cursed him, before starting in on herself. Only a masochist, only an orphan with a terrible opinion of self, racked with guilt about the lies she'd told to get where she was and filled with enough self-hatred to throw over marriage to a lord for a tawdry affair of the heart, could have attached herself to a permanently hopeless lush of a man who refused to come up with a Plan B for his life.

"Was there ever a time you say to yourself," Maryvonne asked, "this is not my responsibility, I have done all I could do for my wife?"

She had led them across the beach toward the runoff of the waves, professing her desire to walk in the shallows and feel the undertow, strong in the wake of the storm.

"You go ahead," he said, unwilling to bare his feet. "I'll walk parallel to you, and we can bellow back and forth over the surf striking this empty beach. Highly intimate in its own way."

"And I will ask you personal questions and you will tell me?"

Sure, why not?

"Which of you slept first with another person? After your marriage, I mean."

Zelda, most likely. In retrospect she often denied that the affair of 1924 had been sexual, but Scott knew his wife only said that to spare his feelings.

"Can you remember his name?"

Of course he could.

"Why not tell me? As a nurse I met so many soldiers and pilots. Maybe I have heard of him."

All the more reason not to utter it.

"You are still pained by her infidelity after all these years?" she asked. "And yet you are the one now who leads the life of duplicity."

Only by necessity, that was the crucial difference.

"Maybe there is choice too in your necessities, maybe it helps if you see it this way. It is only an affair, after all, this first infidelity of Zelda."

Except he knew that his wife had been ready to leave him for the Frenchman. She had asked for a divorce, her timing terrible. He was trying to finish a novel, his *Gatsby*, and angrily refused the request, in part because his pride wouldn't bow before an arbitrary rival, in part because he saw what she couldn't—that her heroic aviator didn't want her permanently, that he wasn't prepared to establish her safely in the world.

"Zelda wasn't someone who could make her own way in life," he explained.

"Did you want to leave her?"

"It wasn't an option."

"How can you be certain?"

He didn't reply. It was too hard to bring himself round to the idea that the code by which he had lived these many years might have been in vain, that Zelda might have managed just fine, or just as well, without him.

"I have not seen a soul for a long mile," Maryvonne observed. "Would it not be marvelous to take off all our clothes and swim far out in the ocean?"

"It's tempting," he said. "If I were to stay on this peninsula much longer, you would become very hard to resist. Ask me in a few days, if I'm still around."

"Oh, look," she cried, gesturing toward the water, where not thirty feet from shore swam a school of porpoises, breasting the waves in playful, arcing dives. "Do you not see what we have missed? Next time I will be more insisting."

As they neared the hotel patio, Scott could see Aurelio sitting alone, drinking a coffee and reading a newspaper on a bench beneath a stately palm.

"I almost forget to tell you, my message, the reason I must

search for you. You remember, yes, that my husband wishes to escort you on an excursion to the cockfights? *Moi,* he cannot escort to such a place, even though I offer to cut my hair like a boy. So it is still a plan, he asks me to tell you."

"I'm looking forward to it."

"He is going to pick a winning bird for you," Maryvonne promised, waving to Aurelio who had spotted them from the patio, then taking Scott aside by the arm, rising on her toes to whisper to him, her lips practically touching his—all of this in front of her husband, what audacity. "Let me walk you back to your room and encourage you, do not say no yet, to think about my proposal."

As they crossed the lawn, his socks soaking up water from the wet grass, he heard his name called and lifted his gaze to discover Zelda leaning forward over the balcony. He envisioned the scene through Zelda's eyes, the Florsheims dangling from his fingertips; and the image of himself walking beside a strange woman for whom he'd taken off his shoes made his face redden as if he'd been caught in an illicit act.

Maryvonne called out to say she hoped Zelda was better today, suggesting they might have a cup of tea this evening while the men watched birds kill each other, but Zelda, refusing to address Maryvonne by name, answered only, "I'm not feeling at all well."

"Scott, another thing," Maryvonne said. "A man stops me this morning and asks if I know you, how long, many such things. There is nothing to it, I tell him, we are new friends and why should he always ask such things."

"What did he look like?"

"Long, beautiful hair, the color of *argent.*"

"Silver hair and a milky eye?"

"Exactement."

"Scott, are you coming inside?" Zelda called again from the balcony.

"Is he a friend of yours?" Maryvonne asked.

"Scott," Zelda called.

"Not a friend exactly," he said, "but I suspect he's relatively harmless."

The Frenchwoman kissed him adieu as Zelda again called his name, and Maryvonne now waved to her, saying she hoped they would all get together soon.

"Aurelio did not think so," Maryvonne replied. "I thought it is better to tell you."

13

SHIVERING IN THE EVENING AIR, HIS CHEST AND FOREHEAD SOAKED with sweat, he slid along the sheets, contorting his hips like a snake, lifting the limp doll's arm draped over his stomach, sidewinding until he was out from beneath Zelda. He checked the time, sat up abruptly, and rose into flashes of dizzying color, mostly reds and purples, his entire body heavy as sand, wanting nothing so much as to succumb to the drowsy pull of the bed. He took several steps, yawned, felt a rush of emptiness come over him as though he were blacking out, his balance thrown so that he had to catch himself to keep from toppling. The room was dark, the heavy curtains shutting out all but a dim radiance that settled on the floor near the desk. Zelda hadn't stirred. Without flicking on a light he slipped into the bathroom, pulled the door shut behind him, wrapping his hand in the dark on the shower knob, its four prongs like the steering wheel on a sailboat. Stepping inside a drizzle that had all the intensity of water sprinkled from a watering can, its cold jarring, brisk, he tucked his head into the stream and withdrew it several times, waking himself. Gradually the water warmed, and though he knew he should step out and get dressed, he lingered under its spray, the heat easing his tired muscles.

He wanted to steal from the room before she awakened. Maryvonne and Aurelio would be waiting for him on the patio downstairs. He was still planning to attend the cockfights because it was the type of thing that might make for a story someday and because he was tired of Zelda dictating the terms of his experience, tired of a life lived for so long without choices. It was a matter of principle. Here was something he wanted to do, an activity he might enjoy. Yesterday belonged to her, the hours squandered on her maniacal fit. Still, as he pulled on clothes he'd laid out neatly on the cool tile of the bathroom floor—all donned earlier this morning, still relatively fresh—he worried that she wasn't well enough to be left alone.

She was the only thing he truly loved in the world, but his love was twisted and wounded, and he could never again make it a simple, straightforward thing. He saw himself standing over her, demanding the gun, threatening violence, and he wanted a drink, he wanted to forget. There was no way of taking anything back, ever. It was out there in the world and even if she forgave him, she could remember it at a later date, in the middle of some fight, recalling the exact words he'd used, recounting what he'd done and hurling it back at him.

Scott traversed the room in the dark, checking the closet, his suitcase, rummaging through the dresser, on the hunt for chocolate, Benzedrine, stimulants of any kind, something to pull him through the fatigue.

"Why are you nervously pacing?"

He had thought she was still asleep and waited a moment before replying. "I can't find my other jacket."

"On the balcony."

He found the damp sport coat stretched over the back of a

white iron chair. Searching the outer pocket, his fingers sinking into a morass of Baker's German's sweet chocolate that had melted into the lining, he traipsed through wrapper and foil until he found a stout stump, like a severed plant stem, extracting the pieces of wrapper embedded in it. The candy tasted stale and bitter, laced with musty lint, with tiny scraps of wrapper. Still, he licked his fingers clean and again plunged his hand into the pocket, digging amid the frayed wrapper until he found several newly chocolate-coated pills, bennies, popping them into his mouth.

"I would never have remained silent for so long about your problems," she said as he reentered the room. "You let me slip too far down—you saw I was in decline and did nothing."

She was sitting up in the bed, back propped against the headboard, lost in the whirligig of her obsessions in which time was all of a piece, in which this morning was interchangeable with the day they met; yesterday, with her first breakdown in Paris. Even the smallest of his freedoms was a commentary on her captivity, their reunions in one exotic place or another merely sentimental. He had a life elsewhere, another woman waiting for him, worrying about him, pining for his safe return.

"We've been here before, Zelda," he said, conscious of the fact that he was running late.

"Except I can't remember."

"I can."

"I don't want you to, I don't want that anymore."

"What?"

"Can't you just forget me? I want to be forgotten, I want to be new again. Do you think that's even possible? Not just for me, but do you think it's ever possible, for anyone?"

"Of course I do," he said hastily.

"You don't, though, I can tell. For what it's worth, neither do

I. But you don't know how hard it is to fight what's inside of you as though it were your enemy—"

"I was there, Zelda." He assured her he had seen her through it all, from the onset of the illness, and he would help her if she were ever again to sink beneath its waves.

"And yet you're going out on the town with them tonight."

He sighed and stole a glance at his watch.

"To gape at birds killing one another. You'll be horrified by the result, you'll be unable to decide if you feel worse about betting on a winning, murderous cock or watching the loser writhe in helpless agony."

"Oh, for crying out loud, look, if you're so damned lonely, I told you that Maryvonne's not joining us, she wanted to meet you for tea on the—"

"Please drop it," Zelda interrupted, resignation in her voice. Then, springing from the bed, launching herself into his arms and resting her cheek against his chest, she said, "You're still angry. How long are you planning to stay mad?"

At dinner Aurelio appeared to be wearing his wife's foul mood, waiting for the portion of the night when he would be free to do as he pleased. The couple had taken the liberty of ordering for Scott, though the meal was cold by now: chicken smothered in garlic and herbs, dressed in mango and avocado, the dish altogether too pungent and spicy for his palate. Scott drained his Cuba libre and reached for his beer. The ale with its bitter hops was pleasant going down, the temperate brown-gold liquid staving off the cotton-mouthed sensation. The double dose of alcohol gave him a jolt. For days he'd been running on adrenaline, on the stirrings of this new place and the good healthy sweat of humidity cleansing his body, so that he was never quite fully drunk, not in

Havana, not here on Varadero. He ought to put something in his stomach. He took several bites of the chicken, coating his seared tongue with beer and water.

"So, no Zelda, what is the story here?" Maryvonne asked sharply. She was irritated at both Scott and her husband, for their willingness to abandon her. "How am I to pass this night alone?"

"Mi compañero," Aurelio said, ignoring the tenor of his cousin's complaint, "my wife tells me that you do not live with Zelda in the United States. How often do you see each other?"

Before he could defend himself, Maryvonne protested. Aurelio of all people, she said, should understand that couples must arrive at arrangements suited to life's difficulties.

"Zelda has trouble with her health," Scott said, giving away as little as possible, "so she resides in a hospital in Asheville, North Carolina."

"Yes, yes," Maryvonne said. "Of course."

"Whereas I make my living writing for the movies, and there's only one place to do that, in California, on the West Coast. As Maryvonne says, it's a difficult situation, but we manage, spending time together between films."

The waiter came to the table and Scott ordered another drink, loathing himself for saying even the little he'd just said, hoping the alcohol might shut him up. By the time the waiter returned with his second Cuba libre, one of the clerks from the front desk had circled round behind Aurelio to impart a message.

"Our ride is here," Aurelio said to Scott. "Did you get enough to eat?"

"I'll take my drink with me," Scott said, standing, as Maryvonne got to her feet and leaned in for a quick word.

"You wish I should visit her perhaps?" she asked.

He appreciated the offer but, no, it wasn't necessary.

She kissed him, first the right cheek, which was visible to her husband, then the left, catching the corner of his mouth at a discreet angle, her moist lips lingering there a second, her wine-sweet breath whispering, "Maybe I will see you later."

In the black Oldsmobile with the long, elegant hood that ascended in the front into a brilliant chrome grille and bumper, Aurelio teased him about the aside with Maryvonne, asking whether secrets had been traded. "Mostly about Zelda," Scott replied noncommittally. It was hard to tell whether the Spaniard suspected a liaison, and if so, whether he was encouraging or preventing it.

"I always have exceptional relationship with my cousin," he said, impossible to read one way or the other. "Never nothing to complain about. We share different views about marriage, about a new life in Cuba, but what is this? Nothing, I say. Everything change for me since the war, that is all." He was trying to confide in Scott and doing a poor job of it, or maybe it would be more accurate to say that Scott was doing a poor job of earning the man's confidences, partly because he couldn't understand what was being asked of him.

They drove along the same road Scott had traversed only last night, Aurelio asking whether Scott had money on him. When he confessed to carrying a large sum of cash, the Spaniard smiled and clapped him on the back. "Do you trust me, *mi compañero,* I will make a rich man tonight of you." The strategy, as far as Scott understood it, was to place bad bets early, throw money around, let their betting appear risky and haphazard, as if they were merely fumbling along on intuition. They must lose more than they won on the early fights. You couldn't waltz into a foreign town and clear out the house bet after bet without provoking the locals' resentments. Aurelio had spent the day scouting the cockfighting scene on the peninsula, angling for the skinny on several birds to be fought tonight, including one that was well-bred and to be pitted by an expert handler, a bird that might score them a tidy sum, though it was up against stiff competition. Scott couldn't afford to gamble and wasn't any good at it. He was the last man in the world who ought to be scheming for an easy score in a foreign land by betting on a sport he knew nothing about.

There had been no time to collect her thoughts because he'd left in such a hurry. No chance to tell him about the demons that hovered over her while she slept last night and again this afternoon, their presence more electrical than substantial, waves moving in and out of focus, pulsing in red like a strobe light or flickering like fire, spirits looming behind the flashes of light inside of inchoate blackened orbs. They were ambient, distorted shadows of noise, except for every now and then when one of their bone-white faces obtruded for an instant, then retreated. She prayed to banish them, but the whispers persisted, buzzing in her ears, contemptuous of her prayers. They were used to being banished. Too cowardly to speak with clarity—she accused them of cowardice aloud—the spirits left only hints. Though never in whole sentences, they brought news of illness, death, awful occurrences.

Alone now as dusk fell, she turned on the light beside the bed. If she stayed awake, the shadowed beings might be unable to find their way into the room. Still, the night ahead was long and beset with worry. She picked up the novel by Rachel Field, but it couldn't hold her attention. She rummaged through her luggage, through assorted items on the dresser—her Mason Pearson brush, silk ribbons, cosmetics, several pieces of good jewelry Scott had purchased for her over the years—fondling a bracelet with silver charms from places they had visited together, only then remembering the issue of *LIFE* borrowed from Maryvonne. She regretted her harsh behavior toward the Frenchwoman this afternoon and hoped she might have a chance to make up for it later. Here again was that blonde girl in the jumper, who might have modeled for a Nazi propaganda poster except her face was so stern and joyless, her eyes eerie in resemblance to those of the doll on her lap, sharp yet somehow lifeless, as though the girl had been conceived in imitation of the doll rather than the other way around. The more Zelda studied the photograph, the more it spooked her. Flipping open the magazine, she vowed not to return to the cover, but every now and then, with index finger keeping her place in an article, she would fold the journal shut to study the girl's empty eyes, perfect nose, and pouty lips. Fanning through pages of a magazine completely visual in its conception, each of its stories spare on the order of advertising copy or news-reels that merely skimmed the surface of world events, Zelda set-tled on a layout that caught her eye: the Nazis taking Prague without a fight. *LIFE* characterized the lies told by the Nazis to justify their actions as "stupid" and alluded to their practice of leveraging atrocity tales no one else believed. The politics of terror could be inferred, but just barely, from photographs of German tanks rumbling into Prague, of military processions filing down cobbled, conquered streets, the Czechs lining up in gray-black overcoats and berets, witnesses to their own capture, a few of the women jeering, perhaps cursing at soldiers with Mausers strapped across their backs who paid them no attention.

On another page she found a quiz and filled it out on Scott's behalf. It was about how people behave in automobiles, drivers mostly. She answered the first three questions, giving Scott the lowest score twice, the middle score once, and saved the best for last: "When you become tense and nervous during a trip, do you . . . ." Instantly she ruled out Option C: "Try not to let it affect you?" Clearly, the answer was either "Give sharp answers to the people traveling with you?" or "Sulk and refuse to talk?" She split the difference—A worth 5 points, B worth 15, so Scott received a 10, bringing his grand total to 35. The index at the end of the advertisement suggested that any score below 70 described a person tagged by doctors as a "nervous irritable," the reasons for irritability many: ill health, worries, modern life, coffee. Readers suffering from a sub-70 score were advised to try Postum, a coffee substitute made of oats.

"Scott," she said to the empty room, remembering how she used to leave the light on in his study when he was away so that when she awoke she would think him near. She imagined him in the car, swigging rum with Aurelio. Hard enough to get him off the booze, never mind weaning him off coffee for some drink made of oats. "Please," she said, "no more recollections of how I was when we first met, when I made you so happy."

An article about Charles Lindbergh gripped her longer than it should have; she found his reclusiveness appealing. He didn't enjoy being in the public eye. How could he after what had happened to his firstborn, stolen from the nursery of the Lindbergh mansion? For several years the American press wouldn't stop pestering the family, and what finally drove the Lindberghs from the country and across the Atlantic to London and Paris was a photograph taken by a journalist (reproduced here in *LIFE*) of their second boy in the backseat of a limousine, on display for the next psychopath with a vendetta against them.

Scott would be at the cockfights by now, she imagined. What did he know about gamecocks anyway? Why was he always feigning interest in some sport he knew nothing about? As when he took up boxing after Ernest, trying to prove something to himself: he had even brought that unbearable Parisian back with them to the States in '28—oh, what was his name?—who stayed with them for almost a year, serving as Scott's waiting man, sparring partner, and drunken companion. Was Aurelio trustworthy? she wondered. Were the cockfights even legal? One way or the other, though it hadn't occurred to her until now, there must be seedy sorts involved.

From the top of the dresser with its fine brown-black burnish (she made a mental note to ask someone about the wood, what kind it was), she scooped her rosary up and rolled the beads nervously between her fingers. She felt no desire to pray, but she couldn't leave him unprotected. So she turned to her devotion, counting beads, contemplating the sorrowful mysteries, knocking out Our Fathers, Hail Marys, Glory Be's, and O My Jesuses in an effort to keep her husband out of harm's way.

Roughly a quarter-mile beyond the church, the Oldsmobile turned south on a dirt road that split embankments of palms, acacias, and cedars, and before long it approached a ramshackle cottage. One of the men from the bodega yesterday, the sly one with the barklike skin, waited for them on the porch, seated on a battered wooden bench. He rose and advanced toward the car with his black gamecock cradled in his arm, the bird swelling and unfurling its wings as Scott and Aurelio climbed from the backseat.

"Here he is," Aurelio said to Scott, speaking of the bird, which was a Spanish black. "In my opinion, *lo mas bello* of the gamecocks." He introduced the stocky indigenous villager as Maximiliano, Max for short, and Scott thought, What a marvelous name for a peasant.

Only this morning Max had taught Aurelio the ins and outs of cockfighting in the region, reviewing, for instance, how the bird before them had been kept, when it had been dubbed (this referred to the act of slicing off the wattles beneath the beak and ear lobes, then trimming the fleshy comb, all of which must be done expertly in the first year and healed properly so that there were no pouches of skin where a rival cock might seize hold with its beak). The two men also discussed what Max fed the bird, where and for how long it had been walked, Aurelio preferring birds that passed the pen walk fending for themselves.

A gamecock was to be watched over from a distance by those caring for it, diet supplemented now and then as necessary with protein, mostly eggs, scraps of meat. Since a cock must never encounter rivals during the formative months, the land it trod had to be kept clear of cocks young and old, also of adult male birds such as the Muscovy duck. Hens were off limits during the game-cock's celibate initiation into a world artificially emptied of rivals and other distractions so that he might perceive it as his own. As Aurelio ran through the basics of raising gamecocks, Max stroked the handsome black bird with the bright red face, massaging its feathers, kneading the neatly cropped flesh of the comb. Occasionally he would dribble onto his fingertips and rub the spittle into the clipped skin beneath the beak, eliciting a ripple of sound from the bird's chest.

"Listen to this story," Aurelio said to Scott, and then to Max, "Tell Scott the story of the bird you lost last year," speaking first in English, then also in Spanish. Max grunted and smiled at the prompt, then subsided into a babble of Cuban-inflected Spanish, Aurelio letting him go on for over a minute before recounting the highlights for Scott. "It was during the walking period. He had fenced off a long stretch of land, free from predators." Scott caught pieces of Maximiliano's excited story, the repeated mention of the bird, *"un gallo de pelea,"* also the term *"pequeño estanque"* used over and over again. "What is that word?" Scott asked. "Pond," Aurelio muttered, then translated more of the story, how the cock grew in his own estimation daily, still not dubbed, his comb and wattle as yet brilliant and full. Max had heard tales about gamecocks and water before but never given credence to them. He would soon learn his lesson. For the walking pen included a small pond, and one day his prized gamecock, the best he'd ever bred, lingered near the pond and while nodding forward to drink, peered into the face of a gorgeous bird, which stared back at him. *"Tan lindo es un gallo de pelea en sus propios ojos,"* Aurelio said, possibly repeating Max's words, possibly adding a layer of commentary. So handsome to himself is the gamecock that all he perceives in his own reflection is the threatening beauty of another bird encroaching on his turf. He spreads his wings and lifts himself off the ground, the rival bird matching him move for move, all their tactics instinctive; and now one of Max's sons is racing for the pond, while a younger son sprints to get Max, who seizes a burlap sack always on hand (because a riled cock, especially before the spurs have been sliced off his feet, can shred clothing, flay skin, even take out a man's eye), and he makes a dash for the pond, already too late. "Despite his haste, his worry, his time and training," Aurelio said. It was often the way with tragedy. Maximiliano discovered the most beautiful of any bird he'd ever raised drowned in shallow water, having fought and been defeated by its own reflection.

Aurelio laughed as Max and he together concluded the story, but Scott detected a hint of sorrow in the villager's joviality. It had been his best bird, after all. Scott heaved his chest into a laugh, feeling the tickle in his esophagus and bronchia, the involuntary roll of the hacking cough, as he raised a fist to his mouth. Max walked back to the porch, speaking over his shoulder to Aurelio, who translated, "He says the drowned one was the most gorgeous bird ever. But does it mean he can fight? Not always. This bird he will pit for us tonight, which we are wise to bet on, is a fighter like no other."

"Has he won many times?" Scott asked, wiping his hand with his handkerchief and tucking it into his pants pocket.

"I'm sure the record has been exaggerated for our benefit," Aurelio said. But the gamecock had been pitted and fought well and survived without injury. Always a good sign. It was, in Aurelio's estimation, a bird with the right instincts.

"I would not spar my own bird the day before a match," he informed Scott, referring to the scene they'd witnessed outside the bodega yesterday. "Still, let us bet on Max's bird, why not, one of our coquettish bets. We tease the local tournament for fun, find out how and where cash flows, though he is not a bird we will win on. You wait, I will show you the bird I select for this task, in your name, in honor of Mr. Scott Fitzgerald."

Max returned from the cottage with a bottle of Bacardi rum, cracked the cap, splashed some of the gold-brown liquid at their feet, then passed the bottle, first to Aurelio, who took a long swig, then to Scott, who did the same, the rum smooth and warm, tasting of oak and molasses, though its finish was on the thin side. The men shared the bottle, and each time Aurelio took a swig he praised the bird and its owner, saying, "To your fearless game-cock," or "To the gameness of the birds tonight." Scott kept eyeing the gamecock ensconced in the nook of Max's arm, which stared grimly out into the yard. It bore the shape of a raven, except for the red-orange hue of its reptilian face, except for those intensely bright, protruding brown-black eyes and the trimmed ridge of the comb that reminded Scott of nothing so much as the scales crowning the head of a lizard. The cock showed little interest in the men, but its eyes were alert, looking to take offense.

The three men loitered near the high-end automobile Aurelio had procured, the driver leaning against its hood, awaiting further instruction. Several times the bottle of rum made the rounds, Aurelio and Max exchanging pleasantries and barbs in Spanish, Scott no longer listening, trying to suppress another fit of coughing. Sputtering, he twisted away from the others, feeling the cough subside even as a raw ache lingered in his lungs. He took another swig. The rum sat heavy in his stomach, making him tired and sad rather than forward-looking. It occurred to him that he shouldn't be sharing the bottle, not if his tuberculosis was kicking in, but it was difficult to be vigilant about the treatment protocols of a disease his friends and family refused to believe he suffered from. The spotting on the handkerchief, the red spittle on his hands, the hollow burning in his lungs, what did they mean if no one believed him?

"He'll ride with us to the fights," Aurelio announced as the villager ventured inside the cottage, returning with a pen for the bird and a topless wood toolbox filled with equipment: twine, leather swatches, water, herbs, scissors, and sundry other sharp metal implements. Aurelio sat in the middle with the toolbox, Scott flanking him on one side, Max on the other with the bird in his lap, the pen on the floor. After stuffing a wad of tobacco into the corner of his mouth, Max offered some to his companions, the Spaniard politely accepting a small pinch. The driver, though, refused to start the Oldsmobile. He complained of the cock's getting loose inside the car, knowing how much damage a gamecock could do—if it saw a rival out the window, if they were to hit a rough patch of road—not only to the leather interior of the Olds but to the men trapped there in that enclosed space with an enraged bird. Agreeing to pen the bird, Max slipped out of the backseat, and when he returned to the car held the pen in his lap, the cock peering forward through its steel cage door. The driver whipped the Olds down the uneven, jagged road, tires popping on gravel and branches as the tropical blue-gray evening descended into the trees ahead.

"What's that?" Scott asked.

"It's the gaff," Aurelio told him, "you know, which replaces the spur after it is shaved down."

Scott studied the curved spike, designed for no purpose other than to puncture flesh with facility, an instrument that might have been conceived by Spanish inquisitors in their spare time.

"It's so long," he said. "How long is the spur above the cock's heel naturally?"

"Not quite half this length," Aurelio said. "The gaff increases efficiency."

As they rode through woods onto the main dirt road, the car's headlights now and then washed over the glowing eyes of road-side animals. All he could think of was Zelda, alone in that hotel room or wandering long moonlit beaches, tempted by the tides. He was crazy to have left her alone so soon. He extended his palm to receive the bottle from Aurelio, swilled the rum, letting it clear his throat and burn his tender lungs, then shook his head, feeling the buzz, dazed, bleary-eyed, muttering, "God damn me"—his remark drawing a query from the Spaniard as to whether he was all right.

The Oldsmobile now drove along a golf course and soon a white stucco mansion came into view, from the front this time, but still Scott recognized it right away, the same house he had admired from the beach yesterday afternoon. Its many faces, its windowless walls and high parapets, yielded the impression that it was defending itself against something.

"Whose house is that?"

Aurelio posed the question to Max, but the driver spoke up first. "It is the estate of American tycoon, Mr. du Pont."

Tonight's series of cockfights was unsanctioned, since the family was not in residence. But cockfights on the peninsula often took place at the du Pont stables. The driver pulled the Olds behind a small line of cars and trucks, several of them in metallic greens and reds with fine chrome bumpers and white roofs, others among them rather obviously weather-beaten and dilapidated.

Once inside the stables Scott scrutinized the pit in the foreground of the barn, the open dirt floor swept clean of hay and impediments, strewn with sawdust, and a two-foot-high fence concocted of wire and burlap having been rounded into a ring of twenty feet in diameter.

An in-progress match drew lackluster shouts from the crowd.

The novice bird they'd observed sparring outside the bodega yesterday (Scott wouldn't have recognized it if not for Aurelio's prompting) was fighting and in bad shape. It had been billed in the head. Now in runaway mode, it refused to engage its rival, bandying about the arena in an uneven gait. Sometime prior to getting brained, the bird had managed to gash an eye of its rival, which circled the pit in a disoriented frenzy, unable to locate its opponent. The standoff had lasted for more than five minutes.

"Soon they move the match," Aurelio explained, "to the drag pit." This was a smaller arena where matches that had become uneventful could be carried to their end.

"Why don't they pick the damned birds up and let them live to fight another day?" Scott asked.

"There has to be a result," Aurelio said. "For the sake of bets, for the sake of the birds. Probably the winner of this match will also suffer the hatchet."

Scott was appalled by the crudity of the logic whereby a bird might survive, even perhaps win a fight, and still surrender its life.

"What good is he if he cannot fight?" Aurelio reasoned. "If eye is hurt, the bird is of no value. A broken leg can be reset, maybe, probably with success, but only if *un gallo de pelea* shows itself first to be a fighter."

On the other side of the pit Scott caught sight of—he should have been more surprised, but he wasn't—Famosa García, crouched low along the wall and cheering on the bird with the gashed eye. Maybe he knew its owner or handler, but more likely he had bet on the bird. Now the referee summoned the handlers to retrieve their cocks and move them to the drag pit. In the midst of the commotion, another villager approached Maximiliano and the two men traded heated words. Apparently, the Spanish black had been scheduled earlier on the bill than expected because a bird had been disqualified. Max wanted time to prepare his bird, to draw out its aggression with the sparring mitts. He spat a long gob of brown saliva at his feet, perhaps in disgust at the news.

"We have to bet on him," Aurelio said. "Give me some money, I will place our bets."

"How much?" Scott asked, taking out his wallet.

"Twenty American dollars," the Spaniard said. "This should be fine."

It seemed like a large bet, especially given the strategy Aurelio had outlined earlier of wagering mostly to lose on the initial bouts. Almost all the money Scott could lay claim to in the world was on his person, a small reserve stashed in a suitcase at the hotel, no fees due him from the studio or from magazines, his royalties at a standstill, next to nothing in his bank account. The money he drew on for this evening's revelry had been calculated in terms of the time it bought him: five to seven days here in Cuba, several weeks afterward to scramble for new footing in Hollywood, maybe a month and a half total if he was lucky and frugal, if Arnold Gingrich took another piece or two for *Esquire* on commission and Scott managed to scrounge up patchwork editing jobs on a few movie scripts. It wouldn't be long, though, until he was flat broke again and begging from whomever would still float him cash, the circle of candidates ever smaller, shrinking by the year. He was back to surviving on speculation, betting on his next novel to pull him out of hock. Earlier in the day, when Aurelio had boasted that he was sure to win big, Scott played it cool, pretending he didn't care one way or the other, but of course he did.

Still, the prospect of an easy score tempted him. If he could double the cash laid out tonight, somehow pocket even a hundred bucks, well, winnings like that weren't small change at this point in his life. Which was why throwing away twenty on a first bet didn't sit well. Which was why, as he handed over the cash, he was secretly miffed at the Spaniard for making him bet more than he could afford to lose. He hated it when other people were reckless with his money; he'd done enough damage to his finances on his own.

"Yes, for first bet this is fine," Aurelio repeated as he walked away with Scott's cash.

Only afterward did Scott think to ask the Spaniard how much of his own money he was wagering, and only after that did he consider that by throwing cash around carelessly he was putting Zelda's vacation at risk.

"The match was difficult basically from the beginning because it is a really hot night," someone said to him from behind. Scott turned to meet the familiar, unflappable gaze of Famosa García. "Once a bird loses his cool, it is all over."

In the company of Matéo's emissary stood a blond-haired man in a white linen suit—white apparently never out of season in the tropics. He was a German, Famosa García explained, without introducing the man. Scott shouldn't have been surprised. Roosevelt hadn't declared war on them yet, and it was well-known that Germans with treacherous politics vacationed and transacted business in America's neighboring nations to the south, crossing borders with impunity. Maybe he was an anti-Fascist, one never knew. Scott studied the man's grim smile, his blanched pinkish lips and slightly twisted nose, his thick white-blond brows set over burrowed eyes. For whatever reason, the anonymous German chose to stand a foot or two behind the Cuban's shoulder at all times.

What bonded the men in the barn, what allowed them to put aside political differences, was a common passion for watching one gamecock square off against another, each descended from birds whose brave genealogy and deadly notoriety went back to antiquity, before the time of Christ's crucifixion. Fiercely territorial, unyielding, an inspiration to warriors from the classical age on up to the present, the cocks were biologically designed to brawl; even their handlers couldn't instill the spirited hate in them. It was either in the bird or it wasn't, what the cockers called gameness. Get Darwin or Herbert Spencer to explain that to you if he could, but you might just as soon blame God.

"The bird I bet on," Famosa García said, "he fights with fine and clean movements, his blows straight to the breast, hitting hard, then backing off, again rushing his enemy—except it is not an easy game always. Straight out his opponent struck a lucky blow to the eye, always such things are possible, and now my bird fights desperately, aggressively, he lands a brainer, and *al instante,* in a flash, there is no beauty left in the way he must kill his rival."

"But you're confident the fight will go your way?" Scott asked.

"It is the only way," the silver-haired emissary replied. "I overhear your conversation minutes ago—you bet good money on the Spanish black, a long shot, I believe you say. I did not take you for a gambler, Mr. Fitzgerald."

What was Famosa García still doing here anyway? Scott wished to be free of him. Had Cardoña paid him to stay on and attend tonight's event? But, then, he couldn't have known Scott would turn up at the cockfights.

"Your wife, she does not join you tonight?" Famosa García asked even though there was not a single woman in the crowd. He led Scott and the silent German toward the drag pit, the tighter space having worked wonders for the bird that still had gameness.

Though ruined for subsequent battle, the one-eyed bird had cornered its rival and now lifted itself to drive the gaffs into the lame bird's chest. Scott looked away. Focusing too much on the sloppy, brutal end to this bout would only ruin the next for him.

Afterward the handler of the slain bird, the other man Aurelio had spoken to outside the bodega yesterday, the one with the pug nose and flat Amerindian face, rambled on in Spanish to Famosa García and the German, apologizing for his bird's sad performance.

"I should tell you, Mr. Fitzgerald, I have not yet heard from Señor Cardoña," Famosa García said to Scott. "But the man who died, it turns out, is not a nobody. So, of course, the police must solve this crime."

"I appreciate the news bulletin," Scott said coolly, then extracted his Moleskine, remarking that it was a professional vice, forever scribbling observations about your experiences, never knowing what they might amount to. "Of course," Famosa García said. Scott retreated several steps, unfolding the journal, but as he did so a piece of green stationery slipped from its pages, eddying on an ocean-backed breeze and landing in a strip of rippled, grainy dirt, probably smoothed-over manure. He stooped for it, bending at the waist instead of crouching, dizzied for a split second as the wind again caught the letter, and now also fumbling the Moleskine; and though he nimbly slipped his other palm beneath the falling journal, he failed to make the catch, its pages splaying open into the dirt, papers scattering as he cursed himself and crouched to the ground to gather strewn contents: a negative of the photograph taken with Famosa García, directions to a restaurant here on Varadero, several notes scratched on hotel stationery. Zelda's letter was no longer in sight. He searched in vain for it, distraught, impatient with himself, as he moved along the wings of the crowd that fanned out toward the stables.

He could smell the hay and sense it prickling in his lungs, breathing in the stink of manure and horse urine but also the vital stench of the horses themselves, their hides like fresh leather on new shoes except different because there was sweat and blood and oxygen in those hides. It was the odor of animal existence in its raw prowess, of yesterday's black mare on the beach in the sun, still capable of finding her legs when spurred.

Back at the pit, his head clearer now but also troubled by the loss of the letter, he saw Max seated on a stool, holding the Spanish black across his lap, outfitting the bird for its bout. Aurelio had agreed to serve as an assistant of some sort, and as Scott drew close, he watched the Spaniard wrapping small swaths of leather around the bird's right shank, securing the patches with twine snug against the spur stub, now sliding the gaff with its large curved spike over the leather, fitting it wide so that the point was positioned lower on the heel but in the same basic direction as the shorn spur. Max grasped the bird firmly, one hand clamping its thighs together, the other up along the bird's cape, and in one swift motion he flipped the bird and Aurelio walked round behind Max to outfit the other shank.

"Why is that damned thing so long?" Scott asked about the gaff when Aurelio stepped over the wall with the stool and box of equipment, leaving Max alone in the pit with the bird.

The look Aurelio shot him contained a hint of scorn, as though he was tired of Scott's ignorant doubt. In the pit, under the watchful eye of the referee, the handlers exchanged birds, checking that wings and tails had been duly clipped, the gaffs positioned correctly. Satisfied, they swapped birds again, each retreating a few steps to groom and primp the feathers of his fighting cock one last time.

"He never tell me he is also the handler," Aurelio said, rocking side to side, his weight tilting on one foot, then the other, his voice heavy with disapproval.

The referee summoned the handlers and the crowd clamored in anticipation of the bout. Each handler urged his bird forward, holding it by the tail feather as the gamecocks collided and exchanged pecks, their feathers ruffled, wings spread, striking at each other without yet inflicting any damage. This practice of breasting and billing enticed the birds to engage right away. You could see the fight enter their eyes.

Withdrawing until he stood by the low burlapped wall, Max smiled at Scott and Aurelio, saying, *"Deseale suerte a mi gallo glorioso."*

"He boasts again of his handsome bird, asks for our blessing," Aurelio said.

"It's what the birds might say," Scott suggested, "all that strutting and attitude, it's what they might say of themselves if they could. We are handsome, therefore invincible."

Aurelio smiled at the remark, but it was a grim smile, forced or insincere, maybe both. So Scott asked what troubled him.

"He should be concentrating on the bird," Aurelio snapped, and Scott was relieved to find that he wasn't the source of the Spaniard's displeasure. Clearly, though, Aurelio had his doubts about Max and his bird. Had he too laid down a large bet on the beautiful Spanish black?

Again the referee beckoned the handlers, ordering them to pit the birds, so Max set his handsome black bird with the bright red face in the dirt before him, hovering above and behind the bird, far enough away that it could focus solely on its rival. Instinct told the bird to swagger, pontificate, prepare for onslaught. Its opponent, a stunning white gamecock with bluish-gray breast feathers, came in low and aggressive. The birds measured each other, one craning its neck forward, the other lunging for a quick strike, their wings raised and flapping in sharp, violent motions, each parry and riposte sounding like a percussive slap. As the Spanish black sprang into the air, leading with talonlike feet and the torturous metal gaffs, it flared its wings above its nape angelically, slanting forward, such grace in the low-to-the-ground flight of the two opponents that for a brief interval it was as though they floated in an image torn from someone's elegant dream.

The white gamecock was swifter, mercurial in its movements. It slipped past the talons of the Spanish black, dodging thrusts, then billing it hard and stiff in the neck, the two birds propping themselves and rotating on their tail feathers, raising talons and bounding forward, gaffs held high, searching for angles at which to strike. The Spanish black's responses and adjustments lagged behind those of its rival. All at once it became clear that Max's bird couldn't win. When Scott glanced again at Aurelio, he saw defeat written on the Spaniard's face.

What happened next—in a manner of minutes, in a splash of time in which all incidents blur—was one of those events in life people often say are best forgotten. You might spend half your time wishing to remember exactly what you'd done (unable to rid yourself of the belief that even forgotten actions contain hints of the true self), the other half feeling grateful that the mind is so marvelously porous (so much of everyday experience slipping almost immediately beyond our apprehension of it). There may be occasions on which we ought to be thankful for what we can't remember, but always there is the allure of shame, a sense that here lies one more thing that must remain hidden from sight, even perhaps from yourself.

This much Scott would remember: how the white but blue-breasted bird rose above his rival in full plume, able to get higher all of a sudden, how its steel gaffs plunged into black feathers, frenzied, loosened, floating free as a gaff snagged in the other bird's breast. Even in injury, Maximiliano's bird was undaunted, its plumage gorgeous, the feathers from crown to cape standing on edge like frightened hair, wings raised and awful. With the gaff caught in the chest of the black bird, the referee called for the handlers to separate the cocks, Aurelio striding into the pit with the stool and box, Scott pressed against the low burlap wall from the outside, studying the bird. Max tended to his gamecock by plucking a choice feather or two, cooling it with water, applying salve to the wound, but mostly by holding the bird upright so it might crow and jut its neck, gagging on the blood clots in its chest. "If it hacks up a chunk of blood," Aurelio said to Scott, "that is good." But as far as Scott could tell the blood merely curdled in the bird's punctured lung.

Next he must have walked out wide along the wall, for he could remember Famosa García saying, "The beginning is full of the end. *Es portentoso,* an opening of ill portents for your bird, *compañero,*" and though possibly it wasn't intended as such, Scott heard the remark as a taunt. The referee called for the birds to be pitted again, their fury and hatred for each other evident in their reptilian eyes, and when Max set the Spanish black down, it glared with bright-eyed hauteur at its rival. Almost immediately the white bird inflicted further damage, descending swiftly, a gaff tripping on the edge of the Spanish black's wing before glancing off. After that, Max's bird could no longer lift itself off the ground, and the white gamecock came in once more, feet raised, gaffs aimed at its rival, already tilting badly to the left, nearly prone, and as the blows landed Scott felt them as if they struck his own chest.

It must have been that which led him to hurdle the burlap wall amid a frenzy of shouting, the order of events from here on out arbitrary, as if a spirit of chaos had descended over the pit. Maybe the referee turned and signaled for help (in memory Scott possessed an image of the man's contemptuous gaze), but in any event before he reached the bird, Famosa García's German and two locals came out of nowhere to tackle him and he fought back, fists raised, swinging wildly, inaccurately, believing he had to get to the black gamecock if only to spare a single proud bird this rite of barbarism. He took several blows to the head, clenched fists at first, then wild shots to the stomach, one to the solar plexus that knocked the wind out of him and brought him to his knees, gasping, coughing up phlegm even as someone kicked sand in his face. His nose was bleeding. In the confusion he lost track of his opponents, until his gaze latched onto the man in the white suit and he rolled toward him, designing retaliatory damage even in defeat, if only for one of his opponents, if only by bloodying his white linen suit. Scott grabbed at the linen ankle cuffs, attempting to pull the German to the ground, and as the other two assailants increased the severity of their blows, he tried to rub his bloodied nose against the fine clean fabric of the suit of the man who stood above him kicking his leg to free it. Eventually, Scott collapsed, as someone ground a knee high into his clavicle, as someone else plunged a thumb into his eye, the spray of sawdust and granules of sand grinding across the surface of the cornea as he clamped the lid shut and only lamely fended off blows. He rolled free, beyond the kicks to his stomach and groin, the point of someone's boot catching the bad eye, the pain shooting to his temple, the eye throbbing, difficult now even to open it. Soon he lay in the dirt a few feet from where the gorgeous white gamecock stood over its rival, strutting, taunting, driving its beak into the wounded bird's chest. A gamecock with any fight left might have held up its heels, offering a well-aimed gaff as a last defense against certain death, but the Spanish black only lay on his side, the reptilian head lifted in a show of defiant dignity as he waited for the rival to come at him again.

Above Scott the handlers of the birds pled with the referee and cursed the man at their feet, Max more viciously than the other handler, who now held the white gamecock in his arms, turning the triumphant bird away from the rival it hadn't yet finished off. Several men joined the circle of Scott's assailants, who while relenting in their attack kicked him every now and then for good measure. A boot pitched at his shoulder glanced off the clavicle instead, so that he felt a sharp twinge in the same area where he'd shattered the bone in that diving accident several years ago. He tucked his wounded arm under his body, fearing the worst, wincing in pain but trying to prevent greater injury, wishing somehow to get beyond this moment so he could assess the damage to himself.

Among Scott's attackers stood Famosa García, not so much intervening as helping to decide what should happen next. At last Aurelio arrived, maybe he had been there the entire time, and he shouted that the *Americano* had rightly paid for what he had done. Scott wanted to protest, tasting blood in his mouth, but since he seemed to have been forgotten for the moment, he felt along his waist for the Smith & Wesson revolver, ready to pull it on the next person who tried to kick him, except it wasn't there, that was yesterday, the gun was back in the hotel room with Zelda. If only he'd thought to bring the damned gun. Was this their idea of a fair fight in Cuba? His head dizzied by pain, anger, and alcohol, his mouth filling with blood and saliva as his lungs burned from the effort to catch his breath, he pressed a palm into the sand to raise himself, afraid to use the other because of the sharp stinging in the clavicle on that side. Please don't let it be broken again, he said to himself.

He would remember later that he had tried to do a one-handed push-up to get to his knees, but the heel of a boot descended, digging into the small of his back so that he was flattened against the ground once more, the boot stepping on the hand by which he'd tried to raise himself. Facedown in the dirt, he felt split open, unprotected: the jagged pain in the clavicle, the raw sear in his lungs; but worst of all was the eye, swollen shut, constantly blinking, fluttering, and he could feel a scraping along the surface of the eye, as though a piece of coarse fabric were embedded beneath the lid.

Some of the pain and outrage would subside within the hour, the parameters of the event blurring until Scott reached a point where he could hardly see himself as an actor in the scene that had unfolded in the pit. It is often this way with our greatest humiliations. Leftover feelings (indignation, embarrassment, remorse) persist, but gradually they detach themselves from the event itself. Later it even becomes possible to treat the episode, if only in the way we talk about it in our heads, as belonging to that which is unreal.

Aurelio kept arguing with the men, saying that Scott's transgression was irrelevant, that the cockfight was long over, the Spanish black clearly done for after the second injury. Only then did Scott remember to search the floor of the pit again to locate the gamecock, which lay maybe four feet from him, slick and greenish black through the chest, the fine sheen of its coat glistening like oil on the surface of water, the bird no longer attempting to lift its head, since no antagonist stood above, taunting it with the knowledge of its own dying. Max protested, shouting at Aurelio, spewing tobacco juice at his feet, claiming that his bird still possessed a reasonable chance of winning. But one only had to look at the Spanish black, prone on the floor of the pit, and listen for the gurgling noise emitted from its perforated chest to know better. The bird kept kicking his legs, spinning, scattering sawdust, trying to recover and fight and kill whatever it was that had done this to him, but he couldn't right himself.

No one could understand what Scott had done or why he had done it, Aurelio least of all. "I told you this was not the one," he said, practically spitting with anger, pleading with him in hindsight, wanting answers—but this remark must have come after they extracted him from the pit, half-carrying him to the Oldsmobile, Scott supported on the shoulders of Aurelio and Famosa García. "I told you our winner comes much later," Aurelio said. "I do not see why you have done this, Scott Fitzgerald." It seemed to him that Aurelio's wrath, though contained, was greater even than that which Scott had suffered in the pit. Expecting consolation from his friend for the way the German and the two local Cubans had come at him all at once, hardly a fair fight, Scott instead met with disgust. Now it was Famosa García who spoke up on Scott's behalf, "It is a weakness in *Americanos* I have met. To watch an animal dying, it is something they cannot do. It does not fit with their image of themselves." All Aurelio could say in response was *"¡Ay, cabrón!"* They had been banned from the cockfights, Aurelio as well as Scott. "You cost us money, Scott Fitzgerald, do you understand? You owe us money." He spoke with contempt, as if dressing down a soldier who had panicked under fire. "Why did you try to rescue that no-good bird? It is acceptable to lose the early bets, remember, I tell you this." But somewhere in the middle of the Spaniard's lecture the night went black.

14

NEAR THE END OF ANY VACATION SHE WOULD START TO WANT THE hours back, reclaiming whole days in her mind, the ones squandered on bad company and poor restaurants, on visits to art galleries that displayed nothing but minor talent. Mostly, she regretted the mistakes she made with Scott, episodes during which she tried his patience or ran off spur of the moment without telling him where she was headed. He might promise not to hold them against her, but they hung over them—how could they not?—as further proof of her illness. She refused to dwell, however, inside the betrayals and recriminations. "What's done is done," she whispered to herself, a mantra reminding her that sorrows and regrets mattered only insofar as they placed limits on what might happen next. Still, a sickly envy infected her behavior, an envy not so much for other people's lives or the adventures that remained open to them as for her own better days.

Dejected, she spent the night in bed, drained of expectations, wondering how much of it was her own fault. Maybe she really was asking too much of him. She knelt for a while at the foot of the bed, read from the Field novel, dozing off with a finger in the pages of the book only to be visited by silhouettes adrift on the weak orb cast by the lamp, glinting in splashes of red and gold. She prayed, still not fully awake, Dear God, we'll try again, please say we'll try again, but her petitions provoked the sibilant whispering. In half-sleep she pulled herself up in the bed, listening for words from guests in an adjacent room, from revelers in the room above, trying to locate a source, any source, that might account for the noise. She tried to evaluate herself objectively. The voices were bothersome but not yet ominous, she reasoned. Saying aloud to herself: "It's my choice." And: "It's not yet illness as long as there's choice involved."

Sometime after midnight she awoke with a start and walked onto the second-floor terrace to inspect the courtyard, leaning on the balustrade to peer down into the recesses of the arched portals, the cement cool beneath bare feet. Rather than returning to bed she pulled the chair from the desk onto the terrace to keep watch on the courtyard staircase. Without dread or fear, with only the grim certainty that she must stay alert for what came next, she kept herself erect in the stiff-backed wood chair.

She was still sitting, just so, as a buzz mounted from the courtyard. "Which room is it, which is Mr. Fitzgerald's?" "Will we wake her, do you suppose?" Scott's was not among the murmuring voices. "This staircase, are you certain?" Now a woman's voice in a French accent, Maryvonne most likely: "Yes, it's the only one possible because their balcony faces the sea." As the voices climbed the stairs, someone asked whether after yesterday's events the wife would be able to handle the news, and another member of the party replied tersely, in Cuban-inflected English, "I do not see that there is another option."

Zelda braced herself for the worst. Two men rounded the corner, stumbling forward as they supported a wastrel of a man between them, but they started at discovering her sitting there alone, in that stiff-backed wood chair, the door of the room propped open as she gazed into the dark. She could only have been waiting for them, yet she said nothing. They called her by name, "Is that you, Mrs. Fitzgerald?", then more formally, "Mrs. Zelda Sayre Fitzgerald, is that you?" Several additional people now gained the terrace, clustering behind the two men who shouldered the slumping figure who was most likely her husband, though she couldn't be sure from here, the eaves of the terrace projecting long shadows over the faces of those assembled at the top of the stairs.

"It's about Mr. Fitzgerald. He is hurt," a distinguished, statuesque stranger announced. The panic rose in her chest. Time to face it again, time to see what her husband had done to himself. The stranger asked permission to enter the room and lay Scott on the bed, and as he drew close she could see that his companion was their handsome guide from Havana, who raised a finger to the brim of his hat and nodded politely.

"Zelda," Scott mumbled, recognizing her, trying to raise his arm, but it only flopped uselessly against his body. His face a bloody pulp, lips swollen, a white gauze bandage taped over his eye, he was covered in cuts and blood that had seeped into the cloth of his fine blue shirt. "Zelda," he whispered as though she alone could hear him, "you have to help me, we have to get the bastards who did this."

"Revenge is a dish best served cold, Mr. Fitzgerald," counseled the distinguished man in the beige linen jacket who had placed himself in charge of delivering Scott to safety.

"Or at the very least sober," Famosa García said.

"Serves them right, though," Scott remarked, more or less in conversation with himself.

"Scott," she whispered as the men carried him through the small foyer, embarrassed by her own words, ready to take them back even as she spoke them, "if you can't take care of yourself, who's going to take care of me?"

The strangers, though, didn't need to hear any of this. She wished them gone at once, out of her room, out of sight, but first she wanted answers. Someone owed her a story: who had done this to her husband? Just then Maryvonne rushed into the room, straight to Scott's side, now propping pillows behind him, now raising his head and his chest, announcing that she would need to inspect his wounds again.

"What's she doing here?" Zelda asked, addressing herself to Scott, though he was the person in the room least capable of answering.

"I am a nurse, I can help him," Maryvonne insisted.

"Did you do this?" Zelda said and the Frenchwoman straightened, misunderstanding the question until she perceived the finger pointed at the bandage over Scott's eye.

She had been enjoying a drink on the hotel patio, she said, when her husband and these men came back from their night out, recounting Scott's preposterous attempt to break up a cockfight. So Maryvonne truly hadn't been with Scott at the cockfights. Immediately Zelda's jealousy subsided. Maryvonne could be of use, for a while at least.

"I ask the man behind the desk please find medical supplies," Maryvonne explained.

"Naturally, he was beginning to do this very thing," said the stranger who had carried Scott up the stairs and dragged him to his bed.

"I am the most competent medical professional," Maryvonne continued, "in *la voisinage*, in the region, perhaps you say."

The stranger in the beige linen suit and Panama hat introduced himself, tipping the hat: Colonel Eugenio Silva, owner of the Club Kawama. Zelda remembered the couple on the beach speaking of a wedding involving the daughter of the resort's owner, who was a military man.

"Your daughter was married only this past weekend," she said. "I'm awfully sorry, I wish you did not have to bother with any of—"

"Oh, no," Maryvonne cried dramatically, hustling toward the French doors, scolding Famosa García as he swung them open to let in cool night air. "The wet air cannot be good for him," she said, nodding toward Scott, who lay on the bed succumbing to spasms of hollow hacking that ebbed into a moist, sputtering rumble. His lungs, his lungs, she lamented. Famosa García might choose to step outside or stay put, but at any rate the doors to the balcony must remain shut.

"This is solid advice. We have sent for a doctor," the owner of the Club Kawama informed them.

Maryvonne began to recount what she had heard about Scott's ill-fated protest of the ceremonial slaughter of a Spanish black gamecock, her voice thick with admiration. It was noble, in her opinion, to stick up for tortured birds. Zelda didn't bother to argue the point. She did notice, however, that Maryvonne hardly spoke to Aurelio, who several times floated into the room to gape at Scott before retreating from the reproachful glance of his wife to the terrace, hovering near the door, sharing a cigarette with Colonel Silva.

"I hold my husband responsible for this," Maryvonne said, struggling with the buttons as she tried to remove the shirt of her patient, who in fitful drowsiness slapped playfully at her hand. "He must take better care of Scott."

"How could he know his guest would dart into a cockfighting pit—"

"It is a stupid sport, the gambling, the violence."

"But really how could he know that my husband, bolstered

by infallible drink, would try to bring an end to a tradition with more than two thousand years of cruel pleasure behind it?"

"I suppose you are correct," Maryvonne whispered, not wishing to let Aurelio hear this concession: though he might eventually be exonerated, it wouldn't happen all at once. So she reviewed for Zelda's benefit the steps taken on Scott's behalf, how she had rinsed his eye with water and administered an analgesic to keep Scott from writhing in pain before exploring it for damage. No lasting injury to the cornea as far as she could tell, though it appeared to be scratched rather badly, the swelling in a three-quarter moon along the orbit of the eye a cause for concern. Also Scott winced in pain anytime someone touched his left arm or his chest near the clavicle, and, of course, there was the cough, sounding worse and worse. She recommended a hospital, preferably tonight.

"Let me check the bones," she said, "to see if they are broken. Would you help me calm Scott in case the pain alerts him?"

"Couldn't you ask Aurelio to do it?" Zelda suggested. "He'll be better able to hold Scott still. My husband can be fierce when drunk, especially after he's been wronged."

Laying a palm on her shoulder, Famosa García asked if he might speak with her on the balcony. She hadn't known this man was even on the peninsula, and she couldn't begin to understand how Scott had ended up again in his company. It might mean Matéo Cardoña was still tracking them, though whether to keep the Havana police off or on their trail she couldn't have said. Still, she followed this man with the square, strong chin onto the balcony, distracted for several seconds by the chatter of the palms. He returned Scott's wallet to her after describing how the assailants had rolled her husband while he was on the ground in the pit. It had been a struggle to retrieve the wallet because the men felt cheated. Choosing words carefully, Famosa García impressed on her that the men who'd done this to Scott were not in the wrong. "It was no easy matter," he said. "If not for the friendship with Señor Cardoña, I might be forced to wash my hands of this matter."

She flipped through the billfold, still a large amount of cash inside, though considerably less than before. She had no way of measuring how much might have been pilfered.

"How much do you suppose is missing?"

"One thing at a time," Famosa García said. "I have made arrangements for a car to transport you to Havana this night." He also recommended a call to Señor Cardoña, who could arrange for Scott to be checked into one of Havana's finest hospitals. It was a lot for Zelda to take in at once. It meant packing up the room in a quick hour or so; it meant leaving the beach and sun behind before they'd even had a chance to enjoy them. But Scott's health could not be left to chance. For the next few hours at least, while her husband was too enfeebled to protest her decisions, it was up to her to assure his well-being.

"What you propose makes sense."

"Would you like to speak with Mr. Cardoña first?"

"Order the car, if you would be so kind," she said.

"I have done so."

"Please arrange for the hotel to ring Mr. Cardoña," she said, exercising an authority that depended on her former life, on reserves of charm and worldliness but little else. "Perhaps a half hour from now, when things have calmed down."

"Did I ever tell you who you remind me of?" she asked, kissing the Cuban on the cheek by way of thanks. It was impossible to say which of them now held the upper hand, whether she was charming him to procure his assistance or whether she was being baited, drawn along some course charted by Matéo Cardoña for inscrutable reasons. "Remember, the other day, I mentioned your resemblance to a friend of ours? After studying the photograph and your strong chin I noticed it. Ernest Hemingway, you have heard the name?"

"Of course; he is a famous American author who lives in Cuba. You know him?"

"One of my husband's oldest and dearest friends," Zelda said formally, glad that Scott could not overhear her dropping Ernest's name to increase their standing in this man's eyes.

Inside the room chaos had erupted, or rather, Scott had erupted in the form of chaos. Roaming between the bed and the dresser unsteadily, tilting over his suitcases, ransacking hers, he muttered, "I demand to know where it is." Maryvonne apprised Zelda of what had happened. She had been examining his wounds, the clavicle that made him wince whenever she touched it. Nothing broken as far as she could tell: a series of bruises shaped like the toe of a boot formed a kind of necklace on his skin, several bearing the imprint of a medallion, and also there were open cuts where the boots' metal toes had sliced into the skin. As she next sterilized the wounds, the sting of iodine stirred Scott, prompting him to curse Famosa García and Colonel Silva, accusing them of being in league with his assailants and vowing to avenge himself once he found a weapon. It was for this reason he now tossed the contents of the luggage, glancing up every few seconds to threaten the two men, warning them they would be sorry if they hung around much longer.

"Was it wrapped in his shirt?" Zelda interrupted.

"What?"

"The medallion?" she said, staring at her husband's bandaged ribs and naked, bruised chest. "It was around his neck, strung on a piece of twine, a gift from me."

"I did not see it, I am sorry," Maryvonne said.

"Somebody has hidden it, obviously," Scott protested abstractly, rummaging through the suitcases.

"Perhaps all of you could step out onto the terrace for a minute," Zelda said, and lest they mistake her order for a request, added, "Immediately, please."

"What did you do with it?" Scott complained, turning on her now.

Famosa García herded the others out of the room onto the central terrace in the courtyard, Maryvonne professing reluctance to leave Zelda alone with Scott.

"He is not himself," she reasoned.

"He is my husband and I know all his selves," Zelda assured her as Famosa García ushered Maryvonne outside and shut the door, which Zelda locked from the inside.

"Did you hide it on purpose?" Scott said, hovering over his suitcase.

"It's on the damned desk where you left it this afternoon," she replied. He followed the trajectory of her finger and skulked across the room, hanging his head, eyes averted, cupping the handle but aiming the gun at the ground, away from her. He cursed several times, threatening to go after the men who had done this to him.

"Problem is," he said, slurring the phrase, taking a swig from a flask of brandy, "simple problem's this: I don't know who they are."

"It does make them difficult to target," she said lightly, and he smiled at her, tickled by the absurdity of his predicament.

"Where did you get that?" Zelda inquired, merely nodding at the flask.

He was pleased enough with his deception, with his well-kept secrets, to indulge her brief sermon on why he shouldn't be pouring liquor on his misery, not after the drugs he'd been given to quell the hurt in his eye. "Fair enough," he said, but he would keep the flask for now, also the gun in the event that the men from the cockfight came looking for him. He shuffled bare chested through the French doors onto the small balcony overlooking the beach, the winds off the ocean sharp and raw, the moon-bright sky scrubbed of clouds.

"Do you know how easy it is to kill birds?" he asked as he turned to her.

"How easy?"

"Watch this. See the gull perch there on top the palm." He aimed the gun and fired at the tree, the shot ringing out in the air as the startled bird flew off. Her body lurched, the percussive explosion echoing in her chest as Scott turned to warn her, "Cover your ears." Immediately there was pounding at the door, followed by desperate shouts from the courtyard terrace, the words muddled, predictable, exactly the kind of cries, she thought, that people utter in emergencies to compensate for their helplessness.

"Scott, won't you please put the gun down?" He fired a second round into the trees as the gulls clawed and circled in the air above the palms, crowing chorally, warning one another.

"Apparently not that easy," he said as though considering a change in philosophy. "It's tougher when you can only see out of one eye."

"How is your eye, Scott? May I look?" she asked, approaching him, the pounding at the door of their room urgent now, Maryvonne's high-pitched clarion call carrying over the male voices.

"You're just trying to get the gun," he said, pulling away from her.

"Scott," she cried, losing patience. "I must ring Havana to arrange a doctor for you. Can you promise me not to harm any gulls while I'm gone?"

"I can do that," he said, smiling sadly. "If you had ask' me to kill one, not so sure."

Leaving Scott on the balcony, walking through the hotel room to unlock its door, she joined the party nervously assembled on the courtyard terrace, Maryvonne immediately rushing to her side with a barrage of questions, the others joining in. Are you harmed? Is Scott okay? Where did the gunshots come from? Guests cracked doors along the terrace, poking their heads out to cast inquisitive stares, wanting to know what all the damned noise was about but hesitant to complain, not wishing to put themselves in danger.

"Would you be so kind," she asked Aurelio, "as to step onto our balcony and help me separate my husband from the gun he is using to shoot at seagulls?"

"Surely Scott would not be shooting at birds," Maryvonne protested.

A veteran of the Republican Army of Spain, stronger and in-finitely more sober than Scott, Aurelio followed Zelda onto the balcony.

"Scott, Aurelio has come to stop you from making a fool of yourself and most likely hurting an innocent in the bargain."

"Can I have the gun, Scott?" Aurelio said, stepping in, pre-pared for a fight if Scott drew on him.

"Oh, it's out of bullets anyway," Scott replied.

"Where is it, Scott?" Zelda asked, staring at her empty-handed husband, observing that Maryvonne now stood just inside the French doors. "Give the gun to him."

Scott, elbow propped on the balcony rail, gestured toward the base of a palm tree. "See over there, hard to see in dark, but I threw't in the yard, tired of that damned Smith 'n' Wezz'n, doesn't shoot straight anyway."

Aurelio announced to no one in particular that he would retrieve the gun.

"I just kept the gun loaded with one or two bullets," Scott continued, surveying the desolate beach, shirtless, shivering as he spoke, interrupted by his own hacking cough. "I just kept it on hand all this time, in case you slipped away, in case things got too terrible for us."

He was referring, of course, to the years when she had seemed past recovery. He could be so maudlin when he drank. Maryvonne glanced at Zelda, sympathy and embarrassment in her smile. Aurelio, standing near the doors, tilted his head to beckon Zelda into the room, and Maryvonne stepped aside to let them pass, then hastened toward Scott, cooing his name, coaxing him to come out of the night air because it wasn't good for his lungs.

"I do not recommend putting trust in this Famosa García, whoever he is," Aurelio said as Zelda listened to Maryvonne pleading behind her. "Scott," the Frenchwoman implored him, "you must obey me because I am a nurse," as Scott forlornly, half-flirtatiously replied, "My own nurse?"

"He is friends with men who did this, you understand," Aurelio said. "For a long time he talks to them in the pit as Scott lies on the floor, beaten and bleeding. I do not expect him to assist me afterward and I cannot figure out what he is doing. I do not trust him, that is all."

Zelda conceded that she had already enlisted Famosa García's help in arranging transportation to Havana tonight. Maryvonne, arms wrapped around Scott's torso, palms clamped to his naked chest as she rubbed his stomach and kidneys, led him out of the night air.

"Be careful what you ask," Aurelio warned, before hurrying off in search of the gun.

Matéo Cardoña lifted the receiver of the phone on a small table in the corner of the lobby of the Hotel Nacional. His network in the city was extensive, and when he wished to be found, he was not a difficult man to find.

"Hello," he said, in a tone that suggested he had been expecting the call for several days. "How can I be of further service to you, Mrs. Fitzgerald?"

Famosa García had rung an hour earlier from the peninsula. On hearing his report about what had transpired at the cockfight, Matéo applauded his associate's plan to have the wife speak with him as soon as possible. "Resourceful of you," he remarked, not wanting anyone else to lay claim to the Fitzgeralds, wishing to make sure that he was the one to help them, the one to whom they were indebted. And when Famosa García asked to have his own assistance remembered to Mr. Fitzgerald, Matéo replied curtly, "Of course," assuring his underling that he kept a mental log of favors received, favors paid out.

"Can you help me?" the woman on the other end of the line asked after explaining her predicament, blunt but altogether dignified in her directness.

"Did your husband truly try to break up a cockfight?" Matéo replied, laughing. "He is most imprudent in his bravery. Those are dangerous men he crossed, lots of money in play, it is a serious sport. He seems to have a talent for finding trouble."

"It was you who took us to that bar on Saturday," she said.

"I did not intend any insult," Matéo replied quickly, adopting a tender if paternalistic tone. "It is good to recall who your friends are, Mrs. Zelda Fitzgerald. Do I not deserve your gratitude for the assistance I have rendered so far? Our acquaintance is brief, and though I have not known your husband long, I feel not unlike a brother toward him."

"Well, then, you'll help us," she said.

"For just such an emergency, my man is there on the peninsula."

"Why is that, may I ask? Why exactly is Señor Famosa García here in the first place, and why was he also at the cockfights?"

"Oh, this is not so important—Famosa García conducts business of mine. I often use him as courier, as a liaison, since he is reliable, discreet. As for cockfights, they are a passion of his, none of my affair."

As she ended the phone call, she wondered which of her own words were genuine, how much of Matéo's persistent hospitality honest. She wanted to believe in the generosity of other people, but Aurelio's warning not to trust Famosa García or anyone he knew lingered in her thoughts.

"Should I have asked more questions?" she muttered to herself, hanging up the phone.

"Did you say something?" Maryvonne asked from the bed, where she continued to dote on Scott, having removed the old bandage, now in the midst of rinsing the rapidly blinking eye with a mixture of water and boric acid.

"You have been so awfully helpful, Maryvonne, and we will not forget your kindness."

Zelda cleared out the bathroom first, next the dresser drawers, pitching Scott's personal items into her luggage, flinging hers in with his, vowing to sort them later at the hospital. She found his soft Alpagora overcoat in one of his suitcases and set it aside.

"I wonder whatever has become of that doctor," Maryvonne mused aloud as she applied some sort of gelatinous salve to the eye, preparing to dress it. It was as though she was attempting to prove herself indispensable. "He might at least do something for the pain."

Soon Famosa García knocked at the door to announce that the car was waiting below, but Zelda wasn't ready. Panic washed over her. She didn't know where Scott had stored the return plane tickets, where the rest of their money was, what he'd done with the passports. It might all turn up later in one piece of luggage or another, but still she combed the room, the desk, the dresser, the bathroom, asking Maryvonne to help perform a quick sweep. "Look under the bed, could you," she instructed. Her inability to locate the medallion saddened her, but there was too much else to do and she could not concentrate on its loss.

Downstairs a maroon four-door Nash sedan waited before one of the archways of the villa. Neither the colonel nor a hotel manager anywhere in sight, Zelda decided their bill was most likely paid several days in advance. There would be no way to recover the money. She and Maryvonne lowered Scott into the backseat of the car, while the driver and Famosa García loaded bags into the trunk.

"I will ride with you, as far as Havana," Maryvonne offered.

"So kind of you, but altogether unnecessary," Zelda said.

"He needs tending, he needs someone to monitor the pain and make sure there is nothing unexpected in the next few hours."

"I will look after my husband," Zelda snapped.

Aurelio still hadn't returned from his search for the gun, and his absence made the reproof of Maryvonne seem harsher somehow. Like Zelda herself, Maryvonne was an exile—banished from all who had once constituted the core of her life, from familiar sorrows, from acquaintances new and old, set adrift on the currents of things done and those she might still do if given the chance. She wished only to be of use somewhere in the world.

"We do not have a permanent home in Cuba," Maryvonne said. "It is hard to say where we will settle. I would wish to write to you and Scott. At which address, though?"

On principle Zelda refused to give out the address of the Highland Hospital. Maybe the couple had extracted the story from Scott, maybe they hadn't, but Zelda wasn't about to advertise herself as someone enrolled in the ranks of the mentally wounded. She couldn't recall Scott's address at the studio and didn't have an address for him in Encino, so she suggested that Maryvonne write them at Scribner's, care of Max Perkins.

"Well, goodbye," Maryvonne said, bowing forward robotically, her puckered lips brushing the soft skin above Zelda's jaw, before she leaned into the car. "*Bon voyage,* Scott," she said, bending to kiss him, her lips lingering at the corner of his. "Please take care of yourself."

Zelda was surprised to discover that Famosa García was nowhere in sight. She had expected him to travel with them to Havana, and the prospect of riding off into the night with a complete stranger worried her. The tires of the car rolled slowly forward, gravel popping, when all of a sudden headlights shone behind them, brighter by the second, Maryvonne jerking open the back door with the car still in motion and jumping onto the runner to stick her head in and announce, "I will see who is this arriving, perhaps the doctor."

Sure enough, it was Colonel Silva with news of the village doctor, whom he expected to appear within the next five minutes, not much longer than that. Maryvonne strongly recommended waiting, since it was best to be armed with as much information about Scott's condition as possible. "Is he bringing morphine?" Zelda asked, having encouraged the colonel to make the request earlier, but no one knew anything for certain. "It's the only reason to wait," Zelda said, overriding the Frenchwoman's frustrated objections, her confidence mounting with each small decision. For the first time all night she felt as though she were truly in charge. "Besides, I'm certain the doctor is strictly small-time, and Scott will soon be a patient at an excellent hospital in Havana."

"He is in considerable pain," Maryvonne repeated. "If we could give him a shot of morphine, maybe it is wise to wait."

She was just stalling, though, buying herself a few more minutes with Scott. Zelda affectionately squeezed the Frenchwoman high on the arms, saying it was okay, she would get Scott to a hospital. Only as she started to pull the door shut did she consider again everything Maryvonne had done for Scott. This refugee couple, though honeymooning at a resort their first week here in Cuba, probably didn't have much in the way of funds.

"I should pay you for your help," Zelda said. "I don't want to insult you and we're hardly in high cotton ourselves, but would you take something as a gesture of gratitude?"

"But I did exactly no-thing," Maryvonne protested.

Zelda pulled her husband's billfold from her purse, extracting a twenty and a ten-spot. Maryvonne refused to extend her palm, but Zelda held the bills forward, saying, please, as a favor, so they wouldn't feel so bad. Still the Frenchwoman's hand didn't move, so Zelda stuck the ten back in her wallet and said, "Here, a fair compromise," extending the twenty-dollar bill by itself. "Maryvonne, please, it's hard to go through life never paying one's way."

"But, of course, it is not for money," the nurse protested.

"Of course not," Zelda said kindly, and the Frenchwoman slowly unfolded her arm, palm upward, accepting the cash, embracing Zelda again, wishing her luck in Havana. "You know where to reach me the next few days," she said, not mentioning Aurelio at all, "if you require advice on medical matters—there can never again be a question of money."

As the car drove off, Zelda flipped through the diminished cash in Scott's wallet, estimating there might be a hundred dollars left, a hundred and twenty at most. She prayed Scott had stashed money elsewhere, or they might run out within the next two days, stranded in Havana without a friend in the world. What would she do if that came to pass? Whom could she wire on short notice? Maybe Scott had scribbled the numbers for Harold Ober and Max Perkins in his Moleskine. She searched the pockets of his sport coat, and on finding them empty realized that the men who'd filched his wallet might also have stolen the journal or that Famosa García, recovering it, might have kept it for himself so as to have something on her husband.

In a stupor Scott snarled, "Why is someone trying to wake me?"

She fell back against the seat of the car.

"Where are we going?" he asked repeatedly, though she was certain she'd told him several times already. He protested that he couldn't make it all the way to the city without alcohol or painkillers. Squirming in pain, he demanded that the driver turn the car around this instant. If she hadn't emptied the flask back at the hotel, and then for good measure left it behind, she might have given him a drink just to quiet him for a while. "Stop the car," he commanded as she tried to imagine what the driver would do if Scott became ugly, unruly, and altogether too much to handle. "Where's the luggage?" He had Luminal in his bag, which would take the edge off. So they pulled to the side of the road and Scott tore through the luggage in search of the pills. The driver kept saying it was dangerous to be parked roadside, and Zelda couldn't tell whether he was worried about a speeding truck coming wide off the curve ahead to smash into their car, or perhaps marauders from some nearby village finding them undefended in the night. *"Esto es peligroso, muy peligroso,"* the driver murmured over and over. *"Por favor, date prisa, porque ésto es peligroso."*

"Scott, get into the car," she pleaded. She was near tears. "Why are you doing this? I keep waiting for you to get on your feet, some stroke of fortune that will tell you everything's okay again—"

"Enough," he shouted, his words echoing from inside the trunk of the car. "I won't listen to any more. It all started with your dis'ppearing act. Everything els's just neurotic chatter."

He was right on some level, she decided. It was a bout of nerves and she mustn't let it get the better of her.

"But I'm tired too," she said. "Tired of your fears of me, for me, about me. And even if the big break came tomorrow, if you finished the novel and made it a bestseller, there'd always be one more thing, Scott, the latest in a long list—"

"Zelda, it stops this instant or I'm not getting back in that car. Next week you'll be writing me saccharine-sweet letters, saying I'm so sorry, saying you had a nice time on holiday, you didn't mean to be so ungrateful, but I won't open them. Stop this now or it's the last trip we ever take."

Ah, there it was, the bottle of Luminal stashed in one of her silk purses. He swallowed three pills without water, tucking the bottle into his jacket for safekeeping, the clothes scattered across the floor of the trunk as he slammed it shut. She worried he had taken too many pills, but his tolerance for narcotics was high.

"Is that supposed to be a threat?" she murmured, more for her own ears than his. "Because you're such a joy to travel with? Showing up drunk at the Highland to pick me up."

She gestured for the driver to get back into the car.

"Which I'll hear about from the doctors and other patients at the Highland for weeks after my return, don't think I won't; and then to top it off you go and befriend dubious characters, drag us to a dangerous juke joint, get beaten up at a ghastly cockfight, leaving me to manage you and your rummy friends."

The echo of her voice trailing in the dark as she got into the car made her sad. Scott stayed conscious long enough to say he was sorry for being irritable, he had been in tremendous pain. He was so much more peaceable when sleepy. Also he didn't want to check into a hospital in Havana, he was okay, truly, his eye stung but not unbearably, nothing permanently wrong with it. And then there was the tuberculosis, and the drinking, what if the doctors recommended treatment, attempted to hold him over here in Havana?

"Because it would be terrible to have to recover from illness in a foreign country," she said as he nodded off.

Scott's head slanted, bobbing against the leather seat, his own snores every now and then awakening him. "Don't worry, I won't let them commit you," she said, sliding a finger along his jaw, pulling together the lapels of the overcoat she'd retrieved from his luggage earlier. His head now rested on her shoulder, the un-bandaged side of his face smooth and fleshy against hers. Something in her still enjoyed taking care of him, experiencing herself as necessary, but it felt like long ago. "Being in love with you," she said aloud, her hand tucked beneath layers of jacket, stroking his stomach in circular movements, "is like being in love with one's own past."

As her thumb circled the cotton fabric of the shirt near his belt, it caught on something, maybe a stray thread, but, no, it was too coarse to be a thread. Eagerly, she followed the woven twine into her husband's pants, parting the two jackets to unbuckle his belt, loosening the slacks, fingers exploring his lap while Scott slumbered on, dead to the world, the twine leading her to the waistband of his BVDs, catching there, some of it looping down like a lasso along the crease of his groin. And as she tugged at it, she whispered the beginning of a novena to St. Anthony taught to her by one of the patients at the Highland, able to remember only a few key phrases ("glorious Saint Anthony" and "conde-scension of Jesus"), but improvising others ("obtain for me this medallion, a sign of my devotion to my husband and my trust in you and God and the company of saints"), promising someone— God, the saint, or only herself—to look up the words later and say a weeklong novena all the way through once back at the hos-pital in Asheville. Then she heard the tinking of metal against the belt buckle and suffered, yes, on a smaller scale, but nevertheless something akin to the blissful rapture of the saints—Lazarus spared the grave and walking back into the light; his medallion spared the filth of the cock pit, cradled in the waistband of her husband's BVDs to be returned to her, so that she might get it properly blessed by a priest, secure it on a sturdy silver chain, and present it again to Scott.

15

WITH MODEST, FAINTLY GRIZZLED LIGHT, DAWN CREPT OVER the seawall of the Malecón as they pulled up to a discreet roadside square that gave access to the Plaza de Armas. Stray revelers made their way home to hotels from all-night joints such as Sloppy Joe's, still boisterous and frolicsome, outraged by the suddenness with which the dance floors had been pulled from beneath their feet. Small shipping vessels headed out of the harbor, huffing on choppy waters, the wake of each curling off the stern in an apron of froth, the barreled voices of the men aboard saluting soldiers on watch or fishermen on the docks who embraced their role as harbingers of day. At this quiet hour several taxis and a long white Cadillac nestled against the curb of the roadside square. The driver said to her, "That must be the car of Señor Cardona."

Her stomach flipped with worry. In her haste to leave the peninsula, she had failed to negotiate a price with the driver. She had no idea what Scott might have paid for the trip to Varadero or what a reasonable surcharge for the emergency circumstances under which they left this morning might be. It was possible that the driver was yet another courier in the employ of Matéo Cardoña. Should she leave the matter of payment to their benefactor? How far into his debt could she and Scott afford to sink? Short on cash, considering that she still hadn't tracked down the return Pan American tickets and had no idea how much the hospital might cost or how much she might have to dole out for new plane tickets or subsequent train fare to New York City—the only place she could think to bring Scott for rehabilitation because she couldn't inflict him on her elderly mother in Montgomery—she decided to assume the car ride had been paid for.

Cardoña stepped out of the white car and strolled across the cobblestone plaza with the air of a man greeting the day rather than riding out a long night. "Ah, Mrs. Zelda Fitzgerald," he called, "I hope the drive was pleasant." Without invitation, he slid into the backseat to examine Scott and she didn't protest. Instead she seized the opportunity to ask the driver to open the rear, so she might shuffle and repack the clothes strewn everywhere by Scott during his pain-induced rage, delving once more through interior pockets of the luggage in search of cash, plane tickets, the Moleskine, passports, turning up only the last of these. She checked the sport jacket worn to the cockfight, still smeared with dirt and blood: nothing inside its pockets. It made her recall her lost dress.

"His eye is very bad," Cardoña hailed her, and she came forward to find the Cuban reclining in the backseat beside her husband, the bandage now dangling loosely from Scott's eye. "I boxed in my youth, and I have not seen an eye in that shape in a long, long time."

"Scott also boxes, or used to," she said, not sure why it was relevant.

"Let us head to the doctor next. I have made arrangements at a clinic affiliated with a club of which I am a member. These clinics provide the finest care in Havana. I will find a room for you at an appropriate nearby hotel," he said, his tone solicitous. "You must be positively tired after—"

"I have decided against the hospital," she said, making up her mind only as she spoke the words. She was terrified that they would be marooned in this city without funds if the doctors remanded Scott to their care.

"This is impossible, I have made arrangements with a doctor, a bed awaits Mr. Fitzgerald."

"We need to go home," she said studying the look of surprise on his face, aware that she had altered the script on him. She wondered what Cardoña had been able to infer about their financial situation while they were away on Varadero. After all, their reduced fortunes were hardly a mystery, Scott's adversities well chronicled if by no one other than himself, easy enough to track if you had access to an independent news services such as Reuters. Did he still believe them to be members of the American leisure class? Was he blindly unaware how close they skated to broke, ever along the edge of irrevocable collapse?

"This makes no sense," Cardoña protested, roused to anger, clearly someone who did not like to be defied. "This is not what you requested hours ago. I have gone to great trouble on your behalf yet once more. You are tired and upset and you are not thinking clearly."

"Señor Cardoña, I appreciate your efforts more than I can say. I still require your help in leaving the country." She resented his last remark but was determined not to let it show. "We're a short plane ride from Miami, from family in Alabama. It makes no sense for us to stay on here as strangers, imposing ourselves on your hospitality, when a flight will solve everything. There we will have access to money and can repay you for all you've done for us, and when Scott is better, he can negotiate whatever business the two of you have begun."

She was aware, of course, that the last part was a lie, that Scott was in no position to transact any business with Cardoña and had probably tried to make this clear to him.

"It is unsafe for him to fly in this condition, before his lungs have been checked."

Cardoña's concern seemed to be heartfelt, and yet it was most likely meant to intimidate her or make her second-guess herself. Refusing to take no for an answer, he dropped his voice into a softer register, into what she could only have described as a seductive lilt, offering to escort them in his own car to the clinic where Scott would receive the highest standard of care.

"Again, I thank you for all you have done," she said. "It is above and beyond the call."

Their driver transferred their luggage to the white Cadillac, while Cardoña and his chauffeur hoisted her husband from the backseat onto their shoulders and dragged his slack body across the plaza, his brogue shoes scraping on the cobblestone. She wasn't sure whether Cardoña had agreed to her terms or not. For all she knew, she was being abducted. She wished for more information, about what Scott and Mr. Cardoña had discussed, about what agreement if any they'd come to in the wake of Saturday's violent crime. What was it exactly that Scott had asked this man to do on their behalf? All she could be sure of for the moment, as she glanced across at Cardoña, conducting himself as though he would ultimately make the decisions, was that he had settled her account with the driver, one less matter for her to worry about.

Inside the Cadillac, as her husband slouched between herself and Cardoña, she repeated her wish to return to the United States. Cardoña said nothing as the car drove out along the harbor, banking into a curve that hugged the seawall. Was it possible he had enough influence in this city, she wondered, to check her husband into a clinic without her consent? The Cadillac turned inland, up a street that ran parallel to a magnificent tree-lined promenade they'd walked only days ago, the splendid white dome of the Capitol visible up ahead, the pink and yellow neocolonial theaters, hotels, and mansions framing the street on which they rode. Soon they diverted onto a smaller street, the car rattling through a neighborhood of colonnaded porticos that fronted colorful three-story buildings with multiple stone balconies or heavy black iron balustrades along the second- and third-story windows, the ride so rough and dramatically uneven she found it hard to reconcile the architecture and the roads.

"I would make excuses for our streets," Señor Cardoña smiled, "but what excuse can there be? It is simply deplorable, loose blocks everywhere, potholes the size of small gullies."

On cue they were jolted into the air, Zelda gasping in surprise, Cardoña hitting his head on the roof of the car, then swearing softly in Spanish as he warned the chauffeur to be more careful. Through all the jostling, Scott slept on, unperturbed.

"Perhaps this is the condition in which one must drive our streets," Cardona said, nodding toward her slumbering husband, but almost instantly eating his words—"I mean no disrespect, of course"—and telling her the story of the city's new Capitol building, of the diamonds in its floor. He seemed oddly talkative. He held a newspaper in his hand, folded shut, as he listed off the morning's headline news: Mussolini had scorned FDR's proposal for a conference to curb Italy's aggressive economic expansion; the U.S. president was rebuking not only international leaders but also dissenters from his own political party, suggesting that anti–New Dealers among the Democratic party resign; and here in Cuba, Colonel Fulgencio Batista expressed a willingness to stand for the presidential elections if it became necessary for him to do so.

"He is already running the country, of course," Señor Cardoña remarked.

"I am sorry," she said, unable to feign interest. "I'm distracted this morning."

"I have an errand that will take but a second," he said as the car pulled sharply to a curb, Cardoña opening the door before they had even come to a complete stop.

The more she thought about it, the more she resented Cardoña's officious manner, his presumption in asking her to wait while he ran errands and refused to tell her where they were headed. She might easily coax Scott into a cab and demand to be taken to the airport. But what if the return tickets really had gone missing? What if after paying the taxi she needed to haggle over the fare or customs fees? What if she lacked the funds to leave the country?

"Scott," Zelda whispered, shaking his arm, "Scott, dearest, won't you wake up?"

The lid above the undamaged eye fluttered. "Zelda, that you?"

"Do you remember where you stored our return tickets?"

No sooner had the words left her mouth than the door opened, Cardoña standing above them framed by bright sunlight, the doctor at his side.

"I want him to look at the eye, listen to the lungs, that is all."

Zelda wondered if this was a stratagem of some sort, but she didn't protest as the doctor slid in next to her husband. The doctor listened to the lungs with a stethoscope, lifted the bandage from the eye to examine it as he asked questions of Cardoña, who leaned into the car, now and then shooting her a few conciliatory words.

"He runs the clinic of the club of which I spoke, with its roster of patients that includes some of Havana's oldest families."

Immediately alarm shot through her and she said before she could gather her thoughts, "Really, we can't afford a clinic," stopping herself, feeling flustered by her mistake, finding it uncouth to have spoken so frankly of money to a man she hardly knew.

"What do you think about morphine?" Cardoña asked, ignoring her remark. It took her several seconds to understand that the question had been addressed to her.

How much would the doctor charge, she wondered, for a shot of morphine? Scott's complaints had subsided, the Luminal having cast its spell. Maybe the morphine shot wasn't a good idea after all, especially with so many substances already in his system. Besides, if Cardoña intended to overrule her and check her husband into a hospital, she would need him vaguely coherent, able to stick up for himself.

"Will it present a problem for the airlines?" she asked, making the tactical decision to proceed as though Cardoña intended to cooperate with her wishes.

"You let me worry about that," he replied.

"And it's safe?" she asked, listing the substances Scott had ingested within the past twelve hours, almost too many to count.

The doctor administered a mild dose of morphine, assuring her it would keep the misery at bay for hours but would not prevent her husband from traveling.

As the car pulled from the curb, leaving the doctor behind, she breathed easier. She had been sure he would declare Scott in need of emergency care and insist on escorting him to the clinic. Still, she was at the mercy of a man they hardly knew, riding down streets she couldn't recognize, Scott passed out and unavailable to help in any way. Cardoña said little as the sun brightened behind them; and now the landscape grew familiar, no longer dusty as it had been on the ride into the country, here and there splashes of dark red clay, the countryside around them ordered in long green rows of neatly irrigated fields. The tightness in her chest released, giving way to gratitude, then triumph. They were headed toward the airport.

At the terminal, Matéo Cardoña was a whir of efficiency, bypassing one line after another, working officials, skipping baggage and passport checks, preempting objections before the airline staff could raise them. He produced a letter from the doctor, waved it in front of several peons, and when they sought the advice of their superiors soon overrode all protests. "He has been given a few sleeping pills because he is ill," he explained, setting aside objections that the passenger was in no condition to fly, "and his wife can easily wake him in case of an emergency." When she tried to explain about the lost tickets, Cardoña dismissed her concern. "It has been taken care of." His solicitousness did not end there. He would not allow her to wait for the airplane alone, but instead ordered his chauffeur to transport the luggage to the tarmac, then helped her settle Scott on the plane, as a patient rather than an inebriated man who had been badly beaten in a fight.

She was prepared to give Cardoña all the money in Scott's wallet if it came to that. God only knew how much they truly owed their benefactor. She studied him with a new appreciation for his angular face, slender in the jaw, darkened ruggedly by stubble from a sleepless night. She would promise to send him money once they were home, not knowing what they could afford to pay or when. Or, she supposed, she might ask him to bill Scribner's. Max might not be pleased, but over the past couple of years Scott had resolved his personal debts to his editor as well as his publishing house. He was good for the next loan.

"I wish we were leaving right away," she said once they had

boarded the plane, empty of passengers. It was not scheduled to depart for an hour still.

"Time is only the enemy if you see it as such," Cardoña said.

He was too much of a gentleman, she realized, to bring up money. So, versed in the etiquette of the Southern lady, exploiting codes against which she'd once dramatically rebelled, she summoned those social graces by which women procure favors without recompense and pay benefactors in flattery for kindnesses and benevolence. She couldn't believe how easily she managed the aristocratic Cuban. And whatever his original intentions might have been, whatever he'd once wanted (perhaps still wanted) from them, he rose to the codes of a lapsing era and received her extended hand as if he'd never expected anything more.

"How can I ever pay you back?" she said, making it clear by her tone she could not.

Scott spent the flight wrapped in a morphine haze, experiencing only a lightheaded sense of being airborne, the pricks and aches of injury. From time to time he rose to consciousness, aware of the eye obstructed by gauze, the lid and lash flitting wildly against the cotton like a trapped insect, the visible world smeared in thick gray dabbings like the excess paint at the edge of an artist's palette. When at last he opened his eyes, stinging, enmeshed in wrappings, he was on a train, able to remember (if only in faintly humiliating images) that he had lumbered in his sleep through an airport terminal before subsiding into a taxi.

"How did we get here again?" he asked his wife, seated in the booth across from the sleeping berth.

"Can't you remember any of it?"

"Sure, I lost a cockfight, and the nurse Maryvonne tended to my eye. Were we in the city with Matéo?"

Portions of the night might eventually come back to him, though he wasn't sure he wanted them to. Still, there was the terror of having gone missing from your own life— not just the wondering what you might have done, what you might have said, whether anything had taken place with that Frenchwoman, but the sense of having been rendered completely open to harm. An ambiguous terror, in truth attractive on some level: to lay yourself open to the cruelties and mercies and whims of other people. How many times had Scott seen drunks robbed, beaten, more or less ravaged? He'd even watched as such things were done to himself. Inside every true drunk was the desire to be punished for some crime you couldn't remember having committed.

"Are you really awake? Will you remember this?" Zelda asked, and he said he was and he would remember, without knowing if his statements were true, still under the spell of the morphine.

Much of the conversation, she understood in advance, would slide back into his drug-hammered unconscious. Nevertheless there were things she needed to say. "The hardest part," she said, studying him as he tried to memorize the words, "I wish you could understand this, Scott, the hardest part is never knowing whether these trips are experiments in starting over, if there's anything at stake in them except killing time."

"I'm sorry, Zelda," he said. She had pulled him through a tough spot, all on her own. "The lengths you went to there at the end, I won't forget, I won't."

He slept again, so she composed a note to him, organizing her thoughts: "Please believe me, Scott, the happiest I ever was was when I was with you. I do best that way, I think, in your arms and full of myself, and maybe I will again someday? Devotedly, Zelda." She folded the note into the pocket of his shirt, vowing to scribble a whole series of notes over the next few days, if necessary. On a train traveling up the Eastern seaboard, through cities such as Charleston, Baltimore, and Wilmington, cities in which they had vacationed, reveled, or lived together, she began to plan the immediate future: how to manage Scott once they arrived in New York, how to get him checked into a hospital, what she must say to her doctors when she returned to North Carolina alone, the letter she would need to send Scott from the sanitarium covering for his failure to escort her safely home. Composing lines in her head, she tailored the story for the ears of her doctors, who read all her correspondence, who monitored every twist and turn in the drama of her private life. They must never find out what had happened in Cuba, not if she wanted to see Scott again anytime soon.

He took the news of the lost Moleskine fairly well. How could he not? It was his own fault.

"A lot of material in that journal, things people said, some nice sentences too," he lamented. "But I suppose I'll get most of it back."

"I wonder if there are any words you can never get back," she said, teasing him with the memory of her lost love letter.

"Zelda, why so cryptic, I can't make sense of what you say when you talk like that," he answered. "You've been spending too much time with clairvoyants."

She laughed, giggling at first, then letting the thought expand in her mind, the laughter building as she dwelt on it. He liked her newfound confidence, her way of seeing herself as someone who could make things happen. "You have a winning air about you," he said. "I should let myself get beat up more often."

"Well, then, about California, when can I come?"

He showed less surprise than she expected. She told him how during the flight they had talked extensively of her visiting him in California within the next few months, of her helping him put his life in order. The truth was she had alluded to the possibility during the few minutes in which he'd opened his eyes, then drifted off, but while falling asleep he had said, "There's room at my cottage, you could stay with me"—and that was all the encouragement she needed.

"You remember inviting me to come, don't you?" she said, then stopped, changing tactics. She asked him if he was in much pain and stood up to fetch another pillow, propping it behind him. Even in the sleeping berth, wrapped in blankets, he still wore the two coats, feeling the cold all the time, the hacking in his chest erupting in unexpected fits that seemed to her to last longer each time.

"Of course," he said automatically. He was lying, she knew he was lying, but it didn't matter.

Zelda hadn't liked Hollywood when they'd stayed there as celebrities a decade earlier. This time, though, it would be a private experiment, the two of them off the radar, in a cottage in Encino, in the hills outside Los Angeles. She was no longer afraid of what that city represented. She had lost too much this past decade to bother competing with beautiful darlings who relished the fickle favor of fame, likely to be tomorrow's castaways before they had even realized it.

"When will I visit?" she asked again.

"Maybe in July, so we can celebrate your birthday, also the anniversary of our first meeting."

"And, Scott, you do think I'm almost better? Truly?"

"I know it," he said with all the conviction he could muster.

She stared out the window, the flat green land and the happy blues of oceans, glades, and marshes blurring as she held her forehead to the cool glass, overcome with fatigue. She hadn't slept even an hour last night, and it was already past noon.

"Scott, you look cozy in that berth," she said, "and I don't feel like climbing up into mine. Do you think I could come and lie there beside you for a few minutes?"

"Of course," he said. His bad arm was closer to the wall, so she, also fully clothed, wearing a long white frock, could rest her head on his shoulder.

"What about our shoes?" she asked, kicking her feet. "Shouldn't we take them off?"

"Not yet," he said. "Let's just lie here perfectly still for a few minutes."

These hours spent sleeping by her side on the train—these and the scurried, muddled days ahead in New York City—they are the last he will ever spend in her presence. Summer will pass with Scott on the mend, Zelda's visit to Encino postponed, replaced by talk of his coming East, but those trips also put off. He will become immersed in his new novel, while Zelda is discharged from the Highland Hospital into her mother's care—and for a year and a half there will be letters and imaginings, about how they will see each other as soon as circumstances permit, about how work progresses and finances deteriorate, and yet somehow he will always scrape together money for her expenses. It will be the longest span of not seeing each other in their entire life together, since they first met in the month she turned eighteen. Their love lies in the rhythm of written declarations of loyalty, in repeated vows of steadfast belief in each other and a future that remains within reach. He'll write and tell her he's under contract again, their money woes soon to be alleviated. And she'll believe that this is the year in which he'll get his life on track and at last make room for her somewhere, anywhere, since she now requires so little to be happy. Out of consideration for his illness, she'll propose visiting him in California at a later date, when his lungs are recovered, when he's making progress again on the novel.

And in December, on the mend from a heart attack weeks earlier, only two days after sending Christmas presents for Zelda and Scottie, he will sit down across from Sheilah Graham to read about the Princeton football team in an alumni magazine, by some accounts having also just consumed a piece of his favorite chocolate, and he will stand up to stretch his legs, licking his fingers, reaching for the mantel as he collapses at her feet, dead by the time Sheilah returns with help.

In the berth she slept contentedly, certain that the spirits couldn't chase her on a train that was moving so swiftly. She awoke beside him having dreamt two dreams, the one melting into the other. She was dancing in a professional ballet company and attaining on stage greater height and arc in her leaps than ever before; then she was standing on a bluff above a white-sanded beach, her body turned out toward ocean, knowing Scott (though in the dream she couldn't see him) was somewhere down below watching out for her. The dreams were exhilarating and she wanted to talk to Scott about them.

"You were the one who saw what I was going to be," she said, not yet sure if he was awake, already saddened to have left the world of the dream. "But then one day I felt you giving up on me."

"The lengths you went to there at the end, Zelda," he started to say.

"Scott, you never have to thank me," she said, interrupting him. "In the afternoons after you have worked on the novel, and I have taken long walks in the hills of Santa Monica, we will lie like this on the couch in your living room."

Whenever she spoke of what might still happen for them—how things would soon get better, how her month's stay in Encino might bring about a reunion not only in affections but in practical solidarity—he yielded completely, considering how much her hopes had cost her, how difficult it was in the face of decreasing dividends to talk herself into optimism. He received her words as though they came from someone who might look into the future and tell his fortune. It would be easier if she were to stay on for a few weeks, without the pressure of planned vacations, the implicit demand to fill her life with adventures—instead just the two of them getting by, day to day. It might make all the difference. In her hopes he intuited the structure, rhythm, and ritual certainty of faith. It was not mere self-deception—if only because they were never more earnest than when talking of the future. If only because, even in the wake of disaster, they meant every kind word they said.

"It's strange," she observed, "that there are so many homes you've made for yourself, hotels, apartments, all these places I can't even begin to imagine."

"Oh, they don't matter." Sheilah had found the cottage for him, of course, but he beat back that thought, concentrating only on what Zelda wished to hear. "Some of them were so tawdry, I'd be ashamed for you to step foot in the door. But every time I choose a place I truly like, where I could see myself staying a while," he said, happy to be speaking freely now, without holding anything back, "I ask myself, 'What would Zelda think?' and I imagine what you will say when you visit me next."

"Tell me again about California," she said, "why I will like it so much better this time around. Why I will enjoy evenings on the captain's deck of your small cottage. And what about the walks, are they marvelous, you know how I love long walks, Scott."

He wanted her to believe in an existence that was quiet and ordered, in expectations that were safe rather than wild. So he described for her the hills in the immediate vicinity of his home, the trees undulating in lush green on the Santa Monica Mountains, how the sun settled down into them in the evening.

ACKNOWLEDGMENTS

'VE INCURRED MANY DEBTS IN THE WRITING OF THIS NOVEL. THANK you to my agent, Leigh Feldman, whose enthusiasm and vision for this book were tremendous from the very first read and who guided the manuscript expertly through several drafts. Thanks also to her assistant, Jean Garnett, whose editorial contributions were similarly deft and precise. I am fortunate to have had the opportunity to work with the fine staff at Overlook Press, and wish especially to thank my editor, Liese Mayer, whose insights and ideas refined the novel on every level. Thanks to my publicist, Theresa Collier, and to Melody Conroy, both of whom understood the power of the Fitzgeralds' story—and this untold portion of it—right away.

Every writer needs a place to call home (as the itinerant Fitzgeralds had to learn the hard way), and over the course of the past two years, that place for me has been the Iowa Writers' Workshop. My thanks to Connie Brothers, Deb West, and Jan Zenisek for all they do to allow writers to live as much as possible in their heads. I'm honored by the relationships and conversations I've enjoyed with the terrific faculty at the Writers' Workshop while completing this book: Ethan Canin, Charles D'Ambrosio, Marilynne Robinson, Andrew Sean Greer, ZZ Packer, and Samantha

Chang. From each of you I've learned much about the art of fiction. A handful of writers have long served as mentors and inspirations: Mark Costello, Leon Waldoff, Harriet Scott Chessman, Martha Serpas, Kevis Goodman, Leslie Brisman, and Richard Powers.

My thanks also to the following people for specific and important contributions to this novel along the way, often on writing matters, often on historical details pertaining to everything from architecture to cockfighting, from ballet to Cuban music of the 1930s (you know what you did): Andrés Carlstein, Paul Jaskot, James Molloy, Don Waters, Robin Romm, Deborah Kennedy, Curt Armstrong, Susannah Shive, Mario Zambrano, Robert and Patricia Ream, Avantika Mehta, Jeff McCarthy, Lala Mooney, Celia Rosa, Angel Pérez, Emilio Cueto, and Jonathan Hansen. The staff at the Firestone Memorial Library provided expert assistance on several separate visits during which I dug through portions of the vast archive of Fitzgerald's letters and papers housed at Princeton University. And a special nod to the extended Spargo clan, for being part of this journey from the start.

Finally, there are three persons without whom this novel might never have existed: Amelia Zurcher, whose flawless ear for the English language couldn't purge all my flaws (I choose to call them style), who read, commented on, and edited this manuscript at the earliest and latest stages, her improvements to the story too many to be counted; my sister, Jennifer Mitchell, a kindred spirit in literary taste, who brought that taste to bear by helping to shape this story and carry it out into the world; and Anne Ream, who shares my love of all things Zelda and F. Scott Fitzgerald (first expressed in long-ago happy hour conversations devoted to *Tender Is the Night*) and whose fine sense of historical detail, dialogue, and narrative pace helped bring focus and clarity to many a scene.

R. CLIFTON SPARGO is a Chicago-based novelist and cultural critic who writes "The HI/ LO" for *The Huffington Post*. A graduate of the Iowa Writers' Workshop and the doctoral program in literature at Yale, he has published stories and essays in *The Atlantic, The Kenyon Review, The Antioch Review, Glimmer Train, FICTION, Raritan, Commonweal*, the *Chicago Tribune*, and elsewhere.